BUD'S
JOURNEY HOME

OTHER BOOKS BY
LINDA SEALY KNOWLES

Journey to Heaven Knows Where

The Secret

BUD'S
JOURNEY HOME

Linda Sealy Knowles

TATE PUBLISHING
AND ENTERPRISES, LLC

Published by Tate Publishing & Enterprises, LLC
127 E. Trade Center Terrace | Mustang, Oklahoma 73064 USA
1.888.361.9473 | www.tatepublishing.com

Tate Publishing is committed to excellence in the publishing industry. The company reflects the philosophy established by the founders, based on Psalm 68:11,
"The Lord gave the word and great was the company of those who published it."

Book design copyright © 2016 by Tate Publishing, LLC. All rights reserved.
Cover design by Joshua Rafols
Interior design by Shieldon Alcasid

Published in the United States of America

ISBN: 978-1-68270-787-6
1. Fiction / Family Life
2. Fiction / Romance / Western
16.03.18

To

Pete Knowles, my son

1

A s Rosie sat on an old weather-beaten wooden dock with her head tilted back, she allowed the bright sunshine to wash over her dirt-smeared face. She sat with her auburn hair, hung with knotted crusty dreads, tossed behind her shoulders. With her emerald green eyes shut, she loved the feel of the warm breeze off the slow moving river. She dangled the tips of her nasty toes in the water. This was her favorite fishing hole to come to and catch fish to help feed her two younger brothers. As she sat daydreaming, she heard a noise rustling in the brush close by. Feeling a little uneasy, she sat straight up and immediately felt a jerk on the fishing pole that she had placed under one side of her backside. A big catfish was flapping and tugging for its freedom at the end of her cane pole. The noise in the brush seemed to be closer as she stood, pulling on her washed-out, colorless shift. Standing very still, she looked around but didn't see anything. Remembering the fish, she pulled it up onto the dock. She carefully slid her hand under the catfish's fins and threaded it onto the long thin rope with the other fish she had caught and eased it back into the water to keep them fresh.

Standing straight up and listening to the sounds surrounding her, she heard the noise again. She tiptoed very softly across the dock stepping down onto dry sand. Slowly she crossed the river bank, looking through the tall thin trees and bushes. Being as quiet as she could, she was surprised to see a horse trying to make its way through the underbrush to the water's edge. The big, brown horse had a saddle and dark leather saddlebags strapped across its back. A rifle hung down in the side holster. The animal's reins dropped to the ground, dragging in the mud and dirty water. Rosie looked all around for the owner of the horse. There didn't appear to be anyone nearby.

"Whoa, boy, it's all right. I won't hurt you," Rosie said as she walked slowly toward the big, brown buckskin. The horse tossed his head back and sidestepped into the swampy water. Continuing slowly toward the horse in the gooey soft mud, she quickly reached for his reins and secured them.

"Where's your master, boy?" asked Rosie, not really expecting an answer. As she pulled on the horse's reins, he tossed his head and gave her a hard jerk, causing her to lose her balance and go down on one knee in the murkywater. As she attempted to stand, her bare foot stepped on something soft.

Rosie quickly sucked in a scream as she looked down on a man's body lying with part of his face in the swampy marsh. She immediately turned the animal loose and let him go to the river's edge. Slowly, Rosie eased away from the man and squatted down near his head.

"Hey, mister," she called but received no response. Using her hands, she turned the body over and saw that the man was young and appeared to be a good-looking critter. As she glanced at the man, she noticed the bloody water surrounding his body. She took her dirty, fishy hand and pulled back his leather vest and plaid shirt. Powder burns and blood surrounded a big hole in his side. Continuing with her examination, she hoped that the bullet had made only a flesh wound.

"Lord, I'm thankful that this fellow is out cold because he's gonna be in awful pain when he wakes up," Rosie said to the high heavens.

Realizing that she would need some help to carry this man to the shack, she walked slowly through the muddy marsh and grabbed the horse's reins. Leading him over to the dock proved to be almost more than she could handle. He was a big, strong animal that had been well taken care of, and he didn't like strangers. She hurried to the end of the dock and retrieved her long line of flapping fish. Leading the horse over to a fallen tree stump, she stepped up onto the tree stump and climbed up on the saddle. The horse didn't appear to be pleased with a strange rider, but after sidestepping a few times and not wanting to move forward, Rosie managed to guide him to the trail that led to her home.

Rosie lived in the Louisiana Bayou near the Texas border. Her home was an old rundown shack that was hardly fit for animals to live in, much less a young girl and her two brothers. The frame of the shack leaned to one side, and boards were tacked on over holes in the roof.

"Tater, I need your help," Rosie yelled as she rode the big horse into the clearing of the shack. Tater, Rosie's thirteen-year-old brother was sitting on the front steps whittling pieces of wood to help start the fire in the fireplace. He was thin as a reed with big green eyes and a dirty face sprinkled with brown freckles. He had long, reddish-brown hair that he tied back with a piece of thin leather. His face and neck were tanned, but he hadn't seen a bath in a month of Sundays.

"Gosh, Rosie, where'd you steal the horse?" asked Tater.

"Tater, you know better than that! I ain't never stolen a thing in my life. I found a man down by the river that's been shot. We've got to bring him here or else he'll die. He might die anyways, but we got to try and help the poor fellow."

"Why didn't you toss him on the horse?"

"He's a big son of a gun. You and me together can't lift him on this tall horse so run around to the garden and get the little wagon. I'll go in and get Boo."

Tater headed away to do as Rosie asked while she hurried into the house and walked over to the baby's crib. Looking down at her darling two-year-old brother playing with a pan and a wooden spoon, she untied the rope that secured his ankle to the crib. He wore a long, white nightshirt and a dingy white nappy. Boo had to be watched or tied every minute of the day or he would wander out of the house and be out of sight in a flash.

"Up you go, Boo! We're going for a ride in the wagon," Rosie said as she lifted him onto her hip. "Oh crackers, you're soaked." Grabbing a dry nappy, she quickly changed the baby as he repeated the word crackers. "I wanna…ackers!"

Rosie placed Boo into the wagon and pulled him as fast as she could while he held on for dear life. He was laughing and squealing as his beautiful brown curls blew in the wind. Rosie hit every bump on the sandy dirt trail. Tater was bending his thin frame over the back of the wagon, pushing to keep Rosie on course.

Approaching the man's body in the thick brush, Rosie checked again to make sure he was alive. Lifting his eyelid, she could tell that he had beautiful green eyes. She pressed her face to his bloody chest to see if she could hear a heartbeat.

"He's still alive, Tater. Let's get him into the wagon. Sure wish we had something bigger to haul him in. Oh well, we'll have to manage with what we got. Now you grab his feet and I'll get his shoulders."

"I'm going to take his big boots off first. Hey, if he dies, maybe I can wear his boots. They're sure fine ones," Tater said while thinking of the prospect of getting something new to wear.

"Tater, hush that kind of talk and get his feet. I'm going to set Boo on the ground and lay the wagon over on its side. Let's push him into the wagon and then turn the wagon back up on its four wheels. He's one tall drink of water, I'll tell you that. Boo!" Rosie yelled as she grabbed at the baby. "Stand beside me, now you hear!"

After what seemed like an hour of struggling to pick up the giant, Rosie and Tater managed to get the fellow into the wagon without taking in too much swamp water. His side had begun to bleed again as his long legs hung over the back of the wagon. Rosie and Tater were both as muddy as two old pigs.

"Tater, put this wet young'un on your back, and I'll pull the wagon. We've got to hurry so I can try to stop the bleeding and get him cleaned up so he won't get an infection in his wound."

Once the trio made it home with the lifeless body of the cowboy, Rosie very gently turned the wagon onto its side and dumped the man and water out onto the ground. Blood was oozing out of the young man's body as he lay on his back in the wet dirt.

Tater had carried the baby back inside and changed his wet nappy. He placed him back in the crib and retied his ankle. He walked over to a jar and got Boo two crackers to nibble on while getting several to eat for himself.

Sitting down on the step of the porch to rest, Tater was breathing hard while attempting to eat his crackers. "How are we going to get this man into the house, Rosie?"

Rosie had flopped down on the ground next to the cowboy, trying to catch her breath too. Before she could answer him, Justice, an old black Creole friend, walked from around the back of the shack. Justice claimed to have the power of voodoo.

The old woman looked at the man lying on the ground and then looked at Rosie and Tater who were both out of breath and muddy from head to toe. "What yo' doing with that body? Where'd you find him?"

"Thank goodness you're here, Justice," said Rosie as she slowly stood up from the ground. "We sure can use your help to pick this big boy up and get him in Pa's bed. I found him in the swamp near the dock where I fish every morning. He's been shot and is bleeding badly."

"Guess I had a feeling you needed me," she responded by reaching her arms up into the air as if she could feel the spirits.

"Come on, boy. Let's grab his legs while Rosie holds his head up. Let's get this body on the porch, and if need be, we'll drag him in the house," instructed Justice, looking down at the man's bloody body.

After what seemed like forever, the three of them were finally able to place the young cowboy on the bed. Rosie told Tater to bring her a pot of hot water while she looked for some clean rags to make a bandage. Rushing over to the large pan of cold water, she washed the mud off her hands and arms. After gathering some of Boo's clean nappies, she continued to look for something to tie the bandage up on to his side. Glancing at the pretty flour sackcloth that she had gotten last month with the fifty-pound bag of flour, she sighed. She'd have to use it, but she really wanted to make herself a skirt. She didn't know when she would be able to purchase more flour and get more material.

Oh well, we all have to made sacrifices sometimes, she thought.

Justice was busy removing the man's vest and shirt. The hole in his side looked bad, but over the years, she had seen worse. She loosened his belt buckle and slid his denims off his long hairy legs and tossed them in the pile with the other wet clothes. Grabbing a blanket, she quickly removed his white drawers. Rosie got an eyeful as she approached the bed just as Justice was covering up his bottom half.

"Tater," Rosie said, "please take his wet, muddy clothes outside and put them in the big pot that is ready to wash. Go ahead and start the fire under it so the clothes can be washing. There are a few more of Boo's nappies that can go in it too."

"Shucks, sis, I wanted to go through his saddlebags that I got off his horse."

"You can do that as soon as you put the wash in the pot. He will need his clothes soon, and I want them to dry today. While you're out there, unsaddle the horse and hobble him in that tall grass."

After giving the young stranger a thorough cleaning, Justice reached down into her bosom and pulled out a small sack that contained some special healing herbs. She requested a real clean hot pad to place on the open wound.

"Rosie, fetch me that bottle of rye whiskey that you have hidden in your special place. Thank the almighty that drunken fool of a papa of ya' ain't found it yet."

Rosie leaped off the front porch and raced around the house and removed a bed of moss from an old tree stump and retrieved the bottle. If her old pa knew that she had this bottle, he would have drank it up in one sitting. Thank the Lord he wasn't home today. He hadn't been home in months, but she and Tater didn't give a hoot.

Justice laid the hot compress onto the gunshot wound, and the young man sat straight up and yelled. "Damn!" he screamed and then laid back down, unconscious.

Justice continued with the cleaning of the wound on the front and back of his side. Once she was sure all the particles of the gunpowder had been removed, she sprinkled some of her medical herbs over the hole. "These herbs will help the wound to close and keep the infection from entering his body. He's healthy and strong. He will live because of you, Rosie."

"Me? You're the one caring for him."

"True, child, but you found him and brought him home—if you call this place home. He could have stayed out there and died in that swamp."

2

L ATER THAT EVENING, as the young cowboy slept, Tater placed his saddlebags on the table and emptied everything out of one of them. The first thing he pulled out was money— lots and lots of paper money. Rosie and Tater stood over the table, glancing back and forth at each other. Tater stacked the money in several piles, not bothering to count it. He reached in the other saddlebag and pulled out some folded papers, two decks of playing cards, and a handful of letters.

"This here paper says James Abraham Downey is the owner of a farm in Limason, Texas. So I guess this fellow's name is James Abraham Downey."

"That's a nice name, James." Rosie looked over at the cowboy and said that he looked more like an Abraham than a James.

Justice asked Tater if he had ever seen that place called Limason on the map.

"Can't rightly say, but I bet that's where he's headed 'cause he has a piece of land there." Tater held up the paper with signatures on it. Tater was proud of the schooling that he had received from Rosie these past few years. He hated going to the town school because he never fit in with the other boys. They picked on him every day until he brought a snake to school and told the boys that it was his pet and he could make him bite on command.

Tater continued to pull out more of the man's personal items. There was a comb, a straight razor, toothpowder, and a bar of used soap. There were several letters addressed to a James A. Downey.

"These letters are addressed to the prison outside of New Orleans. He's been in prison! I wonder if he escaped." Tater's voice rose to a high pitch.

"No, he's no jailbird. He's not dressed in prison clothes," said Rosie with a big sigh. "Look for a date on the letters. The one letter I wrote I remember putting the day and the time I wrote it. You know they teach you to do that in school."

After scanning the letters, Tater declared that they were old letters. "Here are his release papers from the prison. You're right as usual, Rosie. He ain't an escaped convict."

"Thank goodness for that," she replied.

Justice walked over to the table to look at all the items that had been taken out of the saddlebags. "In the morning, Tater, you'll need to go into town and get some grub for this place. Rosie, let him take twenty dollars out of this man's money to fetch some food. You've earned a little of this money for saving his life and this place needs food and other things. Sit a spell and make out a list for him to take to the store."

"Oh, Justice, I can't take the stranger's money. It ain't right."

"What's you going to feed him when he wakes? You need food for the baby, I'm sure. Don't be a ninny now. Do as I say."

"You're right, of course. He'll need food to gain his strength back from all the blood that he has lost. Let's get busy, Tater. You'll have to help me decide what all we may need. Before we get started, we need to hide the saddlebags just in case we have unwanted visitors." Rosie prayed that her old pa didn't chose to come home anytime soon.

Early the next morning, Tater took the little wagon into town to purchase some fresh food and canned goods. Rosie instructed him to say nothing about the cowboy being at their place just in case whoever shot him might still be around.

"If that nosy Mr. Hatcher asks where you got the money, you tell him that I sold some things to a peddler that comes through here. If he keeps on pestering you about it, just come on back home. I'll go and get the things we need." Mr. Hatcher was the owner of the little store in the nearest town, and he was always up in everybody's business.

The young cowboy felt as if he was drowning into a pit of darkness, and his body was on fire. Was he in hell? No way. He was lying on something soft, and he could hear a sweet voice humming. Was he caught between heaven and hell? Was there such a place? He was struggling to rise and open his eyes. He felt as if he was dreaming and being tortured. He was miserable lying down. He needed to get up and go relieve himself, but something or somebody was holding him down. He knew that he couldn't still be in the prison camp. He didn't hear the stomping of the guard's boots as they patrolled on the high catwalk around the camp. There was no screaming from someone being whipped, which seemed to happen every hour of each day. The smell of something good was cooking—fried fish. He could hear something running nearby; the pitter-patter of small feet or a large dog, maybe. There was a child's voice speaking about something being in the room. A mouse, *have mercy, a rat* maybe?

"'ie! There's a 'ouse! Get it!" Boo raced by the bed where Bud laid.

"Oh, Boo, he won't eat much! Just leave him be and *please* be quiet. We've got a sick man in the house."

I'm dreaming, the young man thought as he tried again to raise his head, but he couldn't lift it.

As he lay on the bed trying hard to wake up, he began to hear a sweet soft voice singing *Amazing Grace*. Lord, have I died and someone is singing at my funeral? Lying still, he drifted back off to sleep.

After a few hours, he woke up, and finally was able to raise his head and look around. He heard chanting. Someone was chanting about *trouble*. He looked straight ahead out the door that was pushed wide open. There standing behind a large tree stump stood the ugliest black creature he had ever seen. A small, wiry-looking black woman with colorful rags sitting on top of her head appeared to be in some kind of trance. There were a cloud of white feathers flying all around her. In one hand, she held a bloody ax and in the other hand, which she held high above her head, was a big, headless chicken. Blood was streaming down her arm as she shook the fat, bloody bird while chanting something about *trouble, double trouble!*

The shock of seeing the headless bloody chicken was too much for the young man. He mumbled something about a nightmare and fell backward on the bed in a dead faint.

"Justice," Rosie yelled, "the cowboy woke up for a minute and then he went back out."

Justice was in her own little world as she prepared a chicken for the stew pot.

Tater arrived back home after a few hours of walking to town and purchasing the much-needed supplies. Rosie was right about old man Hatcher. He had cornered Tater and drilled him as to where he got a twenty-dollar bill. Tater told him that they had picked cotton to earn the money. He had been so nervous that he had forgotten what Rosie told him to say.

Mr. Hatcher knew that old man Jourdian had been gone for months and had left those kids to fend for themselves. The church in town had offered them food and clothes, but the girl, Rosie, wouldn't accept charity. Her pa was a drunken bum who loved a jug of moonshine more than he did his family. One night, he had been seen at a cockfight, betting what little money he had on a big red rooster. After he lost all his money, he just up and disappeared. Somebody said they heard he jumped on a wheel boat and left the area.

Early the next morning, Tater milked their poor cow. After letting Rosie strain the milk, he lowered it down in the well to keep cool. With some of the money, he had purchased a bag of oats and some chicken feed for their animals. Thank the good Lord for the few farm critters that they owned. The cow gave them milk, and the chickens supplied eggs each day. As Tater came into the house, he could smell bacon frying. He was very thankful that Rosie had found the stranger because he didn't know how much longer they could keep eating fish. Justice had brought over the chicken that she cooked yesterday and made a stew. Every time Rosie had to kill one of their own chickens, she would cry and not eat a morsel.

"That bacon smells mighty good. I hope you're cooking a big batch of those flapjacks 'cause I can feel my backbone this morning," said Tater.

"I could cook all day and never fill you up. You've got a hollow leg!"

"Maybe so, but I'm ready to eat," he replied as he picked up his little brother and placed him in his high chair. "Now sit still or I'll tie you in."

Boo squealed with laughter and banged on the table. "Jacks, jacks!"

"Please go out to the well and get the milk. We're ready to eat."

As Rosie was waiting for Tater to return with the milk, she cut up some flapjacks for the baby and gave him a small piece of bacon. "Chew good now, Boo, I don't want you to choke."

Rosie walked over to the bed and looked down at James Abraham Downey. He had slept all night. He tossed and turned and made moaning noises, but he didn't ever wake up.

As Rosie turned to walk back to the table, the cowboy had been peeking out of his eyelids at the girl. He reached out and grabbed her arm and jerked her to the floor. Rosie screamed to the top of her lungs as he attempted to sit up. The blanket slid off his naked body.

Tater heard Rosie's cry for help and raced into the house, slogging milk on the floor.

He immediately took in the problem. "Hey, mister, turn my sister loose before I deck you one. Man, cover yourself up too."

Rosie slowly stood and straightened her dress. She looked down on the angry man and gave him a sweet smile. "It's so good to see you're awake. You've been out for nearly two days. Please, let me look at your side to make sure it's not bleeding. You've got to be careful and not move around like you just did for a while."

The young man was looking at the young girl who had the voice of an angel and the dirtiest auburn hair he had ever seen. "Where am I? Who are you?"

"You're at our place, mine and Tater and Boo's. Well, my name is Rosie Jourdian and this here is my two brothers, Simon and Peter, but I call them Tater and Boo. You're near the big town of Lafayette. We live at the edge of the river and the entrance of the swamp."

He never took his eyes off Rosie and the two boys. He watched them and they looked at him wondering what he was going to do next. Finally he spoke, "I've got to piss, I mean, I need to go to the outhouse."

"Oh, you can't get up until Justice says that you can and she ain't here right now. Tater, get the can and help Mr. Downey."

"How do you know my name?"

"Well, we…" Rosie mumbled.

"I went through your saddlebags and looked at some of your papers. They had your name on them. I hid your saddlebags. I'll get them whenever you want them. Your horse has been taken care of too," said Tater.

"I see." He was very pleased that his things had not been stolen. "Get the can and you get your little butt out of here while I take care of business."

"Of course," Rosie said as she turned to Tater. "Can you watch Boo eat while you are helping him or do I need to get him out of his chair?"

"Nah, leave him."

After a few minutes, Tater called to Rosie that she could come back into the room as he carried the can outside to empty it.

Rosie got a bowl of hot water and a clean rag and carried it over to him. "Mr. Downey, let me help you sit up for a few minutes while you wash your face and hands. I have a big breakfast cooked, and I know that you must be hungry."

"Bud," he said.

"What?"

"Bud's my name. My father is Mr. Downey. Call me Bud."

"Sure thing, but the papers say that your name is James Abraham. Why Bud?"

"I don't remember being called anything else. I guess like your brothers, Simon and Peter."

"Can you place your feet on the floor. Justice will be here shortly, and she will dress your wound again and put more medicine on it. The medicine takes some of the pain away."

Bud turned, and using the blanket to cover his lower body, he put his feet on the floor. Taking the clean washrag and dipping it in the hot water he wiped his face and hands. "This feels so good."

"I'm glad. I'll mix you some soda water to rinse your mouth out with and I can help you shave after you've eaten."

"I can shave myself and I have some toothpowder in my saddlebags. How did I get to your place? The last thing I remember I was being chased by two men who were trying to steal my money."

"Well, I was fishing, and I heard your horse in the swampy grass trying to get to the edge of the river to get water. While I was trying to catch him, I stepped on you. Nearly scared me to death, I tell you, when I saw you lying there all dead-looking and all!"

Giving her a once-over, he said, "You couldn't have picked me up and put me on my horse. How did you carry me here?" quizzed Bud.

"Tater and I rolled you into our little wagon and when we got you home, we rolled you out of it. Sounds awful, don't it?"

"Doesn't it?" Bud corrected her.

"Doesn't what?" Rosie asked.

"Never mind," Bud said, trying to be polite.

"Anyways, Justice came and she helped us get you up on the porch and into the house. Justice is very good with healing folks with her special powders and herbs. She has taken real good care of you. You haven't got any infection and that's because she cleaned you up good. The bullet went into your right side and came out the back."

"Damn, no wonder I was on fire. I thought I had a hot poker touching my side."

"Please don't swear." Rosie requested very sweetly.

"What?"

"You know…the children. Boo repeats everything he hears. I don't want Tater thinking that he can talk that way."

"Please forgive me. I've been around a rough bunch of men, and I have forgotten my manners."

"Why were you in prison?" Rosie asked.

"You don't beat around the bush, do you? I guess you've seen my release papers in my saddlebag. Listen, you mentioned food. Can I eat first and we'll talk later?"

Bud ate a large stack of flapjacks and a half dozen pieces of bacon. He drank some cool milk. In less than ten minutes after filling his stomach with the hardy breakfast, he was yelling for a bucket. His stomach rolled, and he heaved. After he finished throwing up his guts, Rosie gave him a glass of soda water and said, "Don't swallow any of it."

Bud laid down on the mattress holding his stomach and instantly went to sleep. Justice wasn't a bit surprised by what had happened to him. She instructed Rosie to give him some of the chicken broth that she had made the day before. "His stomach wasn't ready for heavy food," she said.

While Bud was sleeping, Justice attempted to remove his bandage. Bud woke up and looked at the old black Creole woman in the face. *What the hell?* he thought.

"Well, young man, I see you lived. That's good. I hate it when my herbs don't work."

"You must be Justice." Bud scrutinized the little woman from head to toe and remembered seeing her in his *nightmare.*

"That's me. How does your side feel? Has the burning gone away?"

"Yes, it was better until I spilled my guts this morning after I ate."

"I need to remove this bandage and replace it with a clean one. Can you sit up?"

"Where are my clothes? I would like to put on some drawers," he said with a cocky grin.

"Rosie will get them for you. She washed and ironed your pants yesterday."

"Where is everybody?" Bud had been looking around the shack and didn't see the girl or the boys.

"Rosie took them fishing. She fishes every day. The fish helps with the food supply. Every day one meal will be fish," explained Justice.

After examining Bud's wound, Justice was pleased to see that her medicine was working and the bullet hole was closing up from the inside out. There was no sign of infection.

"You need to take it easy, boy. No picking up anything heavy or riding that big horse of yours," instructed Justice just like a real doctor.

"How long?"

"How long for what?" Justice asked with a frown.

"How long will it be before I can ride? I've got to get away from here, well, I mean I've got to be on my way. I'm heading home to see my folks and I've got a farm to start working."

"The person who shot you is still after you? Is this shack of young people in danger 'cause they found you and saved your hide?"

"Lord, I hope not. As for the men who shot me, I believe that they are still looking for me. They were plenty mad that they lost a big pot of money to me. But I won it fair and square and I'm not going to surrender it to them."

"You best not have put these young'uns in danger. They ain't got no protection, and Rosie would die for her little brothers. She's awful pretty and no telling what those men might do to her."

"Pretty, you mean dirty don't you. The whole bunch of them needs to be thrown in the river for a good bath," said Bud as he lay back down on the bed.

"Dirty or clean, you best not let them come to any harm," warned Justice.

"Where are their folks? How come they live here alone?"

"Their Ma up and ran off with a peddler right after she was strong enough to get out of bed from having little Boo. Their pa is a drunken sot who would sell his soul for a drink of rye whiskey. Once, a few months ago, he tried to sell Rosie to some men who came by for a drink of cold well water. She heard him making a deal with them so she ran off into the swamp. The men weren't interested, praise the Lord. I was shore glad that I didn't have to put a spell on them."

Bud was upset learning about the children's folks, but he was very concerned that this old black woman said that she could cast spells on people. *Wonder if she really could?*

"Can you really put spells on people?" asked Bud.

"I try not to 'cause it drains my strength, but yep, I can and I will if I have to."

Bud laid on the bed looking at Justice as she moved around in the little shack. She squatted down in front of the fireplace and built the fire up to take the chill out of the room. He drifted off to sleep as he watched her mix a batch of cornmeal to make cornpones to go with the fish.

Rosie returned home with the two boys. She scooped up Boo and changed his nappy and laid him down in the crib. He had played at the water's edge until he was ready for his morning nap. Tater was outside cleaning the five catfish that they caught for dinner.

"How's our patient today? Did you change his bandage?" Rosie asked.

"Yep, he's fine. I told him to take it easy. He can get up and go to the outhouse, but that is all."

"Justice," whispered Rosie, "I seen some riders looking around in the swamp area nearby where I found him. I grabbed the boys and got away from there before they saw us."

"You think that they were looking for this…Bud?"

"Afraid so, I heard them talking, but I couldn't make out what they were saying. I didn't stick around. I told Tater to keep his ears and eyes open while outside. Sure hope they don't come here."

Tater brought in the fish, and Rosie prepared them to be fried.

"Sure wish we could have something besides fish," grumbled Tater.

"Hush complaining. We had bacon and flapjacks yesterday and tonight we're having chicken and dumplings, your favorite!" Rosie smiled at Tater as he grinned and went back outside.

3

AFTER A LONG morning nap, Bud sat up on the bed and glanced around the shack. There wasn't anyone in the house. He needed to go to the outhouse so he pulled the covers back and placed his bare feet onto the swept floor. This was a pitiful place for anyone to call home, but surprisingly it was very neat and clean. He pulled the thin blanket up around his waist and tried to stand. He was light-headed, and he swayed a little after the first step or two. He balanced himself by using the wall of the shack and walked bent over to the front door. His side was very sore, but he didn't have the burning, stabbing pain that he had before. Once he made it to the front door, he saw Rosie beside the house in a fenced area. She had a straw hat covering her long dirty hair, and she was chopping at some high weeds. Boo was trapped in the fenced area with her. Tater had moved his horse out of the barn. He had several buckets of water, and he was washing him. He glanced out over the yard and saw the path that led to the outhouse. Slowly he made his way onto the porch and down the one step that led to the ground. He was trying to keep the blanket wrapped around his near naked body.

Rosie removed her straw hat and used the back of her hand to wipe the sweat off her brow. She couldn't believe that Bud was attempting to make it to the outhouse by himself. He was naked except for his knee length drawers. He had wrapped the bottom part of his body with the thin blanket off his bed.

"Tater, go help that stupid fool before he falls flat on his face!"

Tater looked in the direction that Rosie was pointing, and he threw down his soapy brush and rushed over to grab Bud by the arm. Bud had heard Rosie yell for Tater to go and help him.

"I don't need your help," Bud said through clenched teeth. One more step and his knees began to fold under him as Tater offered his arm for support.

"Well, maybe I do…this time." As Tater opened the door to the clean little outhouse, Bud twisted around, jerking his blanket that covered his backside inside with him. Tater couldn't help but give Bud a big smile as he pulled the door closed with a bang. Tater stood waiting for Bud so he could help him back inside the house.

Rosie and Boo had come back inside the shack. Rosie walked over and handed Bud his freshly washed clothes. "Sorry about your shirt. It was pretty much ruined with the bullet hole in it so I washed one of Pa's for you. He ain't needing it now."

"Appreciate it," said Bud. "I'll feel better wearing my pants in the presence of ladies." Bud gave Rosie a big smile and asked if he could have some privacy so he could dress.

"Why? You ain't got nothing I ain't already seen?" replied Rosie.

"I may have been unconscious when you were gawking at my bloody body, but I'm fully awake now, so get your little ragtail out of here before I toss you out!"

Rosie walked over to Boo and said, "Come, my boy. We're not needed here any longer."

Rosie stayed outside most of the afternoon as she worked in her little vegetable garden. Boo raced around the yard, chasing butterflies with the bottom of his nappy wet and black as soot. He was a very happy baby who could entertain himself with a stick or a roly-poly bug. Rosie had taught him not to eat the bugs, but she wasn't sure that he didn't.

Rosie pulled the big washtub down off the wall and walked to the well and pulled up two buckets of cold water. She poured the water into the tub to allow the sun to take the chill off the water. Boo loved a bath. When the water was warm, Rosie placed Boo into the tub. He kicked and splashed.

Bud had laid down after he dressed himself in his clean clothes. He could hear the sound of laughter, so he pulled himself up off the bed and walked to the front door and looked out. There in the middle of the yard was Boo playing in a big tub of water. There was more water on the ground than in the tub, but he appeared to have had his hair washed and his face was shining clean. Rosie was kneeling down beside him as he attempted to splash water on her.

Now, that's one little gal who needs a bath. Splash her good, Boo, thought Bud. Rosie glanced up and saw Bud standing at the door.

"Come on out and I'll get a table chair for you to sit. Fresh air and sunshine will be good for you," she said while going into the house to get a chair. Rosie placed the chair on the porch for Bud to sit on while she went back out into the yard to watch Boo play a little longer.

"I'll be glad when I can bathe all over. Boo makes his bath look so inviting," Bud said.

"He has always loved the water so he doesn't mind getting a bath or a good scrubbing. Now Tater ain't fond of a bath no time," she explained.

"What about yourself? Don't you like a good bath?"

Reaching up and stoking her long dirty hair, she said with a sigh, "I do, but it's better for me to look like this especially when strangers come upon us."

"Do you get many strangers dropping by here?" Bud was getting concerned that this place wasn't a very safe hideout for him.

"At times. Well, a few men came by here a couple of months ago, but none since." She remembered how angry and sad she felt when she heard her own pa trying to sell her to those men. Thank goodness they weren't interested or they might have caught her as she ran away and hid.

"I'm going to need to leave here soon. When I'm able to ride, I'll go into town and get some supplies for my trip. I think I'm about a week away from home."

"How long has it been since you've been there?" Rosie asked.

Bud was thinking that it had been way too long since he had seen his pa and ma. His little brothers were almost grown now. He had missed everyone so much.

"It has been nearly two years. I really miss my folks and my two brothers."

"Must be nice to have a ma and pa that you miss."

Bud remembered what Justice said about Rosie's folks, and he could see the sadness in her eyes. *This kid has really had it rough,* he thought. *It's a shame that she has had to raise her two brothers all alone. She has to fish and hunt and live off a small garden to feed herself and her little family. She has never had anyone to care about her well-being unless it was Justice, her old black friend. There were no decent clothes to wear, and they were isolated from town out in this hidden swamp home.*

Bud couldn't help but think about how easy he had it at home when he was Rosie's age. He had chores to do, but he never had to worry about anybody, not even himself. There was always plenty of good food and nice clothes to wear. His Ma and Pa made sure that he had a nice horse to ride. He went to school and church and didn't have a care in the world. He wished now that he had realized how good he had it. His folks were good to him, and they didn't deserve a rotten son like him.

As Bud continued to talk with Rosie, he realized that she wasn't a person to feel sorry for herself. She wasn't an angry or rebellious young girl. She got up every day with a smile on her face and took charge of her two brother's care. The few days that he had been here, she took excellent care of him without the first complaint. He was beginning to realize how fortunate he was to be found by her. *He owned his life to her, that's for sure*, he thought.

"You know you never did tell me how come you was in that prison?" asked Rosie. "Did you kill somebody?"

Bud laughed and said no, that he didn't kill anybody. "I don't want to talk about it, but I will tell you this. I did something stupid, and fortunately for me, I had some friends that helped me out. But I've paid for my stupidity, and I certainly don't intend to go back to prison again."

"All right. I won't ask again. I don't like folks meddling into my business either." Rosie grabbed a towel off the clothesline and reached down and wrapped Boo in it.

"No, down, down!" Boo screamed to the top of his lungs and pushed and pulled at Rosie to put him back in the tub.

Rosie whispered something in Boo's ear, and he settled down and grabbed her around the neck. He placed his thumb in his mouth and laid his head on her shoulder. "Such a sweet boy, my Boo," she cooed to him as she walked past Bud to enter the shack.

Bud's side was beginning to ache, so he stood and walked back inside to his bed. He eased down on the side of it and slowly lay down onto his back. "Oh, this feels good to just lie down," he said to Rosie as he watched her feed Boo some homemade soup with a few soda crackers.

"When I'm finished feeding Boo, I will dish you up some soup too. It's got a lot of fish and wild onions in it, and I thicken it with flour. Justice taught me how to make it. She calls it chowder. It will hold you until I can cook chicken and dumplings for supper."

"You're a mighty fine cook for a young girl your age," Bud replied.

"Had to learn or starve. No one else hereabout to help me but old Justice. I don't know what I would've done over the years without her friendship."

Rosie glanced over at Bud, and he was fast asleep. She smiled down at him, thinking he was just plain pretty. He had a head full of black hair, deep green eyes with thick eyelashes, straight white teeth, and a fine straight nose. His body was lean and firm. Not an ounce of fat on him anywhere. *He was a mighty fine-looking man for shore*, she thought.

Justice came walking into the house later that evening. She was carrying a big basket that contained two loaves of homemade bread. "Here you go, honey," she said to Rosie and she took the bread out and placed it on the shelf over the stove.

"Where in the world did you get the fresh bread?" quizzed Rosie as she reached for a loaf and sliced a thin piece for Tater and Boo. She cut herself a slice and dipped it in Boo's bowl of chicken and dumplings. "Gracious, this is so good."

"I bartered for it from an old lady. She wanted me to help cure her big toe. It was about to rot off. After a few days of my special medicine, it was so much better. I told her my payment was some bread."

"Oh, Justice, you're too good to us."

"How's the cowboy? Is he getting up and moving around?"

"I sure am, thanks to the wonderful care that I have had from both of you girls." Bud was awake and sitting up on the side of the bed. "Something sure smells good."

"Sounds like he's better for shore," winked Justice at Rosie.

"This morning, he walked out to the outhouse and then sat in a chair on the porch after he dressed himself. Finally, after tuckering himself out he went to sleep before eating."

"Hey, you don't have to talk about me like I'm not here," he said with a big smile.

"Come on over and sit at the table, and I'll dish you a heaping bowl of chicken and dumplings and a big piece of fresh baked bread," said Rosie.

After Bud was comfortable at the supper table, Rosie placed Boo in his crib and Tater went out to care for Bud's horse. Justice pulled up a chair and sat across from Bud.

"I'm afraid that I got bad news for you," Justice said as she looked at Bud, who was practically shoving food in his mouth.

"Give it to me straight." Bud placed his spoon down beside his bowl and looked at Justice.

"Two men were in town last night. They were going from saloon to saloon asking questions about a tall guy with black hair riding a big buckskin horse. An old black man got in their way and one of the buzzards stabbed him just because they bumped into each other. His daughter fetched me, and I was able to help him. He told me about these men. I know they are looking for you."

"Sounds like it," Bud replied softly. "Listen, I've got to leave and head on toward Texas before they make their way here. I'll leave at first light."

"Justice, make him stay longer. You're not well enough to ride!" cried Rosie to Justice and Bud.

"Child, he's got to do what he must."

"It'll be better for all of you if I'm not discovered here." Bud stood and walked slowly to the door. He walked down the step and headed to the barn.

Bud walked into the old barn and saw Tater giving his horse a good rubdown. Tater was talking to the horse just like he was speaking to a person. Bud stood in the doorway listening to the young man as he whispered his dreams out loud.

"One day, I'm going to have a fine animal just like you. I'll take good care of him too, just like I'm caring for you, boy. I'm going to ride away from this stinking place and never look back. Well, I'll have to take Rosie and Boo with me, but we'll leave this place, never to return." The buckskin tossed his head, and Tater noticed Bud standing nearby.

Tater immediately stopped his chatter and said hello to Bud. "You shore got a fine animal here. I sure would like to ride him one day, if you don't mind."

"You've done a mighty fine job taking care of him for me. I know that he liked the bath and all of the good rub downs you have given him every day. I know that he's going to miss you. I've got to leave in the morning, son. I do thank you for all of your help."

"Why? Why in the morning? You're not well enough to ride yet," said Tater.

"It's for the best that I head on out. The men that shot me are in town looking for me and it won't be long before they'll be coming out this way. I don't want to have to kill them, but it could come to that if I stay and have to confront them."

"Tater, do you have a gun on the place?"

"Got an old shotgun but no shells for it," he replied with misty eyes.

"Damn." Bud thought for just a second. "Well, I have two pistols and a Winchester repeating rifle. I'm afraid the rifle will be too much for you to handle, but one of my handguns should be all right. Do you think that if I showed you how to load and shoot it that you'll remember how to do it after I've gone?" Before Tater could give Bud an answer, they both heard horses and men shouting in the front yard. They rushed over to the window to see what the commotion was.

"Damn it," Bud swore. "I've got to get out of here. Listen, Tater, in a few minutes I need for you to push this door open and then run into the swamp as fast as you can. I'm going to get on my horse and lay low and ride like hell. I'm sure they will follow me and leave all of you alone. Got that, boy?" Tater shook his head yes while Bud was tossing the blanket and his saddle over on the back of his horse. He grabbed his saddlebags and quickly secured them. Next he shoved his rifle into the leather scabbard and gave his saddle cinch another hard pull.

In the house, Justice looked out the front door and saw the two men from town. "Rosie!" she whispered. "Those bad men are here looking for Bud."

"Hey, in the house! Get your asses out here *now*! Bring that sorry low-down snake of a gambler with you. If you ain't out here in one minute, we're going to burn this shack down around your ears!" The two men were pulling on their horses as they circled around in the yard.

"Justice," whispered Rosie as she rushed over to the crib and jerked Boo up into her arms. "Take Boo," she said as she shoved the baby into Justice's arms. "Go out back into the swamp. Hurry, I will stall them a minute. Wonder where Tater and Bud are right now?"

"I saw Bud walking out to the barn, and I bet Tater is in there too."

"Hurry, now. I'm going out to the porch and try to talk to them," said Rosie.

"Lord, child, be careful!" she said softy as she slid out the backdoor and raced into the tall grass behind the shack.

"Time's up in the house. I've got a torch—" He stopped screaming when he saw Rosie step out onto the porch. She was smoothing down her hair with one hand and running the other hand down the front of her shift.

"Well, well, lookie here, Jasper!" One of the angry men rode his horse closer to the porch. As he started to get down, the other man gave him an order.

"Make her tell us where that fool of a gambler is hiding!"

"I'm gonna make her do more than that." As he got off his horse, he gave Rosie a big toothless smile as he ambled toward her.

In a flash, Tater pushed the old rotten barn door open, and Bud rode his big, brown buckskin out of the barn. Lying low on the horse's back, he gave him a hard kick in his side and the horse practically flew out of the yard. Bud gave a loud yell so the men would follow him down the old dirt trail that led away from the shack.

"There he goes! You sorry piece of trash!" The nasty man bellowed at Rosie as he tossed the fiery torch inside the door of the shack and remounted his horse. Both of the men took off in pursuit of Bud as fast as their horses would carry them.

Rosie was so beside herself with worry about Tater that she didn't take time to try to put out the fire inside the shack. She followed the direction where she had last seen him headed; she ran while screaming his name at the top of her lungs.

Tater came out of the brush and grabbed Rosie as she raced by him. "Here I am!"

Rosie hugged her brother who had been so brave to help Bud escape the awful men. "I was so afraid for you when I didn't know where you was. Justice said she thought you was in the barn with Bud. Thank goodness you were together out of sight of those men."

"Where is Justice and Boo?" he asked, and before she could reply, he pointed. "Look at all that smoke! Come on. Let's go see what's happened."

When the two returned to the front of the shack, they saw Justice and Boo standing in the yard watching the last of their home go up in smoke. Rosie walked over to her old friend and took Boo out of her arms. They all stood while watching the old rotten boards go up in flames. The old boards that covered the roof were crashing down, sending ashes and sparks high into the sky. The shack crumbled and disappeared right before their eyes. Not a tear was shed for their loss.

"What are you going to do, child?" Justice asked as she was looking at the pile of charred boards with black smoke rolling up into the clear blue sky.

Rosie looked around at her surroundings and saw the clothes that she had washed earlier and hung out to dry. "Thank goodness, I had some wash on the clothesline. Boo has clean nappies at least." Rosie walked over and sat down on the big tree stump with Boo in her arms.

"The barn is still here," said Tater. "It's mostly dry." Tater was very mature for thirteen. Rosie had raised him to always look on the brighter side of life.

"That's true. We've got the little garden and some of the money that we took from Bud. We'll be all right."

"Maybe that cowboy will come back and see how you fared," Justice said.

"I just hope he's safe somewhere out there away from those nasty men. They sure scared me."

4

B UD HAD NEARLY run his buckskin into the ground before he had to stop and deal with the two scalawags that were determined to rob him of his winnings. He had won the money fair and square, and he wasn't about to give it up to these two sorry losers.

He rode his horse behind some big rocks and secured him to a tall thin pine tree. He climbed up on the rocks and lay low waiting for them to come around the bend. His side was on fire again and hurting like hell. It was too soon to be riding, and his body was screaming with pain. The men were about fifty yards behind him. He allowed the lead horseman to get about twenty yards from him when he took aim and fired his rifle. He made contact and hit him in the right shoulder. He screamed and fell off his horse. The other rider was directly behind him and nearly ran over his partner. Bud fired again and shot several times with his repeating rifle hitting the other man in the arm and leg. He fell off his horse screaming and cussing a blue streak. Both of the men's horses kept on running down the trail without their riders.

Bud walked over to where the two men lay. He placed his rifle into the stomach of one of the cowboys and reached down and retrieved the colt .45 out of his holster. He looked at his wound and he knew that he was in excruciating pain. He didn't have sympathy for him because he was sure that he was one of the men who had shot him.

"I'd say that we're even, wouldn't you?" Bud asked the man as he lay moaning.

"What'd you mean, you bastard? You still got our money."

"You shot me and now I've shot you. But the difference is that I'm going to go into town and report to the sheriff that you tried to kill me and I had to defend myself. Just maybe he might come looking for you and help you back into town before you bleed to death or before some hungry, wild critter comes by this way."

Bud walked over to the other man who lay unconscious. He had fallen hard from his horse when he got hit. "Your partner is in a bad way." Bud reached down and turned him over on his back. He pulled his revolver out of his holster and walked back to the rocks where his horse was waiting.

Bud stuffed the men's two guns into his saddlebag and got onto his horse. He sat and studied his situation. He knew the right thing to do was go back to the shack and check on Rosie and the boys. He really had not thanked them properly for all the care that they had given him. He really owed Rosie and Justice his life, but how did you repay someone for doing that? After studying on the problem, he decided to go back to check on the little family before heading for town.

Bud rode into the yard and looked around at the pile of smothering wood. The shack was burnt to the ground, and black smoke was still floating into the air. The barn seemed to be intact. Bud got off his horse and held onto the reins as he yelled, "Rosie, Tater!"

"Here we are!" voices called from the tall brush behind the barn.

Rosie came from behind the barn carrying Boo in her arms. Tater was helping Justice as they walked into the front yard. "Oh, Bud," sighed Rosie. "We weren't expecting you to come back here, but its shore good to see that you're all right."

"I had to make sure those idiots didn't hurt ya'll. I had to shoot both of them, but they aren't dead. They don't have any guns or horses so they won't be bothering anyone for a while."

Looking at the pile of burned wood, Bud asked, "What happened to the house? How come it's burned to the ground?"

Justice spoke before Rosie could get out an answer. "Those men threatened to burn the house if you didn't come out. See, they thought you was hiding in there. When they saw you ride away, they threw their fiery torch inside the house. Rosie went in search of Tater while I hid in the swamp with the baby. When we all returned to the shack, it was burning to the ground. Now these poor young'uns got no home cause of you," Justice said softly but sternly.

"Justice! That ain't fair and you know it. Bud couldn't stop them men."

"It's all right Rosie. Justice is right. This is my fault," he replied as he looked at the dense smoke.

"Papa!" Boo screamed as he flapped his small arms and reached for Bud to take him.

"Lord, help me," Bud said as he took Boo out of Rosie's arms. "Darn it, you're pissy again."

Rosie's face blushed a bright pink. "Here, give him to me and let me go change him."

"Well?" Justice said as she walked over to the tree stump in the middle of the yard and sat down. Looking all around the place, she looked at Bud as he stood surveying the area.

"What you going to do now that you brought those heathens here. There's little food, no clothes, and no shelter except that fallen down barn that leaks like a sieve with it rains."

"Hey, old woman, I didn't ask to be brought here. I didn't ask to be bushwhacked by those bastards. If you remember I was unconscious, and I had no say as to where my carcass was being carried. So don't go blaming all this mess on me!"

Bud's temper flared, and his anger had quickly gotten out of control. He knew that he never intended for any of this to happen, and he felt guilty for raising his voice and speaking ugly to the old woman. But damn it, he didn't ask to be shot and left in the swamp to die. He didn't ask Rosie to drag his half-dead body here to this shack. He stormed over to the well, and he dropped the bucket down the shaft. After watering his horse, he led him toward the barn.

"Sorry, oh, boy, but you aren't going to be bedded down in here. It looks like this place will have new boarders," Bud said to his horse as he tied his reins to a post.

Rosie and Tater had walked over to the garden and began digging small red potatoes. Bud watched the two young people. Instead of Rosie crying and carrying on about her home being destroyed and this awful situation she found herself in, she was getting ready to prepare something to eat for her little family.

Bud walked off into the swamp area and found a fallen log to sit down on. He looked up into the sky. Taking off his black Stetson, he wiped the sweat off his forehead. Looking back toward the black smoke coming from the shack area, he knew that he was responsible for these children being homeless. They didn't need to remain here any longer, but where would they go? If they went to the city, they had no money for lodging so they would be living on the streets. Rosie was a beauty under all that dirt and grime, and it wouldn't be long before she found herself flat on her back in some brothel trying to earn a living. The boys would be taken away from her and placed in an orphanage. Bud couldn't imagine what that would do to her. Bud hung his head down between his knees and thought about praying, but he hadn't done that since he had been in prison. For the first six months, while in prison he thought that he wouldn't live to see the next sunrise. The guards in the prison made life a living hell every day for new prisoners. He prayed to God that if he helped him get out of the hell that he was forced to endure, he would never ask for anything else. God answered his prayers. That was one promise he never intended to break. He would never ask God for another thing.

Bud walked back into the front yard and went over to the well. He dropped the bucket down into it and began pulling up buckets filled with cold water. He tossed buckets of water onto the smoking charcoal boards. He wanted the remaining burning boards to be put out completely. He was out of breath as he placed the wooden round cover over the top of the well.

Justice walked over to the well and spoke softly to Bud. "Come over here and sit down on this big boulder and let me look at your side. It's bleeding again, and I know it must be paining you something awful." Bud placed the bucket on top of the well and unbuttoned his shirt and pulled it out of his pants. The bandage was soaked with blood. Justice retrieved one of Boo's nappies off the clothesline and tore it into small pieces. She wet part of it with cold water and wiped the wound clean. She sprinkled some of her healing powder on the open wound and wrapped it with the other half of the soft white material. "The pain should ease off in a little while," Justice said.

"Thank you for taking such good care of me. I want to beg your pardon for the way I spoke to you earlier. My Ma raised me to have respect for my elders. I'm sorry, madam." Bud gave her a small bow and then he walked over to the fire to speak with Rosie.

In the center of the yard, Tater had built a nice big fire surrounded by rocks. Rosie had washed the potatoes and hooked the pot onto a tripod over the fire. Both Tater and Rosie worked together very well, unlike most brothers and sisters.

"Rosie, can you go for a short walk with me? Here, let me carry this young man. He's almost asleep in your arms," Bud said as he took Boo and laid his head on his shoulder and patted him on the back. The pain in his side was not as bad as earlier.

The two walked away from the others and sat down on the fallen log where he had sat earlier. "We need to talk about what I can do to help make things better. Would you want to move into town?"

"No," Rosie said without hesitation. "We need to stay right here where we have lived all our lives."

"But, Rosie, you don't have any shelter except the barn and that looks like a strong wind would blow it down."

"Well, in time, Tater and I will have it all fixed. We'll patch the roof and secure the door. We can cut some of the smaller trees and make us some furniture. Please don't fret over us, Bud. We'll be just fine." Rosie gave him a small smile, but the sparkle was gone out of her green eyes.

"Listen to me, Rosie. If you're determined to stay here, I'll go into town and get some supplies like blankets, clothes, canned food. I'll help repair the barn before I leave too."

"You probably have done too much already."

"For goodness sake, woman, don't be fretting over what little I have done when your home is lying there in a pile of ashes!" Bud couldn't believe how calm this young girl was about her situation.

"Come on. Let's get back to the fire." Bud was very frustrated.

Once they got back to the fire ring, Bud said that he was going into town, and he would be back before dark. He was going after food and much-needed supplies.

"Tater, if you wash your face and hands, you can go with me. You can ride behind me on my buckskin."

"Golly, I'll like that. Can I go, Rosie?" Tater asked as he ran over to the well.

Bud handed Boo back to Rosie as he went over to his horse and adjusted the saddle and secured his saddlebags. Tater hurried over to Bud with water dripping down his face and wet hands. "I'm ready," he said.

Bud reached into his saddlebag and grabbed a soft clean rag and handed it to the eager boy. Bud ruffled the boy's hair and laughed. "Let's ride, young man," said Bud, and he reached for Tater's hand and swung him up behind him on the horse.

Rosie and Justice watched them ride out of the yard headed toward town. Justice took the small wagon and filled it with hay and covered it with three of Boo's clean nappies. Rosie laid the baby in the wagon. She pulled it slowly over to a log and sat down.

"Justice, what do you think that I should do? Bud asked if I wanted to move into town. I ain't never lived among city folks before and I don't think that I would like it. I think me and the boys should stay right here. The fishing is good. We've got good, clean water, and I have my garden already planted. I have you nearby." Rosie looked down at Boo and smiled. "I guess I know my answer. I just need to stay here."

"The boys could go to school if they were closer to town. Maybe you ought to let him set you up in a little place."

"You mean like a *kept woman*?" Rosie stood up with both hands on her thin hips and stared at Justice.

"Child, that man ain't going to be sticking around. He could buy you a little place. He owes you that much for bringing those buzzards down here."

"Please stop blaming him for all our troubles. He feels bad enough. I can tell that about him. He's a good person and I know it, but..." Rosie stopped speaking and sighed.

"But what?" Justice quizzed.

"But he's gotta go home, back to Texas, somewhere." Rosie looked over at the cow.

"I best milk Betsy. With all the excitement this morning, I plum forgot all about her. I bet she's about to bust." Rosie walked over to the well and retrieved a clean bucket and walked to the barn. Humming the Christian hymn "Amazing Grace," she placed the milking stool next to cow and began milking.

As Rosie began to sing the hymn, she heard the sound of a horse and some loud singing coming from outside the barn. She eased over to the door and peeked out. Justice was waving at a mule to get back away from the little wagon. On top of the ornery mule was her old drunken Pa.

"Lord, when it rains, it pours," said Rosie to herself. She hurried out into the yard near the fire and grabbed the mule's reins. Her crazy drunken Pa was straddled on the mule facing backward. He held the mule's tail with one hand and a jug of rye whiskey with the other.

When her Pa realized that he had made it home, he yelled, "Thar's my darling! Help me down off my carriage and into the house. I need my bed!"

"You need your skull busted wide open if you ask me, you old fool," Justice said as she watched the man try to get down off the mule. He pulled on the mule's tail as he slid off his back, causing the mule to kick his hind legs. The mule gave several bellowing sounds loud enough to be heard a mile away.

Standing before Rosie was a short, fat man with full rosy cheeks, a stained beard, a big blemished nose, glassy green eyes, and a cowbell hanging around his neck. He was a sight to see, and he was demanding his bed. The old man was Edouard Jourdian, and he was Rosie's Pa. He whirled around twice and hit the ground. Rosie and Justice stood watching him. As funny as he appeared, the two ladies didn't crack a smile.

The old drunk pulled himself up onto his feet swaying back and forth. After he got his eyes focused, he could tell that the shack, his home, had burned to the ground. "Well damn, what happened here?"

"What do you care? You ain't never here," shouted Rosie.

Before Rosie knew what hit her, the old man slapped her across the mouth, busting her bottom lip. "Shut that stinking mouth of yours, girlie, before I shut it for good. I'm your *Pa* and you got no cause to speak like that to me."

Rosie placed her hand over her mouth and jumped away from him.

"Get me something to eat and you," he swayed while pointing at Justice, "*old voodoo* witch doctor, fix me a bed!"

Justice stared at the old fool. "I'll fix you a permanent bed if you hit that child again."

"You ain't nothing but full of old crazy talk, and I find you real amusing," replied the old man.

Rosie walked over to the fire and speared a long fork into several of the little red potatoes. She placed them in one of the tin cups that she had recovered out of the fire's rubbish.

"That ain't enough to feed a big, healthy man like me. Give me some more and something else to go with them taters," he said as he shoved the cup back into her hands.

"There ain't nothing else to eat," she screamed at him, "and if I give you more potatoes, then no one else will have any dinner."

"That's just too bad, ain't it? Do as I say now or I'll take a strap to your backside!"

Rosie dipped all the potatoes but two large ones out of the pot and took it to him. The old fool didn't even let them cool before he was shoveling them into his mouth. He took the jug of whiskey and turned it up to take a big drink. Some of the liquor dribbled down into his nasty beard. He belched real loud and turned around in the yard as he took the back of his hand and swiped it across his mouth.

"Where's my bed?" he shouted.

Justice looked at the old, drunken fool and told him to go sleep with the hogs, and she walked off into the swamp. Boo started crying so Rosie picked him up out of the wagon and followed Justice.

5

Bud rode straight to the sheriff's office and gave him a report about the two men that followed him out of town. He told the sheriff all about how they had shot him, but he had gotten away from them before he fell off his horse in the swamp. He described how they followed him and demanded their money back from the poker game, but because he fled from them, they burned Rosie's shack down. He told the sheriff where he had stopped and confronted the two men and that, after a short scrimmage of gunfire, he had wounded both of them.

"They are without horses and guns. You can go after them if you want, but I'm not going to be here to testify against them. I'm going to stay a few days and help repair the barn so Rosie and the young'uns can have shelter. After that, I'm headed home."

"Thanks for telling me about those two sorry no-accounts. If by some small miracle they make it back this way, I'll run them out of here so fast that their heads will spin. We don't need that kind of trash in this town," said the sheriff.

Bud and Tater walked his horse down to the mercantile store to purchase some food and blankets. After giving his verbal list to the clerk, he walked toward the back of the store where the shoes were stored. He picked up several different styles and finally asked Tater which pair he liked.

Tater's eyes widened as he eased closer to Bud and whispered, "You gonna get me a new pair of boots?"

"I believe I am, if they have your size," smiled Bud as he looked at the surprised expression on the young boy's face. Bud wished then and there that he could afford to buy him a dozen pair.

Slowly, Tater's smile faded and he said very softly, "I don't need any boots but Rosie shore does. Why don't you pick her a pair out?"

Bud couldn't help but smile and shake his head at the boy. "If that doesn't beat all? Look, Tater, if I select a pair for Rosie and some things for Boo, will you try on some boots for yourself?"

"Golly! That would be just fine," Tater replied as he started looking at all the shoes and boots. Once Tater had chosen a pair of brown leather Western boots, he paraded back and forth while Bud stood laughing at him.

Bud asked the lady clerk if she would chose a good pair of boots for a young lady about so high. Throw in a pair of soft slippers to wear inside a house too. Once he left her to make the selections, he led Tater over to the denim pants. He tossed Tater a pair and told him to go behind the curtain and try the pants on. Once Tater's size was determined, Bud chose three pair of denims and three nice plaid shirts. Bud piled the clothes on the counter and tossed in several pairs of short white underwear and a half dozen pairs of socks.

Bud chose a bolt of soft white muslin cloth for new nappies for Boo. The lady salesclerk asked how old the baby was, and Bud had to look to Tater for the answer. She quickly showed Bud some little denim overhauls and some shirts. He chose several long night shirts for the baby to sleep in too.

Everyone was all set except for Rosie. Bud walked over to the ladies' dresses and picked three that looked plain and suitable for everyday wear. He asked the lady again for her assistance in choosing some undergarments for a young lady. The salesclerk raised her eyebrows but didn't make a comment.

"Look, madam, a family's house burned down, and I want them to have some clothes. You understand how it is?"

"Yes, sir. I don't ask questions or make judgments on what our customers purchase here. Ain't no business of mine," she replied matter-of-factly.

"Good then! Just get me what I asked for and I'll be out of here in a flash." Bud's face was fiery red from embarrassment.

As he waited for the items to be added up and wrapped in brown paper, he decided to get Rosie several pair of denims that she could wear with her new boots. He knew she worked in the garden, hunted and fished. He had a beautiful young friend at home that wore her brother's britches to go riding. Rosie didn't ride, but denims would be very practical. He reached out and got her three simple blouses.

As he headed to the counter, he saw some lovely soft scarves. He was sure Justice would like to have a few to wear around her hair. She also could use a pair of shoes. He thought that she was too old to be walking around in her bare feet. A pair of shoes was a cheap price to pay someone for saving your life. He marched to the rear of the store and chose a pair of soft brown moccasin boots.

Once all the necessary items were chosen, wrapped, and carried out to the horse, Bud decided that he needed to rent a wagon down at the stable. He was going to need one to help carry the lumber back to the swamp area.

After renting a flatbed wagon and two strong mules to pull it, he purchased a few dozen long boards, hammer, nails, and a handsaw. He bought several hundred-pound bags of oats, some chicken feed, and a half dozen new buckets. The cow would need good feed to help produce healthy milk, and the mules would need something to eat while he had them.

Before heading back to the swamp area, Bud stopped the wagon in front of a bakery. "Something shore smells good," Tater said as he looked at the delicious cakes and pastries in the bakery window.

"You just sit right here and guard our supplies, and I'll go in there and get us something good to eat on our way back," replied Bud.

Tater watched Bud disappear into the bakery. He was holding the reins of the big, sturdy mules as he looked up and down the street at the people who passed him by. Everyone seemed to be in a hurry to get somewhere. No one paid him any attention. Thinking about how surprised Rosie was going to be with all of her new clothes made him feel good all over. Bud was a nice man, and he was sure going to hate to see him leave.

Bud returned with a large bag of delicious-smelling treats. He had homemade fresh bread and several pastries. "The things in the bag are for the girls and Boo. This is ours," he said as he held out a sandwich and a fried doughnut with a white powder dusted on top for Tater.

Tater was sure that he had died and gone to heaven. He had never had anything as delicious as his sandwich. As they ate their doughnuts, the light breeze blew the white powder all over their face and clothes. The two looked at themselves and at each other and laughed. This had been the best day of Tater's life.

After a couple of hours of slow driving, they finally arrived back to the burnt home site. Tater spoke with much sadness in his voice.

"I knew this day was too good to be true," he said as he saw his Pa lying on the ground near the well, snoring like a big, fat sow.

Bud could hear the disgust in Tater's voice and he asked, "Who's that man?"

"That's our Pa," Tater replied as he was looking around for Rosie and Boo. "Wonder where they're hiding?"

Bud glanced at the barn, and he noticed the fishing pole was not leaning up against the wall where he had last seen it. "Tater, I bet Rosie took Boo and went fishing. Why don't you hurry to her fishing place and tell her to come home. Fish is good, but we don't have to have it for supper tonight."

Tater raced down the worn path toward Rosie while Bud got down from the wagon. The old man heard the jiggle of the mules' harnesses. He sat up and looked at the tall young man and the big flatbed wagon.

"Well, howdy, young man?" the old man said as he grabbed hold of the well to help himself stand. "What brings you to these here parts? Are you selling something?" The old man staggered across the yard to get a little closer look at the visitor. "You interested in purchasing something special?" The old man needed a drink badly, and he was out of ways to get more. The only thing of any value on this godforsaken, burnt-down place was his lovely young daughter. He was tired of her smart, sassy mouth. He sure would hate to have to take a strap to her and bruise her all over. Nobody would want to purchase damaged goods. But he needed a drink, and damn, he needed money. That old fool at the saloon wouldn't give him anymore credit until he paid his current tab. As he looked at the wagon loaded down with lumber, feed, and other wrapped supplies, he thought that this young man certainly must have money.

Bud stood looking at the old fat fool swaying as he walked toward him. "Now, young man, what's your business here? Are you just passing by or you selling them wares you have on that wagon? Or just maybe you're looking for some *female* company?" His words were slurred, but Bud didn't have any problem understanding him.

"I don't see any females around here, mister," Bud said, wondering what Rosie's Pa was up too.

"Well, you'll be surprised in just a little bit. There's one here and she's pretty, young, and *ripe*, if you get my meaning. She's a hard worker and a very good cook, when there's something to cook at this hell hole. Excuse me, at this home."

Rosie, Boo, and Tater were walking around the barn when they heard voices. They knew it was Pa and Bud talking. Tater raised his hand for them to stop and listen.

"Mister, are you offering me your daughter's hand in marriage?" Bud asked.

"Marriage, h*ell no!*" Rosie's Pa waved his hands and said, "Now if you want to marry up that's fine with me, but I want to do a little bartering with you. You can do whatever you wish with her once you give me the price I'm asking."

"What's your price?" Bud asked through clenched teeth. He was holding himself in check because he wanted to beat this old man to a pulp. He didn't deserve to be called Pa.

"I want fifty dollars in green backs, and I won't take a dime less," he spewed out the words. Before he had finished his sentence, Bud tossed the fifty dollars on the ground at his feet.

The old drunk couldn't believe his luck. He immediately fell to the ground, gathering up his manna from heaven. He could already taste the fine liquor.

Rosie was breathless and had heard enough. She gave Boo to Tater and marched around the barn. She looked at her Pa and then to Bud as she screamed at the top of her lungs.

"You can't buy me! I'm not someone's slave that can be tossed upon the block and sold to the highest bidder. I'm my own person. Nobody will ever own me!"

"It's too late. You belong to me. Bought and paid for. Your fine upstanding Pa just sold *you* to me!" Bud had never been so mad in all of his young life.

Bud stormed over to his horse. He reached down into his saddlebags and pulled out a piece of paper and pencil. He scribbled on the paper and called to the old man to get up.

"Sign this bill of sale!" Bud demanded. The old man looked at Rosie through his bleary-eyes. Even in his intoxicated state, he knew that she was angrier than he had ever seen her, but he didn't care. He wouldn't ever have to lay eyes on her and those other brats again.

Rosie's Pa took the pencil out of Bud's hand and marked his "X" on the paper.

Bud snatched the paper back, folded it, and placed it in his vest pocket. He immediately grabbed the old man and shook him hard.

"Listen to me, you old lush. If you ever come near me or anything that belongs to me, I will make you one sorry old man. Do you understand me?"

"You ain't got no worries there, mister. I don't ever want to see them brats again as long as I live," he said as he weaved over to where his mule was tied. The poor critter had never been watered, fed, or untied since he had arrived earlier that morning. The tipsy fool managed to get onto the mule's back and rode out of the yard, never looking back.

Justice had slowly walked up behind Rosie and whispered, "You gonna be just fine. Hope that's the last we ever see of that drunken fool."

Rosie looked at Justice with tears flowing down her dirty cheeks and instantly raced off into the swamp. Bud quickly asked Tater to watch the baby while he went after her. "Listen, son, get the fresh food down and feed Boo and Justice. It might take a while to talk some sense into your sister."

Bud trailed Rosie into the swamp and found her sitting on the low branch of a tree. She was crying silently. "Rosie, come down," Bud instructed.

"Why, so you can have your way with your property?" Rosie was so hurt by her Pa's actions. She knew that one day he would succeed in getting rid of her, but to Bud. She couldn't believe that Bud actually gave him money and had him sign a bill of sale.

"Come down here this minute and hush that kinda talk. Have I ever laid a hand on you?" Bud needed for her to trust him for he had instantly formed a plan for the care of this family.

Rosie walked down the branch until she was at the bottom of it. She immediately tried to walk away from Bud. "Oh no, you don't, I'm going to talk and you're going to listen."

"Say your piece and then leave! We don't need any more of your help."

Bud paced back and forth in front of Rosie before he finally spoke. "You know things could be worse. That old man has already tried to sell you once before this. Justice told me that. If you did escape him again, have you thought that he might try to sell Tater next? There are a lot of farmers who would love to have a young boy like him so they could work him to death in their hot cotton fields. If not Tater, what about Boo? He's an adorable little tyke that some rich couple that can't have children might want for their very own. That crazy man you called Pa is desperate for money, and he would sell his own sainted mother if she was still alive! All he can think about is where his next jug's coming from."

Bud watched the expression on Rosie's face and saw the tears slipping out of her emerald green eyes. He ached for her. His Pa never turned his back on him even when he robbed the train and shot Will Maxwell. While in prison, he received letters from his mama expressing their concern and love for him. This old man that sired Rosie and her two brothers wasn't fit to live on this earth.

"Rosie, I had planned to repair the barn for you, and I bought all of you some supplies and clothes. But since that old man is so dangerous I want to take you and the boys' home with me out of his reach."

Her head snapped up and her mouth flew open to speak, but Bud raised his hand and told her to keep quiet until he finished. "I have a nice farm with a small two-bedroom house located on one hundred acres. My folks live nearby, and I want to take you and Boo to their home. I'm sure my folks will take you in because they have the room. Ma's getting older, and I know that she could use your help. Tater can live at my place and help me."

"So you can work him to death!" she sneered. "Listen, Bud. I'm sorry. I didn't mean that. I thank you for wanting to take us home with you, but I better stay right here. Our mama might come back to get us and we won't be at our place."

"I thought she ran off with some man. Why would she want to come back?"

"I don't know why she'd want to come back except to get us. When my Pa was drunk, which was most of the time, he was a mean devil. He beat my mama until she couldn't see or walk. Me and Tater would jump on him or throw rocks to make him leave her alone. He would have killed us if he could have caught us. Mama was good to us young'uns. She taught me to read the Bible. She worked hard at keeping food on the table. There were many days she didn't eat a mouthful so there would be enough for us. She was awful scared of dying. She would say I sure don't want to die. I know that is why she ran off with that old peddler. But, Bud, don't you see. She could come back for us."

"Rosie, Justice said that your ma left you kids when Boo was about six weeks old. That's nearly two years ago. Has she returned? No, and I don't believe she will if she thinks your Pa is still hanging around the place." Bud looked straight ahead and sighed real big. "Rosie, you know that I will take good care of Tater. He can go to school during the day and help me out in the evening with a few chores. Justice can come along with us, if she would like too. She can stay with me and Tater. She could help out with the cooking. Tater would appreciate her cooking over mine."

Bud stood watching Rosie as she let his plan sink in. "What do you think? You won't ever have to worry about your Pa coming here again, drunk with a buyer." Rosie still felt bewildered and unsure of what had just taken place.

"Would everyone know that I'm your property?"

"Rosie, believe me. I only gave him money to get rid of him. I made him sign the paper so he would know that he could never try to sell you again."

"I need to talk this plan of yours over with Tater and Justice. This moving to another place, with strangers, will affect them too. But first, before I decide to take my family off with you, I need to know why you was sent to jail."

"It's a long story, and I will tell you one day, but not today. Just know that I did something stupid and I have paid for it. I'm asking you to trust me that I will keep you and the boys safe from harm."

Rosie stood still and looked at him. She knew that he was a good man. He had only showed kindness to Justice, and he had been patient with Tater. Boo was already attached to him like a puppy to a mama dog. There were still so many unanswered questions about this stranger.

"Let's go and get something to eat while you discuss this move with them. I believe that Tater will be happy to go with me."

"I wouldn't say anything about him going to school, if you want to win him over on your side," Rosie smiled at Bud for the first time that day.

6

AFTER TWO DAYS of packing the covered wagon with their meager supplies, they were ready to travel to Limason, Texas. Home. Bud was very excited to be heading to his home and family that he hadn't seen in two years. After his arrest and trial, he was sent to the Louisiana State Prison in Lafayette, Louisiana. He was very fortunate to have been sentenced for only two years. He knew that if his family and friends, especially Will Maxwell, hadn't spoken up for him, he could have spent ten years or more in that hell hole. He had been working on a trail drive when he met up with an old man who had the bright idea to rob a train. Being desperate and without funds, he decided to go along with his plan. During the robbery, he went into the passenger car to get a hostage. He needed a hostage to force the soldiers, who were guarding the payroll, to open up the baggage car and give the money to them. To his surprise, Hope Summers, a childhood friend and her fiancé, Will Maxwell, were in the passenger car. Hope recognized him. When he decided to take Hope as a hostage, Will jumped him, and during the scuffle, his gun went off and he had shot Will. He was badly hurt, but once Will recovered and with some encouragement from Hope, Will told the judge that the shooting was accidental. At his trial, he knew how blessed he was with a wonderful family and good friends. After receiving a pardon for good behavior, he was set free. Instead of heading straight home, he decided to try and earn some money for his future. As a gambler, he was very good at cards and reading his opponents' faces. He learned to quit the game while on a winning streak and leave with money in his pockets. After months of playing the tables, he won a big hand with four deuces. That was a sign for him to pack away his playing cards and make plans for his future.

While preparing to make the long trip to Limason, Bud announced to his little trio that all of them needed a good bath. He told Rosie that she wasn't in any danger of men coming around and bothering her any longer. He suggested that she take a nice long bath and wash her hair.

Tater declared that he had gone swimming in the river a few days ago, and he didn't need a bath.

Bud walked over to the well and tossed the bucket down into the water and told Tater to build up the fire. They all needed a good hot bath and either they could bathe themselves or he would lend a helping hand. Boo was the only one who appeared happy with the idea.

Justice walked into the clearing looking like royalty. She was dressed like the Creole women in New Orleans with four long necklaces that dangled to her waist. Her hair was wrapped high above her head with the lovely scarves that Bud had given her. Her blouse and long skirt swirled with bright colors, covering her knee-length moccasin boots. She was scrubbed clean. Bud couldn't help but smile at her as he walked from the well and took her hand. He stood in front of her as he bowed and kissed the back of her hand.

"You're a sight for sore eyes, Ms. Justice," Bud said. "I see you're packed and ready to go," he said as he took her carpetbag and placed it in the back of their covered wagon.

Bud and Tater had gone back into town the day before and returned the flatbed wagon and two mules to the livery. He returned with two sturdy horses and a big, covered wagon. He had purchased a big army tent to take along and some cooking utensils. He figured that it would take five to seven days to make it to his home while traveling with the wagon and children. They could hitch Rosie's cow to the back of the wagon.

Bud selected a couple of the thinner blankets and walked over to two slim pine trees and tied the blankets to them. He carried the tub over and set it behind the makeshift screen.

Once the water was hot, he poured it in the tub and went back to the well to get a bucket of cold water to mix with it. Rosie and Tater watched Bud's every move.

"Who's first?" Bud looked to Rosie and then to Tater. "Now this can be done the easy way or the hard way—don't even think about running, *Tater*! We're not leaving this spot until you three are clean." Looking first at Rosie and then at Tater, he said, "I'm beginning to run out of patience."

"All right, I'll go first," Rosie said with a sigh as she gathered up her new clothes. She selected a shirt and a pair of denims. "Nobody better come near those blankets!"

Bud couldn't contain his laughter, and with a grin on his face, he told her that she had made a good choice of clothing but not to forget the unmentionables. Justice walked over to the blanket screen and stood guard. Bud continued laughing as he pulled up another bucket of water and placed it over the fire to get warm.

Bud signaled to Tater to come with him and help gather some pieces of firewood to place in the back of the wagon. "We need to have a supply of dry wood in case it rains while traveling. A nice fire always makes you feel better at night while out on the trail."

As the two returned to the clearing, Tater walked over to the wagon and lowered the tailgate. He turned to Bud who stood staring straight ahead with empty arms. Bud couldn't believe his eyes. His mouth had fallen opened as he dropped all of the firewood at his feet. Bud was looking at Rosie as she stood close to the fire drying her mass of beautiful red hair. The glow on her hair from the firelight made her appear like a vision. She was a beauty even wearing boy's denims and Western boots.

Tater walked toward the fire where his sister stood. "Golly, Rosie, I ain't never seen you looking like that before. You're shore pretty."

"Well, thanks I guess," she mumbled. "Now it's your turn and I don't want to hear no fussing either."

Bud immediately shook himself out of his trance and picked up the firewood that lay at his feet. He walked over to the tub and poured out the dirty water. He pulled up another bucket of water and put it on the fire to warm. After Tater had gotten his bath and washed his hair; his freckles shined along with his clean, bright red hair. Boo giggled and splashed while enjoying his turn. Rosie dressed him in a new pair of blue overalls. He paraded around in the yard looking like a big boy instead of a toddler. He ran over to Justice and said, "See!" pointing down at his pockets.

Bud could see how proud all three of them were of their new duds. He was thankful that he had the money to purchase them.

"All right, I believe we're ready to move out." The two tubs had been secured to the side of the wagon. "Does everyone have everything that they want to take because we aren't turning around and coming back this way? Since we have to go through town, I'm going to stop at the bakery and get us something good to eat. That will hold us all until supper time."

"Tater, you did fill the water barrels, didn't you?" Bud asked as an afterthought.

"Sure did! Oh, let me get Rosie's favorite fishing pole." He ran over to the side of the barn and retrieved it.

"Thanks, Tater," Rosie whispered. Rosie was excited about their new adventure but she was nearly in tears. She was leaving her home. Even though there was no home or never had been much of one, it was still where she had lived all of her life. It was hard to leave.

"Tater, you can ride the buckskin this morning. I'm going to give Rosie a lesson on how to drive this big wagon. We'll all take turns driving so the trip will be more enjoyable for all of us," explained Bud.

Once they arrived in town, Bud stopped the horses and wagon in front of the bakery. The sheriff was strolling down the old weather beaten boardwalk and waved at Bud.

"I was heading to the stable to get my horse and ride out to these young'uns place," said the sheriff, looking real serious.

Bud reached up and helped Rosie down to the ground. He reached into his pocket and gave Rosie some money. "Take the boys and Justice into the bakery and get whatever everyone wants. Get a little extra to have on the trail later too. I'll be in there in just a minute."

"I want to hear why the sheriff was coming out to see us. What's the problem?" Rosie asked quickly.

"Well, Ms. Rosie, I don't believe I would have known you if I had met you anywhere else. You're sure mighty pretty today," said the sheriff as he tipped his hat to her. "I have some business that I need to discuss with Mr. Downey. It won't take much of his time."

Bud gave Rosie a gentle nudge to go on into the bakery. He turned back to the sheriff as he watched the little group file into the doorway. The smell of fresh bread and sweet pastries coming out the door was wonderful. He was hungry and his stomach growled.

"What's the problem, Sheriff? Have those bastards that I shot showed up here already?"

"No, nothing like that, but something bad has happened. Those young'uns pa was found dead in the alley behind the saloon. His throat had been cut. He had been seen earlier with a big wad of cash, and he was buying drinks for everyone. He was killed for his money, I'm sure of that."

"Damn," Bud said, shaking his head. "He got that cash from me. He was at their place when Tater and I returned from town a couple days ago. Drunk, and spouting off his mouth about needing money, and then he offered to sell Rosie to me. He wanted fifty dollars cash so I gave it to him." Bud looked down at the ground. "He took that money so fast and then high-tailed it toward town. Rosie and Tater both heard him. I really hated that."

"Well, I had heard rumors before that he tried to sell her, but she won't have to worry about that any longer," said the sheriff.

"Where's his body now?" Bud was concerned about the old man for the kid's sakes.

"He's stored in the icehouse with two other bodies that are waiting to be buried. See, the cemetery is almost under water so the undertaker has to wait for the water level to go down. This place is practically all swampland. It will be a few more days before the men can dig graves deep enough for the bodies," explained the sheriff.

"We need to be moving on, but let me pay for the old man's funeral expenses." Bud pulled out twenty dollars and gave it to the sheriff. "For your information, I'm taking Rosie and her brothers' home with me to Limason, Texas. Rosie seems to think that her ma might come back here to get them. If she does, you know where they'll be. My folks will take in Rosie and Boo."

"I'm sure glad to hear that. Rosie is a nice, hardworking girl. She deserves a better life. The old woman will be a big help," sheriff said, referring to Justice. "She's might scary looking, but she knows how to care for the sick." He looked toward the bakery and said for them to have a safe trip.

Bud thanked the sheriff and entered the bakery where the aroma was heavenly. Rosie was holding Boo while he ate a sweet pastry. She held a big cup of milk in her other hand.

"Is everything all right?" Rosie asked. When Bud didn't answer her, she asked if he was going to get something to eat. He nodded yes and walked over to the counter and ordered a big piece of cake and a strawberry pastry to take with him. After paying for his order, he led everyone back out and into the wagon.

Once he had driven the wagon out of the town, he waved at Tater to stop. He needed to tell them about their pa. "Rosie, Tater." Bud cleared his throat before he could begin. "The sheriff told me some news about your pa. He was found dead last night in an alleyway. I'm sorry. But you both know that he wasn't much of a pa to you. Still, I know that you loved him."

"Ain't so, I hated him and I'm glad that he won't ever be around to hurt us again!" shouted Tater as he lowered his face down under his chin while the buckskin stepped back from the wagon. Rosie sat very still and quiet before she said anything.

"So, with Pa gone I don't have to leave and go with you. Me and the boys can stay here," said Rosie, pondering over the news about her pa and now her new changed situation.

"That's what you think," Bud replied. "If you think you can stay here you just try it! You and the boys belong to me now, and I'm responsible for all of you."

"*I don't belong to you*, and I can take care of my brothers. I'll take them back home and hide out." Rosie was so angry that she was nearly screaming.

Bud reached and grabbed Rosie by her narrow shoulders and turned her to face him. "You just try and hide from me out in that dangerous swamp. There's no place where I won't find you. When I do get my hands on you, I'll tan the daylights out of that stubborn hide of yours. Now shut that talk up about not going with me before I decide to paddle you right this minute."

"So now, you're a wretched woman beater," she mumbled for his ears only.

"Not yet, smarty-pants, not yet, but don't push me." Bud snapped the reins and the horses started moving down the trail toward his home.

After the first stop for a short rest and a bite to eat, they formed a routine of what had to be done around the campsite. First, the horses needed to be unhitched and hobbled away from the wagon. Water buckets needed to be filled and carried out to the horses. They weren't going to cook anything for lunch, so there wasn't a need for a fire. Rosie changed Boo and allowed him to run and play. He needed to spend some energy so he would be willing to take a nap after they got back on the trail. She and Justice walked a ways into the bushes for some privacy. Tater unsaddled the buckskin and gave him a good rub down. Bud got out a blanket and spread it on the ground under a small oak tree. He stretched his long form out and dozed off for a short nap.

Boo was marching around the wagon when he spotted Bud lying on the blanket. He ran and jumped in the middle of Bud's stomach. "Papa, fly me," he screeched. Bud laughed and grabbed Boo around his small waist and held him high over his head. Up and down he pushed the little fellow until his screeches became hiccups.

"Come on, little man," Bud said. "It's time for this group to hit the trail."

After traveling a few hours, they came upon a small town called Jackson, Texas. At the entrance of the town was a nice horse corral and stable. The blacksmith was standing in the doorway pouring a dipper of cool water over his face. Bud hopped down off his wagon and asked if they could water their horses. The man took a dirty rag out of his back pocket and made a big production out of wiping his face.

"Shore, help yourself. Water's free," he said with a big smile of welcome.

"Appreciate it, mister," replied Bud. "Would this town have a telegraph office?"

"Shore do, but that's not free," the big man said, laughing at his own joke.

Bud laughed as he helped Tater water the animals. "Thanks for your help."

Bud drove the wagon down the middle of the street until he came to Jackson's Mercantile Store.

Reaching into his pocket, he gave Rosie a few dollars and told her to go into the store and get some fresh bread and hard candy for everyone to enjoy. "If you see something else we need, go ahead and get it too."

Bud continued on down the street, looking for the telegraph office. He pulled to a stop in front of a small building and tied the horses to the hitching post. "Can I send a telegraph to Limason, Texas?" Bud asked the old man behind the counter.

"Be glad to help you for a fee. You got the money, I got the means." Bud laughed and told the little man that he had a few dollars.

After he completed his business in the telegraph office, he returned to the store and loaded up his little caravan. Bud noticed that Justice and Boo were both fast asleep in the back of the wagon. As they traveled out of town, Bud saw rain clouds in the distance. After hearing thunder not too far away, he decided that they better make camp for the night. With a small child and an old woman traveling with him, he was concerned that they might get sick from the cold, rainy weather.

Tater and Bud, along with Rosie's help, made quick work of securing the animals to a picket line and putting up the army tent. Justice and Rosie made a small fire and brewed a pot of coffee and warmed a few cans of beans. After the beans were good and hot, Rosie tossed in a long link of smoked sausage. This wasn't an ideal supper, but it would be warm and plentiful. It wasn't long before the cold rain came down in sheets. Bud, Rosie, and the others had gathered in the covered wagon to eat and have their coffee.

"Bud, what will your folks think about all of us coming home with you?" Rosie asked as she stirred her beans around in her tin plate.

"What do you mean?" Bud asked, stalling for time to think of a good answer.

"Well, you said that you haven't been home since you got out of prison and you've been free for awhile. Now you're coming home and bringing a wagon full of strangers. You plan to dump me and Boo off on their door step. Surely, I want to know how they're going to like this here plan of yours."

"Now, Rosie, it isn't going to be quite like that." Bud looked into the worried faces of Rosie and Tater. Justice was just sitting back without showing any expression on her face. He felt that she would know if he was telling a lie or speaking the truth.

"I think I would feel better if Boo and I could go to your new farm with you and Tater," Rosie explained.

"Rosie, a young, unmarried girl cannot live with an unmarried man. The good citizens of Limason would string me up if I let you stay with me without marriage." Bud chuckled to make light of the situation.

"What's wrong with marrying up with her before we get there?" Justice asked with a grin on her old black face.

"No!" Rosie and Bud spoke at the same time. Rosie could feel her face turning red as fire.

"I mean, Rosie is too young to be married right now, and I have a lot to take care of before I can be responsible for a wife," Bud stuttered.

"She might be too young to you, but she is as old as they get when it comes to taking care of a family. She's reared these two boys every day of their young lives and took care of herself too," declared Justice.

"I'm sure you know what you're talking about, old woman, but when we get home, my folks will gladly take them in. Rosie won't have to work so hard and she'll have a nice room. My folks will treat her good." Bud peeked out of the back of the wagon and saw that the rain had stopped. "I better go and check on the animals and our tent. Hopefully, it didn't leak during the storm."

Tater jumped down out of the back and trailed behind Bud. Rosie told Justice that she was going to get a pail of water. Since it was dark, she needed to wash and dress Boo for bed.

"Papa!" Boo screamed as he clapped his hands together. Justice laughed and wondered what in the world were the Downeys going to think when they heard Boo calling their son papa.

Early the next morning, Bud laid in the bedroll watching the baby as he slept between him and Tater. The youngster had pretty brown curls and eyelashes that fanned out on his face when his eyes were closed. His skin was so clear a person could see tiny blue veins in his rosy cheeks. *This baby was too pretty to be a boy*, thought Bud. As if on cue, the baby opened his eyes and smiled. His tiny hand reached for Bud's face as he said, "Papa." Bud shook his head as he felt the baby's nappy. "Hey, big boy, you're still dry. Come on and let's go outside and pee," Bud said as he stood him up and removed the nappy from his little body. Bud squatted on his heels as he untied the flaps on the front of the tent.

"*Oh*," screamed Bud as he felt a stream of warm water hitting his bare back.

"Hey, little man, don't pee on me." Bud couldn't help but laugh as he picked up Boo and carried him outside the tent. Rosie and Justice were standing at the fire as they listened and watched the man and baby. "Pee pee, 'osie." Boo clapped his hands. The baby's smile told everyone how proud he was of himself.

"Well, I guess you learned a good lesson this morning about babies. Never take his nappy off until you're ready for him to do his business," Rosie said while trying to hold a straight face. It didn't work. Justice looked at Rosie, and they both laughed and laughed.

"You two can just stop that howling," Bud said with a smirk on his face. He knew that this damn situation was funny, but he didn't like being the butt of any joke.

"All right, heat me some water so I can take a morning bath. I don't care to smell like an outhouse all day," he said and the two girls laughed that much louder.

7

AFTER A SLOW week of traveling, Bud pulled the big covered wagon to a stop on the outskirts of Limason, Texas—home. He was excited and nervous at the same time. Tater noticed that Bud had stopped driving the wagon so he turned the buckskin around and rode up to the wagon.

"Why are you stopping?" asked Tater, looking all around.

"We're home. My home and now yours too," he commented while looking at Rosie. "In a few minutes, we will be driving down the main street of my hometown, and I have to admit I'm a little nervous. These good people haven't seen me since I was carried out of town headed to prison."

Rosie's heart was pounding in her chest. While Bud had a case of nerves, she was scared to death. She couldn't even imagine what Bud's folks were going to think about her and the boys. And Justice! Most people were scared to death of her until they got to know her.

"So, Bud, why are we going into town? What about your folks? You know that they're eager to see you," said Rosie.

"I need to stop at the doctor's office and get my house key. Dr. Tim helped me purchase my farm and he has the key. I want to get it and thank him. We need food supplies for us and feed for the animals. Afterward, we'll head for my farm and then later I'll go and visit with my folks and tell them about you and Boo. How's that sound to you?" Bud asked as he started moving the wagon into town.

"That's good. Give them fair warning that we're coming and make sure that they don't mind having us stay a spell."

"Hey, you're going to be staying more than a spell. Their place will be your new home and Boo's too," Bud said with much authority in his voice.

"As you say," whispered Rosie. Rosie had been making plans as they traveled to Limason. She had no intention of staying with Bud's parents for the rest of her life. She was a strong young woman who could work and earn her and Boo's keep. Tater would be just fine at Bud's farm for a while, and then later, he could come and live with her again.

Bud drove the wagon up to the front of Dr. Tim's office. He told Rosie to stay on the wagon, and he would only be a minute. After waiting a little while, she jumped down off the tall wagon bench and stretched her legs. Tater had gotten down from the big buckskin horse and walked it over to the water trough. Rosie didn't notice the two young cowpunchers as they watched her walk around on the boardwalk in her tight denim britches.

Bud entered the doctor's office. He saw Esther, an older black woman, who had worked for Dr. Tim ever since he settled in town many years ago. She was folding sheets when she noticed Bud standing quietly watching her.

"Well, Lord, have Mercy! If it ain't our little Bud done come home." Esther dropped the sheet and walked over to him. "Welcome home, boy. Let me tell Dr. Tim and Ms. Hannah that you're here."

Esther hurried into the back, and it wasn't a minute before Tim and Hannah came out of the back with her. "Well, well, Bud. It's so good to see you, son. You're looking mighty healthy. Have you seen your folks yet?" said Dr. Tim.

"Thanks, Dr. Tim," Bud said as he gave a nod of his head to Ms. Hannah. Bud looked at the beautiful woman standing beside Dr. Tim. He couldn't believe his eyes. Ms. Hannah had not changed one bit. With her pretty red hair and green eyes, she was as lovely as he remembered.

"Oh, Bud," Hannah sighed. "Your folks are going to be so happy when they see you. Your little brothers have really missed you too. You aren't going to believe how big Samuel has gotten. Hurry, Tim, and go get his key so he can head on home and see his family. We weren't sure when you would get here."

Lot of laughter and several screams came from outside of the office. Bud walked over to the window and looked out. He couldn't believe his eyes. Rosie was fighting off a dark-haired cowpuncher as she waved a knife around in front of his face while Tater had straddled another young man's back. He had a handful of hair as he clamped down on the man's ear with his teeth. The man was screaming as he twisted and turned trying to buck Tater off his back.

"On my Lord," said Bud as he jerked open the door and rushed outside, grabbing Rosie and pushing her behind his back. Hannah raced after Bud. She quickly attempted to pull Tater off the other man's back. When Tater slid off, he took Ms. Hannah to the ground with him. Both of them were sitting on the ground with Tater in Hannah's lap when Sheriff Murphy came running up to stop the brawl. He fired his pistol in the air to get everyone's attention and make the little group stop fighting.

"What in the blazes is going on here? Well, Bud," sighed the sheriff. "You haven't been in town an hour and there's already fighting in the street. What you gotta say for yourself?"

Bud didn't even look at Sheriff Murphy. He gathered Rosie into his arms as he pulled her close to his body and asked if she was all right. "What caused you and Tater to be in a fight with these men?"

Rosie didn't answer him. Tater scrambled off the ground, off Ms. Hannah, and told Bud that those cowpunchers were trying to kiss Rosie and make her go to the saloon with them for some fun. She told them to leave her alone but they wouldn't listen.

"Are you all right?" Bud asked Tater as he touched the blood on his new shirt.

"This here ain't my blood. It's his," Tater said, pointing to one of the men lying on the ground, holding a hand over his bloody ear.

"We just wanted to have a little fun with this here, gal. She was out here twisting her tail all around in those men's britches. She didn't seem to be with anybody, and she kept looking our way, like inviting us over," said the young man as he tried to form his words. "She's just the prettiest thing that has hit this town in a long time. We just wanted to show her a good time."

"Well, this pretty thing belongs to me!" Bud pulled Rosie up against his side as he noticed that they had drawn the attention of many of the local townspeople. He looked into the crowd and recognized a few faces.

"What's you mean? She belongs to you?" One of the cowpunchers was standing looking at Bud like he wanted to shoot him for grabbing the beautiful young girl.

"Just believe me, she's mine and you just keep your distance."

"Just because you say she's yours don't make it so! You can't just claim a gal on your say so," sneered the young cowpuncher. "Let's draw for her," he proclaimed, swaying a little from having too much to drink. He had pulled his colt out of his holster. "If I shoot you, she's mine and if you shoot me, well, then she's yours!"

Bud was losing his patience with this drunken cowpuncher. "I don't have to see who the fastest draw is. This young lady belongs to me and that's the end of it. Go back to where you come from and leave us be." The sheriff stepped in between the two men and said, "Come on now and break it up."

"Let the little lady say who she wants to be with. You might just be surprised when she chooses me," sneered the handsome cowpuncher. Several of the townspeople snickered as he straightened up his clothes and spit on his hands and wiped them through his hair.

"I'm going to tell you one more time." Bud pointed his finger at the cowpuncher as he stepped around the sheriff. "This little lady belongs to me and me alone. I have a paper that says she belongs to me!" Bud stood still for a second, not believing that he actually said those words. He turned to look at Rosie as her face flared a bright red.

Rosie couldn't believe Bud. He had just told the whole town that he had purchased her like a slave, even though he didn't actually say that.

Rider, a ranch hand from Jesse Maxwell's ranch, was in the crowd and when he heard Bud say that he had a paper, he thought he had a marriage certificate. He couldn't believe his ears. Rider pushed himself to the front of the bystanders and shouted.

"Well, this is great news! Hey everybody. Listen up! Bud's come home, and he has a beautiful little bride! I think congratulations are in order."

Rider turned to the drunken young man and gave him a little shove. "Get out of here before the sheriff puts you in his jail to sober up. Leave this man's bride alone!"

Dr. Tim had finally come outside his office waving the key in his hand. "I found the key," he said to Hannah. "Whatever has happened out here?" he asked as he saw a large crowd gathered around Bud's wagon, including the sheriff and one bloody young man. "Are you all right, honey? You've got dirt all over you."

"You just missed all the excitement. Those two young men grabbed Bud's new bride. She and her little brother fought them off. We better get this one into your office," Hannah said, as she pointed at one of the cowpunchers. "I think that young man nearly bit this one's ear off." Hannah pointed over at Tater as she led the bloody young man into the office while the sheriff was talking to the other fellow.

Dr. Tim walked over to Bud and handed him the key to the farmhouse. "Welcome home again, Bud. If you need anything, please come to me. I may not be able to help, but I'm good at giving advice."

"You will never know how much I appreciate your help already. That lawyer you got me did a great job helping to get me out of that hellhole. I'll never be able to pay you back, but I'm shore going to show you that I'm not that crazy young fool any longer."

"I know you will, son. Your folks are so excited that you're settling down here," said Dr. Tim. "I hope that you and your bride will be very happy."

Bud gathered Rosie into his arms and tossed her up on the wagon seat. "Tater, saddle up and let's head to the dry goods store and get our supplies before something else happens."

Rider was watching as Bud helped his new bride up on the wagon. She was as cute as a bug, and he didn't blame Bud for being so protective of her, even though she seemed to be able to take care of herself. Boy, was he ever going to have a story to tell at supper tonight.

"Bud," yelled Rider, "I'm going to tell the girls that you have arrived and brought a bride home with you. I'm sure you'll be visited by Rae, Hope, and Ms. Ollie. I'll tell them to give you a few days to get settled. But I know that they are going to want to welcome you and your new little family home."

"Thanks, Rider," Bud said as he gave his horses a tap with the reins to move ahead.

After Bud got comfortable on the wagon bench, he spoke to Rosie without looking her way. "Don't say anything until you and I can be alone. I didn't mean to say what I did, but we'll talk later."

"I am able to take care of myself," whispered Rosie. "You and Tater didn't need to help me and cause such a ruckus. Your actions alerted the whole town."

"I said to keep quiet! Do you ever listen?" Before she could answer, Bud continued, "Don't say another word. I've already made a mess of things and I know it."

"Can you tell me about the ladies that will be visiting us in a few days?"

"Rider is a young man who lives on the big Maxwell Ranch that is located about ten miles out of town. The owners are Jesse and Will Maxwell. They have lived here all their lives and both of the men are married. Jesse is married to Rae and Will is married to Hope, Rae's younger sister. Hope and I were childhood friends, and Will has always disliked me. Anyway, Ms. Ollie is an old black woman who has lived with the Maxwell boys forever. She practically raised the men after their ma and pa died. Now that's one woman you don't want to get riled," laughed Bud. "I bet Ms. Ollie will like Justice."

Once Bud pulled up to the store, he told Rosie that he would tell her more about the people of Limason later. He glanced in the back, and Boo and Justice were awake and ready to get out of the back of the wagon. "Look who's awake," Bud said. "Boo probably needs a dry nappy and some more overalls. While you're in the store, pick him up some more clothes. Life will be easier if you have plenty of things to change him into until he learns not to piss in his britches."

"Listen, since I'm wearing these here britches, it might be best if I stay put. Some folks don't take kindly to a girl wearing men's clothes." Rosie had not even attempted to get down off the wagon.

"Come on down. Just this once won't hurt anything. Besides I need your help in choosing the food that you and Justice will be cooking. I don't want to pick out clothes for Boo. Give me your hand so I can help you down," Bud said.

Bud placed his hands around Rosie's small waist and placed her on the ground. He walked to the back of the wagon and lowered the tailgate and helped Justice out of the back. Rosie climbed into the back of the wagon and changed Boo into some dry clothes.

Justice stood out like a sore thumb. Her tiny, slim black frame with her hair piled on top of her head wrapped in colorful scarves was a sight to see. Standing by the back of the wagon, she waited for Rosie and Boo before she entered the store.

Mr. and Mrs. Smith, the owners of the store, stood behind the counter watching as Bud and his little caravan enter their store. "Welcome home, Bud!" Mr. Smith walked from around the counter and waited for Bud to introduce him to the young lady.

"Thank you, Mr. Smith. This is Rosie, her brother Simon, and her little brother, Peter. We call them Tater and Boo. And this young lady is Ms. Justice from Louisiana. She is the children's nanny."

Justice's head popped up and looked at Bud like he had gone crazy, but she didn't say anything. *Nanny*, thought Justice. *Where did he get that idea?*

Mrs. Smith walked from around the counter and asked Rosie if she could help her make some selections. "We have plenty of canned goods and jars of preserves. These things will help you until your own garden starts producing." Rosie stood at the counter and chose several items that would help to cook a meal. Bud walked over and ordered a dozen cans of each from beans to peaches and a large slab of bacon, three dozen eggs, butter, and fifty pounds of flour and sugar.

Bud gave Rosie a little shove and said for her to go in the back and choose some clothes for Boo. "I can finish up here with the food order. Get Tater some more denims and a couple more shirts while you're at it. He will be attending school soon, and I want him to look nice."

"Bud, we heard that you will be living at the old Patterson farm. Is that correct?" Mrs. Smith asked.

"Yes, madam, I own the farm now. I plan to fix it up."

"Have you seen your folks yet?"

"We're headed that way as soon as I finish gathering our supplies."

After all the supplies were loaded in the wagon, Tater rode the big buckskin beside it looking around at the trees and farms. He was so excited about being able to live with Bud on his farm. He had never lived in a real house and a place where he felt safe from the weather or from his Pa. He was worried about Rosie. She seemed so sad and angry since they left the bayou, but Bud had been good and generous to them. He hoped that once they got to Bud's home, she would be happier. Tater listened as Bud talked about the other farms that were near his.

"The farm that we are passing belongs to John and Katie. Katie is Rae Maxwell's aunt, and she and her husband have a flower farm. They sell all types of plants, flowers, and bushes. We'll have to come over in the spring and get some plants for our place."

Bud realized that he said "our place" to Rosie and the others. *Well*, he thought, *it is their home now as long as they want to stay.* There was no way he could have ridden away and left these poor kids to fend for themselves. He knew Rosie had been hurt when she witnessed her Pa trying to sell her to him. Now that he had taken them under his protection, he was going to do everything in his power to see that they stayed happy and safe. Once the kids learned of their Pa's death, they seemed to be relieved that he would never hurt them again. Rosie seemed to think that her mama might come back to their place and get them, but she had been away for nearly two years. Bud wished for Rosie's sake that he felt the same way, but he didn't think the kids would ever see their mama again.

Lord, what was he going to do with Rosie? He let everyone in town believe that she was his new bride. He couldn't tell them different and look like a fool. Declaring he had a paper that said she belonged to him led people to think the paper was a marriage certificate. He should have never said what he did. This was his fault and now he was going to have to live with it.

"Who lives there?" Rosie asked as she pointed to another farm that sat off from the road.

"That's my folks. My farm is about five miles down the road. You can walk from one farm to the other, but I will have a small carriage for you and Justice to use to go back and forth to visit and travel to town."

"Oh, Bud, a carriage, I ain't never rode in a fancy carriage! I've walked everywhere I have ever been," Rosie said.

Tater looked at Rosie as she sat up on the wagon next to Bud. She seemed to be a little excited about the farm and having a carriage. "Lord," Tater whispered. "If you're as real as Rosie says you are, please let us be safe and happy at Bud's farm." He looked back to make sure that he wasn't overheard talking to somebody you couldn't see.

8

J USTICE WAS HOLDING tight to Boo in the back of the wagon. She was a little nervous traveling so far from the only place she had ever lived. But she would never let Rosie leave her home without her. She had met Rosie and her mama when Rosie was only five years old. Rosie had a high fever, and her mama couldn't bring it down. Her pa had ridden into town looking for the doctor. The doctor was out on a call delivering a baby. Her pa seemed to be at a near panic when he realized that there was no one to help his wife care for his little girl.

"I'll come," Justice remembered saying, and she did. Once at the shack she noticed bruises all over the man's wife. When they were alone, Justice asked her how she got all those marks on her face and arms. She replied that she had fallen. Shortly after examining the most beautiful girl child that she had ever seen, she found a wood tick buried in her armpit. After she removed the tick, she applied some herbs and salve under the arm. Justice stayed two days with the mother and little girl. Soon she became a regular visitor to Rosie and her mama. During the years of friendship, she delivered Tater and many years later she brought Boo into this world. The two boys were not brought into this world with desire and love. Rosie's pa had become a drunken, mean man who beat and raped his wife.

Justice hated the old man with a passion. She had placed a spell on him so he couldn't perform his husbandly duties again with his wife or any other woman. Justice figured that Rosie had enough children to care for. Her mama tried to be a good mother.

Over the years, she taught Rosie to read and cipher numbers. Later, Rosie spent many hours teaching Tater to read from the Bible. Her mama would sit in her rocking chair and sing hymns. One day, the old man came home drunk, and when he couldn't have his way with his wife, he beat her and busted her rocking chair into a million pieces. Later, Justice came to visit the family and discovered that Rosie's mama had left. Rosie said that a peddler came by in a big covered wagon and her mama pleaded with him to take her away from her mean husband. The old man looked at the pretty, young woman with long, golden hair and big green eyes and gladly carried her away.

Rosie was sad that day for herself, Tater, and her new infant brother. She pleaded with her mama to take her and her brothers with her, but she never said a word. She just packed what little items belonged to her and climbed abroad the peddler's wagon to never be seen again. But she loved her mama, and she was happy that she didn't have to stay and get beaten by pa any longer. Her pa never beat her or Tater because they would run and hide out in the swamp until he sobered up.

Justice never had a husband or any children of her own, but she loved Rosie and her brothers like they were hers. She would lie down and die for them before she would let anyone harm them in any way. She knew that Bud was a good man. She had looked into his soul.

Laughter and a declaration from Bud got Justice's attention. "We're home!" Bud said. He sat and looked around the farm. It actually looked better than he remembered. He glanced at the front of the house and said a silent prayer that the inside of the house looked as good as the outside.

Bud jumped down and reached for Rosie. He hurried to the back of the wagon and lowered the tailgate for Justice. He reached out and took Boo in his arms.

"Come, little man! Let's get a look at our new home."

"Papa! Papa!" Boo screamed. "Pee!"

Bud hurriedly unfastened Boo's overalls and his nappy and pushed them down around his ankles right out in the front yard. "Do your business," laughed Bud.

"Now you're setting a bad example for him. He will think that he can pee anytime he needs to right out here in the open," Rosie said while laughing.

"Hey, let's get him trained and then worry about where he's supposed to go later."

Bud looked down and noticed that Boo had sprayed one of his boots. Bud laughed and adjusted the baby's clothes. "Ready everyone? Let's take a look at the inside of the house and then we'll unload our supplies."

Rosie stood at the side of the wagon, looking all around at Bud's new home. It was like a dream come true. She felt so proud for Bud that at his age he could own a place like this. Touching Justice on the shoulder, Rosie whispered to her, "Can you believe this place?"

"Nice and clean, that's for shore. Come on. Let's gather up Boo and go inside."

Bud walked up to the front door and stood looking around at the small porch. He could feel a lump forming in his throat from the emotions building up inside. This was his home. Free and clear of a mortgage. He bought and paid for this farm with the money he won gambling. Some might say it was sinful money, but he won it honestly. He was a very proud young man today.

He reached and pulled the screen door open and unlocked the big wooden door that had three black hinges across the front of it. The door was very heavy and sturdy. Once he entered into the front room of the house, he noticed that the floors were pine and were in need of a good coat of beeswax. There was a stone fireplace that had a nice hearth. As he walked toward the kitchen, he heard Rosie and Justice talking behind him in a soft whisper.

"Have you ever!" Rosie declared as she spoke to Justice. "This here is the nicest house I have ever seen. Golly, Justice. You're mighty lucky to be able to live here. Sure wish me and Boo could stay here. Look!" Rosie pointed to the kitchen area where a big black stove stood on the side wall. She walked over and ran her palm across the top of the stove.

"Look at this stove, Justice, and a hand pump at the sink. *My heart runneth over* for you and Tater." Justice reached and took Rosie into her arms when she saw tears misting in her eyes.

"Now, honey, I'm sure Bud's folks have a much nicer place. This place looks like it has stood empty for a spell. Lots of woman's work needed here."

Bud tried to block out Rosie's sad remarks while he continued to survey his new home. He had to talk to her about their situation, but he wanted to think it through first. He went into the two bedrooms and decided that he and Tater could share the front room and Justice and possibly Rosie and Boo the other room since it was the largest. Both rooms had nice frame beds and a wardrobe. There was a big chest in the back room. He walked over to the beds and checked the mattresses. A good airing and beating would make them useable until he could return to town and have Mr. Smith order some new ones. He had slept in his last dirty bed.

Bud left the girls in the house while he checked out the well and walked out back to look in the outhouse. Both, surprisingly, were in good condition. After checking out the empty barn that had four sturdy stalls and a small tack area, Bud walked over to the covered wagon and started bringing in their supplies.

"Hey, Bud, look here, I found a door to the underground of the house. It's really dark down there but nice and cool."

Laughing, Bud walked over to where Tater was standing. He informed him that he had discovered the cellar. "This is a great storage room for vegetables, fruits like apples and berries, and barrels of sugar and salt. In the winter, we can keep fresh meat because it will be cold but not freezing. I wasn't sure the house had a cellar but I'm sure glad it does." Bud was very pleased with his new home. "Come on and help me carry our things in the house," Bud said as he patted Tater on the back. "Let's unhitch the horses and bed down the cow. She will have to be milked soon."

Rosie gathered up Boo, and they went outside to help bring in the supplies. Rosie placed Boo in the back of the wagon so he couldn't wander off. After all the supplies were brought in and placed in their designated areas; Justice asked Bud to show her how to work the big stove. With a quick lesson, Justice started cooking supper. First she filled the blue granite coffeepot with water and set it to brewing. She whipped up a large pan of fluffy biscuits and a skillet of white gravy. Rosie had found dishes on the shelf and washed them before she set the table. The table had been left by the people who last lived there along with six chairs. Everyone sat down and ate their first meal together in Bud's new farmhouse in total silence.

Once supper was completed, Bud thanked Justice for the fine meal. He glanced over at Rosie and asked if she would take a walk with him once the dishes were clean and put away.

Bud had driven the wagon over to the barn and unhitched the horses earlier. He fed the team of horses, milked the cow, and checked his buckskin to make sure that Tater had rubbed him down good. Rosie walked into the barn.

"You want to talk to me, Bud?" Rosie asked while standing with her small hands tucked in her back pockets. "I ain't got much time. I've got to give Boo a good bath and put him to bed."

"Rosie, I hadn't planned to tell everyone about having a piece of paper that claimed my ownership of you. I just got so angry at that drunken knucklehead that I lost control of my wits. Because of what I said, everyone thinks that we're married. I can't believe I have caused this confusion and messed up my plans for you and Boo. But I've been thinking that maybe you and I could pretend to be married. Later—well, maybe, if you like me—we could go to McBain and get married for real. I already like you," Bud said very softly. "No one would ever have to know that we haven't been married the whole time."

Rosie stood looking at Bud like he had grown two heads. She didn't know how to answer him. All of her young life she had taken care of herself and her brothers. She had prepared food for them to eat, taught Tater to read, washed and mended their clothes. Her mama had never been much help at all, especially after one of her beating from their pa. After her mama ran off and left them, she was in complete control of herself and her brothers and all the responsibilities were placed on her young shoulders. Now, this man, this wonderful young cowboy wanted her to pretend to be married to him. Could she give up control of her life and accept a home, protection, security, food, and clothing? She would never have to worry about her little brothers having everything they needed.

Bud said that he liked her, but some of his actions said she was a thorn in his side. But he was kind and generous to all of them. He was very grateful that she and Justice had saved his life. She found him very attractive and had dreamed of him being a knight in shining armor carrying her away on his big white horse. Things like that only happened in books to beautiful young princesses. He was a rich cowboy, and she was only a dirt poor girl that lived in the swamp.

"Rosie, what are you thinking? Do you understand what I am proposing for us to do?" Bud asked as he looked at her lovely red hair that had come loose from her long braid.

"I think I do," she replied softly. "You want me to act like your wife even though we ain't really hitched."

"Yes, that's what I'm asking. Do you think that you can act like you like me a little bit?"

Rosie looked into his face as he gave her a cocky grin. "I guess I can do that. You've been good to me and the boys. I guess I can pretend to be your woman but, Bud, what if you don't like me after a while? I can be pretty ornery at times."

"Oh, honey, I doubt that will happen," laughed Bud. "You and I get along fine now, don't we, most of the time?" He walked over to retrieve his horse and tossed a blanket across his back. Reaching for the saddle, Bud told her to go inside and get Boo ready for bed.

"I'm going to ride over and see my folks, and I will take you and the boys over tomorrow since it is so late. I know that they have probably heard that I'm home, and I brought a bride with me."

Rosie watched Bud slowly ride out of the barn. She walked over and rubbed one of the other horses on the nose and leaned her head into its neck. For the first time in her young life, she would have someone to help her care for her brothers and her dear friend Justice. Tears fell down on her rosy cheeks as she looked up to the rafters and said a sweet prayer of thanks to her loving God.

It was a lovely night for a ride, but Bud was too excited and nervous to notice. He was anxious to see his folks and brothers again. He felt like a renegade son returning home. He prayed silently to himself as he rode closer to his old home that his father would be happy to see him. He knew his mom would be thrilled to have him here because she had written to him often while in prison. He had already changed before he ever went to jail. While on the run from the law, he had attempted to return the payroll back to the army. He had not been raised to be a thief or a killer. He wanted his old life back; he did not want to be an outlaw, always having to look over his shoulder. Now he was home, and he had paid for his wrongful actions. He stopped as he rode up the driveway of his folks' home. It hadn't changed much. All the rooms were lit up in the house. He rode on in and stopped out near the barn and tied his horse to a corral post. He seemed to be frozen in place as he stood surveying the place. Just as he got the nerve to walk up to the front door, Samuel, his youngest brother, came out of the barn. Samuel stopped and looked at Bud's horse, not recognizing it in the dark.

"Hey, boy," Bud said softly. Samuel looked toward the sound of someone calling to him. He couldn't believe his eyes. "Bud? Bud, is that you?"

"Well, you certainly aren't a little fellow any longer. Your voice has changed."

"Bud, it is you!" Samuel raced over to Bud and threw his arms around his waist, forgetting that, as a big boy, he should be shaking his brother's hand. He had loved and missed Bud these past two years, and he was thrilled to have him home.

"Come on in the house! Mama and Papa are going to be so happy to see you."

"I hope so," Bud replied softly back to him.

Samuel ran to the door and opened it wide, yelling "Papa" and "Mama" at the top of his lungs.

Bud stepped into the doorway and saw his pa standing near the fireplace with a pipe in his mouth. His mama was sitting in her rocker knitting. Bud's pa was looking toward the door at Samuel, and his mama had put down her knitting to see why Samuel was so excited.

"Bud." His mama got up from the rocker, dropping her knitting onto the floor, while walking slowly toward her son whom she had missed over these past two years. Her son was home.

Bud practically flew into her arms as he attempted to wipe his tears on her shoulder. His mama squeezed him tight. He felt safe and loved.

"Mama," his papa said. "Let me get a look at my boy. It's my turn for a hug."

Bud turned away from his mama and fell into his pa's big strong loving arms. He instantly knew that everything was all right between him and his folks. They were glad to see him, and they had forgiven him for his mistakes. No words needed to be spoken.

"Here, son, step back and let me get a good look at you. Gracious, you have filled out and you're almost as tall as I am. Welcome home, son. We have been expecting you for a while," said his pa.

"Sure feels good to be home. I would have been home a little sooner, but I got a little detained. I'll tell you about that later."

"Well, well, well. Look who's finally decided to come home." Bud turned toward the bedroom door to see the person who was speaking to him.

"This is a surprise home coming. How are you, Luke?" Bud walked toward his older brother whom he had not seen since Luke finished school and headed out to California.

"I'm fine, sonny boy. How does it feel not to be a jailbird any longer? You got any more trains lined up to rob any time soon?" Luke met Bud in the middle of the parlor as he slurred his words. Bud didn't attempt to give his big brother a warm hug because he could tell that Luke had been into the bottle.

"Luke, honey, why don't you go back to your room and lie down? You can visit with Bud tomorrow when you're feeling better," said their mama.

"What! And miss this sweet homecoming for my little brother. Besides, I'm not sleepy." Luke walked toward the kitchen and looked under the sink for his pa's jug of whiskey.

Mr. Downey walked into the kitchen and mumbled something to Luke. Both men walked back into the parlor, and Luke immediately gave Bud a bow and excused himself. "Until tomorrow, my good man," he said as he staggered back to his room.

Bud, Samuel, and Mrs. Downey watched Luke leave the parlor and go into his bedroom. "How long has Luke been home?" Bud asked, looking at his mama.

"He came home about a month ago without his wife and two children. He said that she wouldn't come with him, but she did go back home to her parent's ranch. He misses his family something awful, therefore he drinks. I don't know how we can help him."

Everyone was silent for a few minutes. Bud's mama told him to follow her in the kitchen and she would fix him a plate of supper. "I know that you must be starved."

"Thanks, Mama," Bud spoke to her with a sweet smile. "I had supper before I came over. You see, I'm settled in at my new place. I arrived earlier today in town and saw Dr. Tim and Ms. Hannah. I got my house key and then I purchased supplies. Hey, where's Matt? He must be grown for sure."

"We planted the south pasture today, and he worked out in that hot sun all day. He took a dip in the creek and came in and went to bed. He's really a hard worker," said Mr. Downey with pride in his voice as he spoke of his third son.

"Tell him I'll see him tomorrow," Bud said, a little disappointed that he didn't get to see him.

"Speaking of tomorrow, I'll come right over and help you with the cleaning of the house. I'm sure its quiet dusty inside." Mrs. Downey was already planning on all the things she could do to help her son fix up his little farmhouse.

"Mama, Pa, I brought some people home with me. I've brought my new bride home."

"Oh my, this is a surprise," said his ma as she laid her hand over her heart.

"Congratulations, son," said his pa, taking his hand and pumping it up and down. "I'm so happy for you."

"Why didn't you bring her here with you tonight? You know that we would want to meet her," quizzed his mama, who hadn't gotten over the shock of the news.

"I wanted to see you all by myself first. I wasn't sure of the homecoming I'd receive and I didn't want to mix her up in our family dispute. But I will bring her over and her two small brothers."

"So, Bud, it sounds like you have a ready-made family," said his Pa.

"I guess it does. Rosie, that's my wife's name, has been taking care of them since they were very little. Tater is thirteen, and Boo is nearly two. They are good boys."

"Tater and Boo? What names!" Samuel laughed as he walked out of the kitchen eating a handful of cookies.

"Tater's real name is Simon and Boo's name is Peter. You and Tater are about the same age. Maybe you can come over and show him around the countryside," said Bud to Samuel.

"Sure, maybe." Samuel was a little jealous that someone else was going to be spending a lot of time with his brother. He had waited so long for Bud to come home so they could go fishing and hunting together again, just like old times.

"There is someone else that came home with us. Her name is Justice, and she is an older black Creole woman. She and Rosie have been like family for years. She's a character. She claims she can cast spells on people," Bud said while laughing. "I probably wouldn't be alive today if not for her healing herbs and powders."

"I'm sure your pa and I can hardly wait to meet your new family. We're so happy that you're home, son. I'm just sorry that Luke is so unhappy, but now that you're here, maybe he will cheer up." Mrs. Downey walked over and picked up her knitting and sat down in her rocker.

"It getting late, so I best head on back over to my new place," Bud said as he kissed his mama on top of her head. "Night, son."

"I'll walk you out," Mr. Downey said as he reached for his hat. "Everyone has been anxiously waiting for your return, Bud. Will and Hope are very glad that you will be living close by."

Bud laughed and shook his head. "I'm not sure that's true about Will, but how is Hope doing?"

"Fine, she's just as pretty as ever. She has one little boy, and now she's in the family way again."

"Sounds like they are happy, I'm glad. I never had a chance with her while Will was around, but that's fine," Bud said as he untied his reins and got on his horse.

"Speaking of fine, this is a nice animal. Have you had him long?" Mr. Downey asked.

Bud remembered that after he won his first big hand at cards, he went to the horse auction and purchased the big brown buckskin. "I've had him since I got out of prison."

"Welcome home, son," said Mr. Downey as he patted Bud's leg. "You tell your new bride that we'll be over first thing to meet her and her brothers."

As Bud rode out of the yard toward his new farm, Luke was standing near his bedroom window, looking out. *Welcome home, you snot-nosed jailbird*, he thought.

9

Rosie and Justice had been busy after Bud rode off to visit with his folks. They carried out the feather mattresses and gave them a good beating. They prepared the beds with the few blankets that they had while traveling. Tater was already asleep in the front bedroom that he would share with Bud. Boo was asleep on a pallet on the floor in the girl's room. Rosie had decided that she and Justice could lock their bedroom door each night and that would keep Boo from wandering around inside and out. Later, they would get him his own bed. Justice had prepared for bed, but she was waiting for Rosie to come to bed with her.

Rosie heard Bud returning from his visit with his folks. "Justice, please go on to bed. I want to talk with Bud, and we may be up for a while. Please go and lie down. You've had a long day too."

"All right, I will because I'm tired, but you remember that I'm right here in this next room. You two may pretend to be married, but I know the truth. Remember that now, you hear me?"

"Thank you for caring about me. Bud's a good man, and I'm sure he ain't planning on jumping my poor tired body." Rosie smiled and gave Justice a little push toward the bedroom door.

"You don't know what he might do. He's a man, ain't he?" Justice closed the bedroom door just as Bud came in the front door.

"Everybody gone to bed I see. Why are you still up?" Bud asked as he noticed the house was quiet.

"Just thought you might want a bite of something before you turned in." Rosie had taken the small shovel and pushed some coals to the back of the fireplace. Bud walked over to the kitchen sink and pumped himself a cup of water.

"What's on your mind? Are you worried about my folks?"

"Well, it has crossed my mind that they might be upset that you brought home a wagon full of strangers," she said with a small smile.

"To tell you the truth, Rosie, my folks were very glad to see me, and my pa seemed to have forgiven me for being a young fool. My younger brother Samuel has grown taller. Mathew was asleep so I'll see him tomorrow. Oh, my older brother Luke is home from California. He was something else. He's very unhappy because he is alone without his wife and two children. He's drinking pretty heavy." Bud walked over and pulled out a chair for himself and one for Rosie. "Come and sit a spell with me."

Rosie walked over and sat down at the table and sighed real big. "What's wrong, Rosie?"

"Well, you haven't said if you told your folks about me and the others."

"I did tell them, and they will most likely be over in the morning to meet everyone. I told them that we would come over there, but I'm sure they won't wait for us to get over to their place." Bud laughed as he rubbed his eyes.

"Bud, you're beating around the bush. Did you tell them that you took a wife?"

"Of course I did. Ma was surprised, but pa seemed to be happy for me."

"Well," Rosie said as she stood and pushed her chair under the table. "I guess we will have to wait and see if they like me. How long do you think we'll have to play act being hitched? It can't be forever, you know."

"I thought I explained that to you. Let's see if we can live together, and if we both have feelings for each other—I already told you that I like you a lot. Anyway, when you're sure that you want to be married to me, then we'll go to McBain and make it happen." He looked at her and hoped she understood. "I don't want you to ever feel forced to be my wife." Bud stood and took Rosie's hand and walked her over to the bedroom door. "Sweet dreams," he said as he placed a soft kiss on her forehead and walked back to the table to turn out the lantern.

Early the next morning, Bud stood and stretched real big. The house was silent, but he could smell coffee brewing. Tater was sprawled out on his sleeping bag snoring very softly. He eased over and dressed for the day without disturbing the youngster. Making his way into the kitchen, he didn't see anyone so he continued to make his way to the outhouse. As he was coming back toward the house, he heard someone singing a Christian hymn in the barn. Walking very quietly, Bud peeked into the barn. He saw Rosie sitting on a small stool milking the cow.

"Good morning, sunshine," said Bud, a little disappointed that she was milking the cow.

Rosie jumped, nearly turning over the small stool and spilling all the milk. "Horse feathers! You scared me to death. I didn't know anyone was up yet."

"I'm sorry. I'll yell next time I come near you," Bud said, laughing. "Listen, Rosie, this here is a man's job. Me or Tater will take on this task of milking every morning and if need be, in the evening too. You gals got enough to do without having to milk and feed the animals."

Bud had noticed that the three horses were eating their morning oats in a very clean stall. "Tater and I will muck the stalls and take care of the animals from here on out."

"Shoot fire, Bud. I'm used to milking and feeding animals and taking care of my brothers. I've been up before the sun came up." Rosie stood and picked up the milking stool and hung it on a big peg on the barn wall. She wiped her hands down the front of her denims. She grabbed up the bucket of fresh milk and started to the house.

"Rosie, you don't have to work like a field hand here. There are plenty of house chores for you to do without being out here shoveling manure. Now, as of this morning, you will not come in this barn to work. I don't mind you wearing those *pants* to work in the vegetable garden or go for a ride, but otherwise, wear one of your nice house dresses. Is that understood?"

Rosie didn't answer as she sat the bucket of milk down on the floor of the barn and walked toward the house. She was so angry with Bud she didn't dare respond to his commands.

"That's better. I'll bring the milk in and strain it up for you. I'd shore like some good hot biscuits this morning."

Rosie walked into the kitchen and found Justice sitting at the table with Boo. He was tied to a chair and eating pieces of soft bread covered with blueberry jam.

"Good morning, my Boo. Are you ready for some eggs?" Rosie walked over and kissed the top of his head as he wiped his jelly hands on her face. "Eggs!" Boo said.

"Good morning to you too, Justice. Did you sleep well?"

"Strange place. I heard all kinds of weird noises, but I'll soon get use to them." Justice got up and walked over to the stove. She lifted the coffeepot and poured herself a cup. "I'll have some hot biscuits ready in a minute."

Justice was watching Rosie as she walked slowly into her bedroom and closed the door.

"I see everyone is up now," Bud said as he brought the milk into the kitchen. "Do you want some milk after I strain it? If not, I'll place it in the well to keep cool. I'm going down into the cellar to make sure there aren't any unwanted critters nesting down there."

"I ain't never lived where there was a room underground. Louisiana's land is so low that it would have caved in," Justice said as she watched Bud retrieve another pail from under the counter.

"Well, we'll enjoy having the root cellar. People store all kinds of canned goods, barrels of sugar and flour, dried fruit, potatoes, cabbage, and turnips in the root cellar. Come wintertime, it's a great room to have. I'm sure happy that this farmhouse has one."

"Have you always lived on a farm?" Justice asked Bud as she rolled out the flour dough and started placing biscuits in a huge skillet.

"Yep, I never lived anywhere else until I left my folks and started working on a trail drive. Then I got in trouble and went to prison. I guess you might say that I made a full circle. I'm almost in the same place I was before I left," laughed Bud.

Justice placed the biscuits in the oven and cracked a bowl of eggs to scramble.

"Eggs," Boo said as he banged on the table with his spoon.

Bud grabbed his spoon and said, "No, Boo, that's not nice. No banging on the table."

Boo hung his head down on one arm, peeking up at Bud. "Would you like a cup of milk?" Bud asked but received no answer.

Tater walked into the room all dressed for the day, rubbing his eyes and declaring that he was starving. "Is breakfast ready?"

Bud and Justice laughed at him as he stood staring at them. "What's so funny?"

"You," replied Bud. "Pour yourself some water and take it to our room and wash the sleep out of those eyes and run a comb through that mop of red curls. Justice is putting the food on the table now."

The door to Rosie's room opened, and she came walking out in her ragged shift dress that she wore at their shack in the swamp. She was barefoot and had pulled her red curls back in a twisted rope. Bud watched her as she walked over to the stove and lifted plates from the shelf built over it.

"What in the Sam hell are you dressed up for?" Bud asked, being very sarcastic as he approached her. He had instructed her to wear a nice house dress.

Rosie turned to him and answered him as sweet as she could, "What's wrong with the way I'm dressed?"

"You've got much nicer clothes in your wardrobe. Go now and change out of that rag and then burn it," Bud demanded.

"Come, Tater, and sit down and eat while it's hot. Leave those two to settle their differences," Justice said. Tater sat down next to Boo and served them both some eggs with buttery biscuits. Justice passed him the sausage links and told him to cut Boo's up good.

"Move out of my way, mister," Rosie said, trying to side step around Bud. "I've got to feed Boo."

"Boo's just fine, missy. Do as I say now. There's no reason for you to dress like a gal from the swamp when I spent good money to purchase you some nice things to wear."

Bud and Rosie were making so much noise that they didn't hear knocking on their screen door. Justice stood and walked over to the door. Standing on the small front porch was a well-dressed older couple with two young boys.

"Are you going to change, or do I have to take you in that damn room and do it for you?" yelled Bud at the top of his lungs. Boo started crying from the excitement and seeing strangers standing in the kitchen.

"Bud," Mr. Downey cleared his throat as he spoke, trying to get the young fighting couple's attention.

Recognizing that voice, Bud froze in place, glaring at Rosie like he would like to throttle her. Turning very slowly and placing a smile on his face, he said, "Pa, Mamma, please come in."

"They are in," Justice commented as she strolled back over to the table and stood next to Tater and Boo.

Mr. and Mrs. Downey, Matt, and Samuel trailed into the parlor, glancing over at the kitchen table. Bud's folks knew that they had come at a bad time. It was very obvious that they had interrupted a dispute between the young, married couple.

"Uh, we're sorry to have come so early, son, but I couldn't hold your mama back any longer. It's not every day a son brings home a new bride. Well…"

"Just hush, James. Bud, I want to be introduced to your wife and the rest of the family." Mrs. Downey walked over and stood between the two young warriors with a sweet compassionate smile on her face. She remembered the first time she met her mother-in-law for the first time—*the old bat.*

"Mama, this here is Rosie." Bud said with much more pride in his voice than he actually felt. Right before they entered the house, he was prepared to do battle with Rosie and help her out of the rag she was wearing. He knew his mama had noticed the ragged shift and bare feet.

"Come here, child, and let me look at you." Rosie dropped her chin down to her chest and stepped forward toward Bud's mama. "My goodness child, you're so pretty! Please give me a big hug."

Rosie moved forward into her opened arms and allowed a big tight squeeze. "Welcome to the Downey family. Now, may I meet your brothers and your *friend?*"

Rosie had not uttered a word as she led Mrs. Downey over to the kitchen table where the trio sat eating. Bud motioned for Tater to stand while he was being introduced to the family.

"Hello, Simon. Standing behind me is Bud's younger brother, Samuel, who is eleven and this tall drink of water next to him is Mathew, Matt for short. He's thirteen."

"I'm thirteen too. People call me Tater."

"Tater!" Samuel let out a howl of laughter and turned to Matt. "You hear that? Tater, like taters."

Tater hung his head and sat back down at the table. Deeply embarrassed from being laughed at, his face turned red.

"Samuel, apologize to Tater immediately," Mr. Downey growled.

"I'm sorry," he mumbled, still with a grin on his face.

"This is my baby brother, Peter. He is two years old. Sorry about the crying, but he ain't used to strangers." Rosie said as she picked him up from his chair and placed him on her hip.

"He's a darling," Mrs. Downey said as she reached to touch one of Boo's blond curls.

"Papa!" Boo screeched as he attempted to hide his face into Rosie's shoulder.

Mr. and Mrs. Downey both looked at each other and then looked at Bud as if to say, "Explain that."

"Boo got attached to me pretty quick, and he has always referred to me as Papa. I'm not his real papa." Bud was stammering as he tried to explain Boo's outburst. "We call Peter Boo."

Quickly as he could, Bud told his mama and papa that he wanted them to meet Justice. "Justice is a dear devoted friend to Rosie and the boys. She lived alone in Lafayette, Louisiana, so we asked her to come and live with us. Justice is very good at healing the sick."

Justice nodded her head at the older couple as they stared at her. They had never seen a black Creole woman before. Mrs. Downey spoke first, "I love your colorful scarves, the way they are wrapped around your hair. Lovely."

"Your son bought me these pretties," she replied as she smoothed her hand over the side of her head.

"I'm sure we will all become good friends," said Mrs. Downey.

"Can I pour you some coffee before you have a seat in the parlor? Sorry, we don't have too much furniture to sit on," said Rosie. Bud's folks refused the offer of the coffee.

"This is a nice place," Mrs. Downey said. "I've never been inside this farmhouse before. I used to see Mr. and Mrs. Patterson at church. The couple didn't get out much because Mrs. Patterson was sick most of the time. She died right after her sweet baby girl was born, bless her young heart. Then later, do you remember, Bud, Mr. Patterson got thrown from his horse and died? The couple had a young son and the new baby girl. On Mr. Patterson's deathbed he asked the doctor's wife, Hannah, to care for his children. That was a very sad time for the community. Dr. Tim and Hannah adopted those children soon after they married."

"Mama, I do remember that happening, but over the years I had forgotten since I was just a kid. Dr. Tim helped me with the paperwork on this property. I am going to work hard and make this a nice place for my new family."

"I need to take Boo in the bedroom and clean him up and put some clothes on him. I'll be right out," Rosie said as she skirted by Bud.

"Rosie," called Bud. "Take care of that other business while you're in there."

"Come on, Bud, show me and the boys around outside and let me see what I can help you with." Mr. Downey opened the front door and motioned for his sons to lead the way out. Tater jumped up and followed.

Mrs. Downey eased over to the table and took a chair while never taking her eyes off Justice. "The next trip over, I'll bring some preserves that I have put up. I'll be sure to bring some molasses. It will be good on those biscuits and wonderful on flapjacks. I don't make butter like I did years ago. Now I get a supply from the dry goods store. And that is so much easier and better than what I made."

Justice was listening to everything Mrs. Downey said. She could tell that the woman was nervous and chatting away. She knew if she said "boo," the woman would jump out of her skin.

Finally, Justice took pity on Mrs. Downey and said very sweetly, "We'll 'pperciate whatever you can spare. I ain't never canned anything, and Rosie never had the means to do it."

"Well, goodness! I'll certainly be willing to teach her. Living on a farm, there's plenty of food that will need to be canned and put up for the winter months."

Rosie entered the kitchen, looking fresh as a daisy wearing one of her three new floral housedresses. She had put on a pair of soft slippers to cover her bare feet. She had combed her hair and tied it with a pretty blue ribbon. Boo was clean as a whistle with a new pair of blue overalls and a plaid shirt. He was carrying his tiny boots as he raced to Justice.

Mrs. Downey was trying hard to hide her amazement as she took in the change in Rosie. She was a beautiful young girl. It's no wonder Bud couldn't resist marrying this child.

Rosie eased into a chair at the kitchen table next to Bud's mama. "Madam, I'm sorry that you had to hear me and Bud feuding. He likes to tell me what to do or what to wear," she said with a shy smile on her face. "I planned to clean the house this morning, and I didn't want to get this new dress dirty."

Mrs. Downey looked at the simple dress that was made out of flour sack material by some poor dressmaker. It was a dress that most of the women on a farm would wear to scrub or wash in. But she could tell that Rosie was very proud of the dress that she was wearing. *God bless her.*

"We should have given you more time to get settled in before we came barging in on you this morning. But, Rosie, I have been without my son for nearly two years, and I only got to visit with him for just a short while last night. I just had to come see who he had brought home with him. James wanted to see what Bud needed to get started with work on his new place. Please forgive us if we have embarrassed you," said Mrs. Downey as she patted Rosie's small rough hand.

"Shucks, you ain't embarrassed me. If you're around much, you'll probably hear me and Bud tangling with each other a lot. He wants me to only work in the house and not outside."

Mrs. Downey stood and started walking slowly toward the door. "I've got to round up the boys and head on home. Would you like to come to supper at our house this evening?"

Rosie looked to Justice and said softly. "You have to ask Bud. If he wants to, I think that would be nice."

"Well, that's settled then. I'll see you this evening around five if not before. Come over any time you want too." Mrs. Downey was smiling as she made her way out into the yard and waved at James, Bud's pa.

As James, Bud, and the three boys made their way over to the wagon, Mrs. Downey told Bud that they were coming to supper this evening, and she would see them later.

"That's mighty fine," said Mr. Downey. "Jump in the back, boys."

As Bud stood in the front yard watching his folks drive toward their home, he saw Rosie standing behind the screen door. He placed both hands on his hips and gave her a big grin before walking toward the corral.

Rosie enjoyed the visit from Bud's family, but she was embarrassed that they had walked in on her and Bud arguing. But they were very nice and acted like they didn't notice anything. Turning from the doorway, she wasn't going to stand about all day long, especially when it was such a beautiful day with the sun shining. A pile of dirty clothes from their long journey needed to be washed and dried. The house needed to be aired so she walked from room to room, opening all the windows. Rosie unpacked all their clothes and placed her new things in a wardrobe in the room that she shared with Justice and Boo. She put Boo's nappies beside his pallet on a small dresser that had three drawers. All his new clothes would fit in one drawer, leaving the other two empty for Justice's personal items. The farmhouse had two bedrooms, but there seemed to be enough space for all of their belongings. Bud had mentioned that once he got the fall crop planted and some of the fence repaired, he wanted to build two more bedrooms on to the house. He wanted the boys to have their own room. After she was satisfied that the house was in order, she took a big piece of beef, cut it up, and placed it on the stove to simmer for their lunch. Later, she would cut up some potatoes and carrots and add it to the pot to make a beef stew.

Now that all the company was gone, she decided to take off her nice house dress and put on her denims. She put on one of Tater's plaid shirts because the blouses that Bud chosen for her were too nice to work outside in. As she was dressing, she couldn't help but think what a burden Bud had taken on when he took them under his guardianship.

Rosie knew it wasn't fair to Bud for him to have taken on a ready-made family because he had been shot and she and Justice had nursed him back to health. Being responsible for four people was a lot for a young man who was just starting a fresh life for himself. If the bad men who had been chasing Bud had not burned down their house, he would have left them in Louisiana. Now, he was in his new farmhouse with a young woman, an old Creole healer, and two young boys.

Bud had spoken of making their pretend marriage a real one if and when she felt that she had feelings for him. He said that he already liked her. Rosie liked Bud a lot, but she had been on her own for several years caring for her young brothers. She hunted, fished, cooked, and took care of her brothers all by herself. She liked Bud's mama and his family. She didn't have to guess how Tater felt about Bud. He hung onto his every word and trailed his every step. But she wasn't ready to allow some man that she had only known for several weeks to have control over her and her brothers. She needed time to get to know Bud well, and she certainly wasn't going to sit around in this house all day like a hot house flower.

Justice had gone outside and had Tater help her with the big boiling pot to wash the clothes. He pulled the water from the well as she placed plenty of wood in the fire ring under the pot.

After the water was hot, she placed the clothes in the boiling water and stirred the clothes with a long stick. Rosie had heard Justice chanting a tune as she washed the clothes.

At the end of their first day of chores, washing several tubs of clothes, cleaning the house, cooking lunch, mending fences, and plowing an acre of ground, Bud and Rosie were exhausted. After a dip in the cold creek that was located behind their farmhouse, Bud came in and dressed to go to his mama's home for supper. After a wonderful supper and a very nice visit with his folks, they made their way home.

Bud could tell that Rosie had something on her mind. She was busy feeding Boo his last bottle before going to bed, but she kept glancing his way. He stood and rubbed his stomach and said that he had eaten too much at his mama's. "I'm tired. That old plow whipped my butt today," he said with pride in his voice.

"Bud, I would like to talk to you before you turn in," she said while walking to her bedroom to place the sleeping baby on his pallet.

"Come on into my bedroom while I get ready for bed. Man, I'm beat."

Justice gave Rosie a nod with her head saying that it was all right to be in Bud's private quarters alone. "All right, for just a minute."

"What's on your mind, my little swamp girl?" he asked as he pulled his shirt out of his pants and then began unbuttoning it.

"Well, I wanted to thank you for all you have done for us... me, Justice, and the boys. I could never start to repay you for all the nice things you have bought us."

"Out with it. You didn't follow me in here to thank me. You've done that many times over."

"You spoke about marriage...for real."

"Oh, Rosie," Bud was surprised and excited all in one second at her statement about marriage. He never thought that she would commit to him so soon. He reached his long arms out and pulled her into his arms.

"Wait, Bud, you didn't let me finish. I'm not ready for this." She gave him a little shove as she stepped back away from his naked torso. His body was so hard, firm, and muscular. "We are—well, you are for sure—rushing things. You know that if we still had a home back in the bayou, we wouldn't be here. You would be living in this nice farmhouse alone. *Not with a household of strangers.*"

"Sorry, darling, but you didn't have a home. It was a leaning, rundown shack."

"It was my home—the only one that I ever knew."

"All right, I'm sorry. I didn't mean to speak so nasty about your lovely home place. But you have to agree that this is a much nicer place to be."

Bud continued to undress. He slipped off his Western boots and removed his socks. He walked the boots over to the corner of the room and began undoing his belt bucket. He pulled it out of his denim's loops and hung it on the peg on the wall. He turned and faced Rosie again with both hands on his lean hips. Giving her a mischievous grin with a twinkle in his eyes he nodded toward the bed and asked if she would like to join him. "I can make a pallet in the front room for Tater."

"Bud, you're bad and you know it. I came in here to tell you that I want to work on this farm. I can't stay coop up in this house all day. If we are going to make a home together, I want to work beside you and help with the milking, feeding the animals, and mucking the stalls."

"Taking care of the house and Boo is a full-time job. I can't believe you."

Bud stood, looking down at her as she took deep breaths and continued, "I want to earn my own way by helping you. I always have and that's the way I am."

"What do you think people will think about me if I *allow you* to work outside like a hired hand? I can tell you what they'll say! 'Oh, that Bud is nothing but a jail bird that is too lazy to work so he puts his wife to working like a field hand while he lays up inside the house.'" Bud was working himself up into a full temper fit. He couldn't believe this little gal. *We haven't been home but two days, and she wants to work like a grown man in the fields.*

"That's another thing, Bud. I hate lying to your folks. Your mama accepted me as her new daughter. I wanted to cry. She offered nothing but kindness to me while I spoke one lie after another to her about us. I hated every minute of it!"

Bud had walked across the room looking out of the window. He was so angry he wanted to hit something. "Go, Rosie. Get out of my room before I say or do something that we'll both regret. We'll finish this conversation tomorrow."

Rosie turned and fled from Bud's room. She didn't realize that he was going to get so angry with her. Tomorrow would be another day. *Yes,* he will understand how she feels about their situation when he isn't so tired, she thought. Later, he would be glad for her help.

10

THE NEXT MORNING, Bud was gone from the house and didn't return until late at night after everyone had gone to bed. Justice left him a plate of food on the stove. This seemed to be the routine that Bud took for several days. He was avoiding Rosie and the future conversation about how she wanted to work outside of the house and do dirty, nasty chores that were meant for men only. After a short visit from his pa, he was told that they were having a small barbecue. This would give the Maxwells and Dr. Tim's families the opportunity to welcome him home and meet Rosie and the boys. Bud wanted to refuse and beg them not to do this, but his pa was so excited about the idea. "This will be good for Luke, too. He hasn't seen anyone since he arrived home."

At supper, Bud walked in the house and nodded to everyone. Rosie and Justice were surprised to see him. Tater had not missed Bud because he had been working beside him every day. Boo was thrilled when he saw Bud. "Papa! Up, up," he screamed. Bud scooped Boo up in his arms and kissed him on the cheek, asking how his little man had been.

"I've missed you. You being a good boy?" Bud asked Boo.

"No," Justice replied sharply. "He has stood at that door and yelled your name over and over for hours, like a little lost puppy. You should be ashamed of yourself."

Bud's face turned a fiery red while he was taking his seat at the dinner table still holding Boo.

"I saw my pa today. We have all been invited to their home tomorrow evening for a barbecue. They have invited the Maxwell family—Jesse, Rae, Hope, Will, Ms. Ollie, and their children along with Dr. Tim and his family. Some others are invited too—should be a nice time."

"What should we cook to take?" Rosie looked at Bud and spoke to him softly.

"Just ourselves, but bring plenty of clothes for this here booger. These parties tend to last a long time. It'll be late when we get home." Bud looked around the room at everyone, and they sat silently thinking about his announcement with grim expressions on their faces.

"Hey, this will be fun! We're not going to a hanging, so let's see some smiles. Tater, there will be boys that you haven't met and, Justice, I know that you'll love Ms. Ollie. Rosie, you will really like Hope, Rae's sister. She married to Will, Jesse's brother. You both are close to the same age. Tomorrow will be a nice, relaxing day for all of us." Bud hoped that all he said was true. He was nervous about seeing Will and Hope again himself, but he couldn't allow his nerves to show. He knew that Dr. Tim and Ms. Hannah would treat him nice because he had already seen them since coming home.

The next morning was full of activity. Everyone was busy with their morning chores. After a big breakfast of bacon and flapjacks, Bud and Tater headed out to the barn. Bud walked the horses out of the barn into the corral while Tater milked the cow. Rosie had rushed out to the chicken yard and gathered the eggs from her sassy, fat hens. As she was making her way out of the chicken yard, Bud came around the barn and spotted her.

"Rosie!" Bud yelled. "I told you that I didn't want to see you in that chicken house again. Collecting those damn eggs are part of man's work. Your work is in the house, and Tater and I work outside." He had marched up to Rosie and was practically in her face trying to make his point.

"There's no reason I can't gather eggs from the chickens."

"There is so! Just look at the blood on your hands and how nasty those eggs are. They need to be washed before carrying them into the house to be used. I don't want to hear any more about milking that blasted cow of yours or those –."

Before Bud could complete his sentence an egg was smashed onto his forehead.

"Now, there's one egg that won't need to be washed," Rosie screamed as she smeared the egg on Bud's forehead.

"What the hell!" Bud shouted while being very confused and irritated at her behavior. He bent forward as he attempted to reach for her. She wriggled away as the egg yolk dripped down the center of his nose and ran down his chin, falling onto his shirt.

Rosie still held the basket of eggs as she lost all restraint on her temper. She turned and threw another egg at him, hitting the side of his head where yellow muck and sticky eggshell collected in his hair.

"Girl, what's wrong with you? I'm not going to let you get away with…" Before he could take a step forward, two more eggs targeted his head in rapid session. Bud's hair was covered with yellow, slimy egg yolks. He placed both of his hands over his head and backed away from the line of fire as he wiped egg slime out of his eyes.

"I don't know what's wrong with you," he shouted. "Shoot fire! Most girls would be happy to have someone else washing nasty chicken *poop* off their eggs!"

"I'm not like most *girls*." With much satisfaction, she jumped out of his reach. "I've been milking my cow for years, and I like gathering eggs and caring for them. If I'm going to live here, then I'm going to do what I want inside and out." Quickly rotating around, Rosie raced to the house, jumped up on the porch, and entered the kitchen while letting the screen door slam.

Justice had been watching out of the kitchen window. "Why in this world was you wasting those good eggs on Bud's head?" Rosie looked at Justice, and both of them fell into a fit of laughter.

"Let's just say maybe he will think twice before telling me I can't do something." Both of the ladies stood at the window watching Bud wash himself off at the well. Tater had come out of the barn with a questionable expression on his young face. Bud just looked at him and said, "Don't ask because I can't explain what makes a woman act *nuts!*" he shouted loud, hoping Rosie would hear him. Tater shook his head and carried the milk into the kitchen.

Bud didn't know what to make of Rosie. After being in prison, he had learned to be patient, think with a clear head and try to be reasonable in most situations. Now with Rosie, he only wanted to make life easier for her, but she didn't see what he was trying to do. He dropped a bucket down into the well and pulled up some water to wash his face and neck. *Damn!* he said to himself. *I got slimy crap in my ears too.* He jerked off his shirt and washed the egg off the front of it and hung it on the clothesline.

"Women," he mumbled to himself as he strolled to the creek for a much-needed dip. "If I live to be a hundred, I'll never understand them."

When Bud returned to the house, he found Rosie, Justice, and Boo all dressed and ready to go to the party. Rosie was dressed in a floral green and white dress. He was surprised at the feeling that had come over him as he looked at her. He felt his breath catch as he took in how lovely she looked. She had taken extra care with her grooming. He felt lightheaded for a second because his little swamp rat had stilled his heart.

Boo had on a new pair of blue overalls with a light blue shirt. He was ready to go as he stomped around the room in his new cowboy boots. His Western hat was swinging loose down his back.

Justice looked like a fancy Creole voodoo queen with her hair piled high. Beautiful scarves adorned her hair and looped at the bottom to stay fastened. She was wearing five long necklaces around her slim neck with a gold chain wrapped around her tiny waist. Her long floral skirt covered all but the top of her knee-length soft boots. She was certainly a unique character to see. Bud hoped that her unusual appearance didn't scare the little ones too much.

Bud and Tater dressed quickly. Rosie and Justice couldn't help but give the two guys a big smile. Tater was dressed just like Bud because he idolized him and wanted to be just like him in every way. Both had on dark brown leather vests over soft plaid Western shirts that were tucked into their dark blue denim pants. They both had buffed their boots to a glossy shine.

Bud stood and gave Rosie a hard look, trying his best to intimidate her.

"Well, missy, I see you're in a better mood than you were earlier." Bud walked past her and told Tater to follow him out to the barn. "Let's hitch up the wagon and get those lovely ladies loaded and off to the party. Since I missed breakfast, I'm starved. I'm sure my mama will feed me when I get there."

The party was in full swing when Bud drove his wagon up to the barn. He jumped down and Hank and Jeremiah were standing nearby ready to assist the ladies from their wagon.

"Girls, I would like you to meet Hank and Jeremiah," said Bud. "Hank is Jesse Maxwell's boss man, and this is his good friend Jeremiah who lives with Katie and John Johnson."

"Howdy," said Hank. "Why don't you let me take that big boy while Bud helps you down?" Rosie dropped Boo into Hank's big arms. Hank lifted Boo over his head and told him that there was another little fellow in the house just waiting to play with him.

Hank walked toward the house with Boo while Jeremiah offered his hand to help Justice down. Jeremiah had never seen an old Creole black woman before, but over the years, he had heard about them. She looked like she could do magic—not the good kind either.

"Where're you from?" Jeremiah asked Justice.

"Why you ask, old man?" Justice replied while never taking her eyes off the short, stocky little man. This man's skin was coal black, and she would bet the whites of his eyes and teeth would glow in the dark.

"Just curious, that's all," replied Jeremiah. "Ollie, who has lived with Jesse and Will all their young lives, is in the house waiting patiently to meet you. I bet the two of you will get along just fine." Jeremiah commented while helping Justice down.

"Bud, why don't you unhitch your horses? You gonna be here awhile," Jeremiah said.

"Right, Tater, you go along with them. I'll be in shortly," Bud said.

"I'd rather help you and then go in when you're ready, if you don't mind."

As Bud was escorting his horses into the corral, Will walked over and opened the big corral gate. Bud continued walking and gave one horse a pat on the rump as he turned to face Will for the first time since the day he was led out of the courtroom and put on the train to go to prison.

"Welcome home." Will walked toward Bud with a smile on his face and extended his right hand for a handshake. Bud noticed that Will was not limping, and he was very relieved.

"Thanks, Will," Bud replied with a lump in his throat. He didn't realize how breathless he was going to feel seeing Will for the first time since he was sentenced to prison for shooting him in the attempted train robbery. He almost wished Will would have greeted him with a sock to the jaw.

"I met your lovely wife as she was going into the house. Man, you are one lucky son of a gun. She's a little beauty."

"Thanks." Bud was frozen into place. He was happy that Will had been so gracious in welcoming him home, but he was still very nervous.

"Come on. Everyone is waiting to greet you and welcome you home. Hope wants you to meet our son, Jacob."

"Pa told me that she's in the family way again. How's she doing?"

"She's just as beautiful and feisty as ever. I'm never going to tame her to be the sweet docile wife that some men have." Will grinned and placed his arm across Bud's shoulder and pushed him toward the house. Both of the men laughed and Bud's nerves seemed to have relaxed. It had not been that many years ago that he was sure that Will hated his young guts for riding and swimming and having a good time with Hope.

Remembering that Tater was nearby, Bud spoke to Will. "Oh, Will, this youngster is Tater. He's Rosie's oldest brother and the best sidekick a man could have. Tater, meet Will Maxwell."

Tater hung his head and mumbled a hello to Will. His face blushed as red as his hair when Bud told Mr. Maxwell that he was his sidekick. That comment made him feel very proud because no one had ever said anything nice about him except Rosie.

As the three men walked up to the house, they were greeted by John and Katie and their pretty young daughter, Missy. Katie was Rae's aunt and John worked for Jesse on his cattle ranch. Years ago, Katie and Jeremiah had come to visit Rae and Hope at the Maxwell's ranch. She met John, and they married several months after Jesse and Rae's wedding. Jeremiah had lived and work for Katie's first husband, and after he died, he stayed as her helpmate and protector. Katie loved plants and flowers so she and John had a very successful flower and plant farm on the property that connected to the Downey's place.

Katie greeted Bud with a big, warm hug while John waited patiently to shake Bud's hand. John introduced his young daughter, Missy, while Bud patted Tater on the back and introduced him as Simon. Tater quickly looked to Bud for him to make a correction to his name but none was forth coming.

"Call me Tater," he stammered as he glanced at the prettiest girl he had ever seen up close. Missy's pretty brown hair was plaited into two long pig-tails and covering her pretty blue eyes were gold wire-rimmed glasses. She had a spray of light brown freckles covering a little turned-up nose. Tater was instantly in love.

Jesse and Rae stood on the porch waiting for Bud to approach them. The last time he had seen them was in the courtroom before he was sentenced to prison. They had hugged him good-bye and wished him well. They had forgiven him for his stupid actions. Now they were waiting to welcome him home with open arms. Bud felt his nerves start to settle down in his gut. Everyone had been generous with their kind words of welcome. God had answered his prayers that he would be accepted back into the fold of his family and friends.

Mrs. Downey came to the door looking out over the yard for her son. "Bud, I was beginning to think that I was going to have to send a search party out for you. Hope wants you to see her baby before she has to put him down for a nap. Hurry on in now, you hear?"

Bud spoke quietly to Rae and Jesse and said that he had best get inside. As he made his way into the room he had to let his eyes adjust from the bright sunlight to the cool, darkened parlor. Sitting in his ma's rocker was Ms. Ollie. She was rocking a big baby boy. As Ms. Ollie gave Bud one of her sweet smiles, he looked around the room. Sitting on the sofa were Hope and Rosie. Hope jumped off the sofa and quickly raced across the room and took both of Bud's hands. Bud stood still looking into the face of his young childhood friend. Hope was still the most beautiful young woman in the whole county. Motherhood agreed with her. Her hair was beautiful pulled back behind her ears while her skin was as smooth as silk. *Will was a lucky man*, thought Bud.

"Oh, Bud, you look wonderful. We have all been so worried about you being incarcerated in that awful place. It's so wonderful to have you home and your new bride is lovely. Rosie and I are already becoming fast friends." Bud glanced at Rosie, and she gave him a sweet smile.

"Bud, come and look at Jacob." Before Bud could move over to the baby, Hope said, "Would you have ever thought that I would settle down and become a mama?" Hope rubbed her hand over her small belly as she suggested that she was carrying another child.

"I'm happy for you and Will. Your boy is beautiful. Wonder where he got that black hair?" Bud teased as he walked over to Boo and picked him up high in his arms.

"Papa!" Cried Boo with slobber dripping out of his mouth. Bud reached in his back pocket and pulled out his clean handkerchief and wiped the baby's mouth.

"This one is cutting some more teeth," said Rosie as she took Boo from Bud.

Ms. Ollie laughed as she told Bud that the two babies had being gibber jabbering at each other ever since they met.

"Jacob got cranky pretty quick because he was up before sunrise this morning. He's cutting a tooth too, and he cries a lot," Hope said.

"Oh, Bud! It is wonderful having you home and living so close to all of us. I'm glad that Jacob and Boo will be able to grow up together and have a playmate so close in age. I always wanted someone my age to play with, but all I had was Will, Hank, and the other guys to play with me."

"If I remember correctly, you mean to say that they played with you and let you have your way. They spoiled you." Bud laughed as he looked at Ms. Ollie. She smiled and shook her head.

"You got that right, Bud. She was so spoiled you could smell her a mile away." Ollie laughed at her own joke. "She's still getting spoiled every day by that husband of hers. That Will would give her the moon if he could reach it."

"Now, Ollie, I'm good to Will too." Hope pouted. "You seem to forget that sometimes. You're always taking his side when we get into an argument."

"You're right, sweetheart. Now take this boy so I can get up. Lay him down on a pallet in the other room. You better watch Boo because he's liable to sit on top of Jacob while he's sleeping," said Ms. Ollie laughing.

"Here, let me have him, Miss Ollie. He's a little heavy for Hope to be carrying." Bud reached and took the baby from Miss Ollie and followed Hope into the front room. After Bud laid the boy down and stood, he looked into Hope's lovely face.

"I can't thank you and Will enough for all that you did for me. I really didn't deserve your help after what happened. For weeks, I wished I was dead when I thought I had killed Will. I knew that I had hurt you so badly, and my folks, too. I had made a mess of things just because I was wild and stupid." Bud shook his head as he remembered how he had tried to rob a train. Will and Hope were passengers, and Will tried to stop Bud from taking Hope as a hostage so he could get away. Will had jumped Bud, and they wrestled over the gun. Will had been shot, and Bud dragged Hope off the train and took her to Laredo, Texas.

"Oh, Bud, that's all behind you now. You're a different person, and this is a new start for you and your ready-made family." Hope paused as she took Bud's hand. "You know I am very happy with Will. I know that you said that I wouldn't be, but I have always wanted to be with him. I can't remember ever not loving him. You know he completed our beautiful home, and now we have our son and another child on the way." Hope stood in front of Bud twisting side to side showing off her rounded belly.

"I'm glad, Hope. You know I was crazy about you but not in the same way that Will loved you. I believe the reason he hated me so much was because he was wildly jealous of us having such a good time together." Bud laughed as he remembered the mean dirty looks he always received from Will.

"Will and I are happy for you too. You have said that you're sorry and you have paid your debt by being in that awful prison. Let's not speak of this again. Come on, let's go and get Rosie and check on the barbecue. I'm starving!"

Ms. Ollie and Justice were sitting under a shade tree in the yard. They seemed to be getting along very well. Ms. Ollie was entertaining Justice by describing each family member. "Now, Justice, you can go to church with Bud and Rosie or you can join me and Jeremiah on Sundays. We pass right by Bud's farm going to our meeting place. I think that you'll enjoy meeting our friends. We don't have as many young people like we used to, but there's still quite a few of us old birds that goes there every Sunday. Jeremiah and I tries to help some of the older ones that live alone. Maybe you would like to help us sometimes when we make our rounds and visit with them?"

"Now, I like helping the sick, but I don't think that I could enter your house of worship. It would be like throwing holy water on the devil," Justice replied with a grin on her old shiny black face.

Ollie didn't know how to respond to Justice's remark about church.

"Like I said, I like helping the sick. I have special potions that I can mix up and give to them. Most feel better pretty quick." Justice looked at Miss Ollie who was staring hard at her.

"I ain't too sure about your 'potions,' but whatever you can do to make them comfortable will be a big help," Ollie said as she shook her head.

"Can you do magic?" Jeremiah inquired as he walked up while listening to the ladies' conversation.

"Depends on what kind of magic you're speaking of."

"Jeremiah, I can see right now that you aren't too sure of Justice and her special healing ways. You just leave her alone. Why aren't you over there mopping that beef with your special sauce? We're all hungry." Ollie pointed to where the men were gathering around the big fire pit laughing and talking.

"Now, Ollie, don't go and put words in my mouth. Her ways are just different from ours. I'm not sure if our folks will take to her. They might be frightened of her special potions."

"I ain't never harmed anyone unless they deserved it." Justice looked straight into Jeremiah's big brown eyes.

"Well, I best go see if they need my help." Jeremiah gave Ollie a grin as he strolled away, whistling a little ditty that he heard Will singing after their trip to Houston several years ago.

"Justice, he means no harm. He is really a good man. You'll soon learn his ways." Ollie clasped Justice's hand and gave it a good squeeze. "Oh good, here comes Dr. Tim and Ms. Hannah with Susie, Mary Beth, and Little John."

After Dr. Tim's family had settled into the house and gave Bud and his family a warm greeting, Mr. Downey rang the dinner bell. Everyone came out of the house and surrounded the makeshift tables and benches. They had been placed under the large oaks trees where everyone could enjoy their dinner in the nice cool shade. After Mr. Downey mumbled a short blessing, Bud and his family were given the honor to be first in line. Jeremiah and Hank stood over the big pit where a side of beef had been slowly cooking most of the night and all morning. As the guests passed their plate, big slices of beef were placed on them. Mrs. Downey had prepared all kinds of garden vegetables along with big bowls of small red potatoes and roasted corn on the cob. Hope had baked two loaves of fresh bread and a pan of golden yeast rolls. Rae had baked a three-layered chocolate cake, and Katie had prepared a big bowl of bread pudding for dessert.

Tater whispered to Rosie that he had never seen so much food in his young life. Boo had been placed in an old high chair that Mr. Downey had brought down from the barn attic and cleaned up just for this occasion. Rosie had changed his clothes and tied a dishcloth around his neck. He was banging on the table with his spoon, screaming, "Eat!" Everyone laughed at him as Bud walked over and took his spoon away and said, "No banging, young man."

Rosie had filled a plate and sat down on the bench next to Boo to help feed him. Bud saw Tater with his plate piled high sitting at the end of another table with Missy, Katie's daughter. Little Jess and Claire, Jesse and Rae's children; John, Mary Beth, and Susie, Tim and Hannah's children, had joined them at the table. Laughter was coming from that way, and Bud was very happy that the young people were making Tater feel welcome. He wanted him to be happy and agree to go to school on his own, because he was going whether it was his choice or not.

Rae and Hannah came over to the table and sat across from Rosie and Boo. Hope joined them and said that Jacob was still taking his nap. Ollie and Justice were in the house eating their dinner and they would listen out for Jacob.

"I'm sorry we were late, but you're never going to believe what happened at the office," Hannah explained. "Esther fell down the back steps and broke her left leg and her right hand. Lord, have mercy! She screamed as she tripped on her own feet. She scared the devil right out of me. Thank goodness, Tim and I were both there in the back of the office."

"How is she? Where is she?" Rae asked quickly. Esther had been Dr. Tim's cook, maid, part-time nurse, receptionist, and loyal friend ever since he arrived in Limason. She was like a mother to him.

"Right this minute, she is in the hospital ward in the back of our office. Her husband is staying with her until we get home. She's sleeping and most likely will be until late this evening."

"Is she in lot of pain?" Hope asked as she wiped barbecue sauce off her mouth.

"She will hurt some, I'm sure, when she wakes up, but you have never witnessed a trooper like her. There she was lying on her back with a broken leg. You could see part of the bone. I nearly fainted. Well, her hand was broken and already starting to swell. Not one sound came out of her mouth. She didn't shed a tear or yell." Hannah shook her head as she laughed and said, "Esther said to Tim, 'Be careful, Dr. Tim. Don't hurt your back picking me up.' She's always thinking of the other person."

"So how long do you think that she will be laid up and not able to work for you?" Rae was very concerned about Esther because Ollie and Esther were the best of friends. She knew once Ollie heard about Esther, she was going to want to try to take care of her.

"She will be off that leg for a spell, I'm sure. Her hand will heal quickly, but she won't be able to do too much with just one hand," Hannah said. "Esther asked Tim to telegraph her sister in McBain to come and help take care of her. She should be here by the end of the week. Until then, her husband can sleep in the infirmary at night with her. I'll have to hire someone to come and stay in the office in case Tim and I have to leave during the day."

"So what are you going to do for help?" Rae asked. "There're not too many people to choose from these days." Ollie would want to go and take care of Esther but the ten-mile trip to and from town each day would wear her out.

Rosie was listening attentively. Maybe this would be a nice neighborly thing to do for a few days. She had the house in good shape, and Bud wasn't allowing her to work outside. Justice could watch Boo and the two of them could cook supper when she got home.

"I could help you," Rosie said very softly.

"What, dear?" Hannah asked, not sure she understood Bud's pretty new wife.

"I could help you out until your friend's sister comes."

Hannah looked at Rosie and then she looked at Rae and Hope. "Why, honey, that's so sweet of you to offer to help, but you have a lot to do at your new place."

"You did say it will only be a few days. I have everything in order at home and I know that Bud wouldn't care if I helped you out. All of you have been so good to Bud and me and my brothers. It's the least I can do."

Hannah sat back and sighed real big. "Well then, I guess that's settled. Could you be at the office around eight and Luther, Esther's husband, will come around five so you can leave for home. How does that sound?"

The family gathering was a great success. Luke, Bud's brother, didn't make an appearance which was a disappointment to Mr. Downey. No one asked about him, so there were no excuses to be made for his absence. He had not come out of his room for breakfast and not a sound came from his room. Mrs. Downey had warned the other boys to stay away from his room and not to disturb him. "He's tired," she said, making excuses for him. Everyone knew he wasn't tired because he had not done anything for days. He had been hanging his hat in the Golden Nugget Saloon in town.

Bud's new family was exhausted as they made their way home from the party. Justice sat on a quilt in the back of the wagon holding Boo in her arms. Tater leaned his head over on her shoulder. Both boys loved her like a mama.

Bud moved over on the bench and whispered to Rosie, "I heard Ollie and Justice talking about you taking care of Esther at Dr. Tim's office. What's that all about?"

"I told Ms. Hannah that I would help care for her friend until her sister comes in a few days. I was going to tell you, but I never got you alone to discuss it," she replied very softly.

"I wish you had asked me about this before you talked to Ms. Hannah. I'm not crazy about you riding five miles to and from town each day by yourself. And besides, Justice is getting too old to run after Boo all day. You should have thought of that." Bud was irritated with Rosie that she had not asked him for his approval.

Rosie could tell that Bud was angry with her, and she really didn't understand why he would be. "I thought that you would be pleased that I wanted to help some of your nice friends. You told me that Dr. Tim had helped you a lot. I just thought that I could return a favor to them for you. If you don't want me to help them, then I won't. But I need to go in and work Monday. I will tell them I can't come back into town…if that's what you want me to do."

Bud drove his two big horses down the road and didn't look down at Rosie. She made him feel bad. He knew that it wouldn't hurt anything if she went into town and helped care for Ms. Esther, but he was selfish. He liked having her around the farm with him. He enjoyed coming into his new home and watching her cook, and playing or rocking Boo. She was a ray of sunshine and a joy to be around. Damn! His days had been so miserable the past two years. He couldn't help feeling that he might lose her to the ways of town once she got used to being there.

After arriving home, he pulled the wagon to the front of the house. Bud helped Rosie down and walked to the side of the wagon. He reached in and took Boo out of Justice's arms and shook Tater awake.

"Hop down, son, we're home. Help Justice out of the wagon and into the house." Bud went into the bedroom and laid Boo in his crib that his parents had brought over the day before. "The bugger is wet," he said quietly.

Bud went outside and placed the two horses in the barn. After settling them down for the night, he gave them both a bucket of oats. Once back in the house, he sat down at the kitchen table and waited for Rosie to join him before getting ready for bed.

Rosie joined him at the table and asked if he would like something to eat or drink. "No, thank you. It sure was a nice party, wasn't it?" Rosie nodded her head yes but didn't respond.

"Everyone enjoyed meeting you and the boys. The men told me how lucky I am to have such a beautiful girl for a wife."

Rosie looked at him and smiled. "That was nice."

"Listen, Rosie, I didn't mean to be such a brute. I've got a lot to learn yet and I'm trying to be a good person. I've been around so many bad…well, anyways, that's no excuse for me to act ugly. If you want to go to town and help Ms. Hannah out for a few days, I'll help Justice with Boo and we'll all pitch in and help each other out. I could take you into town each day, if you like?"

"Thank you, Bud, for understanding. I can go into town by myself. I ain't, I'm not, I mean, afraid." Rosie stood and ran her hands down the front of her skirt. "Well, I best turn in. We've got to get up and get dressed for church tomorrow. Your mama said that she expects to see us there and go home with them for lunch. She's gonna have a lot of leftovers for us to eat."

"Well, we don't want to get off on the wrong foot with Mama now, do we? See you in the morning."

Rosie started to walk toward her room when she stopped and turned to face Bud. She hurried over to him and placed a kiss on his lips and said, "Thank you." She rushed away into the bedroom and closed the door quickly.

Well, damn, thought Bud. *She gives me a kiss for allowing her to go and work.*

11

Early Monday morning, Rosie was up before the sun peeked out from behind the farmhouse. She had dressed in her denim pants and Bud's big wader boots. She had put coffee on the stove to brew before she hurried out to the barn. She gave the shovel a few quick swipes as she mucked the horse stalls. Grabbing the milking stool off the wall, she sat it down beside her cow and, after washing the cow's teats, milked her. Carrying the milk out of the barn, she sat it down and covered it with a nice clean cloth. She rushed over to the chicken house and gathered a basket of fresh eggs from a disgruntled bunch of sitting hens. This was a little early for them to be bothered, but they surrendered their eggs without too much fuss. Pleased with herself for getting some of the morning chores completed before Bud had gotten up, she went back into her room and dressed for the day. She selected a pretty, simple green dress and pulled her red hair back with a green ribbon. She slipped her soft house shoes on her feet and wished she had a pair of more durable street shoes. But Bud had been so generous with her that she couldn't dare ask for anything else.

Making sure that Boo was still asleep and covered well with his small quilt, she opened her bedroom door and went into the kitchen. Bud was sitting at the kitchen table drinking a cup of coffee.

"Good morning, sunshine," he said, using the pet name that he had started calling her.

"Good morning to you too. It's a little early for you to be up. I had hoped to have biscuits cooking before you got up." She had really hoped to have the milk strained and placed down in the well before he got up and saw that she had milked the cow.

"I thought I heard something out in the chicken yard, but I didn't see anything," Bud said as he sipped his coffee.

Wrapping an apron around her small waist, Rosie took the big bowl out from under the counter and filled it with flour, lard, and some milk. She began mixing the biscuits while humming the sweet tune of *"Amazing Grace."* Bud stood and stretched and said that he best get dressed and get the day started. He was going to plant some winter hay in the back field. Tater would do all the other chores and then come out and give him a hand. Later he would send Tater back to the house to watch Boo so Justice could rest a spell. He walked back into his room and closed the door.

Quickly, Rosie washed her hands and hurried over to the dry sink and strained the milk. She rushed out the door and went over to the well. Hooking the milk onto a rope, she lowered it down the side of the well. "Great!" she sighed with relief that Bud didn't catch her doing that chore.

Placing the last of the biscuits in the pan, she opened the oven and slid them in to cook. Justice came out of the bedroom with Boo trailing behind her. Boo ran around Justice and grabbed Rosie's legs, pulling on her to be picked up. "Eggs," he said as he pointed at his mouth.

"Say please, darling," Rosie instructed.

"Pees!" he yelled as he walked over to be put into his chair.

"This rascal is getting heavy," Rosie said as she lowered him into his highchair that Mr. Downey had insisted that they bring home with them after the party.

Justice had poured herself a cup of coffee and was uncovering the bacon when Bud came into the room. "Sure smells good in here," he declared. "I'm going to the barn and I will be back in just a minute. You know I think I will rig up a bell to be placed at the door. This will be a way to tell Tater and me that it is time to eat or we are needed at the house. What do you think of that idea? Hope told me years ago that when Ms. Ollie has food on the table, she rings the dinner bell."

"I like the idea. Better than trying to find you outside," commented Justice.

"Bud, breakfast is nearly ready, so don't go out there. Please go in and wake Tater and tell him to dress and come and eat." Rosie needed to stall Bud from going outside at least until she left for town.

The bacon was sizzling as Rosie poured the eggs into another hot skillet. Justice pulled the biscuits out of the oven and placed them on a platter. She gathered the butter and jelly from the pantry and set them in the middle of the table.

Tater came into the kitchen announcing that he was starving and could eat a whole cow. Everyone laughed because he said something similar to this every time he came to the table. Rosie could tell that Tater was growing and filling out. There was plenty of good hot food, and he didn't have to hunt or skin anything to eat.

After breakfast, Rosie asked Tater if he would saddle one of the horses for her to ride to town. "I'll do it for you," Bud replied as he placed his hand on Tater's shoulder to keep him seated.

Bud walked out of the house, whistling a little ditty that he had heard Jeremiah whistling at the barbecue. He walked into the barn and stopped cold in his tracks. He immediately saw that the stalls were cleaned and the cow didn't need to be milked. "Lord, please forgive me for what I am about to do!"

"Rosie!" Bud yelled as he stormed into the house. Tater, Justice, and Boo's eyes were as big as saucers when they saw Bud marching straight to Rosie's bedroom like a sergeant in the army. He had sparks flying out of his eyes.

"Rosie," Bud said, a little calmer as he made his way to her closed door. "Rosie, I'm coming in." He knocked and opened the door at the same time. He slammed the door, causing her to jump as she stood in front of the mirror, making sure her bonnet was on straight.

"Good gracious, Bud. What's all the fuss about?" Rosie turned to look at Bud with such innocence on her lovely face.

"Don't stand there acting like you don't know why I'm mad as hell. You thought you could sneak around this morning and I wouldn't find out that you've been working outside like an old slave woman. You know that we didn't finish our discussion about your chores. I told you that I wanted you to work in the house and to stay out of that stinking barn shoveling manure!"

"We haven't finished talking about my duties because you haven't been in this house for three solid days before we went to the party Saturday. We were busy with church and visiting your folks yesterday. So there, Mr. Big *Boss Man*. I haven't agreed to anything as of yet."

Rosie swept around Bud and grabbed up her bag and tried to pass by him out of the bedroom. "Oh no, you don't, you little spitfire. You and I will finish this conversation when you return this evening. Don't think for one minute that a wife of mine is going to work out in that dirty barn. You will do as I say or so help me you'll be sorry."

"I'm not afraid of you, mister loud mouth! If I'm going to live here, then I'm going to work. Put that in your pipe and smoke it." Rosie scooted by him and went into the kitchen.

Bud threw up his hands in the air and yelled, "I don't smoke... yet!"

Boo was sniveling while Justice held him in her arms. Rosie rushed over to him. "Oh, baby, I'm sorry if all that yelling scared you. Bud is sorry he was making so much noise, ain't you, Bud?"

Bud just looked at Rosie and reached for the baby. "Come to me, little man, and let's go outside. I've got to go check on Tater and make sure he's got Rosie's horse saddled and ready for her to leave us all alone today."

Bud stormed out the door, carrying Boo on his shoulder as he giggled and pulled Bud's hair. "That's right, Boo baby," Rosie said very quietly, "yank all his hair out by the roots. He ain't nothing but an ornery, old goat this morning."

Justice grinned at Rosie as she gathered up her things to take with her to town. "Rosie child, I want you to listen to me. I'm an old woman, but I want you to know something that I see. Bud cares deeply for you. He may not know it yet. He wants you to be the lady of his house and he be the man. He's trying to spare you from hard work. Don't be so bullheaded. Look at your hands. They ain't the hands of a lady."

Rosie looked down at her palms. They were rough and red with many calluses from hauling wood, washing clothes in hot boiling water, shoveling manure, and hoeing and weeding the garden. She slid them in the folds of her skirt.

"Maybe, Ms. Hannah will give me some cream to put on them. Thanks Justice for helping me with Boo. And I'll—I'll think about what you said about Bud."

Hannah took Rosie into the small infirmary ward and introduced her to Esther. It was love at first sight. Esther took to Rosie immediately.

"You know what, Ms. Hannah?" Esther said as she looked at Rosie. "This child reminds me so much of you when you first came to me and Dr. Tim—small and petite with a mess of glorious red curls and just as pretty. Lord, have mercy, that shore was a long time ago. Come closer, child, and let me get a better look at you."

"Yep, just like you, Ms. Hannah. Look at this child's hand. It's rougher than some of those cowpunchers that come through our door. I can tell she ain't lazy with hands like that." Esther was in her glory to have someone to take care of.

"Ms. Esther, I am supposed to be caring for you." Rosie glanced down at her hands. "Maybe Ms. Hannah will give me some cream to go on my hands, but you've got to lie down and keep that leg still."

As Hannah left the two of them alone she couldn't help but laugh. "Good luck with keeping that old mule still. And yes, I will bring some cream for your hands in a little while. Right now, I have a few patients standing outside the door wanting to get in to see Tim."

"How old are you, child?" Before Rosie could answer, Esther said, "I bet you ain't even eighteen yet? Am I right?"

"No, madam. I am eighteen. I've been full grown for a long time."

"Full grown with a lot of responsibilities, you mean? There's a difference, you know. Some young girls have had an easy life and never had to do anything but sit around and bat their eyelashes at handsome young men. All they wants to do is get married, even though they don't really know how to care for themselves, much less a man. But I heard from Ms. Hannah that you are a hard worker. She mentioned that you are married to Bud, and you have the care of your two younger brothers."

"That's right." Rosie hung her head thinking that she was going to have to tell more lies. "My folks weren't exactly like some of the nice people I have met here."

"Don't make me drag everything out of your mouth, child. Tell me what your folks were like and why you have the care of your brothers. I promise to rest after I know where your folks are."

"Ms. Esther, you are too much." Rosie laughed and pulled up a chair and placed it beside the bed. "My pa was never anything but a drunken scoundrel who was mean as a snake when he was sober. He beat my poor mama until she couldn't walk or even see out of her eyes sometimes. When he tried to beat me and my younger brother, Tater, we'd run into the swamp and hide until he was gone or asleep. My poor mama got in the family way and she had Boo. He's two now. Right after he was born, she ran off with a peddler who came our way once in a while. My mama begged and pleaded with him to take her away. I prayed he would take us all, but that didn't happen. So when I was sixteen, I had the care of an eleven-year-old and a newborn baby boy not quite a month old. Justice, an old Creole woman that lived on the outskirts of town came by almost every day and helped me with the baby. I couldn't have managed without her. Tater was a great help too. Between the two of us, we managed to stay alive and away from our pa. He's dead now."

"Mercy, child, how did you get married up with Bud?"

"Now, Ms. Esther, you said that you would rest after I told you about my folks. That's enough about me. You need to rest, and afterward, I will help you with a bath and a nice lunch."

"That'll be nice, but I ain't finished hearing about how you got hooked up with Bud and how you and those young'uns survived living out in that swamp."

Rosie fluffed the pillow and adjusted it behind Esther's head and placed a pillow under the back of her knee. She placed her broken wrist on top of her stomach as she smoothed the quilt over her small fragile body. "Now, are you comfortable?" Rosie asked as she picked up the breakfast tray to carry it into the kitchen.

"Yes, thank you, child. Now you run along and help Ms. Hannah by starting some lunch. There's a chicken all dressed out in the icebox that needs to be cooked." Esther mumbled as she closed her eyes and drifted off to sleep.

Rosie stood at the foot of the bed and made sure that Esther was settled in for a nice nap. She didn't appear to be in any pain. After a few minutes, Rosie carried the breakfast tray into the nice, well-equipped kitchen. She walked over to a short wooden box and pulled on the handle. "Mercy!" Rosie said out loud. *She felt cool air coming from the inside of the box. This must be the icebox,* thought Rosie. She reached in and pulled out something wrapped in white paper. Carrying it over to the counter, she discovered that it was a chicken all cleaned, ready to be cooked. *I got to tell Bud about this special box.*

After discovering the well-stocked pantry, Rosie made short work of preparing lunch for Esther, Dr. Tim, and Hannah. She had boiled the chicken, and after removing the bones, she dropped dumplings down into the meat and broth. She made a pan of fluffy biscuits and prepared a delicious peach cobbler with a sprinkle of cinnamon on top. The fresh coffee was brewing when Dr. Tim came into the kitchen.

"My goodness, this kitchen smells so good that I was sure Esther was in here standing on one leg cooking. I could hardly listen to my patient telling me all about her complaints as I was sniffing the aroma floating through the office," Dr. Tim said as he stood in the doorway looking at Rosie.

"Well, sir, I have it ready, if you're ready to eat. Is Ms. Hannah going to eat with you?" Rosie hung her head, looking at the floor, as she spoke to the doctor.

"Hannah!" Dr. Tim leaned around the door and called to his wife. "Come and eat."

"Tim, please keep your voice down. You could wake the dead. Esther is still resting." Hannah scolded Tim as she came into the kitchen. "I bet she'll be awake soon just from the wonderful smell in the air. I wasn't hungry until I came in here," Hannah said as she walked over to the table and sat down next to Tim. Rosie served both of them a big bowl of chicken and dumplings and set the biscuits in the middle.

Tim and Hannah watched Rosie as she walked back over to the counter. "Where's your bowl, Rosie?" Hannah asked. Rosie looked at the nice couple sitting at the table and only smiled.

"Please serve yourself some food and come and sit at the table with us. You aren't a servant here."

Rosie brought her bowl and sat down with Tim and Hannah. "I can cook beef stew for your dinner tonight," Rosie said. "It should be ready before I leave."

"The chicken and dumplings are wonderful, Rosie, but we have a young lady that is cooking for us. Since Ella Mae is away, Susie, our daughter, has been helping her with dinner. Cooking us a nice meal for lunch is plenty for you to do. Besides, when Esther wakes, you'll have your hands full," said Hannah.

"This is a nice kitchen," Rosie said. "I shore like that big cold box over there. Esther called it an icebox. I've got to tell Bud about that. How do you keep things in it cool?"

Tim laughed and said that in the bottom of the box is a fifty-pound block of ice. "Since the town has an ice storage facility at the end of the town, we have ice delivered every other day. The ice melts and the water drips down into the large pan under the box. Some people use a large tub down in their cellar and keep it filled with ice, which melts and makes ice cold water. We store ice down in the cellar in saw dust and several blocks of ice will last a good while. This keeps milk and other food items nice and cool. Bud may want to get a tub and a supply of saw dust so he can store ice until he can purchase one." Dr. Tim enjoyed watching Rosie as she studied the icebox. It was like seeing something very magical to her.

"I can't wait to tell him about it," she whispered.

"I hear Esther's bell ringing," said Hannah.

Rosie assisted Esther with her bath, changed her into a clean gown, and fed her some lunch. She had Esther sit up so she could rub her shoulders and the lower part of her back. Justice had said that a person couldn't lie in bed without a back rub. A person can get bedsores if they aren't moved around in the bed. Esther loved the special attention that Rosie gave her.

Later in the evening Luther, Esther's husband, came to spend the night. Rosie warmed him an extra big bowl of chicken and dumplings with several biscuits. After brewing him a fresh pot of coffee, she told them good night. She would return in the morning.

As Rosie walked down to the stable to get her horse, she noticed a large covered wagon parked in front of the dry goods store. It had writing on the side of the dirty canvas. She couldn't make out the words on the side because it was getting too dark for her to see all the lettering. It reminded her of the peddlers' wagon that her mama had left home in. Thinking of home, she could hardly wait to get back to Bud's farm. She had missed him and the boys today. She did enjoy helping Esther, but she was glad that she would only have to be away from the farm a few days.

It didn't take Rosie too long to ride back home. When she rode into the yard, Tater was waiting outside for her return. "Hi, Sis," he said. "Boy, we sure missed you today. Do you have to go back to town tomorrow?"

"When did you start calling me Sis? You haven't ever called me that before."

"I don't know. I heard Little John call Mary Beth 'Sis' and thought it was nice. Do you mind if I call you that sometimes?"

"No, of course I don't. Just seemed a little strange, with me being gone for only one day, I hope too much more hasn't changed," laughed Rosie.

"Bud and Justice missed you too. Boo cried a lot so Bud carried him around the farm on his horse. He loved riding, but Justice had to rock him for hours to get him down for a nap. He cried for you."

"Oh my," she said as she walked toward the house.

When she entered the house, she saw Bud sitting in the rocker holding Boo. The baby had a clean night shirt on and his blond curls were still damp from his bath.

"'osie!" cried Boo when he saw her enter the kitchen. He sat straight up and was waving his little arms in the air for her to take him. "Oh, Boo, my baby, I missed you so much."

"Did you miss me too?" Bud asked with a cocky grin on his face. He leaned forward as to stretch his back.

"Yes, I shore did. I enjoyed helping Ms. Esther and Ms. Hannah but I'm glad to be home."

"Justice is lying down. This young man is a handful. He is a mama's boy for sure. He wanted only you whenever he got tired or hungry," Bud said as he stood. "There's some beef simmering on the stove ready to have some vegetables or whatever you want to do with it for supper. I need to go out to the barn and take care of the animals. Tater has been a big help today."

"I'm sorry, Bud. I can tell this has been a tiring day for all of you. Just another day or so, and we will get back to normal," Rosie said as she sat in the rocker with Boo. Before Bud got out the front door, Boo was sound asleep in Rosie's arms.

The old rooster sat on the fence post and announced that the sun was coming up behind the house. Rosie had made coffee and was sitting on the front porch in a rocking chair. She had always been an early riser when she lived in the swamp. Hunting and fishing for food was best done before the sun came up. She left the boys sleeping, and she would have returned before either one of them was awake. The sounds from the river and the animals that roamed the swamp were very relaxing as she sat on the dock each morning. Now, listening to the sounds of the farm animals was very comforting too. The chickens were beginning to move around in their yard, the horses were ready to be released out into the corral and the cow was waiting for someone to come and give her relief from her full bag of milk. Each animal had a unique sound. Rosie sat back in the chair and rocked while humming a favorite hymn. It felt very strange to just sit and sip her coffee. She wanted to go out to the barn and take care of the morning chores, but she knew that her actions would only make Bud mad. Justice said that Bud wanted to treat her like a lady, not a field hand. Maybe if she sat long enough and relaxed, she might get use to feeling…useless? *Well*, she thought, *I'll give it a try today.*

Justice came to the screen door and looked out on the porch and spotted Rosie. She was sipping a cup of coffee while looking out into space.

"Good morning," Justice said. "I guess you have already done all the outside chores while Bud and Tater are still sleeping the morning away."

"You're wrong for once," smiled Rosie. "I'm being the lady of the house like you said yesterday. Believe me, it ain't easy just sitting here."

Justice smiled and said, "Well, I ain't the queen so I'm going to whip up some biscuits and gravy. Those boys shore like to eat when they rise from the dead."

"Let me lend a hand. I can't stand being a big lazy critter," laughed Rosie.

After Bud and Tater finished their breakfast, they went outside to do their morning chores. Rosie fed Boo and placed him on the floor and played with him. Boo loved to stack several blocks and then knock them over. Rosie was teaching him to count the blocks. He was very smart for a two-year-old. He would place a block down in front of himself and say "two" and chap his hands. He kept calling for "J."

"Want 'J,'" he would scream. It finally took Tater to figure out what he was wanting. The "J" meant Jacob, Will and Hope's baby boy.

Rosie told Boo that she would take him to see Jacob one day soon. Boo was so funny marching around the kitchen calling Jacob, but only the J was said. Once Rosie laid Boo down for a short morning nap, she dressed for her day at the doctor's office.

Hannah came into the kitchen where Rosie was washing the lunch dishes. Tim had seen the pretty slippers that Rosie was wearing, and he told Hannah to find something more suitable for her to wear while working. Slippers are fine for the house in the morning or evening but not sturdy enough for walking and standing or going outside. Hannah chose a pair of nice, brown leather shoe boots that Susie had not worn enough to have even scuffed the soles. They looked to be Rosie's size.

"Rosie, I hope you will accept these shoes as Susie doesn't wear them any longer. I feel that you need something more suitable to wear in the office and outside. Your slippers are lovely and I would hate to see you get them dirty while working here."

Rosie looked at the shoes that Hannah held out to her. They looked brand new. "Oh, Ms. Hannah, I could never take your daughter's shoes. They look like they have never been worn."

"Of course they have, but you need something sturdier to wear while taking care of Esther. Dr. Tim won't hear of you not having better shoes. Had you rather have a new pair?"

"Gosh no, madam. That ain't what I meant a'tall. They're too nice to just give to a stranger." Rosie looked at the shoes but held her hands down by her side.

"Bud is no stranger to us and you are his wife and family now. We take care of our friends in Limason. Please sit down and try these shoes on, and if they don't fit, we'll go over to the store and I'll get some new ones. You're doing us a big favor and now we are doing something for you."

Rosie rushed over to the kitchen chair and sat down and removed her lovely brown slippers. She eased her tiny foot down into the boot shoe, and it fit perfectly. She twisted her ankle from left to right and finally stood and looked down at her foot. "Oh my, how wonderful," she said softly as she sheepishly looked at Hannah. "Thank you so much."

Hannah swallowed the lump that had built up in her throat and said, "Well now, remember to take the trash out back when you finish in here."

Turning, Hannah hurried out of the kitchen before her emotions got the best of her. It felt so good to be able to help someone who truly appreciated simple gifts. Tim had been so good to her and their children. Since meeting him, after she had been put off the wagon train outside of Limason years ago, she had never had to want for anything. She had only just met Rosie, but she could see the goodness in her young soul. She certainly had taken wonderful care of her two brothers. Her friend Justice appeared to be dedicated to her, and Bud was head over heels in love with the beauty. When Rosie heard that Esther needed someone to care for her for a few days, she volunteered. Rosie was certainly a very good Christian girl who, from what she had heard, had certainly done a good job taking care of herself while living in the swamps of Louisiana.

Rosie walked around in the kitchen pulling her skirt up around her ankles so she could see her new brown leather shoes. They looked wonderful and felt so good on her feet. She gathered the trash and walked outside to place it in a big round barrel. The weather was so pretty that she sat down on the porch steps. She immediately held her feet out in front of herself to look at her shoes again. Looking down the alley, she saw a covered wagon parked behind the dry goods store. The wagon reminded her of the one that used to come by their shack. As she sat staring at the wagon, a small, petite woman appeared from around the side of it. She was wearing a nice dress with a white apron and had on a big bonnet tied with a bow under the chin. The woman glanced up and stopped. She stood very still while staring at Rosie. She took another few steps further away from the wagon. Rosie thought to herself that the stranger looked like her mama. Rosie turned to walk back inside the doctor's kitchen when the stranger called out to her.

"Rosie, Rosie. Is that you?" The stranger called softly at first.

When Rosie heard the woman call to her she stopped. "Mama?" whispered Rosie as she realized the voice coming from the stranger was her mama's.

"Oh, Rosie, it is you! Rosie," cried Rosie's mama as she practically raced to where her daughter stood frozen near the back steps.

As both daughter and mama recognized each other, they wrapped their arms around each other and held on for dear life.

Tears of joy streamed down their cheeks. Rosie's Mama was the first to speak while tears continued to flow down her face. "I can't believe that the good Lord has finally answered my prayers. Oh, honey, I have missed you so much."

"Oh, Mama, I can't believe that you're here." Rosie took the tail of her skirt and wiped her eyes.

"What are you doing in this town? How did you get away from Louisiana? Where are my boys, my baby?" quizzed her mama without giving her time to answer one question much less many.

"I could ask you the same. What are you doing here? I see you are still traveling with that man you ran off with," Rosie said a little sharper than she intended.

Hannah called to Rosie from the back door of the kitchen. "Is everything all right out there, honey?"

"Oh, yes, Ms. Hannah. This is my mama. She has found me—at last," Rosie replied.

Hannah had no idea what Rosie was speaking about. *Her mama had found her.* Hannah didn't know that Rosie had been lost.

"I'll be in shortly, Ms. Hannah. I need a little while to talk with Mama."

"Of course, take your time. I will oversee Esther if she needs anything." Hannah walked back into Esther's room and made sure that she was resting well.

"Rosie, are you living in this town working for the doctor?"

"Not exactly, I live on a farm with my…husband, Justice, and the boys. I'm helping out here at the doctor's office for a few days."

"Where is this farm? I want to see my baby. Oh, how is he? I have missed him so much. I bet Tater has grown a foot," said Rosie's mama. "When can I come out there and see them? Mr. Shire will finish his business in town today. I couldn't believe that we were going to come to this town. We traveled back near Lafayette and the sheriff told me that you all left with a young man heading this way. I was praying that I might find you here. Tally, Mr. Shire, brought a farm and a few acres of ground in

McBain before we hooked up together. Now we are going to settle down there." Rosie's mama looked over her shoulder like she was looking for her husband to appear.

"Rosie, did you know that your pa is dead?"

Rosie only shook her head, acknowledging that she knew. A sick feeling was beginning to form in the pit of her stomach. She always prided herself on the fact that she knew when something was very wrong, and today that feeling was coming over her.

"Mr. Shire and I married as soon as we heard that the old man had died. We had been telling his customers that we were married for a long time. It was best for his business if people thought I was his wife.

Rosie's mama paused for a minute, giving her daughter a long hard look. "So my little baby girl is married too. Ain't that something? I want to meet your man. Listen, baby, as soon as Mr. Shire finishes packing our wagon with new supplies, I'll ask him to take me to your farm. Can we come out today?"

"I guess so," replied Rosie very quietly as she looked away.

"Will that be a problem? Is your husband nice, or does he beat you like your pa did me?"

Rosie was shocked into silence for just a second. She couldn't believe her mama would ask such a question. "Yes, he's very nice, and no, he doesn't beat me. I would never let a man do that to me." She knew that she shouldn't have said that, but she never understood why her mama didn't take an ax or hammer to her pa while he slept. He deserved to be punished for the way he treated her.

"Good then. I'm going to insist that we stop at your farm. Tell me where you live."

"Go out of town that a ways and travel about five miles. The main road leads to our place. I will be home in a couple of hours."

Rosie watched her mama walk back to the peddler's wagon and climb up into the back. She watched the old peddler climb up on the wagon and drive off toward Bud's farm. She couldn't believe that she wasn't rejoicing inside after seeing her mama again.

She entered the kitchen where Ms. Hannah stood waiting for her to come back inside.

"Rosie? Do you want to talk? I didn't understand what you meant when you said that your mama had found you." Hannah noticed that Rosie had gone very pale and was trembling.

Rosie walked over to the kitchen table and eased herself into one of the chairs. "Ms. Hannah…I'm more afraid than I have ever been. Even not having enough food, or feeling like the shack we lived in might blow down, I haven't had this bad kind of feeling. My mama ran off with a peddler man soon after Boo was born. My pa beat her all the time. I can't blame her for leaving, but she left all of us. I was fifteen, nearly sixteen, when she left. If it hadn't been for Justice coming out and checking on us young'uns, I don't know what would have happened to us. She taught me how to care for Boo, who was only four weeks old. She stayed at the house while I hunted and fished for food. Tater was just a little fellow, but he was a big help. I thank the good Lord every day for Justice. She has her funny ways and many people are afraid of her, but she's a good person. Anyway, Mama never sent us a note or nothing. Pa came around once in a while, but he was only happy when he had a fresh jug of moonshine to drink. When he really needed money, he tried to sell me to a gambler, cowpuncher, or any man traveling through our area. I always managed to run and hide. When he tried to beat me and Tater, we would grab Boo and escape in the swamp until he left for town. Pa was scared of the swamp."

"Why are you suddenly afraid now that you and your mama have reunited with each other? Aren't you happy to see her?" Hannah asked.

"I don't likely know for sure. I know in my heart that I should be, but I have a really bad feeling in the pit of my belly." Rosie rubbed her stomach and hung her head before she looked back at Ms. Hannah. Instead of the joy she should be feeling, she felt despair.

"She wants to see the boys today. It's the way she kept asking about Boo. Not so much about Tater. I feel in my gut that she may want to take Boo with her now that she has a place. I'm not sure how that man of hers will feel about taking my brothers to his farm, but she kept asking about Boo. Like I said, she might just want to see them."

"Listen, honey, why don't you get your horse and go on home today. If she is going to come by, you'll want to have a good supper cooked for them. Why don't you stop at the butcher shop and get a couple dressed chickens. That will be a big help with dinner. I do it all the time," laughed Hannah.

"Are you sure, Ms. Hannah? I don't like leaving you with so much to do."

"I believe I can handle everything for the rest of the day. Susie can help me after school. Besides, Esther's sister will be here tomorrow afternoon if the stage is on time. If you can, come in the morning. If you don't come in, I will know that something has kept you home because of your mama's visit."

"All right, I believe I will go ahead and go. I want to be at the farm when she stops by. Thanks again for my new shoes. They're the nicest that I have ever owned."

As Rosie walked to the livery to get her horse, all kinds of thoughts were going through her mind. *Tater would be surprised to see Mama. Of course, Boo won't know her at all. He will most likely cry if Mama tries to hold him.*

After saddling her horse, she walked him over to the butcher shop. She had never heard of people shopping for fresh meat. But she wanted to cook a nice supper and having the chickens ready to fry would be a big help. Bud might think that this was an extravagant way to spend his money when they could serve the unexpected guest rice and beans. She wanted to show her Mama that she had a nice home for herself and her little brothers. *Surely, she won't take Tater and Boo with her when she leaves for her new farm. Please, Lord, please don't let her take my boys. I am their mama and have been ever since she ran off and left us to fend for ourselves in that swamp. She left us with that old drunk,* Rosie prayed silently.

When Rosie rode into the farmyard, she could see the peddler's wagon parked close to the house. "Oh my," Rosie said out loud to herself. *They must have come straight out here as soon as Mama's husband came out of the store.*

She rode her horse close to the barn as Tater came running to meet her. He grabbed the reins and held the horse as she got off. "Rosie, Mama's here," he whispered into her face. "She said that she seen you in town." Before she could make a comment, he continued, "Justice isn't happy at all to see her. They have been saying ugly things to each other. Bud asked Justice to start a meal for dinner, but Justice says that they don't belong here."

"Where is Boo?" Rosie asked, very concerned. She wasn't surprised at Justice's attitude toward her mama.

"Bud is sitting in the rocker holding him while he's sleeping."

"Please take care of this animal. I have brought two chickens home to cook for supper." As Rosie turned to walk toward the house, she stopped and called to Tater.

"How do you feel about seeing Mama? It has been nearly two years."

"I'm scared. I don't know why, but I am. How do you feel?" he asked.

"Scared, but we aren't alone now. Bud's here."

Rosie hurried into the house. There wasn't a sound coming from the room except the soft wheezing coming from Boo and the crunching noise of the rocking chair on the wooden floor. Justice was standing at the counter in the kitchen. Bud was in the rocker with Boo, and Rosie's mama and Mr. Shire were sitting on a bench in the parlor.

Bud got up from the rocker and carried Boo to the bedroom. Rosie walked into the kitchen with her bundle of white paper that held the two chickens.

"I see you found the farm all right," Rosie said to her mama. "Justice and I will have dinner fixed in just a little while."

Rosie's mama looked at her husband, and he shook his head side to side. "Rosie, dear, we don't have the time to stay and eat. We will eat later on the trail toward home. Mr. Shire wants us to be on our way in a few minutes. We were waiting for you to come home to say good-bye."

Relief flowed through Rosie's young body. They were leaving, she thought.

"Listen," her mama said as she slowly stood and looked around the room. "We're going to take the boys. I want my baby, and I need for you to pack their clothes. I will make Boo some more things as he needs them, but for now, we'll take what you have for him."

Bud was standing in the bedroom doorway when he heard the words flowing out of the woman's mouth. He looked from Rosie's mama to Rosie. He couldn't believe his ears. Rosie had turned white as a sheet. Tater's roar made them all jump.

"No!" he screamed. "I ain't going nowhere with you. You didn't want us before, so why do you want us now? Leave and never come back. This is our home now."

Mr. Shire spoke for the first time. "Don't speak to your mama like that, boy! I'll take a whip to your backside," he said very sternly as he spit in the low-burning hearth.

"Mister," Bud said very firmly, "I understand young people need to show respect to their elders, but if you ever lay a hand on this boy, I'll break every bone in that tall ugly body of yours." Bud stepped in front of Tater, telling the man that he was the boy's protector.

Justice walked over to stand next to Rosie. She took one of Rosie's hands and gave it a squeeze, waiting for her to speak. Justice's touch seemed to have brought Rosie out of her state of shock. She felt something bad was going to happen, but until she actually heard her mama say that she was going to take the boys, she was praying that she might be wrong.

"Mama, you can't walk into my home and take my brothers. I'm their mama now. You left us all alone in the swamp with that old, drunken fool. I understand why you wanted to leave Pa. I don't understand why you didn't take us with you. I would have been a big help to you and your man," she said as she looked over at the tall, ugly peddler. "You left your newborn baby with me, someone who knew nothing about how to care for a tiny infant. If it hadn't been for this old woman here"—she stopped talking and looked at Justice with love in her eyes—"we might all have died. She taught me to care for your baby. She helped us with food and her medicines. You never looked back after you left us. No note or letters. No money for food or clothes, even though you had plenty after running off with this man. Now you come here and you want to take my brothers away. I will die before I give them up to you. My husband loves your boys, my brothers, who I love as my very own. Leave this house," said Rosie as she pointed to the door. "You will not take my boys."

"Rosie, you have no right to keep my baby from me. I will take you to court. No judge will keep me from having my baby and, of course, Tater."

"Why would you want to take Tater? You know you'll never be able to keep him. He will run right back to me."

"The baby won't be any help on my farm right away, but this youngster can do a man's full day of work in the fields. He will be a big help to us." The old man was thinking that taking the boys wouldn't be so bad after all. He would place chains on Tater's feet like he seen others do runaway slaves that had been captured. He would never get away from him.

"This young man is staying right here with me and his sister, who is his real mama. He will be going to school every day. He will not be some old man's slave and beaten if he doesn't do enough work to satisfy him." Bud looked at the old man as if he could read his thoughts.

"Come, woman," said the old peddler. He knew that Rosie and her husband were not going to hand over the boys to them today, but they would get them soon enough. "We will see the judge in McBain. He will get the sheriff to come and get the boys for us. We won't have to even come back ourselves." The old man strolled out of the house and climbed up on his wagon, not even waiting on his wife.

"Tell that sheriff he'd better bring the whole damn army with him when he comes," Bud said through his teeth.

Rosie's mama hung back as she watched her husband make his way to their wagon. She had to make Rosie understand how much she needed her baby.

"Rosie, please. Please give me Boo today. Let me take him home with me," her mama pleaded. "I promise you I will care for him. I have grieved and suffered every day for my baby."

Rosie looked at the woman who claimed to be their mama. Her mama had been a good and loving person. Not this stranger pleading for only one of her children.

"I grieved for you, Mama. I cried myself to sleep for weeks. I didn't have time to grieve or cry during the daylight hours because I was too busy caring for your baby and young son. See, Mama, I know what it is like to grieve over someone you love. I loved you. But you haven't even asked me how I made out without you. You haven't told me that you missed and worried over us." Rosie looked at the older version of the woman standing in front of her, trying hard to see her mama.

"You aren't my mama that ran off and left me. She is still lost to us." Rosie turned her back as she heard her mama walk out of the house and allow the screen door to slam.

12

A S THE PEDDLER'S wagon drove away from their farm, Bud pulled Tater into his arms and gave him a firm hug. "Please try not to worry."

Tater wiped his eyes on Bud's shoulder and shook his head without looking up. He hurried into the bedroom that he shared with Bud and closed the door. He needed to be alone.

Rosie glanced at Bud as he held his arms open for her to come to him. She hurried into his strong arms and released the tears that she had been holding back. She cried as Bud picked her up and carried her over to the rocker. He sat down and pushed her head back on his shoulder and allowed her to release all the raw emotions that she had been feeling since she saw her mama. He whispered sweet words of encouragement to her while rubbing and patting her back. He remembered when he had been placed in jail and heard the prison doors slam shut the first time, how he wanted to curl up on his cot and cry like a baby. He didn't know why he was so afraid but he was. So he knew that Rosie was feeling the same way he did. She was afraid because she had lost her mama again.

As he sat rocking Rosie, he was afraid for her. He was afraid of the unknown future of her two young brothers—her boys, she told her mama.

Justice busied herself by preparing the dinner meal. She unwrapped the two chickens that Rosie purchased at the butcher shop. She cut one of the chickens into pieces for frying and a part of another one. The few remaining pieces, she placed in a big pot of water to boil. Tomorrow she would make chicken and dumplings for lunch. This was Tater's favorite dish.

As the grease was getting hot for frying, she rolled out a big pan of biscuits. She had already put on a big pot of potatoes and they were about ready. A quart jar of snap beans would round out the dinner. Bud's mama had been very generous to them with her canned goods. Once the chicken started frying, Tater came out of his room and sat down at the table.

Tater looked at Rosie and Bud as they sat together in the rocker. "You shore have spent a lot of time in that rocker today, Bud. First rocking Boo and now you're holding Rosie like she's a baby."

"Are you jealous? Do you want me to rock you next?" Bud asked Tater as he heard a giggle coming from Rosie's throat. She sat up, shaking her head at the two men.

"Now, that's my girl. Why don't you go and wash up for dinner while Tater and I help Justice set the table. It smells like she has it ready," Bud said as he helped Rosie get up off his lap.

As they all sat around the dinner table, they should have been celebrating a joyous occasion. With the return of their mama, they should have been rejoicing that they would be a family again. But the mood was very depressing. Rosie felt that she was grieving the death of her mama. Rosie knew that the woman she spend a little time with this afternoon was not the Mama that ran off and left her in the swamp. Her actions were those of a stranger.

When Rosie and Tater were very young, their mama was very loving. She cooked good meals, washed their few clothes, and played with them. Bible readings each night were a very special time that they shared. She would sit at the side of their bed and read to them until they fell asleep. Later the Bible was the book that Rosie learned to read from. Her mama was very patient with Rosie because she wanted her to have a good education even though she didn't attend school. Rosie's pa wouldn't allow her to go to the school in Lafayette because he claimed the boys would do nasty things to her. When he came home drunk, if she didn't do something fast enough to please him, he would try to beat her. Her mama would step in between them and take the abuse. He was mean as a snake, sober or drunk.

"Justice, thank you for cooking our dinner tonight. I planned to hurry home and cook a good meal before Mama and her man got here. Bud, I spent some of your money on the chickens at the butcher shop. I wanted to show Mama what a nice home we have made for my brothers. I know now that she didn't care about me or this place. She didn't care for me at all," Rosie said as she hung her head down. "All she wanted was to hurry out here and get Boo and Tater." Rosie looked at Tater as she made that comment.

"Listen, Sis, I may not be as old as you, but I know Mama didn't want me either. She never put her arms around me or said that she missed me. All she wanted was Boo, poor little fellow. He ran to Justice and screamed and screamed when she tried to take him. I kept waiting for her to want to hold me. She didn't pay me any attention. I was so glad to see her, but then, she began to act strange. . Not the Mama that I remembered. You know what I mean?" Tater asked with deep sorrow in his voice.

"Rosie, child, I shore didn't like the looks of your mama the minute she knocked on our door. She came marching into this house and demanded her baby. I came very close to slapping her silly. Thank goodness Bud was here," said Justice. "I knew immediately that she was trouble without the first word being spoken. I don't have to have a conversation with a body to know what they're up to. She acted like she was someone important and she came to claim what was rightful hers. Boy, did she get a welcome from Boo. God love the little fellow," grinned Justice as she looked at Bud and then saw a smile appear on Tater's face.

As Justice passed the potatoes to Bud, she continued, "Mrs. High and Mighty saw Boo playing with his blocks and squatted down beside him and tried to pick him up. With eyes as big as a saucer, he screamed like he had been scalped. He crawled away from her right over to where Bud was standing. Bud picked him up, and he hid his face in his shoulder and never gave her another glance. She pleaded and begged, but he only grunted and held on tighter to Bud's neck."

"I finally had to tell her to sit down and leave Boo alone," Bud commented. "I sat and rocked him, hoping that he would go to sleep. He didn't care for his mama or her husband."

"I'm so sorry that all of you had to put up with her. I didn't know that she was going to come right out here, before I got home," said Rosie, wiping away the mist in her eyes.

"After Tater and I do our afternoon chores, you and I need to talk. I don't like what that old man said about getting a judge."

"I'll tell you now! I don't care how many judges he gets. I ain't leaving here, and they can't make me. I'll run away first," Tater said with a definite plan already made up in his young mind.

"Tater, settle down. I told you earlier that Rosie and I will take care of you and Boo," Bud said with the authority of a parent.

As Rosie tried her best to eat some of the delicious supper that Justice had prepared, her thoughts were the same as Bud's. What if her mama's husband gets a judge to agree that she can have her sons back, then she would just lie down and die.

Rosie helped Justice clean the kitchen and place the leftovers in the pie safe that had been left in the house. She bathed Boo in front of the low-burning fire in the front room. He splashed water on the floor while Rosie poured water over his hair. He shook his head side to side like a wet dog. "Oh, Boo! You're making a big mess," laughed Rosie.

Once the baby was down for the night, Rosie walked outside. She noticed the big oak tree that was located beside the house. Someone had made a ladder out of old boards and nailed them to the tree trunk. The leaves were a golden brown, and it had big sprawling tree limbs that were just right for sitting. She loved to climb trees back in the swamp so before she gave it much thought she had climbed close to the top. She realized how very close she felt to God. Looking up at the evening sky through the colorful fall leaves, she prayed.

"Lord, I know it seems like I'm always asking you for things; in the swamp, it was please don't let Pa kill Mama. Sometimes I asked you to help me catch a mess of catfish so I could feed my brothers or please don't let the storm blow our home away. I felt ashamed at times for coming to you so much. But, Lord, in the Good Book, He said to ask and we shall receive. Sure enough, I did a lot of asking and my prayers were always answered. Now, I really need you."

"Rosie," Bud called. "What in the world are you doing up in that tree, and so high? Don't you know that if you were to fall, you could break your neck? Who's up there with you? I heard you talking to somebody." Bud was circling around the base of the tree, looking up to get a better view of Rosie and whoever she was with. Tater wasn't up there because he just went into the house.

"You need to come down, but please be careful. Some of those boards might be rotten," Bud said as he pulled on a board or two while Rosie was backing down the ladder.

Once Rosie's feet were on the ground, Bud glanced back up in the tree. "Who were you talking to?"

"Oh, Bud, I was praying. I was telling the Lord how much we need his help. I believe in prayer, do you?"

He reached for the precious young girl who was stealing his heart. He pulled her up close and placed his hands around her waist. He gathered his thoughts before he spoke.

"I don't think I really did until I got put in prison. That place was so awful I had to get out. I was sure that I was going to die in there. One day, I saw a man with a very old, worn Bible. As I watched him read, I remembered my Bible lessons from going to church. I began to pray. I know He heard me, because Dr. Tim got me a good lawyer and as you see, I'm here—a free man."

"What are we going to do about Mama and that old peddler man who she says she married? I'm scared—really scared."

"Come and let's sit on the porch. There is a nice cool breeze and the mosquitoes won't be bad. We need to make some plans just in case they carry out their threat of going to see a judge."

Bud led Rosie over to the porch. He brushed some sand off the boards and pointed for her to sit. He wanted to make the front porch larger and put screen on the outer walls. Texas was a great place to live, but after dark, it was almost impossible to sit outside because of the bugs.

"Rosie, I'm really sorry that this has happened with your mama. I didn't say too much to her today. She told us that she had seen you in town. You had given them directions to the farm. I know that you hoped that she would come for you and the boys one day. She said that you told her that you were married. She knew that you didn't need her any longer."

"Yes, I did. I was so surprised and happy to see her. I had carried the trash out back of the office in the alleyway, and I had sat down to look at my new shoes. Ms. Hannah gave these shoes to me. See." Rosie held her dress up for Bud to see her nice leather shoes.

"They're nice. But I can buy you all the shoes that you can wear. Ms. Hannah don't need to be buying you any."

"She didn't buy these. They were Susie's, and she didn't wear them. Dr. Tim wanted me to have a sturdier pair of shoes to wear at the office. I had worn my pretty slippers to work."

"We'll talk about shoes and personal items for you another time. Let's talk about your Mama," Bud said, a little concerned that people might think that he couldn't support Rosie and her brothers.

"I looked down the alleyway, and I saw a covered wagon. It looked like the wagon that Mama had gone away in. All of a sudden, this woman walks out from behind the wagon and starts calling my name. Lord, have mercy if it wasn't my mama. We hugged and cried. I couldn't believe my eyes. Standing in front of me was Mama. She began asking about her baby—not me, or

Tater, just Boo. 'Where is my baby? I have grieved so much these past two years,' she kept saying that. I got a real strange, almost sick, feeling in the pit of my stomach."

"She didn't ask how you had gotten along without her or anything like that?" quizzed Bud.

"She did ask me if I knew Pa was dead. I told her I did. Then she said that she and the peddler man got married soon after they learned the news about Pa."

"Rosie, I want to ride into town with you tomorrow morning. I want to talk to the lawyer that has set up an office in town. Pa said that Luke went to see him about his marriage problems. Anyway, I want to see if you have any claim to your brothers. We know that your mama abandoned you, but your pa was still alive."

"You mean, she might say that she left us with our pa and not by ourselves?"

"Yep, she could say that all right. He did come and go whether he provided anything for your welfare or not," replied Bud. "We have to prove that you were the only person to care for your brothers, not some old, drunken sod who tried to sell you every chance he got."

"Oh my," said Rosie as she looked at the serious expression on Bud's handsome face.

"We might have a chance if we can get some people to say that your pa was mean and lazy. Maybe that man that owned the store on the outskirts of Lafayette where you traded could speak up. Of course there's Justice, but I'm afraid they won't listen to her—you know, her being a Creole black woman."

"Without her help, we might have all starved to death," Rosie responded quickly.

"Sweetheart, you and I know that but will the authorities care. We have to prove that you and your brothers were actually left without anyone to look after you."

Bud squeezed Rosie as they sat close together on the steps of the porch. "There's something else that needs to be taken care of. You are a young woman, and the judge will want to know how you are going to care for the boys. You need to be able to say that you have a husband and a nice home that will help you to provide for them. Everything that you tell the judge must be true." Bud was looking out toward his barn wondering if Rosie fully understood what he was saying.

"Everyone already believes that we're married. That isn't enough, is it?" Rosie hung her head, already knowing the answer to her question.

"The judge may ask to see our marriage license, and well, we need to be able to present one."

"Are you saying that we're going to have to get married for real?"

"Yep, that's the way the wind is blowing for sure. Do you object to the idea?"

"Oh, Bud, I hate all this trouble that I have brought into your life." Rosie couldn't contain her tears.

"Hey, come here." Bud pulled her close and snuggled his face into her sweet-smelling hair. "Don't cry, my sweet girl. We both want what's best for the boys. I'm going to do everything possible to keep our little family together."

Rosie looked up at Bud and saw a very determined young man that she could place her trust and faith in to help her to keep her brothers. He was willing to marry her and give up his chance of ever meeting someone in the future to become his real wife. He had already done more for her than any other person in the whole world. Bud said that she saved his life, but truth be known, he had saved hers. God does answer prayers when you least expect it.

"What are you thinking?" Bud asked Rosie because she had become so quiet. The lazy twilight evening was beginning to fill with sounds of different bugs. The mosquitoes had begun buzzing around their heads while the katydids were beginning to make chirping noises. An occasional owl hooted high up in the tree.

"If we are going to get married, where will we go without everyone knowing?"

"I believe the lawyer in town can get us a license, and we can get married by a preacher at some small church. I'll ask about that too while we're in town tomorrow. We want to do this pretty quick."

A bat flew close to the porch, making a clicking and popping sound. "We better get on inside and get ready for bed. We have a busy day tomorrow. I'll ask Tater to stay here and help Justice with Boo."

"I don't have to work all day for Ms. Hannah. Ms. Esther's sister will be arriving on the noon stage. After I help get Esther settled at her home, I will be leaving and heading back here—home."

"This is your home, Rosie." Bud took her arm and pulled her to her feet.

He opened the screen door and walked her into the kitchen. "Well, good night. I'm going to go outside and check on the animals before I turn in."

"Night, Bud. Thank you for everything."

13

AFTER BUD AND Rosie had gone into town, Justice and Tater seemed to get on with the routine chores. Justice put Boo down for a nap and placed a big pot of beans on the stove to simmer all day. Tater went to the barn and mucked the stalls after turning the animals out into the corral. He had been so happy here on Bud's farm until his Mama showed up with her new husband. His Mama had said that she wanted Boo and him to come and live with her. He didn't believe her for one second. She didn't want him—only Boo. He would never leave Bud and Rosie. Once his mind was settled with what the future might bring for him, he whistled as he slopped the hogs.

Rosie helped Esther's sister move Esther back to her home where she could care for her better. Esther was happy to be home where she could sit out on her porch and watch the neighbors go by. Many of her friends would sit a spell and visit. Hannah had a list of instructions for Esther's sister to follow. She told her that she or Dr. Tim would stop in every day to check on Esther. "Make sure she stays off that leg. Thank goodness she will be able to use her arm in a week or less," Hannah said in her voice of authority.

Bud had stopped in at the lawyer's office and asked to apply for a marriage license. He explained to the lawyer his situation with Rosie and requested complete privacy. The lawyer assured him that any business that took place in his office would be kept confidential. He would have the license signed and ready for him in three days. Bud would need to stop by Jeremiah and Ms. Ollie's church and speak with their minister. Ollie had told Justice that he had married Jesse and Rae.

As Bud was leaving the lawyer's office, he stepped out on the old, weathered planks of the boardwalk directly in front of a very familiar face. "Bud, as I live and breathe, I can't believe I practically mowed you down!"

Wiley? Bud thought to himself. Standing in front of him was a young, long-haired man with an unkempt beard. He was slim and spoke with a loud voice, which didn't appear to come from his body. Bud was trying to remember the name of the man, but he knew they were well acquainted. "Howdy, Wiley," Bud said, so pleased with himself that the name finally came to him. "It's been a while."

"Shore has. You're looking great. It seems that prison food didn't hurt you none." Bud noticed several citizens staring at them as they walked past and certainly couldn't help overhearing Wiley's remarks.

"Let's not discuss that place," Bud said as he looked up and down the street. The local saloon, The Golden Nugget, that he had been thrown out of the last time he got drunk and caused a brawl was located a few doors down. He needed to move on away from that place.

"Hey, I'm headed down to the saloon for an eye opener this morning. How about joining me for a few hands of poker for old time's sake? I know we could round up a few fellows and have a good game. Maybe I can win some of my money back."

Bud thumbed his hat back a little off his forehead and wondered what he could say about giving up his old gambling ways. Before he could respond, Wiley punched him in his side and said, "I bet some of the gals will be glad to see a handsome fellow like you. One for sure. She's still here!" Laughing, Wiley pulled on Bud's arm to get him to move toward the saloon.

"Stop it, Wiley." Bud stood stiff and shook Wiley's long skinny hand loose from his arm. "I gave up my old ways. I got a small farm a few miles out of town, the old Patterson's place. I'm married now and my wife has two little brothers that I'm responsible for."

Wiley's mouth dropped open, showing his stained, yellow teeth from chewing tobacco. He stared at Bud like he was seeing something from out of the circus. "You're kidding me," he said when he found the ability to speak.

"No, I'm not jesting with you." Bud needed to go check on Rosie at the doctor's office and head on home to help Justice with the baby.

"I cannot believe that you're actually getting your hands dirty. Why I remember when you wouldn't even go home and help your Pa on his farm. *Now you've become a farmer?*" Wiley tossed back his head and roared with laughter. "I don't believe it."

"You heard me right. Hey…nice seeing you again, but I got a few things to do before I head home." Bud stepped off the boardwalk and circled around Wiley to be on his way.

Wiley stood and watched Bud as he walked away from him. *The next thing I hear that boy will be walking a straight and narrow path down the church aisle to the altar giving his soul to the Lord! Prison must have reformed him,* Wiley was thinking as he walked through the bat-winged doors of the saloon. He couldn't wait to tell the other patrons all about seeing Bud.

Bud hurried toward the doctor's office, hoping to catch Rosie before she finished work and headed home. Maybe they could ride together. He was still a little rattled from running into Wiley. He should have suspected that he would be running into some of the fellows that hung out in the saloon. He had hoped that most of the cowboys and cowpunchers that he had played cards with would have moved on by now. It had been two years since he had been back through the bat-winged doors of the stinking saloon. He did remember being tossed out on his butt into the street by Jack, the big, burly, cigar smoking owner of the establishment. Drinking that rut-gut cheap whiskey had gotten the better of him, causing his mouth to sprout some pretty nasty remarks about the girls giving signals to certain card players. The card players took offense and a brawl took place and busted up the joint. With only a few dollars in his pocket and not allowed back at home, he had got himself hired on as a drover on a trail drive to San Antonio, Texas.

Bud caught up with Rosie at the livery, and after saddling up her horse, they headed out of town to meet with a minister. On the way, Rosie's unhappiness bothered Bud very much. He felt that he needed to do something to help her get through this difficult time. He wanted her to know that he knew that she had done a great job of raising her brothers. Even after his praise of her ability, she said very little.

She returned only a small grunt. He continued talking to her. "I know that you are frightened of what might happen in front of the judge. You are young and inexperienced with this sort of business, so it's natural to be a little afraid, but until we hear something from your mama, let's try to get on with our lives."

Bud and Rosie rode into Jeremiah and Ollie's churchyard. The church was small, but the landscape around the edge of the structure was lovely. The temple was tall with a big bell in the center of it. *This is a very godly place*, thought Rosie. Someone was in the small white building. Bud left Rosie sitting on the big work horse as he glanced through the open double doors. "Anybody here?" Bud called.

The minister was a colored man who had coal black hair with snowy-white sideburns and a large, flat nose. Deep creases on his face told of many years spent out in the weather working the land. His eyes had a twinkle in them when he smiled. No one had to tell another person that this was a man of God. His face shined with kindness.

"Well, hello, young man," answered the minister of the church. "What can I do for you?"

Rosie got off her horse and walked up the few steps of the church porch and met the nice man. Bud explained their situation to him and he instructed them to come back in a few days with the marriage license, and he would be glad to marry them while keeping the service very quiet.

On the way back to the farm, Rosie almost stopped her horse in the middle of the road. "Bud, you don't think that Mama's husband might send somebody to steal Boo away?"

"No, I am sure they won't do anything like that. I could tell that old man felt sure that he had the law on their side. If your mama cries and carries on, he might speed up contacting the sheriff in McBain," Bud said.

Rosie nodded wordlessly. She couldn't help but release a whimper. "I'm sorry. All I do lately is cry."

The weather had begun to turn a lot cooler in the mornings. Bud had finally agreed that Rosie could work with her hens and gather eggs, but she wasn't allowed to muck the stalls or milk the cow. She enjoyed slopping the big black hogs and rubbing the big sows' bellies. Bud had purchased several adult pigs from one of the neighbors who had pulled up stakes and moved on to California. Pigs were moneymaking animals for a farmer, and they were easy to care for. A farmer could sell a big sow or a smaller pig to the butcher in town all year long and have a nice income. He would butcher one for his family and hang it in the smokehouse and have pork chops, sausage, sliced bacon, and ham whenever he wanted it. Soon they would have a whole pen of piglets. Bud had built a new hog pen away from the house where the breeze wouldn't blow the stink from the pigs toward the house.

Rosie and Justice had Bud plow a piece of ground near the side of the house for a small winter garden. They planted turnips, cabbages, carrots, and green onions. A few hills of potatoes, a long row of okra, and a short row of squash were included in the small area. The ladies were so proud of themselves, a weed wouldn't dare peek its head out in their garden. Bud's mama had told Rosie that she would show her how to can when their vegetables started producing more than they could eat.

Bud had been invited to go with Jesse and Will to a horse auction the following week in town. Ranchers who raise horses for a living were ready to sell some of their finest breeds. Bud wanted to purchase a good pony for Tater and a nice, gentle riding horse for Rosie.

The dinner bell rang, and Bud and Tater hurried into the house after removing their work boots on the front porch. "Shore smells mighty good in here!" Bud said as he reached down and picked up Boo to place him in his high chair.

"I hope its fitt'ng to eat. I made a chicken pot pie like your ma said that you liked. I ain't never made one before," said Rosie. "I put everything in it except the kitchen sink and covered it with another pie crust."

"Sounds wonderful," replied Bud. Tater raised his eyebrows as if to say something, but he kept quiet after Bud gave him a hard look.

Rosie quickly said a blessing over her new dish, praying that it was fitting to eat. Everyone passed their plates to Justice to be served. Bud dug into the new creation and was very surprised as to how good it was. "Man, this is good stuff," he said with his mouth full.

"Well, you act very surprised. Don't you think that I can cook?" Rosie asked, being a little put out that he didn't think she could do anything right.

"No—I'm not surprised. You said you were not sure if it was fit to eat. No, I know you can cook real well, right, Tater?" Bud stammered over his words. Bud had witnessed his own pa placing his foot in his mouth over something that his mama had cooked. He wasn't going to make that mistake with Rosie. She was still very upset over her mama's visit and her emotions were all mixed up.

"Tomorrow is Sunday, and I need to go lay out the boys' Sunday clothes and brush an' polish their shoes. Bud, do I need to look your clothes over for tomorrow?" Rosie asked.

"I was thinking about not going. Maybe do a little fishing."

"I hate to tell you this 'cause I ain't your boss, but you can't do that. Your ma will be over here, hunting you down quicker than a snake can swallow a swamp rat. Now that you are home with a family you must set us a good example—church first and then family lunch."

"Shoot fire, Bud! You ain't scared of your ma. Let's go dig some worms now and be ready to go before sunup." Tater was heading for the front door.

"Wait, son. Rosie's right. We should go to church and then have lunch with the family afterwards. *And no, I'm not afraid of my ma*, but I love her. I don't want to disappoint her ever again." Bud never took his eyes off Rosie as he spoke to Tater.

"I tell you what we can do. We'll get up at sunrise and go fishing for a couple of hours. Come home and have breakfast and then go to church." Bud smiled at Rosie and then turned to see Tater smiling too.

"I'll go dig the worms now."

The next morning, Rosie came out of her bedroom with the same dress on that she wore the Sunday before. She had pulled her lovely red hair back and plaited it very softly, allowing it to hang down her back. Bud thought she was prettier than a speckled pup.

"Rosie, I want to apologize to you. I have fallen short in my responsibility to get you some new clothes. The boys have plenty, but you are in need of some nice Sunday dresses with all the other things that go with it. Tomorrow we will ride into town and go see Hope's dressmaker at the dress shop. I think Hope said her name was Nettie."

"I have plenty of dresses. You bought me three when we moved here. That's enough."

"I want you to have some nicer things. The dressmaker will measure your body and make dresses just for you."

"You mean strip out of my clothes down to my underthings— in front of a stranger?" Rosie's eyes were stretched wide open as she looked at Bud.

"Is that the reason you don't want any new dresses?" Bud's roar of laughter filled the room. "I can't believe you are so timid," he said while trying to stop laughing.

"*I ain't scared!*" Rosie exclaimed, blushing bright red. "Have you ever had any clothes made just for you?" Seeing a doubtful expression on Bud's face, she said, "See, you wouldn't like it either."

Bud had stopped laughing, but he said very seriously, "We will be going to town tomorrow, and you will have a new dress to wear to church next Sunday. I don't want people to think that I can't provide for my wife and kids."

"We ain't yours yet," Rosie whispered softly.

Bud walked over and stooped down to her level and said softly but firmly, "Don't get any ideas about changing your mind about marrying me. You're mine and so are those boys. Got that, my little swamp cactus."

Rosie couldn't help but smile at Bud. "There ain't no such flower as that."

Bud reached for his brown Stetson and flopped it down on his head as he walked out the front door, mumbling that she knew what he meant.

The next morning, Justice had helped dress Boo, and Tater was all ready to leave. "You sure you don't want to go with us to church, Justice?" Rosie asked.

"Just stop by and pick me up after church, and I will socialize with your folks at lunch. If I am in that church house, the poor minister won't have a chance at saving any poor souls. Those folk's eyes will be watching me every minute to see if I am going to cast a spell."

"People will never get used to you if you stay hidden out here away from them," said Rosie.

"I don't want them to get used to me. Spells work better if people are a little afraid of you." Justice walked back into her bedroom laughing at her own words.

The churchyard was filled with families from all over Limason. Will and Hope drove up in the yard the same time as Bud.

"Howdy," Will said, and he wrapped his reins over the hitching rail. He reached for Jacob and offered a hand to Hope to assist her down out of their carriage. Her new pregnancy was really showing now.

A loud squeal came from Boo. "J...," he laughed. Boo had spotted Jacob, and he wanted down so he could run to him. Jacob clapped his little hands and spoke a mouth full of chatter that no one could understand.

"Will and Bud stood close as they held the two little boys. "Will! Don't you dare put Jacob on the ground? He will be filthy before we can get him inside."

"Same goes for you, Bud. Boo will be rolling in the dirt because he is so happy to see Jacob." Rosie hugged Hope and told her she looked pretty in her lovely pale blue dress.

"Nettie has a whole bolt of this material in her shop. You need to let her make you a new dress out of this same cloth."

"You wouldn't mind if I had a dress just like yours?" Rosie asked.

"Well, to tell you the truth, your dress will not look anything like this tent I'm wearing. You are so small and petite. No one will even notice the same material, I promise you," said Hope, laughing and rubbing her belly.

"Come on, ladies," said Will as he and Bud walked toward the church. "You two could stand out here all day and talk. Rosie, you need to ride over and visit with Hope so you both can yak yourselves silly and let the boys play together."

"Oh, I would love to do that, if it's all right with Bud," she said while looking at Bud as he walked a few steps ahead carrying Boo.

"Of course you can visit Hope. Just don't go over when Boo needs a nap. Boo can be ornery when he's sleepy," replied Bud like a good father who knew Boo's routine.

Will and Hope agreed that a morning visit would be best. "We can have some coffee, sweet rolls, and a glass of good cold milk," said Hope as she thought of the wonderful rolls that Rae baked all the time. All Hope thought about these days was something sweet and good to eat.

As the foursome entered the church doors, everyone was standing while singing the first hymn. Will led Hope and Jacob down to a front pew where Jesse, Rae, Katie, and John were standing. Everyone shuffled down a few spaces and made room for the late arrivals.

Bud and Rosie with Boo found a pew in the middle of the congregation. Tater had spotted Missy, Susie, Claire, and Little Jess all sitting on the back row whispering instead of singing.

Everyone was seated, and Bud realized that he should have chosen a pew closer to the back. Boo wanted to stand in his lap so he could see. Once he spotted Jacob, he wanted to get down and go to him.

The opening prayer and another hymn were sung while everyone stayed seated, and then the minister got right into his sermon. Bud was listening to the preacher speaking about men who gambled and were not taking proper care of their families. As his mind wandered, the next thing he heard was the scripture being read from the Bible about a man and woman living in sin.

"A man does not take a woman—you adults out there know what I am saying—without marriage in the site of God! It is a man's responsibility to a godly woman to show her the respect that she deserves by having a proper courtship. A godly man shows restrain and waits until they are married to bear children. A godly man doesn't run off and leave a poor innocent girl!"

"I want J!" Boo screamed out his desire for the whole congregation to hear. Bud jumped up quickly and rushed out the front doors of the church, carrying the loud, screaming two-year-old.

Will recognized Bud's situation and carried Jacob outside too. Both of the men looked at each other and started laughing. "Damn," Bud said quietly. "That preacher is on the warpath this morning. I felt like he was going to tell us men that we're all going straight to hell."

"He might before he finishes his sermon. I heard that his middle daughter has gotten in the family way, and she isn't saying who the pappy is," Will told Bud.

Jacob and Boo were down on the grass talking up a storm to each other. Boo had taken Jacob's hand and was leading him out to the carriages and horses. The men followed along behind them, keeping them safe and out of harm's way.

"I hate that happened to his daughter, but I feel better now. At least I know he wasn't preaching to me." Bud and Will laughed and continued to watch the boys play.

Bud and Rosie met his folks in the churchyard after the service. "Bud, I hate you had to miss the sermon this morning, but I'm sure everyone appreciated you boys taking the little ones outside so they wouldn't disturb the minister's message. Everyone, load up and let's head to the house. I have a good lunch ready," said Bud's mama.

"We're right behind you, Mama. I've got to round up Tater and go by the farm and pick up Justice."

"Don't twaddle! I'll have the rolls in the oven by the time you get there."

Bud shook his head and smiled. "Be as quick as I can be with this passel of folks."

Mrs. Downey's lunch was wonderful. Justice and Rosie helped make quick work of cleaning the dishes and putting the leftovers up for supper. The ladies went outside to sit a spell on the front porch as the men walked out to the corral to look at the horses. Luke, Bud's older brother, had not joined them for lunch, but now he stood in the doorway of the kitchen.

"Come and join us, Luke," said his mama. "Would you like for me to dish you up some lunch?"

"No, Mama, I'm fine for now," he said as he gave Rosie the once over. "I believe you get prettier every time I see you, little lady."

Rosie returned a shy smile and said thank-you. She was very uncomfortable in Luke's presence. She was sure he had been drinking, and she had no use for drunks, having lived with one all her life.

Before Rosie knew it, Luke had walked over and slid into the swing next to her, practically sitting on top of Justice. Justice stood and walked over and sat in an empty rocking chair. "Now isn't this cozy," he mumbled.

"Luke, you best go back inside with me and let me fix you something hot to eat," said his mama. "Rosie, why don't you go and see the new pony that Samuel got to ride to school?"

Rosie jumped up and raced off the porch down to the corral. Bud saw her coming and went to meet her. "What's wrong? You looked all flushed. Are you feeling all right?" he asked.

"I'm fine. I just wanted to see Samuel's new pony, that's all," she said.

Bud looked to the house and saw his brother sitting in the swing and his mama talking to him. "Did Luke say anything to you out of line? I'm not going to allow his drinking to give him any excuse to embarrass you."

"Please, Bud. Your mama is taking care of him. Please don't make a scene. He won't even remember it tomorrow," Rosie said as she took Bud's arm and led him to the corral.

Tater was so jealous of Samuel's new pony. He enjoyed patting the young horse and watching Samuel ride it around in the corral. Mr. Downey wanted Samuel to get used to the animal before he allowed him to ride it away from the farm.

Bud walked up behind Tater and placed his arm across his slim shoulders. "How would you like to go to the horse auction with me, Will, and Jesse next week? We might just fine a nice pony for you."

"Oh, Bud, you mean it, my very own horse! Did you hear that, Sis?" asked Tater, looking at Rosie as she wore a big smile.

"Bud is too good to us. You'll need a horse to ride to school. I am going to enroll you tomorrow," Rosie said while she had Tater all excited about a new horse to ride.

Tater looked down and started kicking the ground with his boot. He finally spoke. "I guess school will be all right. Missy said that I would be in her class so I will know someone at least."

Bud and Rosie were thrilled that Tater had agreed to go to school without them having to force him. "A new pony can work wonders," whispered Bud into Rosie's ear. He wanted to nibble on her sweet-smelling earlobe, but he thought he better not with so many people around.

14

THIS WAS GOING to be a very special day. Tater was going to school for the first time in several years, and Bud and Rosie were going to be married. Tater came in from doing his morning chores and washed up. He dressed in a new plaid shirt, clean denims, and polished boots. Rosie had dressed in one of her floral house dresses and new brown shoes. Justice volunteered to stay home and care for Boo and make a few pies.

Once he arrived at the school house, Tater rushed over to the other kids. Rosie met the school teacher, Miss Lucy Ledbetter. She had been teaching at the Limason School for nearly ten years. The children all loved the petite teacher with golden hair who had come from Houston. Miss Ledbetter assured Rosie that she would test Tater and place him in the proper reader and math books. As they prepared to leave the school house, Rosie received a nod from Tater.

"Well, I guess we're lucky to get any kind of good-bye," laughed Bud.

"I wanted to give him a hug and tell him how proud I am of him, but I'm sure he would've died if I had," Rosie said as she walked down the steps toward the wagon.

"He's growing up, big sister. Get used to it!"

Bud stopped in front of the lawyer's office. After going inside and taking care of business, they were off to the little white church in the woods.

The reverend and his wife were not surprised to see the young couple drive up to the parsonage behind the church. "I'm not surprised to see you here today, Mr. Downey," said the minister, but it's very early in the day."

"Is it too early to perform a wedding ceremony?" Bud asked.

"Of course not," laughed the reverend as he called his wife to join them. "Please come inside the church, and we'll have a dandy of a ceremony."

With only the minister's wife as a witness, Bud and Rosie were married. After the signatures were placed on the wedding certificate, Bud thought to himself, *Now this is a legal document, not just a scrap piece of paper showing ownership.*

As Bud drove the flatbed wagon toward home, he glanced over at Rosie's profile. He could see a sprinkle of little freckles across the bridge of her nose. He was so excited his stomach nearly did a flip. She was not an impulsive, flighty girl. She was a hardworking, loving, mature young woman who would die protecting the ones she loved. He wanted her to trust him and to share her hopes and dreams for the future. He wanted her to give him her heart freely and not out of gratitude. He silently watched his new bride as she gazed over the countryside. He was so proud of Rosie. He hoped that he could live up to her expectations of what a husband should be.

"To hold from this day forward, for better or worse" was the part of the ceremony that stood out the most to him. She was his to protect and take care of for as long as they live. Hopefully, he could make her life a lot easier in the near future if she would only let him. She had worked like a man for as long as she could remember, she had told him once. But now that they were married, maybe she would work like a farmer's wife and not a field hand. He wanted to bring joy and happiness into her life. She didn't have to go fishing every morning or pray that she trapped a rabbit or some other critter for the stew pot. He would try to provide everything that she needed but he was afraid that if in the near future things turned bad; well, he prayed that he would be able to take care of it.

The morning was halfway over when they returned to the farm. Justice had a nice lunch prepared. They told her how grown up Tater acted at school and a little about the wedding ceremony. They were married now. Bud explained that this was their home now—all of them, including Justice. As they ate, he said that he needed to go purchase supplies and get started building two new bedrooms onto the house. As a young man, he had always wanted a room of his own, a space where no one was invited in unless he said so.

"So you're going to build the boys their own rooms?" Justice asked. "Boo is still mighty little to sleep alone."

"That's true," Bud said. He could feel his desire to sleep alone with Rosie fading.

"The little fellow can continue to sleep in my room. I'm used to getting up and checking on him every night." Justice grinned at Bud. He was sure she had read his thoughts.

"All right, that's settled! Back to the planning," Bud said, smiling real big.

Later that afternoon, Samuel came riding into the yard with Tater on the back of his horse. "See you tomorrow and thanks for the ride home," yelled Tater as he waved good-bye to Samuel. The boys had a good laugh as Tater yelled "so long" to his new Uncle Samuel.

At supper, Bud told Tater that he could ride one of the work horses to school until they could get him a new pony at the auction this weekend. Tater was pleased to know that he wouldn't be dropped off in front of the school like some of the smaller kids.

"Tater, tell us all about school today. What did you like?" Rosie asked.

"The only thing that I didn't like about school was Ms. Ledbetter insisted that I be called Simon instead of Tater. Everyone has to be called by their proper, legal name. No nicknames," he said. "I guess I should be glad that I don't have a weird name like Cornelius or Willard."

"So school was good?" Rosie asked, trying hard not to grin.

He nodded and said that he better get ready to turn in. "I've got to read a few pages in my new reader. I'm a little behind some of the older kids, and I want to catch up." Bud and Rosie looked at each other and smiled.

Early the next morning, Rosie wrapped her apron around her small waist and went out on the porch to look the morning over. The sky was clear and blue. The dew on the grass sparkled in the bright sunshine. Today, she was different. She was now Mrs. James Abraham Downey. Pondering her new name, she walked over and sat in the porch swing, letting out a sigh. Last night wasn't the honeymoon that she had envisioned. In fact, there wasn't a honeymoon at all. Bud and Tater slept in their room, and she and Justice along with Boo were in their own room. Bud's plans today were to go into town and purchase lumber to build additional bedrooms onto the house. Just thinking about being married to Bud gave her goose bumps. He was a young, handsome, wonderful, caring man. As he was recovering from his wounds while living in the swamp, he had actually cared about her and the boys. Who wouldn't fall in love with such a sweet, demanding, bossy guy like Bud? Rosie smiled at the many ways Bud tried to touch her person. He said that he cared deeply for her. His actions were proof of that. She or the boys didn't need a thing because he was so generous to them. Just remembering how she looked when Bud first met her made her feel so undesirable. How many young men would marry a rag-tail gal like her. *Yes*, she thought to herself, *when the new bedrooms are completed, she wanted to be a real wife to Bud.*

As the weeks went by, excitement was in the air for the newly married couple. There had been no news from her mama and husband about wanting the boys. The fall garden was producing more vegetables than they could eat. Mrs. Downey came over and taught the girls how to preserve the fresh vegetables in jars. It was a long and hot process, but the results were rewarding. Rosie and Tater had picked the last of the wild strawberries, and they were put up in jars. "There is nothing like the taste of a sweet strawberry on a hot, fluffy biscuit during the winter months," said Mrs. Downey. Bud's pa and brothers along with Jesse and Will Maxwell came over on Saturdays and helped with the new addition to their farmhouse. Jeremiah had come on a regular basis and helped Bud nail and saw boards. Bud was surprised and appreciated the new bond of friendship he had gained from the older man. He confessed to Bud that he had always wanted to be a builder. The only things that he had built over the years had been hot houses for Ms. Katie. She had a dozen on her flower farm, and he had constructed most of them along with Katie's husband John. Bud couldn't help but secretly laugh at Jeremiah when Justice was around. He seemed to have one eye on her all the time. It was like he expected her to wave her hands in the air and make the lumber fly into place. Bud was sure that Jeremiah was a little apprehensive of just what Justice could do.

Early the next morning, after Tater had ridden off to school, Bud told Rosie and Justice to get Boo ready because today would be a great day to go and order their new bedding and furniture. Bud wouldn't hear of Justice staying home. "You need to come with us and pick out your new bedding, and I want you two girls to get some more clothes. I want you two to go by the dress shop and order a new dress or skirt, or whatever you want. The fall harvest dance will be the last of this month, and I want my gals to look fine."

Each of the girls started to argue that they didn't need anything, but Bud wouldn't even listen. "You will have new dresses, new under things, new whatever you need! If I have to tag along with you both to Ms. Nettie's shop I will."

He went into the barn and hitched up the flatbed wagon. Never in his life had he met more stubborn women when it came to buying something new for themselves. Most girls wanted something new every time they went to town, but not these two.

Bud laughed to himself because he knew deep down that Rosie would be thrilled to have something special to wear to the dance.

"Bud, tell us about the fall party that you mentioned early. Where's it going to be?" quizzed Rosie.

"You have to ask Hope all about it. It used to be held at the Maxwell's ranch, but I'm not sure if it will be this year. Like I said, ask Hope," Bud replied.

As they rode in the flatbed wagon, Boo sat in Justice's lap and clapped and counted the trees that they passed. He was beginning to talk and speak many words very plainly. Rosie was so proud of how the boys had adjusted to their new way of life on the farm. Tater was happy and growing into a fine young man. His thin frame was filling out, and his voice was beginning to change. Boo was a happy baby. He was practically potty-trained, and he was feeding himself, mostly. He loved to chase the small chicks and hold the new piglets. He wasn't afraid of any of the farm animals. Riding over the fields with Bud was his favorite thing to do.

Bud drove into the town of Limason and pulled directly in front of Nettie's Dress Shop.

"Here's your first stop, ladies. Have fun and spare no expense. I want you to have something pretty to wear. Rosie, have her measure you for a few Sunday dresses. Don't disappoint me now, you hear?" Bud gave her a lopsided grin as he drove down to the livery to get grain and oats.

As Bud was making his way to the dry goods store, he saw Sheriff Murphy coming out of his office. "Howdy, Sheriff," Bud said.

"Howdy yourself, young man. How's the little misses doing and her friend?"

"You mean Justice?" Sheriff Murphy nodded.

"My family is doing fine. We enrolled the older boy in school and he seems to have adjusted real well. You know that Rosie and Hope are good friends now. Will, Jesse, and Jeremiah, along with my pa and brothers, helped me complete the addition to my house. Yes, sir, life is good."

Sheriff Murphy looked down the street and then glanced up at the rooftops of several buildings across the street. He didn't seem to have any intention of moving away from Bud. He looked down at his boots, and finally, he cleared his throat.

"Bud, son, I hate to have to deliver bad news to you, but I got a telegram from the sheriff in McBain. It seems that Rosie's ma wants those boys of hers back. Me or you—those boys have to be taken back to McBain for a hearing to see what is to be done about her request. The hearing is Friday of this week. If they aren't at the hearing, somebody will be held in contempt of court and placed in jail."

"This Friday, you say?" Bud asked to be sure he understood. His heart had fallen to his knees with fear.

"Yep, will you and your misses take them and hear what the judge has to say or do I need to take them? I am supposed to transport them, but I trust you, Bud, to do what is right. What do you say? I need to telegraph the sheriff back and tell him the boys will be there."

Bud stood, thinking about Rosie. How in the world was he going to tell her that her worst fears have come true? She had prayed that her Mama would go back to McBain and decide that she didn't really want Boo. Rosie and Tater knew that she really didn't want "Tater".

"Well, Bud, are you going to drive them to McBain, or am I?" Sheriff Murphy asked in an unsteady voice.

"We'll take them. Don't worry. We'll be at the hearing," Bud said as he walked away from the sheriff feeling like the bottom of his world had fallen out from under him. As Bud passed several citizens of Limason, he noticed that he was near Dr. Tim's office. He opened the door and went inside.

"Goodness gracious, look who's here! Come in, Bud. Is my nurse Rosie with you," Esther asked.

"No, madam. She's over at the dress shop. You look like you are doing well, getting up and around on your leg."

"You can't keep a good dog down too long or something like that," she said, laughing at her own joke.

"Is Dr. Tim here?" Bud asked.

"Let me tell him you are here. You ain't sick, is you?"

Bud smiled and shook his head no.

"Come on back here in his office," said Esther.

Tim stood up from his desk and greeted Bud with a friendly handshake and pulled a chair out for him to sit. "What brings you here to see me this fine day? Are things all right with the farm?"

"Yes, the farm is great. The soil is rich. We have so many canned vegetables we could feed the county with the crops from our vegetable garden." Bud smiled.

Tim leaned back in his big chair and waited for Bud to open the discussion and tell him why he had come to visit.

"Dr. Tim, I may need another lawyer. I hate to have to ask, but it's not for me this time. Rosie's mama wants to take the boys away from us. She abandoned Rosie and the boys soon after Boo was born and now she has returned. We have to have the boys in McBain this Friday for a hearing in front of a judge so he can hear her request."

Tim made no comment as he allowed Bud to continue with his story. "Rosie, along with her friend Justice, raised the boys. Their pa was a drunken old fool who tried several times to sell Rosie to strange men for money. She always managed to escape and hide. He wasn't any help to her with the children. I'm afraid that since their mama has remarried, and they have a place in McBain, that the judge will be lenient toward her and take them from Rosie."

"I'm no lawyer, but judges are funny when it comes to a real mother. We have mamas that leave their babies on the doorsteps of the orphanage and a few weeks later come begging for the return of their child. More often than not, the judge returns them to their birth mother."

"I'm afraid, Dr. Tim. I feel that we should be prepared with as much help as we can get. I'm not sure what this hearing means."

"Let me make a suggestion. Go to the hearing, and if things don't go your way, then I will get you the best lawyer and a detective in Houston to help you. The detective can deliver bad news to you or good news. He might say that Rosie's mama is a good person and cares deeply for her boys and treats them well. Then again, he may be able to prove that she isn't a good mother. I know for a fact that a leopard doesn't normally change their spots."

"Thanks for the advice. I think your plan is a sound one. Now, I have to tell Rosie. But the really bad news is that we will have to travel the next few days to McBain. The trip from Louisiana in the covered wagon was a hard ride with the baby."

"I tell you what I can do to make your trip a whole lot easier. I have a big black carriage that is pulled by four of my strongest horses. Someone referred to my carriage as a hearse, but the thing is so darn big and comfortable inside. My horses will have you there in no time. What'd you say?"

"Well, that's awful nice of you to offer, but are you sure? I would hate to have an accident or have one of your horses comeup lame," Bud said as he was trying to think of other bad things that could happen.

"Don't be silly. Things happen to the best of us. I could take them out and something could happen. It would give me great pleasure to know that you and Rosie are having a good trip for this scary occasion."

"Well, all right then. I'll ride back in to town this afternoon and get the carriage and horses. We'll be leaving at first light tomorrow."

After the trip into town and Boo had been put down for a nice afternoon nap, Bud called Rosie and Justice to the kitchen table and motioned for them to sit. "I've got a bit of bad news, and we need to be away from the farm a few days."

Justice looked at Bud and took a seat at the table. Rosie knew as she slid into a chair at the table that this was the bad news that had been hanging over their heads.

"Sheriff Murphy had a wire from the Sheriff in McBain. Your ma has requested a hearing with a judge to get her boys back. We have to be in McBain Friday morning. The boys have to go with us. Good news. Dr. Tim is loaning us his big black coach and team of four horses. The trip will be faster and a lot more comfortable for all of you. Tater can ride on the top with me. We will probably only have to spend one day under the stars. The big coach will sleep three inside."

"That's mighty kind of Dr. Tim," whispered Rosie as she reached over and took Justice's hand in hers. "What'd you make of this, Justice?"

"I ain't never had no use for courts and judges," she said as she got up and walked outside. She had some important things to do.

"Oh, Bud, I'm so scared! Mama really don't want Tater. She only wants Boo."

"Listen, honey, we'll go and hear what they have to say and if it looks like the judge might be persuaded to give your mama the boys, Dr. Tim is going to hire us a good lawyer and a detective to help us."

"A detective! Why?" Rosie asked, suddenly puzzled.

"You never know what a detective can dig up on people. Now, we need to get ready to leave at first light in the morning. We'll need plenty of food for us to eat on the trip. Pack whatever you think that might make the trip more enjoyable for the boys."

"Rosie, will you ride over to the Maxwell's and tell them where we are going? You'll have a little time to visit with Hope while I ride over to my folks' place. I'll ask Pa and the boys to come over and take care of the animals for us. We shouldn't be gone but three or four days."

Justice watched Rosie and Bud ride out in different directions. She was awful worried about this court hearing thing. She felt in her soul that the judge would give that selfish woman her boys. Rosie was going to be overwhelmed with grief. As she studied the situation, she felt that she should prepare Tater for the worse outcome—the judge could give Boo and him to their mama. Just in case this happened, she needed to arm Tater with special powders to be used against Tally Spire, the peddler man who had married his mama. If that old man believed bad things started happening when the boys arrived on his farm, he might feel different about them living with them. He would have to hear a spell being cast upon him. *That could be arranged*, thought Justice. She would talk to Tater while they traveled on the trip without Rosie overhearing. Tater was only thirteen, but he had to grow up faster than most boys his age. While living in the swamp, Rosie had allowed him to be a boy, but there were times she expected him to help her like a full-grown man in order for them to survive. Tater was a good boy, and he would do whatever it took to help bring them both home.

15

BUD AND ROSIE sat in the crowded waiting room of Judge Sawyer's courtroom. They sat in cane back chairs near an open window where they could feel a nice fall breeze. Rosie was holding Boo in her lap while he reached and pulled on Bud's fingers as he counted them. A baby cried, an old man coughed and took out a hanky and blew his nose, while a young cowpuncher that was handcuffed slumped down in a chair snoring. A hush came over the room as Bud motioned for Rosie to look toward the door. Rosie's breath caught in her throat. Fear like she never felt before rushed over her. Tally Shire and Rosie's mama, Martha Anne, had entered into the overcrowded room.

Her mama, dressed in all her new finery, walked slowly into the room, looking around at the other people waiting for their turn to go before the judge. Tally Shire glared at Rosie and Bud before he took a seat while Martha Anne eased over to Rosie.

"Hi, honey," she said as she looked down at Boo. Fear flowed through Rosie's body as her mama's skirt brushed up against hers as she looked down at Boo. Rosie had dressed him in denim jeans, a plaid shirt, and cowboy boots. He had a wooden horse in his hand, but when he saw the strange woman, he immediately placed it in his mouth and hid his face into her chest.

"Can I hold my baby?" Martha Anne asked.

"He don't take to strangers. I doubt he will let you," said Rosie as she wrapped her arms tighter around the baby.

"Hey, old woman, get your tail over here and sit down. You're going to cause the boy to start screaming." Mr. Shire shouted at his wife. His loud voice made several people raise their heads and stare at the tall, lean man with his long thin hawk nose and dark narrow eyes. His rough tone gave Tater a little fright.

Rosie's mama walked slowly away and found a chair across the room from her kids. Tater never took his eyes off her. His heart was broken, even though he said to himself that he didn't care about her anymore. *She had left him*, he remembered, and now she had not even glanced at him since she entered the room. He swallowed the lump that had formed in his throat and clenched his teeth. *No one would ever see him cry again because of her*, he thought as he stood near the open window.

The door opened, and it banged against the wall and an older short man stood in the doorway. "Rosie Jourdian Downey and Mr. and Mrs. Tally Shire!" The man's voice rang loud and clear, reminding Bud of how the guards yelled in the prison. The little man watched as the group of people stood. "Come with me," he said and led them into the small courtroom.

Judge Sawyer watched the people file in and stand in front of his desk. A nice, young man with a beautiful young girl stood to the right of his desk. The young man held a little boy while the other boy stood next to the girl. An older woman with a nasty-looking man stood to the left.

"I read the request of Mrs. Shire this morning. You want to have your children returned to you. Is that right?" Judge Sawyer asked.

"Yes, sir," she replied softly.

"Why aren't your two boys in your care now?" asked Judge Sawyer.

"Well, Judge, my late husband was a drinking man. He was mean too. He beat me unmercifully all the time for no reason at all. I could never do anything to please him. One day, he came home in his usual drunken state and demanded that I leave. Get off his property. He had no reason other than he was sick of looking at me. I had no place to go where I could take my children. My baby boy was only six weeks old. I could hardly walk, much less travel. Mr. Shire, a wagon peddler came along, and I begged him to take me and my children away with him. He had been by our place before and seen me with black eyes and bruises. He agreed to take me into town. As I started packing up my children's clothes and my few things, my husband returned home and said that I was to go—my children were staying with him. He said that he would kill me if I attempted to take them." Tears flowed down Martha Anne's cheeks as she peeked at the judge to see if he sympathized with her. She was really giving the judge a grand performance.

"So you left your two bigger children and a newborn baby with their low-down drunken pa. Is this your story? Oh, wait, you also ran off with practically a stranger?"

"Your honor, I wanted to die that day," she cried. "I promised myself that when I could take care of my babies I would come back for them. Don't you see? I had no other choice but to go away."

"So after two years, you have finally secured a husband and a home. Now, you have come back to claim your children?" Judge Sawyer looked over at Rosie and the two boys.

"Now, your daughter has married, and she doesn't need your care any longer and your older son is almost a man. It will be up to him to decide where and who he wants to live with. Your children look to me like they have been well taken care of in your absence. Go sit down, Mr. and Mrs. Shire. I want to hear what your daughter has to say about this matter."

Bud was feeling very good after hearing the judge giving Rosie's mama a dressing down about leaving her baby. He was sure that they would be leaving with the boys.

As Rosie's mama and her husband took a seat across the room, Bud took Boo out of Rosie's arms and placed the little fellow's head on his shoulder.

"Now, Rosie Downey, I want you to tell me about what took place the day your mama left and how you and the boys have fared alone with your drunken father."

"Well, your honor, what Mama said about our pa beating her is true. He was an awful mean man when he was drinking and when he wasn't. He did try to whip me and Tater, my brother here, but we would scat and hide. The day Mama left, she did pack her things, but she never packed ours. She told me good-bye and never looked back. I pleaded and begged her to take us along. I told her that I could help out with the boys, but she pushed me away. She got on Mr. Shire's wagon and rode out of the yard. I never saw her shed a tear." Rosie looked at her mama and saw that she was attempting to speak to the judge.

"She lying, Judge! I nearly died from heartbreak. Ask my husband," she screamed.

The sound of the gravel banging down on the desk, and the judge demanding "quiet," made Rosie jump.

"Go on with your story, Mrs. Downey," said the judge.

"Well, after I quit crying, I realized that I didn't have time for any self-pity. My little baby brother needed to be cleaned and fed. My younger brother would need dinner soon. My pa had ran off toward town. So here I was alone with two boys to care for. I was sixteen and really didn't know how to care for a newborn baby. But God answers prayers, Judge. I prayed for help, and the next day, Mama's old friend Justice, who lived on the outskirts of town, came for a visit. She stayed on with us until she taught me how to care for my baby—yes, my baby now. With her help, I was able to fish and trap critters to help feed my little family. Occasionally, our pa would return to demand food and sleep after he ran out of money or moonshine. Several times, he brought a stranger, sometimes a saloon owner, or cowpuncher by our shack, and he would try to sell me to them. He didn't care who bought me as long as they paid him the price he needed to purchase liquor."

"Lord have mercy, child! Are you telling me that your own father tried to sell you for a few dollars to a total stranger?"

"Yes, sir. He offered me to Bud, my husband now, but Bud didn't really buy me, but he gave my pa fifty dollars so he would leave me alone. A few days later, the sheriff told us that Pa had been murdered for that money in an alleyway."

"Later, some mean men came by our shack and burned it to the ground. After that happened, Bud married me and brought me and my boys, along with my friend Justice, to Limason where he has a nice farm." Rosie deliberately left out the part of the story where the men were looking for Bud. If he had asked, she would have told him everything.

"Judge, may I speak?" Bud asked as he moved Boo over to his other shoulder.

"Please do, but make it short. I have a room full of folks waiting for me."

"Well, Judge, it's like this. Rosie is a wonderful mother to her brothers. She is the hardest working young girl I have ever met. She hunted, fished, cooked, cleaned, and protected these boys ever since their mama ran off. She's a good Christian girl who always goes to the Lord with her problems. She has never accepted charity from the townspeople and the boys have never been hungry. I love this girl and these two boys. We have a nice farm, Tater goes to school, and I have plenty of money in the bank. Please, allow us to take our boys home."

"Mr. and Mrs. Shire, please come back to my desk. After hearing both sides of this case, I need some time to investigate both of your stories. The court will need at least two months to decide who will get custody of the boys. Until that time, I am going to allow the mother, Mrs. Shire to take the boys home with her. This is only a temporary decision. We will return on December 15 at 10:00 a.m. That's all. You're dismissed. Next case!" Judge Sawyer yelled.

Rosie stood as still as a stone statute. Her midsection rolled over, and she knew any minute that she was going to empty her stomach. Bud took her arm and led her away from the judge's desk. "Come on, honey. Let's get outside and get you some fresh air. You look like you're going to faint."

"What does he mean? What does that man mean?" Tater demanded. Before Rosie or Bud could offer him an answer, Mr. Shire spoke very firmly. "It means that you and your brother are going to live with your mama for the next two months. Get your things, boy, and come help me with the wagon and our supplies down at the livery."

"I ain't going anywhere with you!" Tater yelled.

"If you do come, you better find some manners, or you'll wish you had," he said very softly for Tater's ears only.

Rosie's mama walked over to Bud, who was still holding Boo. She attempted to take him, but Bud pulled back away from her. "Look, we need some time to get their things together. We'll meet you at your wagon in a short while."

"Please hurry. Mr. Shire is very impatient. He is ready to head home." Martha Anne said as she looked at the young couple. Tater was standing behind them, looking at his mama.

As they made their way back to the hotel, Rosie was blinded by tears that trailed down her rosy cheeks. "Oh, Bud, I can't believe this is happening. What are we going to do?" Rosie said as she held onto this arm.

Justice was waiting to hear the news. Once Bud told her the decision, she asked Tater if he was going to go to his mama's. "No, the judge can't make me go!" he said. "I won't live with that liar and that mean old man."

Justice asked Tater to sit with her while they had a little chat. Rosie and Bud were repacking the boy's clothes.

"Tater, I wanted to have a talk with you while we were traveling, but I could never get you alone. You want to live with Rosie and Bud. You and I have to make those people not want you and Boo. I am going to put a 'spell' on that man with some of my potions. But here is the problem. I need you to go with Boo and protect him from his mama and that man. I have special powders that you will need to put in the man's food. I have a jar of

insects that will eat his garden, but the bugs have to be released."
Justice watched Tater reactions to all of this information.

"Can't you do this 'spell' thing from a distance?" Tater asked.

"No, you need to be near him and on their place. You can't let him catch you putting the powder in his food or drink. I have a chant that I want you to let him hear while he is sleeping. He will think that it's a dream. This may be hard to do, but you'll know when the time is right."

"So you think that if I do all these things, he will think that all the trouble he is having is because of us. To get rid of his troubles, he will have to return us back to Rosie."

"That's the plan. Do you think that you'll be able to do these things and watch after the baby. Boo is going to scream his head off every time his mama gets near him. They both will be crazy."

"I can do this. You give me the 'stuff' and I will do what you say, but how long do you think it will take before they'll be wanting to get rid of us?"

"Maybe two weeks, a little more, a little less, and be very quiet and only whisper to Boo. Silence is the key. Just stare at Mr. Shire every chance you get, and this will make him very uneasy."

After the repacking of the boys' clothes, the little family walked down to the livery stable where Rosie's Mama and her husband were waiting. Bud walked to the back of the wagon and gave Mr. Shire the boy's clothes. "Is this all they have?" he snapped at Bud.

"We didn't plan on the boys taking a two month trip. You wanted them, now you can supply their needs," Bud said as he held his temper in check.

Mr. Shire loaded the items in the back of the wagon and motioned for Tater to climb aboard on the tailgate. Rosie kissed Boo and attempted to give him to her mama. Boo fought his way back into Rosie's arms, screaming and kicking. There was no way he was going to allow that strange woman to hold him. Rosie walked to the back of the wagon as Tater held out his arms to take Boo. She leaned over Boo and kissed Tater on both cheeks, assuring him that she loved him with all her heart.

"You'll be home soon. I'll pray every day and night for your return. If you need us, please try to get someone to telegraph Sheriff Murphy. Bud will come running."

The old man walked to the back of his wagon to check on the boys. He overheard Bud tell Tater that they would be back to see them in a couple of weeks.

"You ain't welcome at my place. You'll see these boys December 15 and not any sooner," he growled.

Bud took a step and stood directly in front of Mr. Shire. Their noses were almost touching. "Tater, you heard me, son. We'll see you and Boo in a couple of weeks. You can count on that."

The old man turned and practically leaped up on the wagon bench. Bud, Rosie, and Justice watched the old peddler's wagon until it was out of sight. Boo was waving his little arms and screaming at the top of his lungs as Tater wrestled to hold him in his arms.

Rosie swallowed hard to clear a lump that had formed in her throat as she attempted to blink back tears. It was no use. The floodwater of tears flowed down her cheeks, and she went down on her knees. Bud lowered his tall form and pulled her back up and held her tight in his arms. "Oh, baby, I know how you feel. I want to cry too, but we've got to be strong."

Bud looked to Justice who stood straight as an arrow with the most sorrowful expression he had ever seen. As she headed to the hotel, he heard her mumble, "That old man is going to be sorry.

16

A FTER TRAVELING THE two days home, Rosie talked and ate very little. Bud was worried about her, but Justice assured him that she would snap out of her slump. "This is the worst thing that has ever happened to her. But seeing your mama drive off and leave you with a baby to care for or have your pa try to sell you to a stranger is pretty bad too. She has always been a strong girl, and she will survive these next few weeks."

The afternoon that Bud and Rosie returned home from McBain, they were sitting in the parlor. It could have been a very cozy scene, a young married couple sitting in the parlor, looking across at each other. They could have been very happy, except for the big dark cloud of doom hanging over their heads. The boys were not home with them. A judge, a legal stranger, would decide who would care for her little brothers the rest of their young lives. Rosie's heart was broken, and she knew that Bud felt the same as she did. How in this world could they convince the judge that Tater and Boo belonged with them? How were they going to survive the next two months without her little brothers?

Rosie leaned her head back against the pretty new sofa that Bud had bought from a neighbor that had fallen on bad times and was moving. It was a lovely sofa. She ran her small hand across the floral fabric of blues and greens and peeked over at Bud. He was sitting in a chair, drinking a cup of coffee that Justice had brewed and brought him. The expression on his handsome face was one of deep sorrow. There was no sparkle in his eyes and no soft smile on his face. He looked like a sad little boy that had just lost his best friend.

As Bud stood to take a seat beside Rosie, he heard a commotion outside. He trailed Justice to the screen door. Parked in the front yard were Hope and Rae Maxwell with Ms. Ollie perched on the back seat. "Rosie, we have company," said Bud as he walked past Justice and went to the carriage to assist the ladies to the ground.

"Oh, Bud." Rae spoke first and gave him a big hug. "Tim told us what has happened and we are so sorry."

"Thanks," replied Bud with a hard knot in his throat. "Rosie's inside."

Bud helped Hope down out of the carriage, and he asked if she should be out and about. *She's as round as an old washtub*, thought Bud.

"Nothing could keep me away from my new friend, Rosie. I know her heart is broken and I came to be with her." Hope adjusted her big tent dress; that's what she called her maternity clothes lately.

"Bud, grab my stepping box out of the back and help me out of this thing. I feel like a trapped bear in a tight cage. They need to make these carriage seats bigger for us old folks." Ms. Ollie instructed Bud as he hurried to do her bidding.

Once Ollie was down on the ground, she greeted Justice, who had walked outside and was waiting. "The girls and I cooked you all a nice big supper. We knew that everyone would be tired from the trip," explained Ollie as she started passing bowls of food to Justice and Bud.

"This food is mighty appreciated, but you all didn't have to do this for us," Bud said as Ollie filled his arms.

"Hush that kinda' talk, boy! Friends and family stick together and helps in whatever way they can. We all have fallen in love with your new wife and those little buggers. Everyone is so worried about them, and of course, you and Rosie," Ollie said while waddling to the house.

Rosie was sitting on the sofa wrapped in Hope's arms. They were whispering to each other as Rae jumped up to hold the screen door open for Bud, Ollie, and Justice. All three had their arms filled with bowls of delicious food. Rae immediately took charge of the kitchen as she helped Ms. Ollie to sit in a chair and get comfortable.

"Now, Bud," Ollie demanded. "Sit down here and tell us what is going on in McBain. How could they take Rosie's boys away from you?"

Bud stood on one foot then the other as he glanced over at Rosie all snuggled in Hope's sweet arms. As he started to speak, a loud pounding came from the door as it opened at the same time. In the doorway stood Bud's parents and two brothers. First to move and speak was Bud's mama. "Oh, Bud dear, is it true? Did the courts give the babies back to their mama?"

"Come in, Mama, Pa. Hi, boys," Bud spoke to his younger brothers, Samuel and Matt.

"Yes, I'm afraid so for now. We have a court date in eight weeks. Then the judge will make his final ruling. But he said that the boys could stay with their mama until we meet again."

"How did Tater take that?" Mr. Downey asked as he remembered how much Matt and Tater enjoyed going fishing together.

"He was only willing to stay because of Boo," Bud said, trying to keep himself from bursting out crying like a baby and falling into his pa's arms. He could still see Tater sitting on that tailgate holding Boo in his arms as Boo screamed for his Rosie. Tater struggled to hold the baby as he fought to get down. His bottom lips were quivering but not a sound came from his lean, young body.

Mr. Downey patted Bud on the shoulder and guided him to the doorway. "Let's take a walk, son," he suggested.

As Bud and his pa walked over to the corral, Bud removed his clean handkerchief from his back pocket. He wiped his forehead and the mist from his eyes.

"Pa, you know while I was in jail, I thought several times that I might just lay down and die. Times were hard, too unbearable to even try to describe to someone who has never experienced a place like that. But yesterday…yesterday was awful. I left my heart and soul in the streets of McBain. I couldn't even console Rosie like I should have because I felt so broken. Like a big failure. I brought her out of that swampy area she called home to protect her and the boys. Now, first bad thing comes along, and I can't do anything. Some provider, protector I am." Bud lowered his head down between his arms as he leaned on the corral fence.

"Bud, you had no way of knowing that their mama would ever return. She ran off and left her children, that's a fact. But women are strange creatures. We'll never know what was going on in her mind when she turned her back on her babies. Now, she feels that she can show up and pick up where she left off. Rosie has been their mama since she deserted them. The court will have to take that in to consideration. You and Rosie are married. You have a nice, stable home and are able to provide for the boys."

"Yep and I'm a jailbird too. It scares me to think that the judge will think that I'm not a good person."

"You have served your time, and besides, there are plenty of folks here that will speak up for your character. Don't let that bother you."

Bud and his pa stood together and watched the horses run and nib each other on the rump. "Bud, I think that you should hire a lawyer to represent you and Rosie when you go to court. Dr. Tim knows plenty of good men, and I know he will help you," Mr. Downey said.

"I have already been planning to do just that. I'm glad that you feel the same way as I do, because Rosie will think that I am being extravagant." Bud smiled for the first time that day.

"Don't worry about that, son. She'll be very happy that you're willing to do anything to help bring her little brothers home. I told you once before that women are funny creatures. You never know what's going to make them happy."

Bud wrapped his arm across his pa's wide shoulders and said, "Let's go in the house and eat some of that delicious smelling food. Mrs. Rae, Ms. Ollie, and Hope brought over enough food to feed an army."

"That sounds wonderful. I want to see the bedrooms too. It's been awhile since I have seen what you and Jeremiah have completed," said Mr. Downey.

After everyone had finished eating the delicious food, the ladies wanted a tour of the new addition to the house. Bud was happy to have something to do, so he was eager to show them the two new rooms and a spacious water closet. He said that he was going to order a big tub. The ladies laughed a little and said that he would enjoy having one very much.

After a tearful good-bye to Hope, Rae, and Ollie, and Bud's folks, Rosie told Bud that she was going to turn in for the night. She was exhausted after visiting with everyone this afternoon. Justice and Bud watched Rosie as she wearily moved across the room and closed her bedroom door.

"What am I going to do to help her get through these next few weeks, Justice?" Bud walked over and gave the rocking chair a little push, remembering how he sat there and held the baby until he went to sleep.

"Keep her busy getting the new rooms ready to live in. There's a lot to be done after the chores. She loves being outside. Teach her to ride properly. Let her ride Tater's new pony. She needs to learn to drive that nice carriage you bought for us to use. Just keep her busy."

Bud smiled at the wise, old, black woman. "I've got to check the animals before I turn in. I'll lock up. Good night." Bud turned to walk outside. He stopped and called to Justice. "I'm really glad that you're here. We all need you."

Justice smiled and said softly to the vacant doorway. "I'm glad that I'm here too."

The following morning, Rosie had awakened earlier than Bud or Justice. She went outside and looked around. Mornings had always been her favorite time of the day. She needed to gather the eggs. She stopped to look around. All the joy had gone out of the farm yard. Rosie looked over at the hen house and watched a few of the chickens as they pecked at the ground in search of a tidbit to eat. The old rooster had flown on top of the hen house, stretching his long neck as he looked around. Pigeons roosted on the barn roof. The slow-moving windmill made a soft creaking noise as it swirled around filling the water tank. The flowers that circled the large oak tree looked sad and wilted. The horses in the corral stood still like they were posed for an artist. It seemed that the animals knew that a big change had taken place.

Rosie slowly walked in the chicken yard, trying to remain calm and go forth like any other ordinary day. But what she really wanted to do was have a conniption fit. She longed to scream, rant, and rave about the injustice of how she felt about the judge's decision. The next thing she knew, she had stormed out of the chicken yard without gathering the eggs. She rushed away from the house. She strolled through a crop of ankle-high wheat. Stopping occasionally, she picked a few lovely bluebonnets that grew wild. Before she realized where she was headed, she came upon a clear blue stream that flowed on the edge of Bud's farm. Her farm now, too, she remembered. She walked to the water's edge and cupped a handful of cool water. Wishing she had a fishing pole, she found a fallen log and took a seat. The sun was peeking up over the treetops. She rarely had time to enjoy her beautiful surrounding. She was always hurrying because her brothers depended on her to care for their needs. Today was different. Today her insides felt tight and twisted like she was dying a slow death. She should have argued with the judge and demanded that he change his mind. Her mama didn't deserve her boys—*my boys!* His decision had surprised her and made her speechless.

As Rosie continued to sit on the log, she prayed, *Lord, what am I going to do?* She cried to the heavens as tears flowed down her cheeks. *There's never been a day that I haven't cared for Tater and Boo. Please protect them. Let them know that you love them like I do.*

Bud spent two grueling hours searching for Rosie. When he found her egg basket in the chicken yard, he was terrified that someone had taken her away. Justice had calmed him and suggested he go and search for her. His heart was hammering so that that he couldn't think straight. Maybe she went fishing, but all the poles were still in the barn. All the horses were in the corral. He called her name until his throat ached.

He couldn't believe his eyes when he discovered her lying stretched out on top of an oak log. Anger flowed through his body. The best thing for her was for him to leave her in peace. Just go back home and let her be, now that he knew she was safe. He wanted to shake her good and proper for the scare she had given him. As he got closer to her, she looked so pitiful. Her eyes and nose were red from crying. Bud stood looking down as she lay so peaceful. He hated to disturb her but the day was getting away from them.

17

Once Mr. and Mrs. Shire had arrived at their new farm, it seemed to Tater that the work never stopped. Tater's mama was indifferent to him except when she needed him to make Boo stop screaming. The old man was happy that he had a new field hand and a slave to do all the work that he didn't want to do himself.

The farmhouse was nice but very small. It had a big kitchen with an area for sitting. There was only one bedroom, but the house had a fireplace with a tall chimney. The front of the house was plain with only three steps leading into the house. It didn't have a big screen porch like most of the houses in Texas.

Boo had a nice, deep crib that was placed in the corner of the kitchen. Tater's room was a stall in the barn. There were two blankets and a small pillow. His mama gave him a large bowl, a water pitcher, a bar of soap, and a soft rag to use so he didn't have to come into the house to clean up.

Tater was gripped with anger. Every morning he was awakened by a kick in his sides or a bucket of cold well water tossed over his head with the demand to get up. After washing the teats of four dairy cows and making sure the animals' milk bags were perfectly clean from any manure, he milked them. He poured buckets of milk into ten-gallon containers to be carried to the pig farmer a few miles down the road. With no breakfast in his stomach, he was pushed out into the corn field to hoe the weeds. After a few hours, he was given a hard biscuit with a cup of warm cow's milk. Once the old man was satisfied that the rows of corn looked good, he made Tater muck out the barn stalls. He fed all the animals and gathered and washed dozens of chicken eggs. Mr. Shire delivered the milk to the pig farmer and rode into town and sold the eggs every morning. While he was away, Tater took the opportunity to visit with Boo. His mama wouldn't allow him to come into the house because he was so dirty and smelled like a barn animal. Boo looked fine, but he was thinner. His mama said that he wouldn't eat.

After returning from one of his early morning deliveries, the old man saw Tater sitting in the shade of a big oak tree playing with Boo. "What do you think you're doing?" screamed the old man, scaring Boo into tears. "Shut that brat up," he yelled, "before I give him something to cry about!"

"You better not ever lay a hand on my baby brother. I will kill you before I let you harm a hair on his head." Tater yelled right into the old man's face.

"So you think that you can scare me, do you? I'll teach you some manners or I'll kill you before it's all said and done."

"That's a laugh!" said Tater. "If you kill me, who's going to be your next slave?"

"Slave? You think I treat you like a slave! I'll show you how slaves are treated."

Before Tater could place Boo on the ground, the old man raised his arm, which still held the riding crop that had a tassel on the tip. His arm came down striking Tater across his back, causing him to fall to the ground. Boo was screaming as Tater used his body to protect the baby from harm. The old man hit Tater another four to five times before his wife hurried to his side and made him stop.

"Please, Tally! You're going to hurt my baby, for lands' sakes. Let the boy up so I can get Boo."

The old man seemed to snap back to reality as he looked down at the two boys. "He needed punishing, Martha Anne. He's going to learn some manners." The old man walked to the barn while she leaned down and touched Tater on the shoulder.

"Stand up, Tater, and let me take Boo into the house." Tater held his breath as he stumbled with the baby in his arms. His back was on fire, and he could feel blood dripping down onto his skin. He held Boo out to his mama, but she had to struggle to take him out of Tater's arms. The screaming from Boo sounded like he was the one who had been beaten.

Tater stumbled over to the well and held tight to keep from falling down. He dropped the pail down into it. He pulled up some cold clear water and splashed water on his face. His arms and back felt like a hot poker was touching him every time he moved. The riding crop had torn pieces of his shirt off his back. He drank a dipper full of cool water and poured some water down his shoulders so it would run down his back. The stinging from the raw gashes brought tears to his eyes.

"Get over here, boy!" yelled Mr. Shire.

Tater looked over to where the old man stood and saw him holding a long chain and two leg-irons. He had seen black Negro slaves wearing them as they rode in a boat near the dock that he fished back in Louisiana.

"I'm going to show you how 'slaves' are treated, boy! You are going to learn to show me some respect or I'll kill you. You understand me?"

Tater looked at the chain and back again at the crazy old man. "I understand," sneered Tater.

"Sit down on that stump and slip your nasty feet into those leg-irons. We'll see how long it takes for you to come begging to be freed from them."

Tater placed his feet into the irons while Tally clamped them shut around his ankles. A three-foot chain dragged between each foot.

"Grab your hoe and weed your ma's vegetable garden. I don't want to see a weed when you're done."

"She ain't no ma of mine!" Tater spit out the angry words.

In an instant, Tater found himself on the hard ground with a split lip. Mr. Shire had backhanded him in the mouth. "You keep a civil tongue in your mouth when you speak about your mama. She may be a worthless, no-account stupid woman, but she did bring you into this world."

Mr. Shire walked off after he demanded that Tater get to work. As Tater got off the ground and wiped the blood from his lip, he thought that there was no love lost between his mama and that old man.

The vegetable garden was located behind the barn. This gave Tater the opportunity to put into effect part of Justice's spell on the farm. She had instructed him to sprinkle the special insects on the plants. Tater couldn't help but smile. Tonight he would try to get under Mr. Shire's open window and say the chant that Justice had him memorize. Next, he had to find a way to pour some of the special potion on Mr. Shire's food. He really hoped that Justice's spell would work quickly. As he worked the garden, he could hear Boo crying and screaming Rosie's name over and over. His heart was breaking for the little fellow. *Please, Lord, help me to keep Boo safe*, Tater prayed and cried.

Tater was fed a piece of white bread with a hard, cold pork chop and another cup of warm milk that was floating with cream on top for his supper. His lip was so swollen it was hard to chew. He drank a dipper of cold well water after tossing the milk on the ground. He was sure that he would never drink milk again. He was so tired from hoeing and weeding the garden that he wanted to lay down and sleep. His back was still stinging each time he attempted to lay down so he propped himself up and leaned his shoulder into the wall of the stall and dozed. Once all the lanterns were out in the house he waited a little longer before he snuck over to the old man's bedroom window. Carrying the chain in his hands, he hobbled with small steps and sat under the open window. He listened until he heard the loud snoring coming from inside. Softly he began to chant what Justice had taught him:

Flame of the candle, heat from its fire, rumble from a storm
Deafen Tally Shire! Confuse, baffle, drive 'im insane
Put a plague on his land—make him feel less a man,
Let the baby scream!

Over and over Tater sung the words like a song. Listening closely, he heard the snoring stop, silence, and then the rustling of clothes being put on.

"What's wrong Tally?" Martha Anne asked, sitting up in the bed.

"Shut your trap and go back to sleep. I heard something that sounded like singing. I'm going to check on that boy of yours."

Tater had made it back to the barn and was propped up on his side against the wall pretending to snore softly by the time the old man got out to check on him. Seeing the boy asleep and nothing out of the ordinary, he stumbled back to the house in the dark. Between that brat's constant crying and the old woman yakking, he was about to go crazy. After crawling back in bed, he grabbed the old woman by the neck and demanded that she pleasure him. She cried that she was too tired, but after he gave her a few slaps across her face, she took care of his desires.

Tater was up before the old man came out to the barn and was already milking the cows His back was sore and the whip marks were still raw, but he didn't dare show how bad he hurt. He wanted the old man to get an early start to the pig farmer's place. He would go in the house and help feed Boo his breakfast and put some of Justice's special powder into the food that his mama would be cooking. His mama welcomed Tater's help with Boo when her husband wasn't around.

After the old man got on his wagon and headed away to do his morning rounds at the pig farmer's and the local store, Tater headed to the house. Just as he planned, his mama was more than glad to let him feed the baby. Boo was thrilled to see Tater, and he wanted him to hold him as he ate his oatmeal. His mama had put a big pot of beans on the stove to cook. She asked Tater to watch Boo while she went to the outhouse. Once he heard the door to the small building close, he walked over to the beans while holding Boo. He reached in his pocket and took out a small envelope that contained the special powder that would cause the old man to become impotent. He dropped several pinches of the powder into the boiling beans. *One more for good measure*, thought Tater with a smile.

After a few nights of hearing the chant, the old man was sure that the boy was making the noise under his window. One night he went into the barn and grabbed Tater's legging chain. He got a big piece of wire and placed it through the chain and wrapped it around a post. "Now let's see if there's any singing under my window tonight." He laughed and stormed away. Tater grinned as he easily slid his ankles and feet out of the leg-irons that wrapped around his ankles. With the lack of food each day, he had lost weight all over his body. His ankles and feet were slim, and he was able to slide his feet in and out of the leg irons.

Later that evening, as the moon moved behind the clouds, Tater slipped under the old man's open window and started the chant once again.

Flame of the candle, heat from its fire, rumble from a storm

Deafen Tally Shire! Confused, baffle, drive 'im insane

Put a plague on his land—make him feel less a man, let the baby scream!

The snoring stopped, the old man jumped up, determined this time to catch Tater. He wasted no time getting dressed and rushed out the door stark-naked. Racing through the small house to the screen door, he lifted the latch and stepped outside. His right leg plunged into the washtub that had been left sitting on the second step. Down he went, tumbling out headfirst into the yard onto the black muddy ground. As he attempted to push himself up out of the mud, one of his big feet slid as he stepped into a pile of slick mud. "What the hell?" he screamed as he slipped back down into the mud. He was cussing to high heaven.

Martha Anne pushed open the screen door, holding a lantern high and saw her husband butt naked lying sprawled on the ground. He resembled some kind of wild animal perched on his all fours in the darkness. Trying hard to stifle back a laugh, she asked what in the world was he doing.

"Where the hell did all this muddy water come from, and what is your washtub doing on the steps?" he bellowed.

"Well, I took a bath before bed and I poured the water out the front door. I didn't know that you would be going back outside." Once more she tried to contain the laughter, but this time, she could not when he stood with globs of mud clinging to his backside and down his skinny legs. "You think this is funny, you crazy ass woman? Get out here and haul up water from that well. I need to wash this shit off me." He reached up and rubbed his chin and mouth. He had landed facedown on the hard muddy ground. "I could've broken my neck, *woman*!"

As Martha Anne scooted past him to do his bidding, Boo stood up in his crib and started screaming at the muddy monster who stood before him. "Osie, Osie!" he screamed over and over.

"Get in here and shut this brat up before I do it!"

"Now, Tally, I can't do everything. Can I get Tater to come and put him back to sleep?"

"I don't care who shuts him up, but he better stop that cat-wailing."

Tater had heard and seen all the commotion outside, and he had to hide his face and cover his mouth to silence his laughter. He knew his mama was coming after him to help with Boo. He made sure his chain and leg-irons were intact before she came into the barn.

His mama came into the barn, carrying a very upset Boo. He was so afraid his mama could see him trembling while his mama put Boo into his arms. "Hold him while I get this wire unhooked." As she worked to unhook the barbwire from the chain, he soothed Boo until he was nearly asleep.

"Come on into the house, but keep your mouth shut if you know what's good for you. Tally is about to lose his mind. He swears that you are out under our window chanting about some spell placed on him. There ain't no way you could be doing that unless you are a magician. Couldn't nobody get out of that chain and leg irons."

As they made it across the yard, his mama was still mumbling about that crazy old man. She didn't know why she had married up with that old, mean fool.

Good, thought Tater. *The chants are working because he isn't a hundred percent sure that it is me making the noise. Wait until he sees the vegetable garden.*

Martha Anne stopped at the well and dropped a bucket down into it. "Go lay Boo down in his crib and come back out here and help me get water to fill the washtub so the old man can get clean. Lordy, he looked so funny," she laughed out loud for the first time. Tater grinned as he changed Boo's nappy and laid him down. Poor little fellow was calling for Rosie in his sleep.

Fresh coffee was brewing on the stove, so Tater removed it from the fire and opened the lid. This was a great opportunity to put more of Justice's special powder in the old man's drink. He sprinkled some of the potion and hurried outside to the well. He was feeling real good with the way things were going. He felt sure the old man would soon be hauling him and Boo back to Limason.

After a day of hard rain Tater was able to lie around in the barn and clean some tack. His back was better but the leg irons had rubbed blood blisters around his bare ankles. Martha Anne brought Boo out to the barn to play with him, so she said. But

Tater knew that his Mama was already growing weary of Boo's constant crying and refusing to eat. "Take care of him for a few hours," she demanded like being with his baby brother would be a chore to him. He was thrilled to have Boo in the barn with him.

"How's my baby brother doing? You hungry? Mama has brought out some food for you to eat. Be a good boy for me and eat your breakfast." Tater coached and pleaded with Boo to eat, and he finally ate part of the oatmeal and hard biscuit. He took a bite and then gave Tater a bite. "Eat," Boo would say while holding his spoon out to Tater. *God love him. Food never tasted so good*, thought Tater.

When the rain let up and the sun moved out from the dark clouds, a bellow like someone was dying came from the back of the barn. Tally came charging into the barn and threw open the tack room door where Tater and Boo were sitting on the floor. "You killed my plants in the vegetable gardens. You!" he screamed, pointing his finger at Tater. "I don't know how you did it, but you did and we both know it. There's not a single leaf on the tomatoes and the pole beans are just vines. I know that crazy Creole woman put a voodoo spell on me and my place, and she has you doing all of her dirty work. I'm not stupid—I see through you, boy!"

Boo stood up from the floor and wrapped his arms around Tater's neck and started whimpering. "Shut that brat up!" Tally demanded as he flew out of the tack room and headed to the house.

Tally stormed into the house and grabbed his wife's shoulders and gave her a good shake. "This is all your fault, old woman. You just had to have your baby."

"What's happened now?" Martha Anne asked as she tried to wipe the pie dough off her hands with a wet cloth.

"Now, you say. I haven't had a good night's rest in days from all that confounded chanting, and now the vegetable garden is eaten alive with some kind of bugs. That boy and that crazy Creole woman has done this, and I know it. When I'm sure that he's behind all this, I'm going to kill him and bury him so deep in the ground he will never be found."

"Now, Tally, you must not speak about killing anybody. Why don't you go in now and lie down on the bed and take yourself a good long nap. The sheets are fresh and clean, and Boo is quiet out in the barn with Tater."

"That sounds like a good idea!" He walked over to the screen door and latched it. He turned and grabbed Martha Anne's hand and started pulling her to their bedroom.

"What are you doing? I'm making a pie for your supper. I don't need to take a rest."

"Good, I don't want you to go to sleep. You're going to take care of me this morning. And you better do a good job, or I'll blister your butt. Now, git in that room!"

After a while, Martha Anne was begging and pleading with Tally to leave her alone. "It's not my fault you can't—do it. I don't know why you are so…small and limp. This hasn't ever happened."

Before she could finish talking, Tally slapped her across the face, causing her to fall back onto the mattress. He jerked her gown and ripped it down the front. He pulled and snatched on her until she was completely nude on the bed. Bringing his big, wide hand down, he slapped her hard on her bare butt. He beat her backside and the top of her thighs until she couldn't scream or cry any longer. Her skin was on fire from the blistering. Hip-cupping and whimpering, she said over and over she was sorry, praying he would go away and leave her alone. It wasn't her fault that his manhood wouldn't perform his husband duties.

Giving his wife a disgusted glance, he stormed out of the house heading to the outhouse. While he was in there, he examined his private parts. After touching and fondling himself, he knew that something was bad wrong. How could that boy cause him to be in this condition?

As the day continued, Boo was hungry for something to eat. Tater moved, slowly holding his chain high as he walked Boo to the front door. Tater knocked and waited. The old man came to the door and looked down on the two boys.

"What you want?" he said as he saw how Tater was holding up the chain.

"Boo's hungry and wet."

The old man disappeared, and in a few minutes, their mama came to the door. Tater noticed that his mama had been crying, and she could hardly walk. *Something bad had happened between the love birds*, thought Tater.

She opened the door and reached out for Boo. He screamed and fought her. She stepped back and asked Tater to bring him in and change his nappy. He watched her move slowly as she dished some little red potatoes and small pieces of carrots on a plate with a slice of fresh homemade bread. Boo shook his head from side to side, disapproving of the food.

"Please be good, baby brother, and eat your lunch. It's good," Tater said as he watched the old man leave the house without a word to his wife.

"Sit, Tater, I'll dish you some beef stew and you can eat while that old fool is gone. You need your strength." Tater was surprised by his mama's sudden generosity to him, but he wasn't going to question her changed behavior. He was starving for something good and hot.

Tater knew by the way his mama was moving around that she had been beaten. "Why did your husband beat you? Why did he turn on you?"

"That's no affair of yours. Eat and then get out. You have many chores to complete now that the sun is shining."

18

As the weeks passed slowly for Rosie, without her brothers, she couldn't think of anything else. But with the passing of time, things seem to get back to normal. People went back to their normal routines and celebrations still took place. All the talk at church was about the Fall Dance that would soon be held at the Maxwell's. Jesse and Rae hosted the big party every year. It was time for all the families to come together to rejoice and celebrate the wonderful summer harvest and share in fellowship with each other. Wagon loads of families would come and camp out overnight in Jesse's open fields. A steer would be barbecued over an open pit. The ladies baked their favorite dishes and desserts. The local band members would play while young couples danced all night. The dancing was the best part of the evening.

Hope had insisted that Rosie wear one of her new dresses and come and be with her at the dance. "Shoot, Rosie! I know you're sad that your brothers are not here with you, but just look at me. I'm a water buffalo, and I'll have to be a wallflower. I love dancing. I'll sure have to watch Will. He's a great dancer, and all the ladies will be dragging him out on the dance floor while I have to watch."

"Oh, Hope, you're too much. You're one of the prettiest girls in this here territory, carrying a babe or not. Will would never look at another gal. You're so lucky to have him."

"What about you? Bud is so tall and handsome. When he was younger, he was so much fun to be with. We went riding and swimming together. Let me tell you something," whispered

Hope. "If I hadn't been so crazy about Will, I would have done everything I could to get Bud to settle down."

"Really?"

"That Bud was wild as a young spring buck. He liked to gamble, drink, and hang out with the ladies, if you know what I mean." Hope grinned at Rosie.

"He's not like that now. He's sweet, kind, gentle, and he loves my brothers." Rosie wiped her eyes with the sleeve of her dress.

"You're going to have to remember to always carry a hanky. Here, use mine." Both girls laughed as Rosie took Hope's delicate hanky and wiped her nose and eyes.

"I know that Bud has changed for the better. It's because of you, Rosie. He loves you so much. His eyes trail your every move when he is around you," said Hope.

"I better go. Bud is over by our carriage talking to his folks. I guess we'll go over and have lunch with them like we do every Sunday," said Rosie.

"Listen to me," Hope said as she reached and took Rosie's hands in hers. "Anytime you want to just talk come over to our place. Rae, Miss Ollie, and I always love to sit and chat."

"Thanks. You're a dear friend. You know," said Rosie, looking down, "I haven't ever had a friend, unless you count Justice, but she's more like family."

"Oh, Rosie." Hope gathered her into her arms and hugged her as close as she could to her plump body. "I'm very happy to be your first new friend."

As Bud and Rosie drove over to his folks' farm for lunch, he noticed that Rosie's hollow cheeks had filled out, and she had more spark in her lovely eyes. There had been many terrible days when she would go without eating. Many nights he had found her walking outside under the stars, claiming that she couldn't sleep. Maybe being away from the farm today and visiting with Hope had helped.

Driving along the countryside, Bud knew how Rosie felt without the boys. At first food was tasteless to him, and he couldn't sleep without having bad dreams about the boys being hurt. He had worked until he was exhausted around the farm and with Jeremiah's help had completed the new addition to the house. Often he felt like he was still in prison, trapped, unable to do anything. There were days he thought he would go insane because he missed the boys so much. He would wake hearing Boo's scream for Rosie. Talking to his pa alone after church helped him to be patient. The court date would be here soon.

Once they arrived at his folks' farm, Bud reached for Rosie. He lifted her down from the carriage, holding her closer than necessary and let her body slide down the front of his.

Rosie looked up into his face as he wore an innocent grin. She gave him a stern look and pushed to make him move away from her. "Stop, your folks are watching."

"Let them watch. I can hold my lovely bride," he replied with a sweet smile. "How would you like to be my date for the Fall Harvest Dance this coming Saturday?"

"Oh, Bud, I don't know if I will feel like dancing and having fun while my brothers are away."

"That's the reason I'm asking you today. I want you to think about it. Everyone wants us to attend and I really hate to disappoint them. Come on, let's go eat. Listening to that old preacher made me as hungry as an old grizzly." Bud led Rosie to the house, laughing for the first time in weeks.

Rosie and Justice worked harder than ever getting the boys' two bedrooms ready for them. Bud and Jeremiah had completed the rooms and all the bedding and mattresses had arrived. Rosie had cut the fabric for the boy's curtains and she sat out on the front porch stitching them together. She was proud of how they were going to look with the new quilts that Mrs. Downey had given them. Justice had stuffed four big pillows using a big bag of scrap materials that Ollie had given her. She normally used duck or chicken feathers, but they hadn't lived here long enough to save enough feathers. The three braided rugs had arrived a few days ago, and they looked grand on the bedroom floors.

"The rugs will feel mighty good on our feet come this winter," Bud said. The wardrobes and chests fit nicely in each room. A mirror was hung on the wall in Tater's room. She wanted to place a chair in each room so the boys would have a place to sit to put their boots on. Bud told her to make a list of all the things she wanted to go in the two rooms, and he would get them for her. The rooms were going to perfect for the boy's homecoming.

Rosie had scrubbed the window panes inside and out until they shined. The new curtains were hung and the rooms were all ready. She was thrilled and sad at the same time. Bud came into Tater's room and looked at the sad expression on her sweet face.

"How's my girl this morning?" Bud said as he strolled over to the window where Rosie stood.

"Bud, I'm so proud of these two new rooms, but I'm scared. I'm afraid that they may never get to use them. I have had a sick feeling for a few days. I want to go see them. I just know that something is wrong."

"You heard that old fool say that we aren't welcome. Dr. Tim hired a detective, and we should be getting a report from him soon. Can you wait a few more days, at least until after the dance?"

The morning of the Fall Harvest Dance, Luke came riding into the farm looking for Bud. Justice told him that Bud was out behind the barn with a sow that was having her babies.

Justice could tell that Luke had been drinking. His voice was slurred, and when he got off his horse, he could barely stand. He didn't even tie his horse to the hitching post.

I need to do something for his folks, thought Justice. Luke's drinking had gotten out of hand, and he was an embarrassment to Bud's ma and pa. Justice giggled thinking about her special potion that she could fix for Luke to drink. It wasn't poisonous, but he would never want another drink of liquor. Turning and going into the house, she told Rosie that Luke was here visiting with Bud. She was going to take them a cool drink to enjoy. Rosie wasn't interested in visiting with Luke, so she went into the bedroom to prepare their clothes to be worn to the dance later. Justice poured cool water into two glasses and mixed a special tasteless powder into one of the drinks. With a wave of her hand over the top of the glass and a mumbled chant, she stirred the mixture. Smiling big to herself, she walked out to the hog pen where the two men were arguing. The men stopped when they saw Justice standing and holding two big glasses of cool water. Bud thanked her and immediately reached for a glass. Luke shook his head, declining the drink but Justice insisted. "You had a long ride over here in the sun. You must drink."

Luke looked at the little weird, old black woman and smiled big. "I guess I better before you cast a spell on me."

"That was uncalled for, Luke!" Bud said as he gave Justice a look of apology.

"Folks say that she can perform voodoo and cast spells on people," Luke said as he turned up the glass of water and drank every drop of it. Justice took their water glasses. She looked down at the mama sow, turned, and walked back to the house, softly singing a chant. She was pleased with herself, and she knew that in the future Luke would be better.

"Listen, Luke, I'll loan you some money if you promise to start working and helping Pa with the work at the farm. He will gladly pay you a salary if you start to earn it." Bud threw his leg over the wooden rail and moved a tiny baby piglet out from under the mama sow. He stood and looked at Luke. "Why don't you go home and take a nap. For gosh sakes, don't show up at the dance already drunk. I'll help you get your family here if and when you sober up."

"You ain't my mama, boy! Don't try and tell me what to do." Luke slurred the words as he turned to get on his horse. "I'll see you at the dance, little brother!"

Later that evening, after Bud had helped the mama sow deliver her nine little piglets, he went to the creek and took a long cold bath. After dressing for the dance, he went outside and hitched up the flatbed wagon. He was going to have to order a larger carriage that would carry all his family, he thought.

When he came into the house, his breath caught in his throat. There standing in the kitchen was the most beautiful girl he had ever seen. Rosie twisted and turned around for Bud. She had pulled her lovely auburn hair back away from her face, letting it fall down over her shoulders. Her new dress was emerald green. The bodice fit tight, showing off her small breasts and tiny waist. The neckline was lower than Bud would have liked for her to wear, but he kept his tongue. On her small feet, she wore black slippers. He let out a whistle and caught her hand in his. He asked her to turn around again so he could see all of her once more.

"You are so lovely. I better wear my gun belt so I can keep the wolves away from you." Teasing her, he reached for her hand and it felt ice cold. "Are you all right?"

"I'm fine, perfectly fine." She mumbled as she forced a smile.

Bud pulled her into his arms and whispered that things were going to work out. "You'll see," he tried to reassure her as he gave her a hard squeeze. Bud's hands were warm and rough, but she felt secure and safe.

"Tonight you are my princess, and I'm your knight in shining armor. You'll be by my side all evening, and I will protect you with my life." He gave her a small bow as he kissed her small, smooth hand.

"Oh, Bud, you sure know how to make a girl feel special. Thank you for my new dress and shoes," Rosie said. "Wait until you see Justice. She's going to be the belle of the ball," Rosie said, smiling for the first time.

Justice walked out of the bedroom, all decked out in a lovely white blouse with a soft lace collar and a long, floral skirt. Her hair was adorned with colorful wrapped scarves with a big butterfly pin holding them tight. She wore one long jeweled necklace around her neck that hung to her waist.

Bud walked over to Justice and took one of her small black hands. He winked at Rosie as he clicked his boots together and gave Justice a little bow and kissed the back of her hand. "You look like a queen."

They arrived a little late for the party. Everyone was already celebrating. There were couples on the dance floor, and people were in line to be served barbecue. Jesse and Will greeted them. Will declared that Bud was escorting two of the prettiest ladies in the county. Jesse guided Rosie and Justice over to the other ladies. Hope was sitting at a big table eating a big slice of barbecue and corn on the cob. "Come and sit beside me, Rosie. Oh my, what a lovely dress. I'm jealous!"

Rosie hugged Hope, trying her best not to get barbecue sauce on her face. "You are beautiful, even with sauce on your nose," laughed Rosie.

"I'm so glad that you came. I know it was hard for you, but we'll have another party when the boys come back home, just for them!" Hope tugged Rosie to her side and said, "I want you to dance with that husband of yours. He's a great dancer."

"But I don't know how to dance. I ain't never been so dressed up before much less done any kind of dancing." Rosie had a look of horror on her face. "I'm nervous just being here with all these strangers."

"Oh, Rosie, you are too funny. Everyone here is just plain, folks. Where's Justice?"

"She walked over to help Ollie and Esther. She's ain't going to sit and be idle."

"How's the little mama doing tonight?" Bud asked as he scooted Rosie down on the bench so he could sit beside her while talking with Hope. "Where's Jacob?"

"Oh, this is a wonderful night for all the young mothers. Ollie gets several of the young girls that attend her church to come over and watch all the babies and smaller children in the house. The mama's go in every so often and check on them, but the girls play with them and later, they put them down on pallets for bedtime."

Bud watched Hope eat a big slice of chocolate cake. He couldn't help but wonder where she put all the food that she ate. "Rosie, let's go get a plate of food. I'm hungry."

"We'll be back in a minute, Hope. Bud hasn't ate in a couple of hours," she joked as they walked toward the food tables.

As Rosie was walking down the food line, Esther and Ollie couldn't say enough nice things about how pretty she looked. "Lordy, have mercy child, you shore pretty as a picture!" said Ollie. Esther shook her head in agreement.

"It's so good to see you up and around, Ms. Esther. How is your husband doing?" Rosie asked as Ollie placed a big helping of potato salad on her plate.

"He's fine. He shore thought the world of you, child. We're so sorry about the trouble with your brothers. I'm praying for their return every night."

Rosie mumbled a thank-you and moved on down the line to Ella Mae. She placed a big dinner roll on her plate and said that she had on a lovely dress tonight. "Both of you ladies look mighty fine," Ella Mae said as she turned to look at Justice.

"What's going on over there?" Rosie asked Ella Mae as she pointed out in the darkness where a group of men stood in a big circle. "I don't know what those men folks are doing," she replied.

Bud saw the men all gathered in a big circle so he walked over to see what was going on. Luke was standing near the circle, bending over and holding his stomach. "You're trying to poison everyone with that stinking rot-gut! How can you call that stuff whiskey?"

"This is some of my finest," said Harvey Fuller, owner of the Golden Nugget. "How about keeping your voice down? You want the women folks coming over here and spoiling our fun."

"You all keep drinking that stuff, and they'll be going to your funerals," Luke said as he walked over to his ma and pa's wagon that was parked near the corral.

As Luke walked away, several of the men sipped the whiskey and were surprised to find that it was some of the best that they had ever tasted. "It's mighty funny that he has drunk gallons of this same whiskey, and he didn't complain about it before," laughed Harvey.

"Something is wrong with that man's taste buds," one of the men said, laughing while asking for a refill.

Mr. Downey had been standing on the outskirts of the group of men listening to Luke complain about the free liquor. Luke was sitting on the tailgate of the wagon, holding his stomach when his pa walked over to him. "You all right, son?" he asked.

"No! I mean no," he said. "There's something wrong with the whiskey. Every time I drink some, it makes me sick to my stomach almost immediately."

"Maybe, you have drank too much and you have hurt your stomach. Better check with Dr. Tim later."

"I think I will ask him to give me something to help settle my stomach tonight."

As Mr. Downey walked away, he couldn't help but feel a little relieved that something might be slowing Luke's drinking down. He didn't want his son to be sick, but if he was, he had brought it on himself. This "sickness" might just be the answer to sober him up for good.

Rosie stood on the side of the dance floor and watched Will and Bud dance with some of the young, single ladies of Limason.

Both of the men were wonderful dancers, and the girls seemed to be standing in line to dance with either Bud or Will.

"You know, Rosie," laughed Hope, "you and I need to be charging money for allowing those women to dance with our husbands."

"I believe the guys will get tired soon. Bud hasn't danced in months, and I bet Will hasn't either."

It wasn't but a minute later when Bud and Will both came over to their wives laughing and joking about how tired they were. Bud admitted to stepping on many tiny toes while dancing around the floor.

"The ladies need a rest from me, and I certainly need to sit right here next to my lovely bride and recuperate." Rosie smiled at Bud while Hope asked Will to go get her a piece of peach pie. They all laughed at the expression on Will's face as he looked down at Hope's big belly.

The band was playing a very slow tune, and all the couples were headed to the dance floor. Bud reached for Rosie's hand and said, "Come, my little beauty, and dance with me. I will lead and we'll move real slowly."

"But, Bud, I can't, I've never danced before. Please..."

"You'll be fine. I promise not to step on your little toes."

"I can't promise you the same thing," laughed Rosie. She walked onto the dance floor and stepped into her husband's big, strong arms. She was terrified.

Bud held her tight as he pulled her into his arms closer than necessary. She felt and smelled so good. In the past, he had only given her a tight hug when trying to comfort her, but this was different. He could feel her small breasts pressed against his chest. He was sure he could feel her heart beating.

As they swayed to the beat of the music, Bud whispered to her that she was doing great. He wanted to shout to everyone that he was dancing with the most beautiful girl in the world, but he knew that she would have been embarrassed.

When the song ended, Rosie looked into Bud's face and asked if he was ready to leave. "Bud, I'm really tired. Do you think that we could go home? It's very late and others are beginning to bed down for the night."

"Of course, Sweetheart, Let's go find Justice and tell everyone good night."

After the long drive home in the open flatbed wagon Bud, Rosie, and Justice had retired to bed as soon as Bud had put up the animals for the night. In the late hours of the night, strange sounds woke Justice. Rosie was having a nightmare. She was moaning and crying out in her sleep. As she attempted to wake Rosie, Bud had come into their room. He stood, looking down at Rosie as she twisted and turned on the bed.

"I'll take care of her," Bud said as he looked down at the lovely creature whose hair had fanned out in all different directions on her pillow. "It's all right. She's my wife."

He reached down and caught Rosie behind the legs, lifting her into his strong, hard arms. He took the few steps to his bedroom and laid her down on the bed. He smoothed back the quilt and covered her.

Justice watched Bud walk out of the room with his child bride in his arms. "It's about time," she said softly. Justice had hoped that one of them would make the first move toward beginning their life as man and woman—husband and wife.

Rosie woke from her deep sleep. She murmured Bud's name and lay perfectly still.

"Are you all right, baby?" he asked.

Bud slid into the bed next to her. He reached and gathered her in his arms. He kissed her on the forehead, on her lovely emerald eyes, and brushed a soft kiss across her half-open pink lips. Whispering soothing sweet words, he wanted to help calm whatever fears were causing her distress.

"I guess I was dreaming. I'll sorry if I woke you and Justice," Rosie said still very sleepy.

"What were you dreaming?" Bud asked, very concerned.

At first there was only silence. Finally Rosie let out a sigh. "It was about Mama. She was leaving. I begged her to take us with her. I was on my knees in the dirt pleading with her. She was going away and leaving us behind. We had no food—no money. She ran over to the peddler's wagon, never looking back at me as I cried her name over and over."

Slowly he assured her that everything would be all right. He made her feel safe, and she drifted off into a deep sound sleep. Bud lay awake for hours with her small body snuggled into his. The lower part of his body was in terrible pain because he wanted to make love to his new bride. Finally, he willed himself to sleep.

Rosie woke first the next morning. She was confused because she wasn't in her bed. She remembered that she had a nightmare and Bud had come to her room and carried her to his bed. Lying very still in Bud's arms, she watched him sleep and listened to a soft purr coming from his throat. Looking out the windowpanes and seeing the first ray of sunshine, she thanked God for sending him to her.

Bud wasn't used to having anyone in his bed. With the slightest movement of the mattress, he was instantly awake. He adjusted the quilt over his chest and looked down into Rosie's face. "Who were you talking to, sweet?" he asked.

"I was thanking God for sending you to me, but I thought I was praying silently."

"Silently or aloud, I thank him too," he said as he attempted to sit up on the side of the bed. He felt Rosie's tug on his shoulder as she said, "I hope you like to snuggle because I liked being here in your bed...with you."

Bud gave her a wicked grin and twisted his body around and scurried back under the covers. "So you like to snuggle? Well, it's still too early to start the day, so why don't you just lay here in my arms." He didn't want to scare her, so he nudged his rough black stubble into her neck, causing her to giggle. He wanted to show her tenderness without alarming her, but she could feel his desire through her nightgown. He kissed her eyes as if by doing it he could make her see the truth that his feelings for her were real. He wanted more than anything to fulfill a wild drive that beat through his blood down into his manhood.

"I love your smell, the way you taste, your beauty, even if your hair makes you look like a wild woman in the morning," said Bud as he ran his rough, calloused hand over her body and through her red, wild curls.

Bud laughed as she pinched his arm and said softly, "Oh you."

Rosie felt safe in Bud's embrace with her head resting on his wide shoulder. It was very clear to her now that she loved him. Her love had begun when she first found him in the swamp, but never having experienced such a thing, she didn't know it at the time.

"Bud, I'm so grateful that I found you," she whispered into the side of his neck.

"Let me show you how grateful I am that you did," he said as his tall, lean body covered hers. Rosie's heart hammered in her chest as Bud held her close and loved her like a woman— his woman.

"Praise be to God," mumbled Rosie. She was finally loved.

19

IT WAS A crisp, cool Saturday morning, and the wind was blowing. Jeremiah, Ollie, and Rae were traveling into town when they passed a broken-down covered wagon. A middle-aged woman was holding the head of the lead horse while a tall, lanky teenage boy was wrestling with a big, wooden wheel. A wheel lay on the ground with a broken spoke.

"Whoa," said Jeremiah as he pulled up close to the covered wagon. Jeremiah handed the reins of his horses over to Rae as he hopped down. "You folks got trouble?"

"Please," said the woman. "Don't come closer. We have sickness here in our wagon."

"What kind of sickness?" Jeremiah asked as he turned and looked back at Ollie and Rae. Ollie is an old woman, and Jeremiah didn't want her catching whatever may be in the wagon.

"My man has taken one of the children into town to see the doctor. I hope he will come out here and look at the other children."

Jeremiah walked over to the back of the wagon and pulled back the white canvas cover. He was surprised to see about a dozen young children dressed in rags. He stepped back and looked at the boy who was standing still watching his every move. He was thin, dirty, and dressed in clothes that were too small for his frame.

The young woman could see that Jeremiah had a lot of questions that he wanted to ask.

"These children are headed to McBain to catch the Orphan Train that is traveling to Houston. We were planning on taking these children to church tomorrow with hopes that some of the Limason's citizens might want to take one or two of them into their homes."

"Mercy, do you hear that, Rae?" Ollie asked. "I bet some of those children are sick too. Let me down from here, Jeremiah! I want to have a look at those babies in that wagon!" Ollie yelled.

"Look," said Jeremiah, "here comes Dr. Tim." Jeremiah was very relieved to see the doc coming because he would have had his hands full with keeping Ollie away from the sick children.

"Jeremiah, pull your carriage away from that covered wagon. These are sick children and I don't want Ollie and Rae getting sick. I have one of their little girls and a man in my office. The child is very sick, and I am sure some of these others are too."

"Dr. Tim, I ain't running from no sickness. There are small babies in that wagon, and I am going to your little hospital and help you and Hannah care for them. Don't give me no sass now. You men get that wheel on that wagon so we can move on toward town," said Ollie.

"Tim, do you have any idea what is wrong with the little girl that you have in your office?" Rae was very concerned for Ollie and her family.

"It appears to be flu-like symptoms with a high fever. This could be a bad case of pneumonia or whooping cough. But if it is whooping cough, it can be contagious."

Once the wagon was repaired, the young man drove the wagon to Dr. Tim's small infirmary. It was located next to the little white church at the end of town. Fortunately, he only had to use it one time so far when the school children all got the measles.

Jeremiah and the young man helped the smaller children out of the wagon. There were seven little girls who looked to be under the age of ten and four big boys ranging from the age of nine to twelve. They were dirty, hungry, and had sores on their arms and legs. Ollie and Rae were both heartbroken as they looked upon the children.

Hannah came out of the infirmary and told Tim that she had bathed the young, sick child and she was resting. "I gave her a cold rub down with alcohol to get her fever down. She is not coughing so much right now. Esther is at the office caring for her. The man who brought her in left and headed for the saloon."

When Hannah saw Ms. Ollie coming through the front door of the infirmary, she rushed over to her. "Ms. Ollie, you don't need to be here. I know you want to help, but we don't want you to get sick. Please let Jeremiah take you home. Between Esther, me, and Rae, along with the lady in charge of the children, we'll have enough help."

"Ms. Hannah, I ain't never run from any kind of sickness and I ain't leaving. These poor children need to be fed, bathed, and put in a clean bed. Now, let me go put on an apron and get busy. I'll leave when I know that these babies are settled and feel safe after receiving our loving care."

The little girls were led into a big water closet. After they were undressed, they got into tubs of nice, warm water. Hannah and Rae washed their bodies and hair. Once wrapped in a big, fluffy towel, Rae put salve on their sores. Jeremiah and Ollie went to the bakery and asked Rebecca for all the bread that she had baked. Pastries, butter, and jam, along with two big jugs of cold milk were placed in the wagon to be carried to the infirmary.

"I'll bake extra loaves in the morning for the children," yelled Rebecca as Jeremiah drove away from the café. "Thanks," he said as he waved good-bye.

Once all the boys and girls were cleaned and fed, Dr. Tim started examining each child. The little girl in his office was very sick. Tim was sure that she had developed whooping cough, which was bad for a small child. After speaking with the woman that was in charge of the children, he was told that Nettie was five years old. She had only had that bad cough for two days.

The other girls were very good patients and were enjoying their full stomachs and clean beds. They all giggled and smiled as

Dr. Tim held their small wrists and listened to their hearts. Some of the children had a mild fever, but that could be from being undernourished and having infected sores.

The older boys fussed about bathing, but Rae could tell that deep down they all felt better once they were clean. They all stood straight and tall while Dr. Tim checked their young bodies. Several of them had big red welts across their backs. When he asked who had hit them, they clammed up.

Mr. and Mrs. Fillmore said that they had agreed to take the children as far as McBain because the driver of the wagon had taken sick in Pine Hill, a town about thirty miles south of Limason. The old man had developed a bad cold and couldn't continue on. The pay was good, and it was a way that they could travel to McBain. They had plenty of time to get there because the train would be passing through McBain Wednesday of the next week.

Sheriff Murphy came over to the infirmary to see what was going on. Rebecca at the café told him that there was a wagon of sick children in town and Dr. Tim was caring for them.

"Thanks for coming, Murphy," said Tim. "You can help me get rid of some scrum." After seeing the welts on the boys' backs, Tim's anger knew no boundaries. He wanted to stomp that drunken fool into the ground. He took several deep breaths and decided that this couple wouldn't get a chance to hurt the children ever again.

Tim walked out on the porch where Mrs. Fillmore was sitting. Mr. Fillmore had returned from the saloon, stinking to high heaven of cheap whiskey. Tim gave the couple a hard stare and said, "I'm taking charge of the children from here on out. You two can get in that wagon and head onto McBain. These children will not be traveling with you. If you deserve any pay, then you can get it from whomever in McBain. I will see that these children are placed in a nice home in Houston. They will not be mistreated by anyone while in my care. Do you understand me?"

"But we have to deliver the children in order to get our money!" slurred Mr. Fillmore.

"You should have thought of that before you took a stick to those small boys. Now, you have just five minutes to leave Limason or Sheriff Murphy will give you a nice clean bed in his jail. I don't take kindly to people beating small, sick children."

"They needed—" cried the old woman, but before she could continue, her husband grabbed her arm and ushered her off the porch and into their wagon. He told her to hush her mouth.

Sheriff Murphy and Dr. Tim watched the wagon as it headed out of town. "Well, it looks like you got a passel of young'uns to look after for a while," Murphy said as he laughed and shook his head.

"After I am sure they're all well, I'll send them to my children's home in Houston. Judd and Patty will care for them. I hate that orphan train. The people pick over the children like they are buying livestock. They are looking for someone to work their fields or be a house servant. They separate brothers and sisters without a care in the world. I attended a church service many years ago and saw how the good Christians chose the children. It broke my heart. I know Hannah and I will have our hands full for the next couple weeks, but I couldn't let that man and woman care for these kids any longer."

"Listen," said Tim. "Miss Ollie is singing to the children." Dr. Tim, Hannah, and Rae looked into the big room where the small girls were laying in beds. Miss Ollie held one of the smaller girls in her lap as she rocked and hummed a lullaby. Everyone was tired from helping to draw water and fill tub after tub with hot water. It was exhausting work, but seeing the sweet smiles on the eleven small children was worth the effort.

"I guess I better get Jeremiah and get our few supplies and head home. I'll bring Ollie some clean clothes in the morning, and I will come after I feed my men folk and help with the children. I'll gather some food and bring it too," said Rae. "At church tomorrow maybe we can get some of the other ladies to volunteer to help us cook and feed the children. We can get Smithy to open his store and purchase clothes and shoes for all of them. I know that Jesse will want to help."

"Listen to me, Rae. Please keep Hope home. Will may have to hog-tie her. I don't want her around these sick children. And as for the expense for the children, I'll take care of all that. If you just help Hannah, I will appreciate it very much. Esther will help too, but I need her to watch the little one in my office. I'm afraid she may be contagious if she does have the whooping cough," Tim said as he helped her in the carriage as Jeremiah was unhitching the reins. "See you tomorrow."

After the church service, Rosie and Justice talked to Ms. Rae about helping with the children. "I want to help out, but one of us needs to stay at the farm and help with the chores. Justice wants to volunteer to help Ollie and Hannah with the children," Rosie said as she watched Justice walk across the street to the infirmary.

"I'm sure her help will be appreciated. The men should be arriving home tomorrow from their trip. Jesse is not going to be happy with me. He won't like it one bit that Ollie is in town caring for those little sick children. He loves that old woman," said Rae as she walked over to greet Mrs. Downey.

"Rae, I will be glad to spend the afternoon cooking some good hot soup for the children. I will have Matt bring it to the infirmary once it is ready. I'll make some cornbread to go with it." Mrs. Downey was hurrying to her carriage eager to be on her way home to start cooking. "Rosie, you hurry along now, you hear. You can help me cut up vegetables after lunch."

"I better go for now. Try to keep those two old women from working themselves to death. Justice never knows when to rest, and I'll sure Miss Ollie is just like that," said Rosie.

After a few days, the children seemed to be better. The fever had disappeared and the coughing only returned if the children were running and playing too hard. Every day, Ollie and Justice put the children outside to play under the big shade trees behind the infirmary while they poured hot water and mopped the tile floors. Dr. Tim had given up scolding the ladies for doing so much manual labor that some younger people could do. Talking to Miss Ollie and Justice was like talking to the wind; your own voice came bouncing back to you with no recognition coming from them.

The smaller child was kept isolated, but she didn't have whooping cough. She had flu that soon turned into pneumonia because of not having proper care. But after receiving good, hot food and cool alcohol rubs several times a day, she was recovering nicely.

Several of the people of Limason wanted to adopt a child, but Tim had refused their offers. Most of the people only wanted one boy or girl. After talking with the older boys, it was discovered that the dozen children had come from only three separate families. Dr. Tim was not going to allow the children to be separated from their siblings. At the children's home, called the orphanage in Houston, the children were never adopted unless the family took all the brothers and sisters of a family. The home was a nice place, and Tim felt that it was more important for the children to live and grow together than have one mother and father. The home had house mothers, Negros, and white ladies that cared for a group of children and most of them grew to love that individual as a mama. They were given everything that a child needed, except their own home. Once the child reached the age of eighteen, he could leave and go out into the world knowing that he always had a place to return to.

The older boys were very thankful that they were going to be allowed to keep their families together. They had endured enough hardships in their young lives, and Dr. Tim was giving them a chance to have a nice place to live, work, and be able to stay together.

Justice and Ollie had worked every day, with Ollie staying most nights at the infirmary. Justice had to travel only five miles home each day, whereas Ollie would have had to travel ten miles to get home. Hope had whined and pouted every day because she couldn't go into town and help with the children. Rae suggested that Rosie and Hope organize the ladies of Limason to cook food and donate more clothes for the children. Ollie and Esther had grown very much attached to many of the children, but they knew it would soon be time for them to leave Limason.

Dr. Tim organized a small wagon train to take the children on to McBain to catch the train headed to Houston. Judd and some of the older boys would meet the children in Houston. Tim, Hannah, Ollie, and Esther hugged each child and wished them well. Tim had assured them that they would have a good home until they were ready to go out on their own. Rev. Anderson came and said a sweet prayer of farewell to the small wagon train of happy, well children. Ollie and Esther shed a few tears as they all waved until the wagons were out of sight.

20

After several weeks had passed, Tater was awakened by a strong arm pulling on him, demanding that he get up and eat. "We'll head for the field in five minutes. Here's your breakfast," Tally shouted as he purposely dropped the food down on the dirty barn floor.

Reaching down in the hay, Tater grabbed up the piece of hard, crusted bread and a cold, fried pork chop. He wiped it clean on his dirty pants. He was so hungry that he stuffed it in his mouth and washed it down with a cup of warm, stale water. He had learned to eat whatever the old man gave him. He needed strength to endure all the work. Some mornings his emotions would get the best of him—fear, hunger, and being so angry it was hard to hold back tears.

"Stop that sniveling, you big, overgrown titty baby before I give you something to cry about." In all the weeks that Tater had been away from Rosie and Bud, he had not shed more than a single tear. He tried to never show any sign of weakness in front of his mama's crazy husband.

Tater's new muscles ached, and the blisters around his ankles hurt so badly. He wanted to collapse back down to the hard barn floor. No matter how much pain he was in, he tried to go about the work in the field without showing any emotion. He was determined to go on until he got the chance to escape. He could have made a run for it plenty of times, but he would never leave this place without his baby brother.

Out in the corn field, the old man gave him his orders. He couldn't stop working until all the corn was pulled from the stalks and stuffed in big bags. The bags would have to be dragged to the end of each row and tossed upon a flatbed wagon. This wasn't a job for one man, much less a single boy. Normally, a crew of neighboring men and boys would help a farmer with this big chore.

Tater was gripped with anger. He wanted to smash the old man's head in with the big sharp tool he held. He dreaded the hard work in the field, but the end of the day was worse. He never knew what mood the old man would be in or if he was going to beat him with his riding crop just to be mean. The least little thing would trigger his anger. Afterward, he would be chained and made to sit in the foul smelling barn until he fell asleep. He might get supper or not.

The barn was filled with unnerving silence. His mind tumbled with memories of home—Bud and Rosie. He missed the farm, his new home; he missed his new friends, Matt, Missy, Lil' Jess, and Claire. He had to continue to be strong so he could escape this nightmare and return home.

Earlier the next morning, Tater's mama visited him out in the barn. She was carrying a crying Boo on her hip. "I can't make this young'un eat or stop crying. There's nothing wrong with him. Here's your breakfast and Boo's. I brought out a couple of nappies. Tally said that you could stay chained and watch him while I ride into town with him." She stood Boo on the ground next to Tater and said, "Make him eat and stop that confounded crying. Tally scares me when he's around the boy. I'm afraid he's going to hurt him. We'll be gone for several hours. Don't you dare let him get away from you and wonder away? I'll beat you myself if you do, you hear me?"

Tater only glared at his mama as she walked out of the barn, closing the door behind her. He couldn't believe that they were leaving him alone to care for Boo. It had been weeks that he had watched and waited for a chance like this; an answer to his prayers—a miracle to say the very least. This would be his chance to take Boo and hightail it away from this hell hole. The old crazy man never thought in a million years that he could get away because he was chained. They were going to leave him alone and be gone for hours. Once the wagon had pulled away from the farmhouse, Tater slipped his ankles out of the leg-irons and peeked out the barn door making sure that they had really left.

"Thank you, Lord! Now is my chance to escape this nightmare!" Tater prayed out loud.

"Come to me, Boo, and eat your food. This might be all we get for a while because you and I are going home. You want to see Rosie? Let's eat and get out of here while the gitting is good!"

Tater changed the baby's nappy and carried him into the house. He filled his knapsack with several cans of beans, a small knife, couple of spoons, and a tin cup. He grabbed a few more clean nappies. Going into the bedroom, he got two blankets, two pair of pants for Boo, and made a bedroll. He found his cowboy boots and tied them around his neck. He tossed the knapsack and bedroll over his head and let it drape down his side. He eased Boo carefully onto his sore back. He swallowed, fighting back the pain and said to his little brother, "We're going home."

Relieved to be away from his mama's farm, he trudged down the side of the narrow road. After several hours of hiking down the pig trail, he began to pant from the heavy load that he carried. He had been starved, and his body didn't have the stamina it once had. The large knapsack with food supplies for several days along with Boo on his back was sapping his strength. Boo had fallen asleep, and his little body was deadweight. The bruising on Tater's back and ribs from the last beating he had taken from Mr. Shire was almost more than he could bare with Boo pressing against the fresh wounds. He was struggling to breathe while carrying such a heavy load. The skin circling his ankles was rubbed raw from the big leg-irons that he had been forced to wear and made wearing his boots impossible. Walking on the uneven ground and thick underbrush had his feet bleeding. But he couldn't think of any of his physical wounds. Getting as far away from his mama and Mr. Shire was foremost in his young mind now.

Feeling almost defeated, Tater realized that he would have to leave Boo somewhere safe. He would never make it back to Limason carrying him. He should have been able to leave him at the farm and then have Bud and the law come back after him. But after he had entered the kitchen one morning and saw Boo gagged and a large red streak across his rosy cheek, he knew that he could never desert him even for a few days. He had heard the old man tell his mama that if Boo didn't stop screaming, he was going to toss him down the well. With the way the old man had treated him from the very beginning of his stay on the farm, he had no doubt that he would soon harm Boo. Mama had run out of patience with Boo's screaming too. Each time she got as close as within two feet of him, he would scream bloody murder. Martha Anne didn't know how to make him stop crying, but she protected Boo from Tally's anger. They were constantly fighting. Shouts of nasty words could be heard all the way to the barn.

After traveling all day and late into the evening, Tater couldn't go any further. He had to stop and rest. After selecting a secluded area, he built a small fire and sat a can of opened beans next to the hot coals. He had taken Boo's wet clothes off and laid them across a big bush to dry. Boo was learning to squat and do his business and pee standing upright. He still had accidents as Rosie would call them when he dirtied his pants. Tater held Boo in his arms and snuggled him close to his chest. He loved the baby more than anything. Tears flowed down Tater's cheeks as the pain of his wounds began to burn and hurt. He didn't know how in the world he could carry Boo any further.

"Help me, Jesus," he prayed silently into Boo's little body as he cradled him in his tired, sore arms. Tater finally decided that crying and feeling sorry for himself wasn't going to help anything. He laid Boo down on the ground in one of the bedrolls next to him and covered him with his favorite blanket.

As Tater sat rubbing his bleeding feet, he felt like he was being watched. Being raised in the swamp, a person had to depend on their senses. Not a chirping sound from the birds, katydids, or frogs. It was too quiet. *Please, please don't let that old man find us*, he prayed to himself. He thought that it couldn't be Tally he heard because he would have stormed through the brush like a wild boar. Quickly he stood and yelled, "Who's there?" Not a sound was heard but the beating of his own heart. Tater was sure he wasn't imagining things.

"I've got a gun, and I'm going to shoot in the brush if you don't show yourself," he yelled again.

A little barefoot black boy with big round eyes stepped out of the bushes. He looked to be about the age of eight wearing dirty overalls and a floppy hat. "Please, mister, don't shoot me," he cried while his bottom lip trembled.

Tater was surprised to see a child. "Where'd you come from?"

The child pointed to the east.

Earlier Tater had noticed an old farmhouse and barn set back off from the main road. "Do you live with your pa and mama?"

He shook his head quickly up and down.

"Are your folks nice? Are they good to you?"

The little boy looked a little confused at Tater's question, but he answered. "Shore," replied the little tyke as he looked at Boo lying on the ground.

Standing away from the fire, the night air had turned cooler. "Look, I need some help with my baby brother. That's him lying over on the blanket. Could you take us to your house—now?" Tater asked the little fellow.

The little boy looked at Tater's bloody arms. He turned to walk away and stopped. He gave Tater a wave that suggested he follow him. Tater quickly put out the fire and eased down to the ground and lifted Boo into his arms. He thought for just a second that he might faint. The pain coming from his back was almost unbearable. He couldn't think about how bad he hurt. He left the beans in the ashes and his knapsack near a log. *Please, Lord, let these people help me*, Tater said to the dark sky.

Tater followed the small child across a knee-high corn field into a clean swept yard. Light was shining from the two front screen windows of the house, casting a glow on the ground. A big red-necked rooster was walking around in the yard while two large geese were flapping their wings and honking. Voices were coming through the screen doorway from inside the house. A big black and gray-speckled hound dog with floppy ears came out from under the front porch showing a mouth full of angry teeth. His hair stood up on his back, and he began to bark. After recognizing the boy, his long tail began to wag, and he started leaping upon the boy.

"Down, Bugger," yelled the little boy to his dog. "Get back, Getty and Louise," he shooed the two big geese.

"Is that you, Zac? You best get yourself in this house this here minute. You have missed supper, and I'm a good mind to let you go to bed hungry!"

"Mama, Pa, I need you," Zac yelled. "Some boy's hurt!"

"Land sakes! You hear that, old man? We're coming," cried his mama.

Tater couldn't continue to stand any longer so he went down on his knees still holding onto the baby with all the strength he had left in his bruised body. He hung his head down and rested it on Boo's small shoulder. The dog raced over and was sniffing Tater. Zac's folks rushed out the screen door into the yard. His pa looked at Tater and pushed the hound dog away, calling for Zac to hold him back.

"Joseph," said the old man to his older son, "take the baby boy out of his arms and give him to your ma. Then we'll carry this young fellow into the house." The older man kneeled down beside Tater and asked if he could walk. Before Tater could answer, he asked if the law was after him.

The older man could tell that someone had beat this child recently because dried blood was still on his upper arms. He couldn't imagine what his back must look like as he noticed his raggedy torn shirt and filthy pants.

Tater shook his head and said that he didn't believe that they had been missed from the farm as yet. "We left early this morning, and I have walked most of the day."

Zac told his folks how he had walked upon the boys in the woods.

Zac's mama took Boo into their bedroom, and she laid him on the bed. She quickly looked him over to make sure he wasn't hurt anywhere. There was a bruise under his right eye, but he looked like a perfect little angel sleeping. She made a pallet for him to lie down on the floor. She didn't need for this baby to pee on her nice clean sheets. Hurrying back into the kitchen area, she immediately ordered Joseph to fletch a fresh pail of water from the well and place it on the stove. Zac told his pa that Tater had a knapsack of items left at his campsite. Pa instructed him to take Joseph and go get his things. "Maybe he had some clean nappies for the baby." It had been years since they had a young baby in the house.

Tater thanked the people who introduced themselves to him as the Brown family. They lived on this place, but Mr. Brown worked for a big farm about a mile away every day. They didn't get too many visitors.

Mrs. Brown warmed a plate of cornbread, lima beans, and several pieces of fried bacon. She poured Tater a glass of cold milk. He gobbled down the plate of food and looked like he was still hungry. A few minutes later, another bowl of cornbread and beans sat in front of him. Laughing, Mrs. Brown told him to eat a little slower so he could taste the food. Tater blushed and thanked her for her generosity. Mrs. Brown wanted to take care of his cuts and bruises, but she felt he needed something in his stomach first. The way he ate his supper proved to her that he had been nearly starved to death.

Joseph and Zac returned with Tater's knapsack and the wet clothes that he had spread over the bushes. "We didn't leave any sign of them at the campsite in case they have been followed," Joseph whispered softly to his pa.

Tater told them about how he and Boo had come to live in McBain. He didn't go into detail about how they had lived in the swamp of Louisiana and how their mama had abandoned them when Boo was only weeks old.

Once he started telling his story about how mean Tally Shire, his mama's new husband, was to him, they never doubted one word. Fresh and old bruises were all over Tater's thin frame. His ankles bore the proof of leg-irons. Tears streamed down Mrs. Brown big eyes as she put salve on Tater's ankles and on his back. She had Tater lay down on Joseph's bed as she cleaned where the whip had cut lash marks into his tan back and upper arms.

"Lord, child, you have endured more than a grown man could have. The good Lord has been watching over you for shore." Mrs. Brown wiped her eyes and then she got so mad she felt like spitting. "You don't have nothing to fear here, son. Mr. Brown and I won't allow that fool man to come over here and get you. Not as long as I got breath in this here body!"

"I need to get home. Back to Limason," said Tater. "My sister Rosie and her husband will take care of me and Boo. They'll keep us safe. Is it possible that I could borrow a horse or mule to ride home? I could make so much better time if I could travel alone. Would you keep Boo here with you until my folks return for him?"

"Mercy, son, you shore got spunk," laughed Mr. Brown. "I tell you what I'll do. I only have one horse, but you can borrow him. Better yet, I'll send Joseph with you." Mr. Brown patted his oldest son on the shoulder. "This here, boy, is a great guide, and he will protect you from harm. What you say, Joseph? Will you see this boy home?"

"Yes, sir. We can leave early in the morning. We can be there in less than two days, if the weather permits," Joseph replied with his chest pushed out. He was so proud of the things that his pa had said about him.

"I shore would like to see him stay here for at least another day or so. His cuts are still raw. They could start bleeding again. But if he can make it home, his folks needs to see what that no-account has done to him," said Mrs. Brown.

21

A FEW DAYS AFTER the dance, Justice and Rosie were working in their fall garden when Dr. Tim drove up in his black carriage. "Morning ladies. Rosie, is Bud around the place anywhere? I've got some news back from the detective that I hired, and I feel you both need to hear what he wrote."

"Sure thing, Dr. Tim. Let me go and ring the dinner bell. Bud will come running 'cause it ain't near suppertime," said Rosie. As Rosie raced around the house, Justice laid her hoe down and watched Dr. Tim get down from the carriage and tie his horse to the hitching post.

"Come on and sit on the porch. I'll get you a cup of coffee," said Justice. As Justice walked into the house, Tim looked at the farm. It had not changed much since Hannah had lived there after Clay Patterson had died and left her responsible for his two children, Little John and Mary Beth. She only lived there about a week before he moved her into his small house in town while he had to go to Houston to settle his uncle's estate. Looking around some more, he saw that Bud had made a lot of repairs to the place and it was looking very nice.

It wasn't but a few minutes before Bud came running across the field and opened the gate. He saw Dr. Tim's carriage and a thought rushed through his mind that something was wrong.

Tim was sitting on the porch in one of the new rockers that Bud had purchased the last time he went to town. He was always bringing a small surprise for Rosie. Tim stood when he saw

Bud and reached out his hand for a handshake. "Welcome, Dr. Tim. What's wrong?" Bud couldn't wait a minute longer without asking what they were all thinking.

"It's like this, Bud. Old Moses at the telegraph office got a telegram from my detective a few weeks ago, and it contained some information that we needed to know. Moses asked his boy to take the message to me. This morning, he found the telegram unopened lying on the floor under a small table. He remembered as he talked to his son about the telegram, the stagecoach driver came in and slammed big bags of mail on his desk. He was madder than a hornet, and he stormed out. Well, when he found this note, he reopened it and hurried it over to me himself. He sure sorry, but at least we know what's happening with the boys."

"So what's going on?" Bud asked with his fist clenched at his side. He felt cold chills run down his back because he knew the news wasn't going to be good.

"Mr. Blackwell, the detective, wrote this: 'Need to come to McBain and get the boys. The older boy is being mistreated. Please hurry. Going to report to sheriff in McBain.'"

Dr. Tim folded the paper and sighed. "Hopefully, the sheriff has already ridden out there and removed Tater and Boo from your mama's home. You never know what authority the sheriff may have since the judge gave them temporary custody."

"I'm going! Let me saddle my horse and fill my saddlebags with some supplies. I'll need to rent a wagon when I get there to bring the boys home, but I want to get there as quickly as possible. I'll take two horses."

"That's a good idea. Two horses will make a faster trip," said Dr. Tim. "When you get there, please send me a telegram and let me know what's going on. I'll send word out here to Rosie."

"No, I want to go with you, Bud! Please let me go and get my boys," she said as tears streamed down her rosy cheeks. Justice stood and pulled her into her arms. "Rosie, Bud can make better time by himself. Let him go. He will bring them home."

Rosie looked at Justice and laid her head on her shoulder and cried her heart out. "I can't believe Mama let that old man hurt my Tater. No one has ever harmed a hair on his precious head. He's such a good boy," Rosie cried.

Dr. Tim patted Rosie on her back as he walked down the porch and boarded his carriage.

Bud rushed over to Dr. Tim and said softly, "What did the detective say about the abuse? Don't hold back. I want to know what that man has done to Tater."

"Bud, I read you the telegram. It has to be bad for the detective to say for someone to come and get them. That's all I know." Tim shook his head. "Bud, let the law take care of him. You just bring the boys home. You're a father now and those boys need you here—not in jail. Tater's a strong young man."

"Thanks for the advice. Pray for me that I have the strength not to kill him."

Bud walked over to Rosie and took her in his arms. "I'm leaving in a few minutes. Please help me prepare for the trip. I'm so sorry, Rosie, that this has happened, but as God is my witness, I will bring our boys home."

Back in McBain, Tally and Martha Anne had been gone from their farm most of the morning. When they arrived home, they were beside themselves when they found the two boys missing. Tally saw the leg-irons lying in the hay. Smirking, he said to his wife, "Look, old woman. I told you over and over that brat of yours was in cahoots with that old voodoo woman. She cast a spell on me and this farm. I don't know how he did it, but he was the one under my window whispering that crazy chant."

"Crazy or not, Tater did a good job on you and the vegetable garden. I don't know how she did it or what he did, but they destroyed your manhood, not me." She threw back her head and laughed like she was crazy as a loon. "I'm glad they got away! My baby *hated me* and I *hate you*! You have beaten me for the last time and I'm gitting as far from you as I can. You can't beat *my son* ever again either."

"You think you're going to leave me? I'll kill you before I let you leave this place." He advanced toward her with his hand raised as to strike her but stopped as she didn't cow down.

"Go ahead and do your worst because if you don't kill me, I'll chop off some of your body parts when you do go to sleep." Martha Anne went to the house and started packing her few items. She was a fool to have married that old man. As long as they weren't married, he had treated her kindly.

"Don't think to take anything from here with you," her husband yelled. "This whole kit and caboodle belongs to me!" *Let the fool woman go—she's crazy as they come*, he thought.

Tally heard a commotion in the front of the house. He came out of the barn and saw the sheriff from McBain. He had seen the sheriff in town earlier this morning while they were there.

"What brings you out here, Sheriff? I saw you in town earlier."

"Well, I would have been out here a while back, but I had to be in Houston for a murder trial that took a lot longer than expected. Just got back last night," replied the sheriff. Looking around the farm yard, the sheriff didn't see any sign of the two boys that he had come to check on.

"Where are your wife's boys, Mr. Shire?" the sheriff asked as he continued to look around the place. "I came out here to see them."

"Well, you know, I ain't rightly sure where they are. We just got home a little while ago and they aren't here. Must be off playing somewhere," he said as he spit a stream of tobacco juice on the ground.

The sheriff got down off his horse and walked him over to the corral and tied him to a fence post. He opened the big barn door and stepped inside. Seeing the leg-irons laying in one of the stalls, he asked, "What are you doing with those things?"

When Tally didn't answer him, the sheriff reached down and picked them up. He saw dried blood all over them. "These have been used recently. Who's been wearing them, Mr. Shire?"

"Listen, Sheriff. The older boy kept running off, so I had to fix it so he couldn't run away. The judge said that he was to stay with us for two months, but he had no manners and was very disrespectful to his mama."

"So with leg-irons on and giving him this nice clean stall as a place to sleep, you taught him to have manners and to show respect to his mama. Is that right?" The sheriff had noticed the dirty blanket and bowl with a dry rag in it.

"That's right. But I tell you he's a stubborn cuss. I had to give him a whipping or two to keep him in line. Young people today ain't like we were when we were growing up."

"So let me get this straight, from the horse's mouth, you might say. You placed him in leg-irons, made him live in a stall near stinking horse manure, and whipped him to keep him in line. Did he help you in the fields and care for the animals?"

"Shore! Can't have no lazy good for nothing boy lying around all day. Now, he's a good worker. He works from sunup to sundown every day. Just about have all my corn ready for the mill," said the old man, bragging on the work being done on his place.

"Mr. Shire, I've heard enough. Now, I want you to go find the boys while I talk to your wife. I'm giving you ten minutes to call them up to the house."

"I ain't sure which way they went!"

"Look for them—or you'll be sorry you didn't."

The sheriff walked over to the screen door and knocked real loud. "Mrs. Shire, please come outside. I need to speak with you."

Martha Anne came to the door and looked at the sheriff. "What's wrong, Sheriff?"

"Where are your boys? Your husband said that they are off playing somewhere." Martha Anne looked over at her husband as he walked out behind the barn.

"Now, I am going to ask you again. Where are your boys?"

"We don't know and that's the God's truth. When we got home a little while ago, they were both gone. I'm thinking that Tater and Boo are headed home—to Limason, to Rosie. Why do you want to know about them?"

"I was sent out here to check on them. I should have been out here weeks ago. Word has it that they have been mistreated by your husband, especially, the older boy. After speaking with your husband, I'm sure of it. I have come to remove the boys from your care and hold them until their sister comes for them. The sister would be your daughter too?" asked the sheriff.

"I hope that you can find them. Tater is a headstrong and determined boy. He will hide and walk every step to Limason if that is what it takes. He took a lot of beatings from my man. That crazy fool has beat me for the last time. I'm leaving him. I done told him right before you rode up."

"I'm going to have your man hitch up a wagon to ride into town just in case we find the boys on our way. If you are ready to leave, you can ride in the wagon. You can say your good-byes to your husband because Mr. Shire is going to spend a few days in my jail. I know that he hurt your older son. There was a detective watching from the woods as he administered unnecessary punishment. I don't allow any man to beat upon his wife and children in my county. He's going to jail until I can talk to the judge who's handling this case."

Once the trio made it back to town, the sheriff locked Tally Shire in his jail. Martha Anne moved into the boarding house after she checked the train schedule. The sheriff went to the telegraph office and sent a wire to Dr. Tim. He told him that the boys were missing, but he was sure that they were headed to Limason on foot.

22

B UD LEFT LIMASON, riding fast and hard to McBain. He
only stopped to water his two horses and let them rest for
a little while. He rode into the town of McBain early the next
morning. He went into the city café and ordered some coffee
and information. The waitress was friendly and told him that
the old Peddler's place was about five miles straight out the main
road. "You can't miss it. But what do you want with the old man?"
she asked.

"I'm got some business with him and his wife."

"Well, I don't like to speak out of turn or get involved in
anybody else's business, but the sheriff locked the old man up
late yesterday afternoon."

Bud looked around and sat down at a table next to the door.
"Why? What did you hear?"

"Why? Oh, you mean, why did the sheriff arrest him? It was
something about mistreating his kids. Shucks, I didn't know a
man could be arrested for beating up on his kids or his wife.
That's a new one on me." Bud was stunned and didn't make a
reply to her comment.

"You may as well have some food with that coffee 'cause the
sheriff won't be in for another hour. He eats all his meals here."

Bud was hungry so he mumbled, "sure thing." The waitress
walked away to go and get him a big, hardy breakfast. The good-
looking fellow looked like he needed it.

The food was good and hot. He didn't realize how hungry he
was. All he could do was ponder about Tater and Boo. Where

were they? Who were they staying with? Where was their mama? It was all he could do to sit and wait for the sheriff to come. Just when he thought he couldn't wait any longer, the sheriff came walking through the door. The jingle of the doorbell made Bud jump.

"Sheriff, I need to speak with you," said Bud.

"Wait just one minute, young man. Let me get a sip of hot coffee and then I can tackle your problem."

"Man, that's good stuff. Come and sit back down and have a fresh cup of coffee," said the sheriff.

"No, thanks," Bud replied. "I've had a few already while waiting for you."

"What can I do for you, Mister...?"

"I'm Bud Downey from Limason. I understand Mr. Shire is in your jail," said Bud.

"I'd put that old bastard under the jail if I could get away with it."

"I've come to get the boys and take them home. I'm married to Rosie, their sister. My wife raised the boys after their mama abandoned them several years ago. One day, their mama shows up with her new husband, Mr. Shire, and she wants them to come and live with her. After going to court, the judge gave her temporary custody for two months. Tater didn't want to go, but he went because of the baby. The telegram that Dr. Tim O'Riley received said that the boys have been mistreated by them. Where are the boys now?"

"Yesterday, I rode out to their farm. Mr. Shire said that the boys were not there, but he led me to believe that they were off playing. He didn't fool me one minute. Once I saw the leg-irons with dried blood on them, I knew that he was lying. He told me how he worked the boy in his corn field. He bragged how he had to whip the boy into shape. He had to teach him respect and manners. After speaking with his wife, she told me that the older boy took the baby and fled while they were gone to town. She seemed happy that they had left. After packing her bag, she rode in the wagon with her husband and booked herself a room at the boarding house. She plans to catch a train today and head as far away from her husband as she can get."

Bud was gripping the table top so hard that his knuckles were white. He wanted to know where Tater and Boo were now. The sheriff was telling him how bad Tater has been mistreated. Anger like he had never felt before began building up inside him. He was struggling to sit still and concentrate while the sheriff rambled on about how he had gone out to the farm to get the boys only to find them missing.

"Please, Sheriff. Tell me where the boys are now?"

"That's what I have been trying to tell you. They left on foot. I'm sure that they are headed to Limason. I plan to get some men to ride with me this morning and scout them out. I know your boy will hide from us. He'll be afraid that Mr. Shire is after him."

"I'll be glad for your help. I'll going to take care of my animals and rent or buy a wagon with two fresh horses. The boys will need a wagon for the ride home."

"Sheriff, I want to go to the jail and see that old man. I would like to have five minutes of visitation with him," said Bud.

"Now, son, you know I can't allow you to get in that cell with him, as much as I would like to see you pound his sorry ass into the floor," said the sheriff with a small grin on his face.

"Never fear now! When I tell the judge how your boy was mistreated, that old man will be run out of this side of the country. He better not ever show his face in these parts again. Now I'll see you back here in about an hour. It will take me a little while to round up some men," said the sheriff.

After renting a wagon and two horses, Bud drove over to the dry goods store and purchased several blankets, cans of peaches, and a bag of hard candy. He wanted to have something for the boys to eat once he found them. He went to the telegraph office and sent a wire to Dr. Tim, explaining that the boys had run away from their mama and were headed to Limason on foot. The sheriff had placed Mr. Shire in jail until the circuit judge came back into town. Please tell my pa so he can start looking for the boys from that direction.

It was midmorning before the sheriff and a group of ten men met Bud. They headed through McBain looking for any signs of the boys off the main road. The sheriff informed the men to look high and low, in ditches and in caves. "This young man is not going to want us to find him. He's running scared."

Bud called to Tater and yelled all morning long as he drove the wagon slowly down the main road. He wished he could ride his horse, but he felt the wagon would be needed once the boys were discovered.

Back home in Limason. Dr. Tim rode out to the Downey's place and told Bud's family what had taken place in McBain. Mr. Downey, Luke, and Matt quickly saddled their horses, while Mrs. Downey prepared some food and bedrolls to be tied to the pack horse. Tim continued over to Jesse and Will Maxwell's place and informed them of the missing boys. Immediately, Jesse, Little Jess, Will, Jeremiah, and John joined in the search. Rider wasn't happy, but someone had to stay home and take care of the ranch.

Ollie and Rae were beside themselves worrying over Rosie's brothers. Hope insisted that Claire drive her and Jacob over to be with Rosie and Justice for a while. Hope knew that Rosie would want to stay home while they waited for news.

Rosie was about crazy with worry. She wanted so bad to saddle a horse and head out to McBain, but Dr. Tim said that she was needed at home. "Bud, the sheriff, and a group of men are looking for them and all of your friends are traveling in that direction. Surely, they will be found soon." Tim tried to reassure Rosie.

As the sun went down on the town of Limason, the only lights that were shining bright were the lanterns and music from the Golden Nugget and Dr. Tim's office. A lantern was on the outside of the sheriff's office, but the place was dark. Both boys were exhausted from riding all day.

"Joseph, Dr. Tim will help us find the sheriff. I want the sheriff to know why I ran away before my mama tells him a bunch of lies and they try to send me back to her."

"Do you trust this doctor?" Joseph asked as he reached back to touch Tater's leg.

"With my life, he's a good man."

Tater and Joseph rode their horses over to the front of the office just as Dr. Tim was backing out of the door. Tim turned and froze. He was never so surprised to see anyone in his life. Tater was sitting behind a tall black boy on a horse. The horse was wheezing and shaking his head side to side. He had sweat and saliva around his nose and mouth and white sudsy foam was caked down his neck and front legs. The poor animal had been rode long and hard. He looked like he was ready to fall. The boys didn't look much better.

"Dr. Tim," whispered Tater as he held out his hand while sliding off the horse hitting the ground in a dead faint.

"Lord, have mercy," declared Dr. Tim. "Help me, son," Tim said to the young man still sitting on the poor animal.

Tim handed Joseph his office key while he stretched Tater out on the ground, checking for any broken bones. Even in the dim light, Tim could see the bruises, red welts, and dried blood on Tater's arms and neck. As gentle as possible, he lifted the young man, who appeared to be skin and bones and carried him into his office.

"Young man, run over to the boarding house and get Sheriff Murphy." Joseph gave Tim a questionable look and he told him that the boarding house was around the corner at the end of the street. "Tell him to hurry."

Tim immediately placed a few sticks of firewood in the stove to start a fire. He placed the tea kettle filled with water on the burner. He needed to clean the dried blood off Tater's wounds so he could begin doctoring them. He grabbed a bowl of chicken stew out of the icebox and set it on the counter.

"Tim," yelled Sheriff Murphy.

"Here! I'm in the kitchen. Thank goodness you were back. Did this young man fill you in on Tater?"

"No. He said to come to your office, that's all." Joseph stood, watching the two men talk.

"Joseph, I need for you to warm this food. Can you do that while I attend to Tater? There's plenty for you to eat as soon as it's hot, all right?" Tim asked. "You can wash up in the water closet down the hall."

"Yes, sir," replied the young man. "I need to care for my horse."

"Let me talk with the doc here and then I will see to your horse. You just sit and eat as soon as it is ready," said Sheriff Murphy.

"Thank you." Joseph placed the stew in a big pot and placed it on another burner on the stove. He was starving for something besides cold beans out of a can.

As Tim undressed Tater, he was glad that the boy was still unconscious. The pain that he must be in would be unbearable for a grown man. Dr. Tim rubbed a place on Tater's arm with alcohol and gave him a shot for pain. He would sleep the rest of the night. While cleaning his wounds, he could only imagine what the boy endured at the hands of his stepfather. The sores and deep cuts around his ankles would take a while to heal, but the whip marks on his back would be with him for the rest of his days. Some of the marks the whip cut into the skin were very deep. He had been beaten over and over and each time the marks would be reopened. By the time, Tim finished cleaning Tater's wounds he was shaking from anger.

"You know, Murphy, if I had that man in my sights right this minute, I don't know what I would do to him. I understand that he has been arrested and jail is most likely the safest place for him to be. I know that Bud will want to strangle him once he sees how badly Tater has been treated."

"Do you think that you could ride out to Bud's farm and get Rosie? She'll want to be with Tater tonight. I'd like to wait until morning and send for her, but she would skin me alive if I did that."

"Sure thing, but let's talk to that young man in the kitchen and get some information from him," said Sheriff Murphy.

After a brief conversation with Joseph about how Tater had come to his house for help, he explained that Boo had been left at his home with his pa and ma. "I'm to ride back home tomorrow."

"You get a good night's rest, son, and tomorrow, I will ride with you to your place and get the baby. I know Bud and Rosie are going to be mighty grateful for all that your folks have done for their boys."

23

Very late in the evening, Sheriff Murphy got off his horse in front of Bud's farmhouse. The house was dark, but the moon shined brightly, casting a light on the front porch. A light in one of the bedrooms shined in the house. Someone had heard him ride up. As his boots clomped across the front porch to the door, it was opened by the black woman that lived with Bud and Rosie. Rosie stood behind her with a double-barreled shotgun.

"Good evening, ladies. It's me, Sheriff Murphy."

"Oh, Sheriff," said Rosie as she put down the shotgun, which seemed to be as big as she was. "Please, please come in. We're here by ourselves so we have to be very careful of strangers calling in the middle of the night."

"No need to apologize. I'm glad to see that you can take care of yourselves," he replied with a smile on his face. "Listen, Rosie, Dr. Tim has sent me out here to get you. Your brother, Tater is here in Limason at Dr. Tim's office."

"What? Now? Tater's here?" quizzed Rosie not understanding that Tater was here and not in McBain.

"Hurry and get dressed. Tater rode double on a horse from McBain with a young black boy. Your little brother Boo is with this boy's family. He is safe and sound. I'm going in the morning with this young boy and get your baby brother and bring him home."

Rosie rushed into the bedroom and changed out of her nightgown and put on a riding skirt and blouse with her new brown boot shoes. The sheriff didn't know it yet but she would be riding with him to McBain in the morning. *How did Tater get away from Mama with Boo?* Rosie had so many unanswered questions.

"Justice, I hate to leave you here alone. But someone will have to see to the animals in the morning. After you milk the cow, hitch up the small carriage, and come into town to Dr. Tim's office. Why don't you stop over at Bud folk's and ask Samuel to come over here to do the other chores?"

"Don't worry, child. I know what to do. You just go with the sheriff here and take care of our boys. I'll see you in the morning," said Justice.

Once the sheriff and Rosie arrived at Tim's office, she jumped off the back of the sheriff's horse and raced into the office. Tim met Rosie as she dashed down the hall looking for Tater. "Rosie, wait a minute. Tater's asleep. So is Joseph, the young man who helped Tater to get home. Tater has been hurt real bad, but nothing life threatening. His deep wounds and cuts will heal in time."

"Oh my goodness! Why did that man hurt him? Tater is a good boy," cried Rosie as Dr. Tim held her in his arms.

Not waiting for an answer from the sheriff or Dr. Tim, Rosie asked if she could sit beside Tater as he slept. Tim showed Rosie into the room where Tater laid stretched out on his stomach. His ankles had been greased with medicine and wrapped in soft gauze and a thin sheet covered his back. Dr. Tim had cleaned each whip mark out and put medicine on the crisscross marks and gashes. Tater's wounds would feel so much better in the morning.

Early the next morning, as Rosie slept in the chair next to Tater's bed with her head slumped over, Esther came in through the backdoor. She walked over to the stove and noticed that the burners were still warm. She lifted the lid off the burner and placed several pieces of wood in the stove and stroked the fire. Placing coffee grounds in the big blue coffeepot, she put it on the burner and started humming one of her favorite hymns. She walked into the front of the office and noticed Rosie sitting slumped over in a straight chair next to a bed. Rosie must have sensed someone because she jumped wide awake and looked at Esther.

"Morning, Ms. Esther. Tater found his way home last night, but he has been hurt by my mama's husband. Dr. Tim has treated his wounds and gave him medicine to help him rest."

"My lands, child. You been sitting there all night in that hard chair? Come into the kitchen and let me gives you a cup of hot coffee and some breakfast. Dr. Tim and Ms. Hannah will be here in awhile."

"I don't really want to leave Tater. He might wake up soon."

"You just sit there, and I'll bring you a tray."

After Esther walked out of the sick room, Joseph raised up from the next bed. He looked around and stretched his arms high. "Hi," he said as he looked at Rosie.

"Good morning yourself. You must be Joseph. I want to thank you for helping Tater get home. I'm Rosie, Tater's sister."

"I need to get up, madam. If you would leave the room while I dress I won't be but a minute."

"Of course, I'll go in the kitchen with Ms. Esther. She's cooking breakfast. I know that you must be hungry."

As Joseph was dressing in his shirt, pants, and boots, Tater stirred from his deep sleep. Raising his head, he saw Joseph dressing. "You going somewhere?" asked Tater.

"Yep, I am. First breakfast and then back home with the sheriff. He is going to my house and get your little brother and bring him back here."

Rosie heard voices coming from the sickroom. She put her coffee down on the table and raced to Tater's bedside. Stooping down beside his bed, she cried. "Oh, Tater, I'm so sorry. Bud and I had no idea what that old man was doing to you. We were coming to see you in a day or two."

"It's all right, Sis," he said as he rubbed his rough hand on top of her head. "I'm home now and Boo is with a nice family. Joseph's folks are taking real good care of him."

"Bud and half of McBain are looking for you from McBain while Bud's folks along with the Maxwell's are looking for you from this end. And here you are—home."

"I'm sure that crazy husband of Mama's is looking for me too."

"No, he isn't looking for you or anyone else. He's in jail in McBain. Dr. Tim got a wire from Bud saying that they arrested him for mistreating you. So you don't have to worry about him ever again."

"I hope they lose the key and never let that animal out," cried Tater.

"Oh, baby, I'm so sorry—so sorry that I ever let them take you and Boo. Did they hurt Boo?"

"No, they didn't hurt him, but he screamed every time Mama got near him. That was part of the spell that Justice placed on the old man. Boo would scream his head off when Mama was close to him and that drove them both crazy," laughed Tater.

"A spell. Justice put a spell on Mama and Mr. Shire?" Rosie asked, not quite understanding.

Tater realized that he shouldn't have mentioned the spell until he had talked to Justice. "We'll talk about this later, Rosie. Joseph and I are both starving, right, Joseph?" Rosie was still confused about what Tater said about a "spell," but she could tell that he wasn't going to talk about it now.

"Let me go and help Esther with the breakfast. I will be back with a tray for you, Tater. Joseph, you may come and sit at the table in the kitchen. There's coffee or milk to drink," said Rosie.

After Dr. Tim and Ms. Hannah arrived at the office, there seemed to be a dozen patients waiting outside and in the front waiting room. Hannah was thrilled to see Tater, and she told him so. "Tater, all the kids sure have missed you. I know that they will be so happy to know that you are home for good."

"Thanks, Ms. Hannah. I'll glad to be home too. I can't wait to go back to school." Rosie came into Tater's room carrying a tray of hot biscuits, oatmeal, bacon, and eggs.

"School will have to wait for a while, Tater. We'll have to get your back and ankles well before you can attend classes. But you can do some studying at home," said Rosie.

Sheriff Murphy came into the office to get Joseph and to see Tater. "Sure good to see you sitting up and eating a good breakfast, young man. Joseph and I are heading to his home to pick up your little brother. Is there anything you want me to tell his folks?"

"Just thanks again," replied Tater. "They saved my life."

Rosie stepped in the room and told the sheriff that she was traveling with him and Joseph to McBain. "Boo don't take to strangers. I want to go and get my baby. Please don't tell me I can't go with you," Rosie said with misty eyes.

"Gosh, darn, Ms. Rosie. You know I can't refuse to let you go while you got tears in your eyes. Let's go and get you a horse. Bud might be angry with me for allowing you to travel that distance, but he will have to take that up with you."

"Tater, Justice will be here in a little while to help care for you. Please mind Ms. Esther and Ms. Hannah. I don't like leaving you, but you know that Boo will be happy to see me."

"I understand, Sis, I do. You go and maybe you will find Bud too. I sure have missed him."

After Sheriff Murphy, Joseph, and Rosie had ridden over fifteen miles on the rough narrow road toward McBain, they saw a campfire with a dozen men surrounding it. The night air had turned cool, but Sheriff Murphy told Rosie and Joseph to stay out of sight while he investigated the camp. Once he rode closer, he recognized Jesse, Will, and Bud Downey.

"Hi, fellows," called Sheriff Murphy as he rode up to the men.

"Howdy, Murphy," said Jesse. "Are you looking for the boys too?"

"No," he answered with a big grin. "I don't have to look because I have found them already."

"What!" Bud raced over to the sheriff's big bay horse and nearly pulled him off it. "What do you mean you found the boys? Where are they?"

"Just a minute, Rosie, Joseph, you can come now," called Sheriff Murphy.

"Rosie?" whispered Bud. "How did she get here?"

Rosie saw Bud first. She leaped from her small pinto horse. "Oh, Bud, isn't it wonderful?" she said as Bud picked her up off the ground in his arms. "Tater's at home, and we are on our way to get Boo."

The other men all gathered around Rosie, Bud, and Joseph. "Tell us how the boy got home," said Will. "Is he all right?"

"Tater took Boo and ran away from Mama and Mr. Shire while they were gone into town. Joseph's little brother helped Tater get to their home and his folks helped them. Joseph took Tater to Limason on their horse while his folks kept Boo until we could come and get him. That's where we are headed now, to get Boo."

"How bad is Tater hurt, Rosie? The sheriff in McBain said that he arrested the old man for mistreating him, "Bud asked.

Rosie just hung her head. She didn't have the heart to tell Bud how badly the old man had hurt Tater. Joseph spoke for the first time. "Tater has good care now, but he was beaten and starved. He could hardly walk and he'll have marks on his back forever, my pa said."

The men all started talking at once. They were very angry. They talked about taking the old man out of jail and giving him some of his own medicine. Bud held up his hand to quiet the men. "Please, fellows, let's not allow our anger to turn us all into animals. We have to let the law take care of a man like Tally Shire. You all know how I feel about this man, but the main thing is the boys are safe and will be home soon—back to a normal life. I can't thank all of you enough for helping me search for them. If any of you ever need help, I'm your man. Please call on me anytime."

"Oh, Bud, we're just happy for you and Rosie. We'll see you at home." Jesse, Will, John, and Little Jess all filed passed Bud and stopped to give Rosie a hug. "Now the boys will get to use their new rooms that we built," Jeremiah said as he gave Bud a big strong hug. "See you at home."

Bud's Pa, Luke, and Mathew said that they were going to stay the night since they were all settled in with a nice campsite. Sheriff Murphy suggested to Bud, Rosie, and Joseph that they should spend the night as well. "Joseph, we'll get up and be able to get you home before breakfast. I bet your ma is a great cook." Joseph smiled and said that she shore could cook biscuits.

Early the next morning, after Bud said farewell to his pa, Luke, and Mathew, Bud drove the wagon into the front yard of the Brown's place while Rosie and Sheriff Murphy rode on their horses. Joseph jumped off his horse and raced in the front door of his home calling to his folks.

Everyone gathered outside in the yard. Mrs. Brown was holding Boo. He was dressed in a freshly washed shirt and blue denim britches. His blond curls were pushed back from his face, and he looked very content. The bruise on his face had faded.

Rosie got off her horse and walked slowly to Mrs. Brown calling Boo by his name. He shouted, "'osie, 'osie," while holding out his arms, reaching and bucking for her. Mrs. Brown could hardly contain him. Rosie took him from Mrs. Brown with tears streaming down her face. "Oh my baby, my baby," she cried over and over. Boo held Rosie tight and patted her face until he spotted Bud.

"Papa!" Boo squealed loudly. Bud rushed to him and took him out of Rosie's arms, lifting him high into the air above his head. Boo kicked his short legs and waved his arms like he was flying. He was one happy little boy.

Rosie walked over to Mrs. Brown and gave her a big warm hug. "Thank you so much for caring for my little brother—my baby. I shall always be grateful. Tater is home. He is at the doctor's office getting wonderful care. He said to tell you again 'thank you.' We all thank you so much."

Speaking of thanks, I want to give Joseph something for helping Tater all the way home. I wish it could be more, but I want him to have the horse that Rosie is riding. Sheriff Murphy has agreed to sell the horse to me, since he only loaned it to Rosie to ride. It is a fine young pinto with a nice leather saddle. I hope, Mr. Brown, that you will let Joseph accept this gift from us. I will write you a bill of sale."

"Well, that's a mighty fine gift, Mr. Downey, but Joseph didn't help your son for no reward." Mr. Brown and Joseph were both very surprised and didn't know what to say.

"That's what makes this gift so special. Your son showed our son kindness and now I want to give him something in return. I know that he can use the pony to travel to school."

"Well, you're right about that. But it just seems too much," but after looking over at Joseph, he said, "but if you're sure, we'll gladly accept the pony."

Bud grabbed the older man and gave him a strong hug. "Thanks! Tater will be happy."

After a big breakfast of fluffy biscuits with scrambled eggs and good, hot coffee, Bud and Rosie got on the wagon to head home. Mrs. Brown gave Boo a big kiss and said that she was going to miss the little tyke. Rosie told Boo to wave good-bye, and he did. Sheriff Murphy said that he was going to go on into McBain and see the sheriff and make a report on the condition of the boys. Both lawmen wanted to have enough evidence against Tally Shire so that he wouldn't be able to have any contact with the boys ever again.

After visiting with Tater at Dr. Tim's office, Bud, Rosie, Justice, and Boo were headed home for lunch and a much-needed nap for Boo.

Later, Rosie would ride back into town and spend the rest of the afternoon at Tater's bedside. As Bud drove the black carriage down the main street of Limason, he met his brother Luke driving his pa's big wheat wagon. Bud pulled up his two horses and sat in the middle of the road waiting for Luke to stop. "Hi, big brother," said Bud to Luke. "What brings you to town today with the wheat wagon?"

"You haven't heard?" Luke asked, remembering that Bud had been away on a trip to bring his boys back home. "My wife and kids are coming in on the afternoon stage. I figured I would need a big wagon to carry them and their luggage to the farm."

"What wonderful news! I'm sure happy for you and for Pa and Ma. They will be happy to see their grandchildren."

"That's right. I will see you later. I better get on down to the stage line in case the stage comes early." Luke drove away with a happy expression on his face.

"Goodness," said Rosie. "I ain't never seen him so sober or so happy."

"It's been awhile since I have seen him that way too. He was killing himself with that rot-gut. Pa said that every time he drank, he would throw up and his stomach hurt afterward for a while. He would have to go and lay down. It was eating away his insides."

Justice didn't say a word, but she had a smile on her face thinking about the spell that she had placed on Luke and his drinking. She was sure he felt that she did something to him, but he didn't want to accuse her. Justice knew that he didn't like her, but his likes didn't concern her. She got tired of him hurting his folks with his stupid self-pity and staying drunk.

Once Bud and Rosie got home and began unloading the wagon, Rosie thought how happy Luke would be to have his children with him.

"Oh, Bud, I was supposed to tell you that Mrs. Rae invited us to have Thanksgiving dinner with them. Your folks are invited to attend their big dinner too. I told her that I had to ask you."

"That's nice. Whatever you and Justice want to do is fine with me." Bud smiled at his lovely wife.

24

Bud's brother Luke stood on the wooden platform at the stagecoach office. He anxiously paced and walked back and forth, waiting for the stage to arrive with his family. It had been almost two years since he had seen his wife. His kids might not know him. He really needed a drink. When he received the telegram that Lisa was traveling to Limason by way of train from New Mexico, he was surprised, relieved, and overjoyed. He was also very angry and out of sorts within himself. She could have given him more notice that she was coming. The telegram said that she was traveling the sunset route on the Southern Pacific train to McBain, Texas, and then taking the stagecoach to Limason. As he took out his pocket watch he noticed the stagecoach was a few minutes late.

A loud noise made Luke look up the street and see the arrival of the noon stage coming his way. His heart was beating so hard in his chest; he thought he might pass out. He was anxious and very nervous. Did he look all right? Would the children know him? All these questions were rushing through his mind.

The stagecoach came to a quick stop and the carriage rocked back and forth. Before the carriage settled down, a tough-looking, dirty driver jumped down and asked Luke if he was Downey. "Yes, I am," he said. "Why?"

"Why?" the driver yelled back at Luke. "'Cause I've got the most gosh darn hardheaded woman in the world in that there coach, and I want to deliver her personally to *you*. I want her out of my coach as soon as possible!"

"Are your referring to my wife?" Luke asked softly.

"If you are waiting on a *loud mouth, stubborn woman* with two young'uns, then I'm speaking about her. There ain't no one else in thar. Now open that door and get her out before I personally drag her out by that stupid hat she's wearing." The driver wiped at his tobacco-stained mouth that held a wad. He spit a stream of tobacco juice at Luke's feet and stormed off into the stagecoach office while his partner got down and began taking care of the six horses. Luke stood stunned and surprised that the driver would speak about his wife in that nasty tone of voice. He looked at the other driver, and he just shook his head and made a chuckling sound from his throat.

Luke opened the stagecoach door and looked inside. His lovely wife Lisa sat on the seat adjusting her small black bonnet with decorative fruit spread on top of it. His baby girl laid on the seat asleep while his son was looking out the window on the other side of the coach.

"Lisa," said Luke very softly. "It's so good to see you. Please give me your hand and I will help you out of this dusty coach."

Lisa moved to the edge of the soft leather seat and looked down at Luke whom she had not seen in two years. Instead of a warm welcome, she said in a very uppity tone, "You could have at least worn a decent suit of clothes to meet me. You look like a field hand." She offered him her hand and he helped her to the ground. As she dusted off her purple velvet skirt and adjusted her fitted vest, Luke reached in and took his son in his arms and gave him a warm hug. "Hello, Luther," said Luke to his son.

"Are you my pa?" Luther asked. The young boy looked at Luke as if he smelled something bad.

"Yes, I'm your pa, and I have missed you and your sister something awful. I'm so happy that you have come back to live with me again." Surprised at Luke's comment, his son screamed. "Mama, are we going to live here? You said that we were coming on a short visit." Luther ran over to his mother and started pulling on her arm to get her attention.

Luke leaned into the coach and pulled his daughter into his arms. She was so tired that she never woke up even with the rough handling he had to do to get her out.

Rider and Jeremiah were in town getting bags of horse feed when they saw Luke meeting his family at the stagecoach platform. They walked over and asked if they could assist Luke with his wife and children's luggage. Luke introduced the men to his wife, but she just stared at them. "I appreciate your help, fellows," Luke said.

As Rider and Jeremiah gave them a salute good-bye, they headed to the livery. As Jeremiah passed Lisa, she held out her hand to him. He was surprised, but he stretched his hand toward hers and she placed a quarter into his palm and thanked him. Jeremiah looked down at the money and realized that she thought he was a man-servant. He clicked his heels together and gave her a low bow. He said, "Thank you, madam." As he turned he hurried to catch Rider. He grinned really big as he tossed the new shiny coin in the air.

Luke was surprised at his wife's behavior toward his friends, but her behavior was different toward him too. She appeared to be ashamed of his appearance. As he attempted to give her a warm greeting, she pulled away from him as if he was a stranger. Something certainly had happened on the trip because the stagecoach driver couldn't get rid of her fast enough. *He would quiz her about the trip later*, he thought.

"Mama and Pa are so excited that you have come home, Lisa. Mama has been cooking up a storm all morning. She has baked an apple and a strawberry pie. She remembered that your favorite pie was strawberry."

"I break out if I eat one single strawberry. I'll eat some of the apple." Lisa sat with one hand holding onto her bonnet while Luther sat on the bench between them on the wheat wagon. The baby, Lucille, was lying on a quilt in the back of the wagon with the trunk and several large pieces of luggage. "Why didn't you drive the carriage to pick us up instead of this big field wagon? We look like a bunch of country bumpkins riding in this thing," Lisa said with a sneer on her lovely face.

"We would have never gotten all the luggage into the carriage. We'll be home in a bit," Luke replied, very disappointed at his wife's attitude. Lisa had always thought that she was a little better than most folks, but she had never been this rude or unpleasant to anyone. He hoped that she was nice to his folks. His mama was a soft-spoken, sweet lady, but she wouldn't tolerate rudeness. She expected everyone to treat each other with kindness.

"Do you have horses, Papa? I love to ride," Luther said as he was looking at the large pastures that they passed filled with cattle and horses.

"There are horses at the farm that you can ride, but most of our horses are working animals. I will see about getting a small pony for you to use."

"I don't want to ride somebody else's old pony. I want my own!" Luther demanded as he folded his arms together and pouted.

"Lisa, I had hoped that you told the children that this farm is their grandparents' home, not ours, but I can see that you haven't," Luke said as he glanced over at his wife.

"I had hoped that these last two years that you would have settled somewhere. Your letters kept pleading for me to return and bring the children. Well, here I am and we are no better off than when we were in California. Why did you want us to leave my folks nice home only to have to stay with your family?" Lisa asked. "If I remember correctly, their place is small and your brothers still live at home. Where in the blue blazes are we all going to sleep and have any privacy?'

"Staying with my folks will be only temporary. I will rent us a place until we can buy our own. You never answered my letters or shared your traveling plans with me. I could have already found a place for us if you had told me weeks ago that you were coming. Now, don't get me wrong. I am happy to have you here and my children. We will manage, but you'll have to have patience and let me earn some money."

"Earn some money! What do you mean? Haven't you been working?" Lisa asked with bitterness. "What did you do with all the money you left with from the gold fields?"

Before Luke could answer, they had arrived at his folks' place. Pa Downey and Samuel were out in the front of the farmhouse. "Samuel, run into the house and tell your ma that Luke is here with his family."

Mr. Downey reached for the reins of one of the big work horses. "Whoa, boy." He pulled the horses to a stop and smiled and waved at Luke.

"It looks like you made good time. Ma's got lunch on the table. She's all excited about meeting her grandchildren!" Mr. Downey said as he approached the side of the big wheat wagon.

Luke jumped down and walked around the side of the wagon where he could lift Lisa down. He reached and pulled Luther into his arms and placed him on the ground in front of his new grandpa. "Hello, young man," said Mr. Downey as he stooped down to the child's level.

Luther looked at his new grandpa and said, "Hello." He placed his fingers in his mouth and twisted his little body back and forth. "I'm hungry. You got any cookies?"

"Yes, sir, we've got a lot of cookies, but we have some real food on the table just for all of you. Look there! Here comes your grandmother." Luther rubbed up beside his new Grandpa and tried to hide behind his tall legs.

After Luke had helped Lisa off the wagon, he walked to the back of the wagon and lifted Lucille, his little Lucy, off the pallet and laid her head on his shoulder. "This little tyke must have been exhausted. She has slept for several hours."

"Welcome, Lisa!" cried his mama as she wiped her misty eyes with the corner of her white apron. We are so glad to have you and the children. Oh my, just look at the kids. They aren't babies like I imagined but they're so darling. This young man looks just like Luke."

"Ma, this young man is starving. Let's get their luggage off the wagon after we feed everyone." Pa led Luther in through the front door of the house where there was a delicious aroma coming from the kitchen.

After breakfast Bud suggested to Rosie and Justice that they get dressed after all the morning chores were completed and go and meet Luke's wife and children. We want to make them feel welcome.

"All right, but I will drive the small carriage and go take care of Tater after our visit." Rosie was so glad that Dr. Tim was taking such good care of Tater, but she would be glad to have him home.

"We have a cake in the oven for our supper, but I think it would be nice to take it over to your folks." Bud raised his eyebrows, but before he could say anything, Rosie hit him with a wet dishrag. "Justice made it, Mr. Smarty Pants!" Rosie couldn't help but laugh at the relief she saw on Bud's face. "Now, Bud, you have to admit that I'm getting better with cooking every day."

"That's true, sweetheart, but we want to make a good impression on Luke's wife," Bud jokingly said as he hurried out the front door, laughing.

After arriving at Bud's folks place, it seemed strange not to see the boys and Mr. Downey outside working around the place. As Bud helped Justice and Boo down from the wheat wagon, Rosie walked over from the small carriage that she had driven and whispered to Bud, "Wonder what's going on?" They could hear loud voices coming from the front room of the house. "Maybe we should leave and come back another time," Justice suggested.

"Come on, now." Bud took Rosie's hand while she led Boo up the steps onto the porch. Boo raced over and banged on the front door. "Grandpa!" he yelled as he hit the front screen with his small hand.

"Mercy, looks who's come to visit, Ma. Little Boo is here with his family. Come in everyone," said Mr. Downey.

Bud, Rosie, and Justice strolled into the kitchen trying to adjust their eyes from the bright sunshine to the darkroom. Luke and Lisa stood in the parlor staring at each other—matched off like a pair of professional boxers that were getting ready for another round. Bud eyed his mama while looking at his pa as he was giving Boo a piece of sliced ham. He finally decided to take matters into his own hands.

"Hello, Lisa." Bud walked over to the couple and stepped in between them to introduce himself. "I'm Bud, Luke's brother. We are so glad to have you here." Lisa didn't acknowledge Bud at all. It was like he didn't even speak to her. Bud continued, "This is Rosie, my new bride and her little brother Boo, who's trying to get up to the table. He thinks he is supposed to eat every time we come over."

Rosie walked over to Lisa and Luke. The couple didn't speak or even look at Rosie or Boo. Anger oozed from the pores of the estranged man and woman. Bud motioned for Justice to come over to him. "Lisa, this lady here is our dear friend Justice."

Lisa glanced over to Bud and saw Justice standing in the front room like an invited guest. "Have mercy!" she screamed. "Not only do you expect me to rise before the sun comes up, you allow Negros in your parlor! What's next?" She turned and raced to the front bedroom and slammed the door.

Bud, Rosie, and Justice didn't move a muscle. No one knew how to respond. Luke finally came out of his trance and immediately apologized for Lisa's behavior. "I'm sorry. Please try to understand her. She's really upset because she has been raised with servants." He turned and followed his wife into the front bedroom.

Mrs. Downey walked over to Justice and placed her arm around her shoulders. Mrs. Downey was a tall woman and towered over Justice's small petite body. "Please—come and have some coffee."

Mrs. Downey was so embarrassed she didn't know what to do or say.

Rosie turned and walked slowly out of the house into the bright sunlight. She strolled over to the hen house, trying to remain calm and go forth like nothing had happened. But what she really wanted to do was have a conniption fit. Screaming, yelling, and throwing things at *Mrs. Wealthy Pants* might make her feel better, but it wouldn't' take away the cruel words that came out of her mouth. Justice had made no reply or shown any sign that Luke's wife had hurt her in anyway. She had to be embarrassed because everyone in the room certainly was, thought Rosie. God love Mrs. Downey. *She kept her words closed behind her angry smile and wrapped her arms around Justice. Mrs. Horse-hockey sure better watch her step. Justice might put a "spell" on her*, thought Rosie as she smiled for the first time.

Bud came out of the house and looked around for Rosie. He spotted her out at the hen house talking—to herself, because no one else was around.

"Rosie, do you want to leave? I couldn't blame you if you did," Bud said. "Luke sure has his hands full with that wife of his."

"I want to leave, but our leaving would only cause your ma and pa to feel worse. Your mama has cooked a nice lunch. Let's go eat and we will make our excuses soon after."

"You're always thinking about someone other than yourself. I could see that temper of yours when Lisa said those ugly words to Justice. You wanted to hit her, didn't you?" Bud laughed as he took her hand and led the way back to the house. As they were ready to enter the house, Bud stopped and said for Rosie's ears only. "Me too."

The lunch was delicious and as pleasant as it could be with only Luke's children joining them at the table. Lisa stayed marooned in the bedroom. Boo wanted to play with Lucy, but she climbed her pa every time he got close to her. Once Boo got cranky from needing a nap that gave Bud's little family an excuse to go home.

Luke walked them to their carriage and apologized again for his wife's behavior.

Bud assisted Rosie into the small carriage and told her to be careful and to give Tater his love. "Tell him I'll come into town tomorrow to see him and play a game of checkers." *Hopefully Dr. Tim will let him come home in a few days*, thought Bud.

Their home place was only a short distance from Bud's folks, but it was enough to rock Boo into a nice afternoon nap. Bud helped Justice down from the carriage and placed Boo in his crib. He told Justice that he would be working on the new corral and would be in later. He needed to work off some of his anger. He mumbled as he walked out of the door. "Don't go to any trouble with supper for me," he said. "I ate too much at lunch."

As he walked out to the barn to start working, he couldn't help but think about Luke's wife, Lisa. It had been a long time since he had run across someone who thought they were better than anyone else. She was a spoiled, ungrateful, mean woman in his opinion. She should have stayed in New Mexico as far as he was concerned. Once he got Luke alone he would blister his ears about his wife's attitude toward Justice. She is really going to be surprised when she meets Ms. Ollie, Ms. Esther, and Ms. Ella Mae. If she says anything rude to one of those ladies, he didn't know how she would be treated in return. Maybe where she came from, Negros and Mexicans were mostly servants or field hands, but here in Limason, people showed respect to each other, no matter the color of a person's skin. Justice was like a family member to Rosie, her brothers and to him. She had been a friend, nurse, and protector when needed. This little black lady was a tough old bird and he had grown very fond of her. No one was ever going to insult her again, he thought to himself.

He grabbed up some posts, a post hold digger, and a roll of wire and drove out toward the area where he was expanding his old corral fence. His mood was as dark as a thundercloud. Bud couldn't ever remember being so upset with a woman. He shook his head as he looked at the five new horses that he had purchased. The animals needed more room to frolic and kick up their hind legs. The afternoon sun had come out, but a cold chill was still in the air. Winter was coming on fast. After digging the holes and sitting the post in the ground, Bud sat down on the ground. His face was covered with sweat and dirt. While wiping some grime off his face, he realized how much he missed Tater's help. Thank goodness he would be coming home in a few days. Bud gathered his tools and headed to the barn, noticing for the first time how late it had gotten. With the big lunch under his belt, he hadn't even thought about eating or returning to the house. Once he entered the kitchen, he noticed that it was dark except for a light in his bedroom.

Bud strolled into their bedroom with the smell of outdoors on his heavy jacket. He went into the water closet and wiped the sweat and grim off his body. After tossing his dirty shirt in a basket, he noticed that Rosie was pretending to be asleep as she watched him through her eyelashes. As he slipped his boots off, he pulled his wide leather belt out of his pants to hang on a peg.

"I know you're awake, sweetheart."

Rosie giggled as she held the quilt high under her chin. "How did you know that I wasn't asleep?"

"Most people breathe or make a soft snoring sound when they're sleeping."

Bud continued to undress until he was completely nude. "Gosh, Bud, you're going to freeze your ass off!"

"Hey, my little swamp girl, watch your mouth," he said as he reached to extinguish the lamp. As he crawled under the quilts, she could feel the hardness of his body as he scooted her over a bit. His body was chilled, but as he reached for her, he felt her warmth as he cuddled her. "How was Tater today?"

"Fine. He misses being home," sighed Rosie as she lifted her arms and placed them around his neck. After placing small kisses over both of her eyes and all around her mouth, he captured her lips and drowned himself into a passionate deep kiss. After coming up for air, Rosie whispered into Bud's neck. "Oh, Bud, I'm scared."

"Scared?"

"I'm so happy, here with you and the boys. Now that we have them back, it scares me to have so much happiness when just a short time ago we were living from day to day, never sure where the next meal was coming from. Now, I have everything. I have you."

"We have each other," Bud said. "You know, honey, I have always had a good home, great parents, pretty much everything I needed. I just didn't appreciate my home and family until I got put in prison. But once I woke up at your place and saw how little you survived on, I realized how fortunate I had been. I'm so happy that you found me," he said. She felt his hard body press against her. In a matter of minutes, his body covered hers and they soon melted into one. Rosie sighed as she took in the manly, outdoor sense of Bud as she placed small kisses over his chest. "I love you."

After Bud's long afternoon of hard work and a night of cuddling into a warm cocoon with Rosie's body, he felt his eyes growing heavy as sleep finally overtook him. Rosie's warm soft body was gathered in his arms. *God had blessed him* was his last thought before he drifted into a sound sleep.

A few days after Bud and Rosie got home with Boo, Tater was still recuperating at Dr. Tim's office. Dr. Tim wanted to keep a close eye on Tater's deep cuts on his back. He assured Rosie that he knew she would take good care of Tater at their home, but he wanted to keep him so he could keep a close watch for infection.

Word had spread like wildfire that the boys had been returned home and everyone was so happy for Bud's family. All the school children were happy to learn that Tater would be returning to the classroom. He was healing very fast, but for the first time in his life, he was enjoying the special attention that he was receiving. Missy, John and Katie's daughter, had found a reason to stop in the doctor's office to visit with him every afternoon after school. She had volunteered to bring Tater his school lessons so he wouldn't be so far behind when he did return. While there, Esther prepared an afternoon snack for the two young people, while Rosie always made herself scarce with an excuse that she had to help Ms. Hannah or Dr. Tim. Missy always straightened Tater's covers and filled his water pitcher with fresh water. Afterward they would enjoy their refreshments while Missy went over his lessons with him. Tater was infatuated with the young girl with long blond braids and gold-rim glasses. She always smelled so nice, and he never wanted her to leave for home.

Matt and Little Jess always stuck their heads in the office and said hi. Tater had grown very fond of his two new friends. Before he had to go to McBain and live with his mama, he and Matt had become fishing buddies. Tater was ready to get out of the sick bed and head out with them to their favorite fishing hole.

The day before Tater was to be released by Dr. Tim, Justice had come to spend some time with him. They had not been alone since he got home. She was eager to talk to him about the "spell" that she had cast on Tally. After Esther had settled in the kitchen making vegetable soup and Dr. Tim and Hannah were busy with patients, Justice sat down beside Tater.

"We need to talk, Tater," said Justice as she slowly closed the door.

"I know!" he whispered very excited. He patted his bed and pulled her down to sit beside him. "I wanted to tell you how the potions and powder you gave me worked. Listen, Justice." Tater looked over his shoulder to make sure no one was near that might hear him. "That stuff that I sprinkled in the old man's food really worked. I put it in his coffee and beans that was cooking. But the only bad thing was that he took his anger out on mama. He beat her so bad one night that she could hardly walk the next morning. I asked her about the beating, but she told me to mind my own business. Tally started saying nasty things about her to me, but once his manhood was *gone*, he was out of his head most of the time. The bugs I placed in the vegetable garden worked quickly. In two days, all the leaves and vegetables were dead. He came at me with the whip and tried to force me to admit to doing something. I thought I might die that night but I prayed and thought about Boo. I couldn't give up."

"I'm so sorry." Justice covered her pink lips with her small wrinkled hands. "I never thought that he would beat you like he did. I would have made the spell stronger if I had known that the devil was in him," said Justice.

"The chanting sounds I made at night nearly made him loose his mind. He was determined to catch me under his window. One night, he didn't even take time to put on his pants. He raced out of the house *naked* and he nearly killed himself. He stepped in a tub and fell out the front door and landed in muddy water. I had to hide my head so he wouldn't hear me laughing. Mama did laugh and he almost killed her later. With my ankles so thin and the leg-irons made for a man, I was able to slip and slide my feet in and out of them. He never guessed how I could move around so fast."

"Tater, I'm so sorry that I was the reason that old fool hurt you. I will never forgive myself for having you do those things to him." Justice wiped tears from her eyes as she squeezed his hands.

"Please don't cry, Justice. He would have found another reason to beat me. Right after we got there, I was sitting in the shade playing with Boo because Mama couldn't make him stop crying. That was the first time he hit me with the riding crop over and over. He wanted to hurt me from the very beginning of our stay. He wanted a field hand—and that was me." Tater remembered how his mama only came to help him because he was holding

Boo and protecting him from the whip. He knew in his heart that his mama really did not care anything about him.

Justice sat with her head hanging down. She was still very upset. "Justice, the whippings were bad. I ain't going to say they didn't hurt me. But to know that we were making his life miserable helped me to endure the punishment he dealt out," said Tater with a sweet grin on his freckled face.

"I guess we better keep this 'spell doings' just between us. I don't want all these people here afraid of me." Justice patted Tater's hand as she got up and walked out of the hospital room.

As Bud rolled out of the bed the next morning, he was in a great mood. "Up, woman," Bud said playfully as he patted Rosie on her rump. "We're bringing our boy home today." After breakfast, Bud hitched the new double seat carriage with two new black quarter horses. Boo sang and chapped his hands nearly all the way to town, chanting Tater's name over and over.

Dr. Tim, Ms. Hannah, and Esther were at the front door beside Tater as he walked out of the office into the bright sunlight. "Wow, it feels so funny leaving here. Thanks, Doc," said Tater as he grabbed Tim around the waist and gave him a big hug. Hannah patted Tater on the shoulder as he wiped his eyes on the doc's chest before turning Dr. Tim loose. As everyone made their way out on the boardwalk, a group of Limason's citizens had gathered out front. When they saw Tater, they clapped and cheered. Tater turned red in the face but gave everyone a wave and a big smile. He was happy that he was going home.

After a few weeks at home, Tater was well enough to ride his new pony to school. Everybody had gotten back to their normal routine. Bud had noticed the change in Tater. He was still a little underweight, but he worked as hard as any grown man. He chopped a core of wood and filled the wood boxes in the house and herded the horses out to the fields before breakfast. Waking up on Saturday morning with the rooster crowing, Tater was the first one out of bed. Bud caught him as he headed out the door with a clean bucket to use for milking.

"Hold on there, fellow," Bud whispered loudly, trying not to disturb everyone else in the house. "This is your day off. You've worked hard this week and today, you are going fishing or do whatever you want."

"Really? I shore would like to get Matt and Jess and go fishing. Maybe I might go for a ride and stop over at Missy's. She was really nice to me while I was at Dr. Tim's." Tater stood looking down at his boots while he was thinking about how pretty she was.

"A picnic would be nice," suggested Bud. "Maybe you could take her on one after church."

"What! Me on a picnic with a girl?" Tater looked at Bud like he was crazy and hurried toward the barn to get his fishing pole. *Bud must be crazy*, thought Tater. Golly, the boys would never stop teasing him about being *lovesick*.

Bud went into their bedroom laughing. Rosie was peeking at him from the bedcovers. "Good morning," said Rosie. "What's so funny?"

"I gave Tater the day off. He said he wanted to go fishing and maybe later go see Missy. I suggested he take her on a picnic but he nearly had heart failure."

"I want to go see Rae, Ms. Ollie, and Hope today. I want to know what their plans are for Thanksgiving. Do you want to go with me and Justice?"

"Thanks, but I want to finish the corral fence. You go without me," he said as he sat down on the bed beside her and ran his hand under the quilts and felt her smooth thigh.

"Papa!" a scream came from Boo's room.

"Oh shoot," mumbled Bud. "He has great timing."

25

AFTER THE MORNING chores were completed, Rosie decided to take Justice and Boo to the Maxwell's house and see what the arrangements were for Thanksgiving Day. They took the new black carriage and drove the five miles. Hank came limping out of the big red barn with a smile and greeted the ladies.

"Sorry, Ms. Rosie, but Rae, Ms. Ollie, and Claire all went into town. Hope and Jacob are up at their house, but Will and Jesse are working in the wheat field.

"We'll ride up to Hope's house and visit with her for a little while. I wanted to talk to her about Thanksgiving." Hank took the reins of one of the horses and turned it around in the yard heading them toward Hope's.

Rosie drove close to the white picket fence and pulled the horses to a stop. She removed her lap blanket and jumped down off the carriage and tied the horses to the hitching rail. She helped Justice to the ground and then retrieved Boo, pulling his jacket close. He raced up to the porch and crawled to the top step. Rosie knocked on the front door. The wind was blowing and the air was very crisp. Boo pounded his tiny fists on the bottom of the door. "Hold your horses, fellow, they'll come to the door in a minute," said Rosie. After another minute, Rosie pulled open the pretty painted screen door and tapped on the big solid front door; still no answer. Rosie walked down to the first window on the porch and peeked in. "Mercy, Justice! Hope's on the floor and Jacob is walking around crying. Help me with the door!" Rosie turned the knob on the door and was surprised it opened. Rosie hurried inside the hallway. Hope was squatted on the floor, holding her breath. She had her hands over her large belly, protecting her unborn child.

Hope looked up through her misty eyes and cried, "Thank the Lord, you heard me."

Justice and Rosie were both bent down hovering over Hope. "Hope, can you stand?" Justice asked. "We need to get you in your bed."

"Send for help please!" she screamed as another contraction hit harder than before. "Get Will, get Dr. Tim!"

"Rosie, go to Rae's and get Hank to go after Will in the field and then get Dr. Tim. I will make her comfortable on the floor until Will gets here. Hurry," Justice whispered.

After getting a pillow off the sofa and a quilt that had been lying on the rocking chair, she helped make Hope comfortable on the beautiful shiny hardwood floors. "Has your water broken?" Justice asked Hope as she gathered a very upset little Jacob in her arms.

"I think so, but it wasn't as much as when I had Jacob."

"Maybe, it's not broken all the way. It will come. If not, Dr. Tim will finish the job for you."

"Justice, I'm scared. The baby isn't supposed to come this early."

"Only the good Lord knows when it's the right time. Now, you just try to lie still. Your little man here is tired," Justice said as she held the twenty-month-old baby close to her bosom and swayed. Just as Jacob's eyes closed, Will came busting through the front door. He had wheat on the front of his shirt and in his hair. "Hope, sweetheart, oh my goodness. I didn't know you were this close to having the baby. I'd never have left you alone."

"Will, calm yourself. Scoop her up gently and carry her to the bed. Has someone gone to get Dr. Tim?" Justice asked.

"Yes, Rider has gone. And he will look for Rae and Ollie while he's there. Everyone will be home soon," he said as he slid his big hands under Hope's back and legs. He lifted his wife and carried her up the staircase, whispering words of comfort.

Jesse had come into the hallway and took Jacob out of Justice's arms. "He needs changing," Justice said as she searched for a dry nappy. "Let me get this one settled, and I will go and take care of Hope."

"I'll take care of this little man," said Jesse. "Thank the Lord that you and Rosie came for a visit," said Jesse while cuddling Jacob close and walking toward the baby's room.

Once Justice went into the room with Hope and Will, she told Will to go and get an oil cloth out of the pantry in the kitchen.

"An oil cloth?" Will started out of the room and stopped, "What's an oil cloth?"

"Get me an old tablecloth—one that can be thrown away. I am going to prepare the bed."

"Once Will had left the room, Justice laid her hands on Hope's big belly. "How are you feeling now?

"The pains have slowed down, and they don't hurt as bad."

"This isn't your first, so you know what to expect. You should be excited and full of joy. You're about to bring a new life into this wonderful world. So let's get ready to receive it."

"I'm feeling better, but Justice I have to tell you something." Hope reached for Justice's hand. "I'm scared. I know I shouldn't be, but I'm not brave. I remember the pain at the end, and it was awful. I promised myself when I had Jacob that I would never go through this again. I have been miserable this whole nine months worrying about this day. Will wants children—lots of them. Well, this is the last one for me! *If he wants more, then he can just have them himself.*"

Justice couldn't contain the laughter. "Oh, Hope, you make me laugh." Justice realized that Hope wasn't trying to be funny at all. She was very serious and afraid of the pain; rightfully so, because childbirth was almost unbearable to many mothers.

"Hope, listen to me. You're going to be fine. I can relieve some of the pain, not all of it. I have some special seeds that I can place under your tongue that will help make giving birth easier, but you can't tell no one. My medicine won't hurt you or the babe. I have delivered many babies and helped the mamas."

"Oh, Justice, can you really take away some of the *torture*? I'll never tell if it will keep me from feeling like I'm being ripped apart. Please give me something. I'll never tell—not even Rae or Ollie."

Rosie came into the bedroom. "Hank has ridden over to get Mrs. Downey to come since Rae and Ollie aren't home yet. Justice, can I help with the bed or help Hope to change into something more comfortable?"

"No, I will help, Hope. You go down to the kitchen and start boiling some water and gather up a big bowl, some cotton, and a piece of string. Get some alcohol, a fresh clean towel, and have Will build up the fire in this room. Dr. Tim will have everything else that is needed. We have plenty of time to get the things that the baby will wear when it gets here. I know Hope has everything all ready."

"I do. Will knows where everything is in the baby's room," Hope said with a sweet smile.

"Where's Boo," asked Justice.

"Jesse took him to his house. He is going to get a sandwich, and he said that he would feed Boo too."

"Rosie, when you finish getting the things for Justice, please come and sit down beside me. Oh!" Hope moaned and grabbed her stomach. "Justice, I feel like I've got to pee. Get me the chamber pot quick!"

Once Will was allowed back in the bedroom, he placed several big logs in the fireplace to take the chill out of the room. He went to sit in a chair beside the bed when Hope sat up and screamed the room was too hot. "It's hot as hell in here! Open a window or throw a pail of water in the fire and put it out. I'm lying in a bucket of my own sweat."

"Now, sweetheart, it isn't that warm in this room. Everyone who comes in here says it's cold," Will said.

"Who's having this baby? Not You! *I am* and it's hot as blazes in here," she screamed. Will walked over to the window and raised it up about two inches, allowing a little cool air in the room. Hope watched him as he sat down again to stand guard over her.

Will was surprised at his precious Hope's attitude. When she gave birth to Jacob, she cried and moaned a lot. She did beg for someone to cut the baby out of her, like that was a possibility. But today, she was acting like a shrew. She was just being hard down mean, especially to him.

Hope's contractions finally stopped, and she went to sleep. While she was resting, Rae and Ms. Ollie returned home and hurried up to Hope. Rae and Ms. Ollie immediately put on clean aprons and washed their hands. They came prepared to do whatever needed to be done. Unfortunately they brought news that Dr. Tim had an emergency surgery. An old man nearly chopped his leg off with a big rusty ax while chopping firewood. The old man was in critical condition when he was carried into Tim's office. Dr. Tim said he would be out as quick as he could. Hannah had come with Rae and Ms. Ollie.

As Miss Ollie stood over Hope, using her hand to brush hair away from her damp face, she commented on how precious her baby girl looked lying on the bed. "It's so hard for me to believe that our baby is going to have another child. I shore hope it's a girl this time. She wants one so bad, but she'll love another boy if that is what she has. She looks so sweet and docile lying here," coughed Ollie.

In less than two hours, the sweet docile new mama was a tyrant. Poor Will couldn't do anything to make her comfortable or please her. She demanded something cold, and Hannah said she could have some ice chips. Will tried to feed her the ice, but she grabbed the cup and threw it across the room. As a hard contraction doubled her over, she screamed that she was dying. "Will, I'm dying! I want Preacher Anderson! I want him to hear my confession! Please get him."

"But, Sweetheart, you aren't a Catholic and he isn't a priest."

"*I can be anything I want to be*—get him here!" She practically stood up in the bed like a wild animal baring her teeth. Will was speechless. He had never seen his precious wife act so crazy.

Justice walked over to Will and said it was time for him to leave the room. "Don't go anywhere. Go and get yourself a cup of coffee. She'll be fine in a little while."

"I ain't never seen her act like this—ever," he whispered to her.

Hannah took Will's hand and walked with him down to the kitchen. She looked at Rae and Miss Ollie and said for them to feed this poor fellow. "He has been put through the wringer. He needs someone to care for him."

Once everyone had left the room, Justice walked over to Hope and told her to open her mouth. "Open wide and lift your tongue. Don't swallow." Justice laid a few seeds under Hope's tongue as she gently pushed Hope back down on the fluffed pillows that Will had fixed for her.

"Just relax and let the seeds do their job. In a minute, your contraction won't hurt you as bad. I wanted to give this to you earlier, but there were too many people around. Remember, you must keep the 'seeds' a secret." Hope nodded her head that she understood.

As the hour grew nearer to supper time, Bud finally showed up to check on Rosie and Justice. They were only going to be gone for a little while. "How's Hope doing? Is her time getting close?" Bud asked. Will only shook his head. He was so worried about his lovely wife because she was having a difficult time giving birth this time. It seemed to be forever since he heard Hank screaming his name this morning out in the wheat field. *There was something very wrong*, he thought to himself.

"I best get back upstairs and check on Hope. She wants me close by one minute and then the next she screaming at me for putting her in this predicament, as she calls it." Will walked up the stairs like he was a man heading to the gallows. He was silently praying that the birthing would be over soon. When he eased the bedroom door open, he couldn't believe his eyes. His precious wife was lying very still and resting peacefully. Once Hope spotted Will standing by her bedside, she reached out for his hand. "Come closer," she whispered. Will sat down on the mattress, feeling it push down a little, making her roll toward him. He jumped up and said that he was sorry if he hurt her in anyway. "No, I'm not hurt. I'm just fine. It won't be long now."

Will looked at Justice to see if Hope knew what she was saying. "Will, please ask Hannah, Miss Ollie, and Rae to come up. I'm afraid our new little visitor ain't going to wait for the doctor." Will leaned over Hope and kissed her rosy lips and her nose and said that he would be outside the door if she needed him. As he turned to leave, he asked, "What about Rosie? Do you want her to come up too?"

Justice walked to Will and whispered, "No, I don't want Rosie to see the birthing. She'd never give Bud a babe if she did." Justice turned and looked over at Hope as she lay upon the bed like a royal princess. "Things are fixing to start happening soon, so hurry the ladies on up here."

"She don't look ready. She's not screaming and carrying on in pain like before," said Will.

"You don't want her in pain, do you?"

"Of course not, but something is different."

"Justice! *I need you*," cried Hope. Will raced out of the room and bounced down the stairs into the kitchen. "Justice needs you girls, now!" He was so excited that he could hardly breathe.

Hannah and Rae circled around Will and hurried up the stairs. Miss Ollie started up the stairs and had to stop and balance herself on the railing. She was dizzy and felt light-headed. Will noticed Ollie standing at the base of the stairs. "Are you all right Miss Ollie?"

"Git over here and give me a hand up these steep stairs. My baby needs me!" she huffed and puffed.

Rosie had been feeding Jacob and Boo mashed potatoes and a hot biscuit. When Will came back down the stairs Rosie had watched the ladies rush out of the kitchen. "Here! Will. Take over for me so I can go and help too."

"Sorry, Rosie." He stepped in front of her with both hands in the air, refusing to take the spoon and blocked her exit. "Justice said that you aren't invited to the birthing. Only the older ladies that have had babies can be up there."

"Shoot fire! Justice doesn't want me to learn nothing important. I need to see what takes place with childbirth. Get out of my way before I run over the top of you!"

Bud grabbed Rosie around the waist and whispered, "Hold on there, you wildcat. If Justice said that you shouldn't be up there, then that's that. One day you'll learn all about having a baby."

"Oh, Bud, you know I need to know what to expect when my time comes. You men think you know everything." Rosie whirled around and folded her arms looking away from Bud and Will.

"Oh, honey, you're needed down here," said Bud as he turned her to face him. He wanted to soothe her hurt feelings. "Mama has been cooking most of the day, trying to keep all the nervous men out of the way and fed." Bud laughed as he looked at Jesse, Hank, and Will. Mrs. Downey had cooked hot fluffy biscuits and fried chicken. The waiting was long, but the food was good.

Rosie told Bud that he should take Tater and Boo home and get them settled in for the night. Mrs. Downey said that she needed to head home and feed her men folk. "Ma, you have Lisa there now. Surely she would have cooked supper for Pa and the boys?" Bud asked.

"Your pa probably sliced some ham and made sandwiches for lunch, but our little queen from New Mexico don't turn her hands for nothing. Luke has his hands full with that one. I'm afraid he's not as lucky as you are son. You have a prize in Rosie," Mrs. Downey said as she was putting on her heavy wrap and gathering her basket. Rosie blushed as she hugged Mrs. Downey.

Hank gave a tap on the side door as he entered and said real boastful, "Look who I found coming down the road?"

Dr. Tim stepped in the door and removed his heavy coat and muddy boots. "Will, how's our little mama doing," asked Tim as he was heading toward the stairs. A baby's cry silenced his footsteps. Soon laughter and praises were heard from Hope's room.

"Looks like I'm too late." Dr. Tim practically flew up the staircase into the bedroom. Will was right on his heels. With the two men stopping in the doorway, Hannah was working on Hope while Rae and Miss Ollie were giggling and washing a tiny baby.

"I'm sorry, Will, but I'm not ready for you to see Hope yet. I'll call you in a little while," said Hannah, like a professional doctor. Tim gave Will a push out of the bedroom door and said, "You heard the doctor," as he closed the door in Will's face.

"But, but—what did she have?" Will stood frozen in place with his forehead pressed on the door when it was jerked opened and Rae stood in front of him. "It's a girl! It's another precious little Hope." Before he could make a response, the door closed in his face again.

"A girl," he repeated to himself. *A girl like Hope*, he thought to himself with a big smile.

"Hey everyone! We have a girl, just like Hope!" he yelled as he bounced down the staircase into the kitchen area.

Hank rushed over and pounded Will on his back, declaring, "Man, are you in for it now!"

"Don't listen to him, Will. There's nothing like daughters," Jesse said as he pulled Claire to his side. "They can run get your slippers…" Before he could finish his talk about daughters, Claire chimed in, "Oh, Papa, you make us sound like a dog!"

Everyone laughed at Jesse as he blushed while grabbing Claire and hugged her tight. "Well, I do love my girls," said Jesse.

"Congratulations, Will," said Mrs. Downey. "I better hurry on home now. I'll see Hope and the baby tomorrow."

"I can't thank you enough, Mrs. Downey," Will said. "We couldn't have made it today without your help. We won't be forgetting it, I can tell you that."

"Come on, Ma, I'll help you with your things and into the carriage," Bud said as he helped her with her cloak. "Would you like me to drive you home?"

"Oh, Bud, that's sweet of you, but you will need to get your own family home now that Hope has had the baby. That child will need rest and I'm sure with Ms. Ollie and Rae, she'll have plenty of help."

As Bud walked his ma out to her carriage, he wondered how Lisa was going to behave at Thanksgiving dinner at Jesse's. "You know, Ma, Lisa has got to change her ways. She can't be allowed to say ugly remarks about Justice, Ms. Ollie—you know who I mean. Shucks, Ma, these people are practically family members. Luke better give her a good talking to or just keep her and the children home."

Mrs. Downey adjusted her cloak and lap throw as she sat on the carriage bench, looking down at her sweet son. "Bud, we have to pray for Luke and Lisa. Something has hurt that child, and she is taking her bitterness out on the people who have never done a darn thing to her. I can't promise how she'll behave, but someone is going to have to give her a good sit down, that's for certain."

"I'll like to blister her butt to where she couldn't sit down for a week!" Bud threw up his hands like he'd surrendered and said, "I know, I know. I won't touch her."

As he watched his mama drive toward home, he looked up at the bright shiny moon with white twinkling stars in the dark sky. The cold wind was blowing the weathervane on top of the barn back and forth. The barn door wasn't closed tight and he could hear the animals. As Bud walked to the barn to check on the livestock, he smiled, thinking about how happy Will and Hope were together with their nice home and wonderful babies. As he busied himself, he thought, *I'm happy too.*

Once back in the house, Bud saw that Rosie and Justice had bundled both boys up in their boots, knitted caps, and warm jackets. "I need to say good-bye to Hope and then we're ready to go home," said Rosie. Bud gave her a nod as he took Boo and walked in the kitchen to say good-bye to Hank, Jesse, and Jeremiah.

Rosie tapped on the bedroom door and went in to see Hope, who was almost asleep. "Come in, child," Miss Ollie said while sitting in a rocking chair. She was holding the new baby who had just received her name: Willow.

"Oh, Ms. Ollie, I love the name. Lovely to be named after her papa," she whispered as she lowered herself beside Ms. Ollie and watched the baby as she tried to put her fist in her tiny, rosy mouth. Rosie looked closely at Miss Ollie. She looked very tired and sweaty. "Are you feeling all right, Miss Ollie?"

"Child, I'm just tired from worrying over my baby girl. Listen, you might have you one of these in the near future. God will bless you and Bud, I'm sure of that. There ain't nothing in this world sweeter than a babe in your arms. You know, Hope was three years old when she and Rae came to live with us. She was the most beautiful little girl I had ever seen. Smart too. She could talk up a storm. Our home was never the same after they came and Jesse and Rae married. Lord knows I have been blessed with sweet babies. Jess and Claire trailed little Hope's every footstep. She had no peace with those two around. Now, just look here. Little Jacob is so precious and now God has blessed Hope with a daughter of her own."

"I came up to say good night, but I'll be back tomorrow to see Hope. Maybe I can hold the baby, Willow, some," laughed Rosie.

"God bless you and Justice for taking such good care of Sweetheart before we got home today." Ollie leaned back in the big rocker and started humming a hymn while Rosie walked over to the bed. She looked down at Hope and over at Will. The couple was exhausted. Will was sitting in a big overstuffed chair with his head back and eyes closed. Hope looked like an angel lying back on her pillow sleeping while wearing a lovely yellow gown. Her long, golden hair had been plaited into a long rope and laid over her shoulder down across her breast. She was a vision of loveliness, thought Rosie.

26

THERE WAS SO much excitement in the air at Bud's home. Rosie and Tater were counting the days until Thanksgiving. They were going to celebrate the special day at Jesse and Rae's ranch with all of the Maxwell family and friends. Bud's folks had been invited and everyone would be together. Rosie and Tater had never had a nice Thanksgiving. With no means to purchase a big turkey, they had a wild prairie chicken or a big fat rabbit, if they were lucky. There were some apple trees at the edge of the swamp that belonged to a poor farmer. Rosie would never climb the trees and steal a few apples to make an apple pie, but the good Lord always provided. There were plenty of rotten apples lying under the trees. She would never take more than she could use. Thinking about all the food that was going to be cooked and served to everyone on Thanksgiving Day made her head spin.

"Justice, what offering do you think we should take to the Thanksgiving table?" Rosie asked as she sat in their small cozy kitchen. "We could roast some nice, sweet potatoes and cook a mess of field peas and green butterbeans together."

"I think that's a fine idea," said Bud.

"Oh, Sis, why not make some delicious cream pies like they have at the bakery."

"Hush, boy," Bud whispered behind his hand. "Sweet potatoes and beans sounds mighty good to me." Bud was smiling as he looked at Rosie and Justice. Rosie watched Bud as he interacted with Tater. "All right, smarty-pants. You don't want me cooking pies because they're not that good. Just admit it, I dare you!"

"Listen, honey. Rae is the best pie maker in this whole county. She'll make all kinds of pies for the dinner. You wouldn't want to be in competition with her, would you?"

"Well, when you put it that way. Of course not, Mr. Smart—but one day I will make pies as good as hers!"

"I sure hope so," Tater grinned. "Look, Sis, Bud is just trying to keep you from getting your feelings hurt. I have eaten pie over at Little Jess's, and man, it was so good. I love your sweet taters and Justice makes cornbread that tastes just like cake."

"Well, I guess that settled then," Justice replied. "We'll be making sweet taters, field peas and butter beans, and two large pans of cornbread."

"Now that we have Thanksgiving dinner all planned, I need to go over to see Pa about something. Why don't we all go over and you girls can try to have another visit with Lisa and her two kids?"

"I want to go," said Tater. "Maybe Matt and I can get in a little fishing before it's too late this evening."

Bud pulled his big black two-seater carriage to a stop beside his pa's barn. Mr. Downey, Luke, and Lisa were outside standing by the well. Mr. Downey and Luke both raised a hand in greeting to Bud and his family. Boo clapped and yelled for his grandpa to come and get him. "Coming, little man," yelled Mr. Downey.

Luke walked to the carriage and held the two horses while Bud jumped down and assisted Rosie and Justice to the ground. Lisa walked slowly over to the horse trough and ran her hand across the water while watching Rosie and Justice walkover toward her.

"Hello, Lisa." Rosie smiled at her sister-in-law as she watched Tater run into the house calling Matt's name. Lisa looked at Rosie and then glanced at Justice and sneered.

"Do you ever go anywhere without this black shadow following you?" Rosie felt instantly angry. Before Rosie could respond, Justice touched her arm and said that she was going to go in the house and see Mrs. Downey. Rosie watched her dear friend walk away, hanging her head down.

When Rosie looked back at her new sister-in-law, Lisa continued with another nasty remark. "I heard that she's an old voodoo woman from the swamps of New Orleans. How *dare* you bring that kind of trash to this farm?"

Before Rosie realized what she had done, she reached for Lisa's long hair and gave it a hard jerk as she pushed her backward into the horse trough. Lisa screamed as her body dressed in a nice frock hit the cold water. Since her head had not gone under the water completely, Rosie took both hands and placed them on her shoulders and shoved her head under. Lisa's legs were flapping and her hands were attempting to grab both sides of the trough. Rosie relaxed her hold and Lisa's head flew up out of the water. With water in her mouth and hair streaming down her face, she attempted to scream and claw at Rosie. Once more, Rosie pushed her back under the water.

Bud, Luke, and their Pa stood witnessing the calamity between the two girls. Bud started walking toward them, but Luke grabbed his arm at the elbow and stopped him. "Let them be," Luke said. "Lisa has had this coming for a while. She needs to learn that she ain't the queen of this farm, and I believe she's getting her first lesson."

The three men stood watching the two girls as Rosie held Lisa in the water trough. "You listen here Miss High and Mighty. If you ever spit another nasty word out of your ill-mannered mouth about Justice or any other Negro woman in this town, I will have Justice cast *a spell* over you. How would you like to have all of your pretty teeth fall out of your head? One day you'll start to speak and the only sound you'll hear is the braying of a donkey coming from your throat. Do you want to live in fear of that happening to you?" Rosie pulled Lisa up and gave her body a good shake until she was standing in the trough and her face was only inches from hers. "Answer me!"

"Please," Lisa started begging as she struggled to get out of the water. "Leave me alone!"

Rosie let Lisa get out of the water, but she still held a strong grip on her arm. "You better heed my words, girl. Something else," Rosie said softly "you get up off your lazy behind and start helping Mrs. Downey. She's trying to be good to you, but you have tried her patience. Luke is working hard every day to please you. You better try *harder* to be a nicer person."

Lisa attempted to pull loose from Rosie, but the small petite girl was as strong as an oxen. "You got one time to mess up and Justice will be working her spells all over you Missy!" Rosie turned the dripping wet Lisa loose and watched her gather up the tail of her skirt and hurry to the house crying, screaming for Luke.

Rosie looked over at the three men who had stood their ground as they watched the show between Lisa and herself. She dried her hands on her skirt and walked over to them. "Luke, I ain't going to say I'm sorry for what just happened. I'm sorry for not being a lady and handling the problem differently, but my temper got the better of me. I'm sorry for that."

"Listen, Rosie, I should have taken Lisa in hand myself, but I was praying that she would change back to the sweet girl that I married. I can't understand how or why she has become so mean-spirited. But after today, if she doesn't change her ways, I'm going to send her back to her parents, but my children are going to stay here with me." Luke turned and walked back to the house.

Rosie stood watching Luke walk toward the house and turned to look at Bud. "Well, have you completed your business with your pa? I'm sure it would be better for everyone if we just went on back home. Tater can stay over and go fishing with Matt. You can ride back over and get him later."

"I think you're right," Bud replied with a silly grin on his face. "Let me go and get Boo. Mama is probably feeding him a handful of cookies about now," he laughed as he started to the kitchen. "Come on in the house and say hello to Mama and then we'll go home."

Thanksgiving Day arrived, and it was a beautiful sunny cold day. Rosie was so excited that while she dressed herself and Boo for this special day, she was humming. Bud watched her as she laid out a freshly ironed shirt and denim jeans for him to wear. Tater had dressed in an identical outfit just like Bud's. Justice took extra time wrapping the scarves around her head and selecting the necklaces that she wanted to wear. Everyone was ready to go to the most important celebration that Rosie or Tater had ever attended.

Bud brought in a crate to place their food in so nothing would spill. A small bag was prepared with extra clothes for Boo. After bundling up everyone in their nice new coats, scarves, and hats, they were off to Jesse and Rae Maxwell's.

Hope had been carried over to Jesse and Rae's home several hours earlier with the help of Aunt Katie and Missy. She was dressed in a lovely green gown with matching robe and slippers. Will had ordered several gowns, robes, and slippers that matched for Hope to wear while recovering from childbirth. Ollie had given her consent for Hope to wear her night clothes in the presence of mixed company. Willow was dressed in a long, flowing green gown with knitted booties to match. Her little blond fuzz was covered with a soft knitted cap with two rose buds on each side. She looked like a small china doll. Ollie had placed Jeremiah over by the baby to stand guard. Little Jacob was fascinated by the new baby. When she cried, she sounded like a newborn kitten meowing.

Before the guests had arrived, Hank, Jeremiah, John, and Little Jess had set up extra tables and benches for everyone to have a place to sit. The aroma of the turkey and dressing was wonderful. The stove was covered with pots of chicken and dumplings, mashed potatoes, gravy and pans of hot fluffy biscuits. When Bud and his little family arrived, Jesse met them at the front door.

He motioned for Little Jess to hurry outside and help Tater bring their things inside. Everyone removed their boots and coats and left them on the front porch.

Boo squealed with joy when he saw Jacob playing in the parlor. He raced over, and Jacob grabbed his little hand. "See," he pointed at the basket with Willow lying peacefully asleep. "Baby!" Jacob yelled. Everyone laughed at the little boys. "Jeremiah, you watch those little rascals now, you hear. Don't let them touch our little princess." Jeremiah grinned at Hope and gave her a nod as if to say, 'I knew she would tell me what to do.'

Dr. Tim, Hannah, Little John, Mary Beth, and Susie arrived. Tim came in carrying a twenty-pound baked ham. Hannah was laughing as she hurried over to see the new baby. "Come John, Mary Beth, and see the prettiest baby in all of Limason. I delivered her, with the help of Justice, Rae, and Miss Ollie. We made a pretty good team of doctors if I do say so myself."

"You have! At least twenty times, believe me, I've heard about this delivery over and over," laughed Tim as he looked around at everyone in the room. Everyone laughed.

"Oh, Little John and Mary Beth, we're so glad you could get away from school. Both of you look so grown up," Miss Ollie declared. "Where is Ella Mae?" Ollie asked, looking around for her. "She's coming. She stopped to talk with Esther," Tim replied. "Esther's husband has a sow down so he won't be coming today."

Mr. and Mrs. Downey, Samuel, and Matt came in the door next. The boys carried a big bowl of potato salad and a big dish of baked apples. Mr. Downey carried a big platter of chocolate cookies. "Where are Luke and Lisa?" Esther asked as she looked behind the Downey's.

"They should be outside now. They were following close behind us," Mrs. Downey said as she looked at Rosie and Justice. "Luke and Lisa have wonderful news. They are going to begin building their new home as soon as their supplies arrive. We gave them forty acres of land so they can have a small spread of cattle and a few horses. Now, we'll have both of our grown boys living close, and we can watch our grandchildren grow up."

Luke and Lisa, along with Lucy and Luther, came onto the porch. They removed their outer clothing and came into the kitchen to join the others. Lucy walked over to see the new baby while Lisa stood back looking at the ladies. She wasn't sure how she was going to be greeted until she heard Mrs. Downey said, "Come on in, Lisa. I'm afraid I spilled the beans about you building a new house. I'm just so happy."

"We're happy too," Lisa said very quietly with a smile on her face. "Rosie, you look very pretty today, and I love your scarves, Justice." Lisa was handing out a peace offering so Rosie and Justice both thanked her for the compliments. "Come, Lisa, and have a look at Hope's new baby girl," Rosie said as she looked over at Bud. He gave her a grin that spoke volumes of appreciation.

Mrs. Esther and Ella Mae told Lisa that they would be glad to help her make curtains and rugs for her new home. "You just let us know when you have picked out the material."

Rev. Anderson and his wife were the last to arrive. Jesse met them out at the barn and unhitched their single horse and walked him in the barn out of the cold wind. Their daughter Mary Ann had married last year and moved to Dallas with her husband. "Jesse, I can't thank you and Rae enough for the invitation to dinner. Now that Mary Ann isn't at home, it's just the two of us. It is mighty lonely at times," Mr. Anderson said as he wiped his nose.

"You won't be lonely today. We have a house full, and we are about ready to sit down for dinner. Do you mind saying grace for us today?"

"I would be honored," replied Rev. Anderson.

Once everyone had visited with each other, they were ready to sit down at the tables. Tater watched Missy as she moved to take a place. He hurried to her side and asked if he could sit next to her. "Of course," she said as she blushed. Little Jess and Matt scooted to the end of the table to be near them. They shoved each other and grinned as they watched the young love birds speaking low to each other.

Claire and Mary Beth helped with the younger children while everyone was taking their seats. Will motioned for Jeremiah to go and take a seat at the table while he sat next to Hope in the parlor.

After everyone was settled down at the table, Jesse picked up his spoon and tapped it on his cup. Once he had everyone's attention, except for the new baby who decided it was time to be fed, he said that he wanted to say a few words.

"First, I want to thank all of you for coming today and helping us to celebrate this special day, Thanksgiving. All of us present are blessed in so many ways and today is a day to say thank you to our Lord and Savior and to our family and friends. I've ask Rev. Anderson to say the blessing, but I want to personally thank my family for all that they have done during the year. Rae, my heart and the reason I live and breathe, I said thank you and I love you with all of my heart. To my children, I say thank you for being the good kids that you are. I'm so proud of Hope, Jess, and Claire. You all make me want to work hard every day. To Ollie and Hank, there aren't words enough to say how I feel about you both. Thank you. I am the man I am because of your love and daily guidance. To my friends, I say thank you for always being there for me and my family. We all need each other, and I have never worried that you wouldn't be ready to pitch in and help in any way that you could. Now, I have said thank you to the ones that I love, does anyone else want to say anything before I turn the floor over to Rev. Anderson?"

The room was silent for a span of thirty seconds when Bud finally got the nerve to rise. "I would like to say something, if I may?" Jesse gave him a nod and politely sat down next to Rae. She reached for his hand and gave it a tight squeeze.

"I want to say thank you to a very special person, Rosie. I wouldn't be here today if not for her. I was on my way home, to

Limason, when I found myself shot and lying in the swamp. I was rescued and doctored back to health by Rosie and Justice. While caring for me, Rosie stole my heart, and I was the happiest man alive when she agreed to be my wife. I love her two little brothers like they are my own sons."

"Papa!" Boo said as he pointed his little finger at Bud.

"Yes, with the grace of God, they are both living with us. One more thank you to Rosie. She cared for me and helped me realize that there is a lot in life to appreciate. The small things are the most important, and I want to thank her and my folks. I want to say thank you to Will and Hope for forgiving me for all the bad I did in the past. I am very fortunate to have such wonderful friends. I thank all of you."

Bud's face was as red as a bright shiny apple. Rosie's eyes were filled with unshed tears as he sat down beside her. She reached for his hand and held it tight. There were no words to describe how proud she was of him.

Jesse stood and asked if anyone else wanted to say anything. Luke eased himself up off the bench seat and said, "I want to thank my folks for being so good to me while I have been home. I know I had made an as—well, I wasn't the most pleasant person to be around. I want to thank my wife for giving me another chance. That's all I got to say."

Rev. Anderson stood after he realized that everyone in the room had said their piece. "To tell you the truth, I don't know if I can say anything more beautiful than what's been said already. Thank you is such a small phase, but when it is said from the heart like it has been today, it is very powerful. So let's bow our heads while I bless this wonderful food and the hands that prepared it." Everyone bowed their heads while Claire placed Jacob on her lap to keep him still.

"Our most blessed Father, we come to you today with Thanksgiving in our hearts. We are thankful for the new life in this family, Willow Maxwell, our homes, friends and family. We are thankful that you gave Bud a bright light so he could be guided back to his family. This is a glorious day that we all have so much to be thankful for. You know what's in our hearts, Lord, and you and only you know how blessed and thankful we are. Thank you for this home, this family, and this wonderful food. In all of Your glory we pray. Amen."

After dinner, Sheriff Murphy leaned back in his chair and rubbed his stomach. I shore hate to leave this good food and wonderful company but I've got to get back to town. "Bud, walk out to the barn with me while I get my horse," said Murphy as he was slipping on his big heavy jacket.

"Sure thing," Bud replied as he grabbed his coat and hat. Once the two men were walking to the barn, Sheriff Murphy told Bud that he had received this letter from the Judge in McBain. It states that he has appointed Rosie guardian of the boys and that they will never have to worry about that old man or their mama again. Sheriff Murphy slowly folded the letter and gave it to Bud. "You know, Bud, there's no law that gives the Judges or lawmen the right to put a man in jail for mistreating his wife or kids. But the judge can order him to get out of his territory. So I understand that Mr. Shire took off in his wagon heading west."

"Thanks so much for bringing this letter out to us. Rosie and Tater will be very relieved. I know I am." As Sheriff Murphy rode out of the barn, Bud placed the folded letter in his jacket and he walked back into the house.

As everyone sat around the table enjoying slices of their favorite pie, Miss Ollie got up to get more coffee. In a flash, Miss Ollie went down on the floor before she could catch herself. "Mercy," she said as she lay on the floor while everyone scrambled away from their place at the table. Dr. Tim and Hannah were on their knees beside Ms. Ollie. "Rae, grab a pillow and place it under Ollie's head. Get a blanket too. Everyone move away while I stretch Ollie out here on the floor."

Ollie opened her eyes and looked up at Dr. Tim. "I'm fine, really," she sighed. "It's hot as Hades in here."

"Yes, it is, but I'll take care of the heat in just a minute. Lay very still. Do you hurt anywhere? Did you hurt yourself when you fell?" He immediately grabbed her wrist and felt for a pulse count. He placed his ear down onto her chest to listen to her heart beat until he could get his instruments.

"Jesse, Will, John! Give me a hand to carry Miss Ollie to her bed. I know that I don't have to tell you to be careful," instructed Tim. The three men reached under Miss Ollie's sides and lifted her like she was a small child and gently laid her in the middle of her bed. Rae raced ahead of the men and pulled a lovely wedding ring quilt back and fluffed up several pillows on Ollie's bed. "Jeremiah, place another log in the fireplace to take the chill out of this room," said Rae. "That's not necessary right now Jeremiah. Ollie is burning up, and she needs the room to be a little cooler until I can figure out what's wrong with her," replied Tim.

Everyone walked around in the parlor whispering to each other. Rosie said that she had noticed right after Hope had the baby that Ollie was a little feverish, but she had said that she was fine. Esther said she had noticed Ollie didn't have any get-up-and-go like she had before. Hope said that Ollie had been coughing a lot and wouldn't get too close to Willow. She questioned Ollie about her health but she just scolded her and said that she was fine.

After a little while and a very thorough examination, Dr. Tim called Jesse, Rae, and Will together. "I'm sure that she has a very bad cold, probably pneumonia. Her lungs are full of congestion, and I've got to get her to cough it up. She admitted to having a mild cold for a while and not getting enough rest so it has gotten worse. She has a good chance of a complete recovery if I can get her fever down and keep it down. And keep her down."

Aunt Katie and Jeremiah had been standing behind Jesse and both of them joined in on the conversation. "She'll stay down if I have to sit on her," said Jeremiah as Aunt Katie shook her head in agreement.

"Rae, you and Hannah change Ollie into her night clothes and give her a good alcohol rub down. She has a high fever, and I have got to get it down. I'd like to move her to the infirmary in town, but its' so cold outside. She'll have to stay here, but keep the children out of her room. No visitors until I say so. She needs complete rest."

Jeremiah stood over Miss Ollie, his dearest friend in the world. He laid his palm on Ollie's forehead. "Will you get your paws off me? There's nothing wrong with me except the room is hot as Hades, and I guess I needed some air. Open that there window a little bit," Ollie said as she glanced at the window in her room.

When Hannah and Rae came back into the bedroom with everything they needed to help bring Ollie's fever down, Justice eased into the room with them. She walked over to the bed and spoke louder than she intended. "Ollie, can you hear me?"

"I ain't deaf, you old voodoo queen. I'm fine, so don't be trying any of your spells or potions on me," she said as she coughed and nearly strangled. "When I think Tim can't do no more for me—I'll call you. Now get out of here and stop looking like I'm ready for you to start tossing dirt on my coffin."

Justice looked at Rae and Hannah and slowly shook her head. She strolled away from her new friend's bed and went outside on the porch. Justice spoke to Bud and told him to go on home and take Rosie and the boys. "Boo's cranky and Tater still needs rest. I'll get one of the men to bring me home later. I'm going to stay until I'm sure that Ollie is going to be all right."

As Hannah wiped Ollie's coal black face, Ollie asked," Did the witch doctor leave?" Hannah smiled and nodded her head yes. "I'm sure she didn't go far. You know she thinks the world of your friendship."

Esther walked out on the porch and stood next to Justice. "You know that Ollie is a tough old bird, and I don't think she's ready to leave this world yet, not with Hope giving birth to that beautiful baby Willow. No, she ain't going anywhere. So try not to worry. Just pray."

A fit of coughing would overtake Ollie's body whenever she tried to lay back and rest. Dr. Tim propped her back up against her headboard with several pillows to help her breathe easier. While she was resting the first night, her fever shot up and the coughing got worse. Each time Rae attempted to feed her something to drink or eat, she heaved it back up. Tears streamed down her shiny black cheeks as she tried to say she was sorry for the mess that she was making. "Remove my quilt before I ruin it!" she cried after she stopped vomiting in a white slop bucket.

After the second night, Tim was very concerned that the medicine he was giving Ollie wasn't having much effect on her recovery. He gave her back a hard rub down several times a day trying to help loosen the congestion. Jesse, Will, and Hope were beside themselves with worry too. They weren't allowed in the room to see Ollie because he wasn't sure if pneumonia was what she had wrong with her. Dr. Tim had ordered Hope to stay home with her two small children. With a new baby only a couple of weeks old, Hope was still very weak and Tim wasn't taking any chances with Hope's health. She was fit to be tied because she wanted to be at Ollie's bedside. Ollie was everything to Hope. She was like her second mama.

After a restless third night, Tim decided to give Ollie a teaspoon of Laudanum to help her rest. She went into a deep, restful sleep. Tim sat down in a big oversized chair and laid back his head. He had not gotten more than a few hours' sleep since Ollie took ill. He was exhausted. It wasn't but a few minutes before Tim was snoring softly.

Will had paced up and down in the parlor and kitchen the past three days worrying and praying over Ollie. He couldn't bear it any longer. He had to see her for himself. He barged into Ollie's room without permission, half-expecting Tim to try to make him leave. He saw Tim asleep so he walked quietly over to Ollie's bedside. He saw her lying still with her arms folded across her chest and big belly. She looked so peaceful. She looked *dead* to Will.

Will went down on his knees beside Ollie's bed and prayed, "Oh, God, please, please, don't take my Ollie. I couldn't go on without her. She's been like my mama my whole life. I love her. My babies need her in their lives. Please." He laid his head down next to Ollie's hip and sobbed like a small child. Slowly, one of Ollie's pink palms lifted and moved through Will's long black hair. After a soft pat and a mumbled "my boy," Will grabbed her hand and held it to his face.

Rae came into the room and looked down at Will but didn't scold him for being in the sickroom. She noticed Tim asleep so she picked up a light blanket and covered him with it. Walking over to Ms. Ollie's window, she pulled back the curtain. On the front lawn singing and kneeling on the cold damp ground were many of Ollie's church members, friends and neighbors each holding a candle or lantern. As the hymn ended, Rev. Anderson prayed. His voice carried loudly in the cool foggy night. After the prayer, a soft humming of a hymn was continued. Will stood and looked out the window. He placed his arm around Rae's waist and said, "I wish Ollie could see all these people. Hopefully, she can feel their love and devotion." He stood and cried silently while looking at the sea of light in the darkness.

Jesse went out on the porch; seeing all of Ollie's faithful friends kneeling while holding a burning candle and humming religious hymns nearly got the best of him. He wiped the mist out of his eyes as he raised his hand high in the air to get everyone attention. John, Katie, Missy, Susie, and Rider stood to one side of the porch, while Hannah, Rae, Will, Hank, and Jeremiah stood behind Jesse.

Justice eased herself quietly into the house and poured a cup of hot water in a teacup. She walked into Ollie's bedroom. She was surprised to see Dr. Tim asleep in Ollie's room. As quietly as she could, she shook Ollie awake. While Ollie was trying to get her eyes open, Justice dropped a teabag in the hot water and slipped a few sprinkles of her special powder into it.

"Ollie, wake up," whispered Justice as she looked over at Dr. Tim. "Listen to me. Dr. Tim has done all he can do for you. I want you to drink some of my special brew. This will make you feel better, open up your lungs, and help you to get better."

Ollie was still a little drugged from the medicine that Dr. Tim had given her earlier. She reached and grabbed Justice's hand as Justice held the teacup up to her mouth.

With her words slurred, she asked, "What's in that stuff?"

"Hush—there's some basil, rosemary, hair of a dog, the tongue of a frog—" whispered Justice.

"Shut up, you old fool. This ain't going to kill me?"

"It ain't ever killed any of my patients. You'll sleep and when you wake you'll be much better, I promise." Justice held the cup and made Ollie drink every drop. "This is my secret potion. You can't tell anyone about it—not even Jeremiah."

"Awful!" Ollie said, shaking her head and sticking out her tongue. She patted Justice on the hand and lay back down on the pillows and sighed. Justice glanced at Dr. Tim and looked back at Ollie. Both of them were fast asleep.

Jesse had the attention of everyone outside. "I want to thank all of you for coming out here this evening. Your devotion and prayers for Miss Ollie are truly appreciated. Words can't express how full our hearts are for all the love you have shown her tonight. I'm sorry to say that Dr. Tim has done all he can for her. Now, her recovery is in the hands of our Lord and Savior." Jesse turned to Rae and buried his face into her shoulder.

After pulling himself together, Jesse and the rest of the family members walked around in the crowd that had gathered. Jesse shook Mr. and Mrs. Downey's hands while Mrs. Downey wiped away tears and said that Bud had to take Rosie and the boys' home. Luke Downey, Mr. and Mrs. Smith from the dry goods store, Sheriff Murphy, and old Moses from the telegraph office were gathered together as Will thanked each of them for coming. Each person was thanked for coming, singing, and praying for

Ms. Ollie. Many of Ollie's church members said that they wanted to stay and be close while continuing to pray for their loved one. Jesse thanked them with a nod of his head, for words were choked in his throat.

As Will started back in the house, he saw one of the big black men and Runner, a small black woman from the Waverly Plantation in the crowd. Ollie was born and raised at Waverly until she came to the Maxwell Ranch at the age of sixteen. "Thanks for coming over this evening. Listen, please settle down in the loft of our barn for the night. It is dry and clean. It's too far for you to ride back home tonight." The nice couple thanked Will for the offer of lodging but said they had a place to stay already. "We just had to be here for Ms. Ollie. We all love her for being so good to us over the years," Runner said. She had known Ollie nearly all of her life.

After a couple of hours of visiting with the people who gathered and prayed for Ms. Ollie it was time to go back into the warm house. The temperature had dropped to nearly freezing, but the people didn't seem to notice as they continued to kneel and pray.

Rae wrapped her arms around Jesse and walked with him back into Ollie's room. Hannah slowly trailed behind them. Hank and Jeremiah walked over to Miss Ollie and looked at her as she lay sleeping peacefully. "She seems to be breathing easier," Jeremiah said as he picked up Miss Ollie's hand and gave it a squeeze. He didn't know what he was going to do without her here bossing him around every day.

Hank looked into Ollie's face. "She ain't coughing either, which is a blessing." Hank had been on the ranch with Ollie for over fifty years. He ate her biscuits and gravy every morning.

Dr. Tim stood and stretched as he walked over to Ollie and took her wrist and felt her pulse count. He grabbed his stethoscope and listened to her heart and lungs. He listened and then he listened again. She was breathing normal and her heart wasn't racing like before. He lifted one eyelid and then the other one. Ollie gave a small snort, smiled, and shook his hand away from her face like it was a pesky fly.

"I cannot believe this," Tim said, whispering to Hannah. "Ollie's fever has broken and all her vital signs appear to be normal. She's going to be all right!" Laughing like a silly young man, Tim called to Jesse and Will. "Look, Ollie's better. She's resting and I believe that when she wakes, she will be on the road to recovery. Praise be to God."

"Jesse, go and tell the people that their prayers have been answered and to go home before some of them get sick." Dr. Tim grabbed Hannah and swung her around and around in the air. He grabbed Will and they beat each other on the back while smiling. Will used the back of his hand to wipe away tears that formed in his eyes. Jeremiah and Hank shook hands and smiled real big as they continued to surround Ollie's bed.

"Golly, I've got to get home and tell Hope, Claire, and Little Jess that Ollie is going to be all right. What a glorious Christmas we're going to have now." Will shouted to the rooftop as he hurried out the front door without his sheepskin jacket. Will passed Rider, John, and Katie as he jumped off the front porch steps. "Ollie is going to be fine!" he yelled.

"Praise be to the Lord," cried Katie as she grabbed John's hand and hurried into the house. "Is it true, Jeremiah? Is Ollie better like Will said?" asked Rider.

"Shore is," replied Jeremiah as he gave Katie a big hug. "She sleeping, but it's a good sleep." The three walked softly into Mrs. Ollie's bedroom to take a look for themselves.

Jeremiah slowly walked into the kitchen as Esther was coming out. "Ain't it wonderful," she said as she hurried into the bedroom where Ollie was sleeping. Justice continued sitting at the table wearing a smug grin on her old black face. Jeremiah poured himself about a half cup of coffee and sat down across the table from Justice.

"There have been some mighty powerful things going on in this house today. Prayers have been answered, that's a fact, but I'm a thinking there was something else besides prayers." Jeremiah sat, staring at Justice and not a word came forth from her.

"I best get myself on home. Now, I can rest knowing my new friend is going to be up and about again real soon." Justice pulled her jacket down from the coat rack and slipped it on.

Jeremiah was sure that Justice did something to help Ollie get better, but he wouldn't dare ask. "I'll take you home in Katie's small carriage. It's cold and dark outside and there are a lot of folks milling around. There's no way I can allow one of God's healing angels to come to any harm this night."

The Sunday before Christmas, Limason's little community church held their annual Christmas play and fellowship supper. Dr. Tim agreed that Miss Ollie was well enough that she could attend the event as long as she didn't get overly tired. At first Ollie enjoyed all the attention from her family and friends, but now she was fed up being told what she could do and could not do. She had Christmas presents to prepare and cooking to be done. She had Claire help her with all her gifts for the children of her church and Will and Little Jess had carried gifts and one of her Christmas hams out to Waverly Plantation.

As Ollie sat in the front pew of the church as an honored guest, she thanked God for her renewed health and for giving her the courage to drink that special potion that Justice had prepared for her while on her deathbed. She shuddered as she remembered that vile liquid going down her throat. Looking around, she watched Hope as she held her one-month-old baby, Willow. Hope was a beaming beauty who looked like she never gave birth to one baby much less two. Will sat up tall, next to her holding little Jacob in his lap. He reminded her so much of

Mr. Jake, the boys' pa. Jesse had his arm around Rae's shoulders, always the loving protector. She was so proud of the young men that she had helped to raise.

As the stage curtain was pulled back, Tater and Missy were dressed as Joseph and Mary kneeling down on hay by a crib. After much consideration, a doll was chosen to be baby Jesus. As the three wise men strolled down the aisle, the children couldn't contain their snickering. They watched Hank, Jeremiah, and Rider dressed in colorful robes proudly holding their heads high with their homemade crowns, carrying their gifts to baby Jesus. Rae had sewn the costumes while Ollie hemmed them. The men complained and grumbled while being fitted, but in the end, Ollie was sure they were proud of how they looked.

Little John, Mathew, Little Jess were dressed alike as shepherds holding tall staffs that Jeremiah had carved from tree limbs. The bright star in the background was being held high by Samuel. After all the lines were spoken, many incorrectly, the rest of the children in the church dressed in white choir robes sang *Away in the Manager*. Boo had been sitting on the pew between Bud and Rosie. He had been eyeing that little baby Jesus since the play started. Before Bud could grab him, he slipped off the pew and crawled up on the front of the stage and flopped down in front of the crib. He took his little fingers and touched the doll's button eyes. "Baby!" He pointed as he turned to Jacob. Everyone smiled and continued to sing along with the children as they sang "Silent Night."

It had been a glorious evening for the town of Limason, especially for Jesse and Rae, Dr. Tim and Hannah and Will and Hope. In a few days, they would be surrounded at their Christmas dinner table with all of their loved ones and close friends. They were blessed with a new life, Willow, into the Maxwell family. Miss Ollie was thankful that her health had been renewed and she gave all the praise and glory to God, and Dr. Tim. And *don't tell nobody, but thanks to Justice too!*

EPILOGUE

A FEW DAYS BEFORE Christmas, Bud and Rosie snuggled in their big bed watching the wood snap and crackle in the fireplace. "We might need more wood before long. That firewood is burning very quick," said Rosie.

"We might just have to steam up this bed ourselves," he said as he placed small kisses under her hair on the back of her neck.

"You're making me cold," she said as she shivered. "You know, Bud, I keep thinking about the Christmas play. Tater was so proud to be a part of that. I could hardly hold back my tears of joy. Everyone here is so good and kind to each other. We're really blessed."

"Come closer and let me hold you tighter. I'll bless that lovely young body of yours with my heat."

As Bud brushed kisses all over Rosie's pretty face, she captured his sweet mouth and kissed him deeply. Tenderly, he returned her kiss as he held her tightly. Rosie's laughter and cries of passion for more were drowned out by loud thunder and torrents of rain.

Early the next morning, Rosie smelled coffee brewing. The next thing she knew, her face was bending over the chamber pot. She felt like all of her insides were going to come out of her mouth. A tap on her shoulder found Justice standing beside her with a cold, damp cloth.

"I wondered how much longer it was going to take before you got caught," said Justice.

Rosie started at Justice, not understanding what she meant. "What have I caught?"

"Mercy me, child, I thought for sure you knew about the birds and bees. How long has it been since you had to spread your rags outside over the bushes?"

"I don't know—you mean I could be with a child in my stomach?"

"I'm sure of it. How do you feel right now? Better?" asked Justice. Rosie wiped her mouth again and said she felt fine.

"What a Christmas surprise I'll have for Bud." Rosie floated over to the bed and lay back down for a little while. "A baby, my very own baby."

Bud had gotten up earlier, and once the boys had finished breakfast, he took them with him into the woods to select a Christmas tree. Tater was having a hard time choosing the perfect tree. Boo raced from tree to tree. Tater told Bud they never had a big tree. "We usually had a small branch. The swamp didn't have much to choose from, and we didn't have anything to decorate it with anyways. St. Nicholas didn't come to see us—not that I can remember no how."

The thought of this young man and his dear sister never having a real Christmas broke his heart. "Well, you can bet your britches that old St. Nicholas will be coming to our home this year. Is there something special that you would like for him to bring you?"

"Are you saying that you can ask for something and he might bring it to you?" Tater couldn't believe that such a thing might actually happen.

"Yep, that's what the old man that wears a long white beard does. He delivers toys, clothes, whatever kids wish for, if at all possible."

"Shoot fire! I'd like to ask him to bring me a gun, my very own gun, so I could go hunting and kill a deer or maybe a wild boar." Tater had thrown up his arms like he held a gun and pretended to be taking aim at a critter. "There were a lot of them in the swamp.

I've climbed many a tree to keep one from getting me. I would have liked to have shot them right between the eyes."

"I can't promise you that he will bring you a gun, but you'll get something I'm sure of that." Bud laughed as he saw the excitement in Tater's eyes as he spoke about owning a gun.

"Well, I really ain't expecting anything. You have given me more than I have ever had in my life. I have everything that I need and then some. Hey, what about this tree?" Tater said, trying to change the subject before he embarrassed himself by shedding a few tears.

The boys placed the tree in the back of the flatbed wagon and took it home. They placed it in the barn to dry out. Tomorrow was Christmas Eve, and they would take it in the parlor and decorate it and then put a few presents under it.

Bud went into the house and discovered Rosie still in the bed asleep. He had never known her to sleep so late. Looking down at her as she lay so peacefully with her red hair spread over the pillow, she looked so young and innocent. Justice walked into the room and assured him that she was fine.

"I need to go into town and get a few things for Christmas. Rosie looks so tired. I really hate to wake her up. She had mentioned that she was all ready for the holiday," he whispered as he walked slowly out of the room. "Do you want me to get anything for you or the pantry?" After writing down what Justice said to get, Bud hurried off to town to see if he could have a talk with ole St. Nicholas before it was too late.

As Bud rode home from town, he wondered if Rosie was up and moving around. Smiling to himself, he was sure he knew why she was being lazy this morning. She had looked a little white around the mouth yesterday and today, and she couldn't get to moving. Yes, she was trying to keep her condition a secret from him. *That's it*, he said to himself with a silly grin on his handsome face.

The trip to town had been very successful. Bud purchased a .22 rifle for Tater. He got several boxes of shells and the tools that would help him to keep it clean and ready to use. He wanted to make sure that St. Nicholas was going to bring Tater the one thing that he would ask for if he'd got the chance. A couple of weeks earlier, he and Rosie had purchased Tater a new Western hat, a pair of cowboy boots, a bottle of cologne to make him smell good, and a man's razor with a brush and cup set. For Boo, they chose a stick horse with yarn for the horse's mane, a new pair of boots, some small wooden horses with a corral to put them in, a warm fuzzy brown bear with black button eyes, and a wooden rifle now like Taters. Bud knew that his Pa had built Boo a red wagon and had a small black and white kitty picked out for him. For Tater, he had purchased a brown and white beagle puppy. "Every boy needs a dog of their very own," his Pa said and Bud had to agree.

The boys were going to have a nice Christmas, and he was thankful that he could afford to give it to them, for if anyone deserved it, Tater did. Nothing would remove the scars that he endured from the hands of his mama's husband. Bud wanted to make sure that he didn't carry any scars in his young heart by showering him with security and love.

While in town, Bud checked on Rosie's gift that he had ordered several months ago. He had chosen a new kitchen table with a matching oak hutch for holding dishes. He selected a nice sofa and two big wingback chairs to match. She had seen the set in the catalog at Smithy Dry Goods Store. He was told that the furniture should be at the store later today. Just in time for Christmas Eve. Perfect!

When Bud arrived home, he unhitched his horses and turned them loose in the corral. As he neared the house, he heard a sweet humming sound coming from the kitchen area. He opened the door and smelled the aroma of fresh bread and hot coffee brewing. He loved coming home and being with his new family.

Seeing Boo in Rosie's lap with her arms securing him to her bosom as she rocked him asleep was one of the happiest moments of his life. If he could have formed words that would have expressed what was in his heart, he would have said them. All he wanted to do was send up a prayer of thanksgiving to the good Lord above for allowing Rosie to enter into his life. She had opened his heart, mind, and soul to appreciate the value of even the smallest things in life. She made him want to be a better son, a good husband, and father. Now with a baby growing under Rosie's breast, Bud could hear Miss Ollie saying, "This is the beginning of a new life for all of you. *You best take care, you hear?*"

CPSIA information can be obtained
at www.ICGtesting.com
Printed in the USA
LVOW04s2057120816
500060LV00016B/273/P